'Moving, engrossing, and richly drawn this is storytelling in its purest form. With lilting, rhythmic prose that never falters, *How To Be Brave* held me from its opening lines. Louise Beech masterfully envelops us in her two worlds separated by time, yet linked by fierce family devotion, bravery and the triumph of human spirit. Mesmerising'
AMANDA JENNINGS, author of *The Judas Scar* and *Sworn Secret*

'Two family stories of loss and redemption intertwine in a painfully beautiful narrative. The relationship between Natalie and Rose is perfectly written – honest and loving, without a trace of saccharine. This book grabbed me right around my heart and didn't let go'
CASSANDRA PARKIN, author of *The Beach Hut*

'Reading *How To Be Brave* is like having a conversation with a very wise friend. Beautifully written, it is also intelligent and moving. This book will stay with you long after you reach the end'
RUTH DUGDALL, author of *Humber Boy B*

How To Be Brave is going to be massive. An amazing story of hope and survival, set both in the present day and the past, it's a love letter to the power of books and stories'
NICK QUANTRILL, author of *The Crooked Beat*

'*How To Be Brave* reminds us of the frailty of the human condition and champions that inner strength we all have when faced with adversity. Beautifully written and emotionally resonant this will stay with you long after you turn the final page'
Liz Loves Books

'Louise Beech is a natural born storyteller, and this is a wonderful story' RUSS LITTEN, author of *Kingdom*

HOW TO BE BRAVE

ABOUT THE AUTHOR

Louise Beech has always been haunted by the sea, and regularly writes travel pieces for the *Hull Daily Mail*, where she was a columnist for ten years. Her short fiction has won the Glass Woman Prize, the Eric Hoffer Award for Prose, and the Aesthetica Creative Works competition, as well as shortlisting for the Bridport Prize twice and being published in a variety of UK magazines. Louise lives with her husband and children on the outskirts of Hull – the UK's 2017 City of Culture - and loves her job as a Front of House Usher at Hull Truck Theatre, where her first play was performed in 2012. She is also part of the Mums' Army on Lizzie and Carl's BBC Radio Humberside Breakfast Show. This is her first book.

HOW TO BE BRAVE

LOUISE BEECH

ORENDA
BOOKS

Orenda Books
16 Carson Road
West Dulwich
London SE21 8HU
www.orendabooks.co.uk

First published in the United Kingdom by Orenda Books 2015
Copyright © Louise Beech 2015

A catalogue record for this book is available from the British Library.

ISBN 978-1-910633-19-9

Typeset in Goudy Old Style

Printed and bound by CPI Group (UK) Ltd, Croydon CR0 4YY

Sales & Distribution

In the UK and elsewhere in Europe:
Turnaround Publisher Services
Unit 3, Olympia Trading Estate
Coburg Road
Wood Green
LONDON
N22 6TZ
www.turnaround-uk.com

In USA/Canada:
Trafalgar Square Publishing
Independent Publishers Group
814 North Franklin Street
Chicago, IL 60610, USA
www.ipgbook.com

This is dedicated to Colin's children, grandchildren, great grandchildren, and many nieces and nephews. He must be up there – with his brothers Alf, Stan, Gordon and Eric, and wife Kathleen – smiling down on us all.

AUTHOR'S NOTE

Truth inspires all stories. A memoir is a true account of the author's experience. A biography is a true account of another person's life. A novel is fiction but it dares to explore the truth more deeply than any other form.

This book is all of the above. Rose and Natalie are based on my own time with a newly diabetic child. The lifeboat story of my grandfather, Colin Armitage, took place in 1943, mostly as is described here. But it was my imagination – merged with memories, newspaper articles, letters, and family accounts – that brought these stories to life.

Sometimes all we can ever know is what probably happened, and that is the truth.

'The sea has neither meaning nor pity'
Anton Chekhov

A SORT OF RECOVERY POSITION

Still two of us left but we are getting very weak.
Can't stand up now. We will stick it to the end.

K.C.'s log

There were two of us that night.

Outside, the autumn dark whispered to me. Halloween's here already, it said. The pumpkins are glowing, smell the whiff of old leaves, of bonfires coming, of changes, of winter, of endings. But I wasn't listening because inside the house my daughter Rose was whispering aloud the words in my current paperback, slowly forming each vowel and consonant as she kicked my kitchen cupboard and twirled her hair about her finger.

'"Vases of jasmine and..."' she began. 'How do you say that? "Vases of jasmine and *s-t-a-r-g-a-z-e-r* lilies barely dispel the urine aroma" ... urine, is that *wee*? "Framed pictures of cities accen– How do you say *that*? A-c-c-e-n-t-u-a-t-e..."'

'Don't read that,' I snapped, taking the book from Rose and putting it in the drawer. 'It's not suitable for nine-year-olds. It's got bad words in it.' To myself I said, 'Plus it's not very good.'

'So why are you reading it?'

'I'm not. I'm going to give it to the charity shop.'

Rose opened and shut the drawer, over and over, until I stopped her. She was wearing a cat costume, with silky velvet gloves and ears, pencil whiskers and a smudge of black polish on her nose. 'You always think I'm stupid,' she said.

'I don't. You're not.'

'I understand adult books, you know,' she pouted. 'I read *Jane Eyre*. I can do *all* the words.'

'I'm sure you can.'

'And *you* say bad words all the time.'

I couldn't argue with that.

She slammed the drawer one last time. 'I'm thirsty,' she said.

'You know where the tap is.'

I was grumpy from spending three hours gutting and carving a face into a lopsided pumpkin. Rose had wanted to make a *Despicable Me* minion, but I'd insisted I hadn't the skill. She hadn't argued, so I'd gone ahead and cut a grinning face, all wonky, with one eye bigger than the other. I swore when I cut the end of my finger, and Rose had said *language* and told me I was a wuss. The blood dripped onto our pumpkin, leaving him with two lines of auburn hair.

'The words were jumping,' Rose said, gasping from having downed the glass of water in one go.

'What words?'

'The bad ones in your book.' She kicked at the kitchen cupboard. Charcoal leggings had ridden up her legs, exposing matchstick ankles. When had they got so thin? Her reddish blonde hair needed washing but I didn't want her going out in the chill air with damp curls.

'Don't kick my doors,' I said.

'Bad words, swearwords, bad words, bastards.'

'Rose!' I touched her clammy forehead. 'Are you feeling okay? You must eat something if you're going out trick-or-treating with Hannah and Jade. What do you want? Beans on toast?'

'Swearwords,' Rose said defiantly, and pushed me away.

I rummaged in the fridge for something that might tempt her to eat, and perhaps behave better. Cold noodles, some tuna, half a tin of beans, custard. That would do it; the magic of cake and custard.

When I turned, the world had changed. It was quiet, slow. There were no whispers, no bad words or swearwords, only Rose falling, her mouth moving, as if she were reading in our book nook. I couldn't hear the swirl of syllables, yet something in their rhythm gave me déjà vu. I tried to read her lips; *What are you telling me?* I wanted to scream.

But I was silent as I watched her fall – down, down, down – and I couldn't move. Couldn't save her.

When her head hit the tiles with a thick crack the spell broke too. I dropped the bowl of custard and ran to her. I shook her limp shoulders and called 'Rose, Rose, Rose' – not what you're supposed to do in an emergency, no sort of recovery position or mouth-to-mouth wake-up kiss, just what comes naturally when you want your child back.

'Jake,' I cried. 'Help me!' But of course he was far away and wouldn't be back for months. 'Help me!' I screamed into the night. 'Somebody – help me!'

The candle in our skewed, grinning pumpkin danced

as though mocking Rose's lifelessness – but where had the draught come from? I felt it on my face too. Had a door opened somewhere? Had someone heard me?

'Who's there?' I called.

But no one answered; it was just us.

And then we were surrounded by the smell of the sea – salty, potent, fresh. I'd been smelling it randomly for days. We live on the Humber Estuary but we're still twenty-five miles inland; yet somehow it had found me; the sea. I'd been getting out of bed at dawn and a briny breeze would greet me, as though wafting up from the bedclothes. I'd hang out wet clothes and it would float down from the trees, the clouds, somewhere.

It faded. So I sniffed Rose's cheek.

I found comfort in her powerful perfume; it calmed my panic a little. Often when she joins me on the sofa for a film I deeply inhale the top of her head, absorbing the hint of school classrooms and sleep and breath. She asks why and shoos me off, but I can't resist. Smelling a new baby is the next thing you do after studying them; so as Rose lay on the floor by the washing machine I breathed in her scent as though it would sustain me through what might come.

Then I dialled 999 and we waited.

❧

An ambulance siren heralded two paramedics. All I can remember about them is that they were male. They came into the kitchen and bent down to check Rose and asked questions and made smudgy footprints like preschool paintings and listened to her heart and took her pulse. We must have looked a curious picture in our Halloween costumes, me wearing a pale-blue nurse's dress stained with beetroot juice and Rose in her black cat suit.

They asked more questions.

So I told them in a tumble of words, 'One minute we were making our pumpkin and then she was talking about naughty words in my book and then I looked for custard and then suddenly she went down, cold. She plays tricks on me all the time, but this wasn't mischief.'

The paramedics gently lifted Rose onto a stretcher, covered her with a red blanket and wheeled her to the ambulance. I followed. Our neighbour, April, came up the path with what looked like a severed head in her hand – 'a pumpkin,' my future, looking-back self would say, 'it was Halloween, remember, and you were going to let Rose go with her friends to the town square, carrying skeleton bags to beg for sweets, you made them promise to stay together.'

I noticed our rhododendron bush needed trimming but remembered the shears were broken; the thought came and went like a rescue flare at sea, flashing and then dying. I climbed into the ambulance after Rose. April was still on our path, so I smiled at her, and was not sure why. Perhaps it was to say I was fine, we were fine, it would all be fine. One of her fingers was hooked through the pumpkin's cut-out eye.

I didn't hear the ambulance engine rev up or the doors close or the sirens start, but I do now, long afterwards, when I think of it in the dark. The world lost its sound again and it was just us two.

I removed Rose's glove and held a cool hand in mine.

It fit perfectly, like they were two warped jigsaw pieces that make sense when joined. I studied her fine lines and traced the scar from when she fell off the shed roof and pressed my nose against her skin. She wouldn't let me hold her hand anymore, and a part of me was glad of unconsciousness, of the chance to kiss it like I had when she was first born.

Then I'd willed her small fingers to be kind, to be gifted, to be brave. To hold a pen or guitar or paintbrush. Now I willed them to ball into fists and push me away – to *wake up*.

At Accident and Emergency I had to let go and Rose was wheeled straight to a private bed area, black tail dangling from the trolley. I hovered by the curtain, not wanting to be a bother. My relief that these medics acted so quickly and knew what to do and did it without pause kept me from absolute panic; alarm at why they needed to never surfaced.

A nurse called Gill took me aside, asking for details and if she could call anyone. Her untidy red hair suggested a long shift. I managed to give our names and tell her there wasn't anyone near enough that I wanted.

'Has Rose had any symptoms?' she asked.

In the din I thought for a second she'd asked if Rose had had any *sympathies* and felt a curious guilt that I apparently had none.

'She's only nine,' I said.

'Yes – they're going to look after her. I just need to ask how she's been in the last few weeks. What kind of...'

And I understood my mistake. 'Thirst,' I said.

'Drinking lots?' asked Gill.

I nodded. 'Oh, lots.'

The thirst came first, beginning softly, like a spring shower and building into a force-ten gale. It had all started when Jake left so I'd thought it was psychosomatic or that Rose was seeking attention. I'd brushed off her grumbles at first, suggested she carry a bottle of water with her.

One night she had come to my too-empty bed; I woke to her ghostly presence, standing at my side. She said afterwards that I was always far crabbier than her dad when disturbed and this had made her watch me for ten minutes until I stirred.

'I'm thirsty,' she said.

'What?'

I didn't turn the light on; when she was a baby I always fed her without one during the night, knowing we'd both stay sleepy that way. It worked and she had been a settled infant. People called me lucky, but I'm just practical. And I like the dark – it's safe.

'I'm thirsty,' Rose repeated, her tone mimicking mine when I feign patience.

'Get a drink then,' I said. 'You don't have to *ask* for a drink.'

'I don't think a drink will work.' Even in the dark I knew the corner of her lip was curling up like old paper.

'Rose, it's late. Shit, I have to get up early.'

'*Language.*'

'I'm allowed to swear when I'm disturbed.'

'Mum, this thirst, it's different. Like it's also *hunger*.'

I sat up. Tried to be kind. 'Maybe you're dreaming. Maybe go back to sleep and you'll wake up fine.'

'No, mum, I won't. I had it yesterday and the one before that and it's totally not going. It's getting *bigger*.'

I smiled at her childlike description, left the bed's warmth and put an arm about my daughter's slight frame. She put her damp head to my shoulder – a place she now reached easily – and her forehead smelt of gravy and her hair tickled my cheek like shampooed spiders and she cried softly, as if I wasn't even there; as if she were resigned to this everlasting thirst; as if she were whispering to someone far away, from long ago.

We went to the kitchen and I watched her messily glug two glasses of juice, realising she had a book under her arm. Always a book – even in sleep. She'd probably dozed off with a finger between chapters and not let go.

I walked Rose back to bed, covered her up and said, 'Sleep now.'

'Still thirsty,' she muttered, but snuggled down.

'Stress can do that,' I said, sudden realisation causing the words to jump from my mouth without analysis. Then, more to myself, I added, 'Anxiety can make your mouth dry so you *think* you're thirsty. I had it when ... well, when I was anxious.' Remembering Rose was there I asked, 'What's making you worry?' It was a stupid question, the kind a stupid mother asks of a child whose father has been away for a month. But she was asleep.

Like now.

Gill the nurse listened to my descriptions of excessive juice drinking, resultant frequent toilet visiting and disturbed nights without interrupting me, but with an expression I couldn't at first decipher. When I finished I realised she was anticipating everything I'd said.

'I've a strong suspicion what caused Rose to collapse,' she

said. 'It'll just take a simple blood test to diagnose.'

'Really?'

She nodded. 'Why don't you take a seat and we'll test her now. Then we can either eliminate it or know what we're dealing with. Treatment is simple if we diagnose her.'

I looked over at the bed – Rose, still in her cat costume, looked too small; almost weightless, as though the mattress had swallowed her. When had she shrunk? Was it baby fat she'd lost? Had she lost it because her father was away? Was it the insatiable thirst and constant hunger and excessive napping after school and at the weekend? Or was it me?

'Her dad went to Afghanistan four weeks ago,' I said to Gill. 'Is that why?'

'No, no, this condition – well, it happens out of the blue. It's no one's fault, I assure you.'

I frowned. 'You sound so sure she has … what *is* it you think she has?'

'Let's just do the blood test first. Would you like a cup of tea?'

I shook my head. Gill walked away; the back of her dress had creased in a lightning shape.

I sat on a plastic seat between a boy whose nose was split wide, like the pumpkin on our kitchen worktop, and a woman with stitches over her cheek. The automatic doors opened and closed, over and over, admitting the casualties of Halloween.

An old man with a face like crepe paper said to me as he got wheeled past, 'They should all wear short dresses like yours, it'd keep me happy. But not the blood – it's like we're at war again!'

I remembered I was dressed as a zombie nurse, my skirt considerably shorter than the staff's, the fabric made bloody with juice, and my skin whitened with face paint and streaked with crimson lipstick.

I remembered also the candle at home, inside the pumpkin. Had I blown it out? No, I didn't think so. Damn. Would the flame burn through the pumpkin flesh? I should call Jake and tell him to do it.

Of course – he wasn't there. If he were, he'd have been here with us. I thought of calling April, but who has their neighbour's phone number on speed dial? She was pleasant enough and we kept an eye on one another's homes when we were away, but I don't feel I have to befriend people whose only similarity to me is where we live.

I worried about the candle. It saved me thinking about Rose. I closed my eyes a moment to shut out the busy waiting area but couldn't block the noise of doors and trolleys and chatter. Rose would want a book when she woke. She'd search under the pillow, be distressed without it.

I covered my ears and put my chin to my chest; a sort of recovery position. In my head was the sea, swishing and swirling and swilling over bleak stony thoughts. I could smell it again, even here amidst injury and pain.

A hand gently touched my shoulder, and I looked up with a start, expecting to see Gill. Instead I looked into dark eyes; in their mirror I saw the ocean I'd heard in my head and a shape like a tattered boat sail and my own face, but drained of colour, as though I were viewing the images through a black-and-white filter.

I readjusted my focus and took in the whole face. He

wore his hair like men in the forties did– swept to one side with gluey pomade and cut short around the ear. A suit with thick lapels kept together by four buttons forming a square was worn over a hand-knitted jumper and striped tie. Two polished medals were pinned to his chest. It was a wartime Halloween costume so authentic he must have borrowed it from an older relative.

'It won't be long,' he said.

He looked a bit like my grandad, seen in old photos. When I was a child, family members used to talk about him. Said he was brave, that he had been awarded medals, and that there was a museum in London with his things in it. Thinking about him used to keep me awake at night – or did it wake me up? I'd hear the sea then, too, and strange voices and accents. I'd smell salt and think he was there at the end of my bed, telling me stories. I never met him properly, not in the flesh. He died long before I even existed. I hadn't thought about him in a long time. Adult life tends to do that – eat up your thinking time, kill your dreams.

'You mustn't be scared,' the stranger said.

'I'm not,' I lied. 'You know, you look like ... well, someone I've only seen pictures of. But it's weird, you're exactly how I'd imagine him if he were alive.' I shrugged, realised I was babbling. 'Your costume's too nice for Halloween. The kids won't know what it is. They're all into wizards.' I paused. 'I hate hospitals.'

'Should be grateful for them.' His accent was beautifully rich Yorkshire, familiar in its flow, like mine only somehow from a time gone by. 'I've a lot to thank hospitals for.'

'No, I hate what they mean. You know, if you're in one

it's not good. My little girl ... she ... *God* ...' I couldn't say anymore.

'She's going to be fine.'

'How can you know that? You can't possibly. It's not normal for a nine-year-old to just collapse, is it? And I should've seen it coming! What kind of mother am I? I should've taken the thirst more seriously. Should've had her at the doctor weeks ago. I thought she was just missing her dad.'

My words ran out and I stopped. Tears built behind my eyes like froth on coke poured too fast – but I wouldn't surrender. If I did I'd be no good to Rose. I tried to apologise for ranting.

'Do you miss her dad too?' The sort-of-familiar stranger held my gaze with what I could only call affection. He seemed too interested in my answer for someone I'd never met before. And yet I didn't mind. In his presence I felt calm and able to be honest. Safe, like in the dark.

'I do,' I said softly. 'He's been away before but not to a place like that. People say you get used to it – their absence. But this time it feels like he's missing rather than gone. Does that make sense?'

He nodded. 'I was missing once – for two months.'

'You were? Did you get to say goodbye?'

'I couldn't.'

He looked down at his palms. I studied them as I had Rose's earlier; they were crisscrossed like an old map, the hands of a labourer, a man who works for a living. I wanted to put one of mine over his, but that would have been forward, and not me.

'Why not?' I asked.

'There wasn't time.'

'Jake had time,' I said, almost to myself. 'The night before he left we sat for hours in front of the TV and he was distant. He's a quiet man in general – you know, polite, affable, but not outgoing. If you talk to him he'll talk back but he'll not seek company particularly. I always thought it odd that he joined the forces – but then he has other qualities perfect for such a life: he's loyal and patient and hardworking. Anyway, we sat that last evening, quietly, until I swore – I'm so bad for it – and I said it was going to hurt enough, him being in a dangerous place, so at least let me have a nice goodbye to remember. And then ... he ... well, you know ...' I shook my head. 'Sorry, you don't want to listen to all this.' I paused. 'Who are you with?'

'My great granddaughter,' he said.

I frowned. Even at a push he looked no older than thirty. 'You must mean your daughter?'

'Mrs Scott?' It was Gill. Where had she come from?

'I'll go and blow that candle out,' whispered the man, so close to my ear that bristly hair tickled me and I smelt tobacco and the kind of aftershave that older men favour.

'Beg your pardon?' I turned to look at him, but he'd gone. How so fast?

I stood, frowned at Gill, and pushed past her to look up the corridor. Porters and nurses and patients and family members filled every space, some sat, some stood by the vending machine, some hurried, some pushed trolleys or wheelchairs. I searched for that mud-brown jacket, for the slick head of dark hair. Even without seeing him I knew somehow that he'd have walked with a merry, must-get-there swing, hands in pockets, and that he'd be whistling a tune I'd know but not be able to name.

'Where did he go?' I asked Gill.

'Who?'

'The man in the brown suit. He was just here.'

Gill frowned. 'I didn't see anyone like that.'

I looked at the boy with the nose and the woman with stitches across her cheek and my empty chair. If they were still there, with me in the middle, how had he sat next to me?

'We should sit down,' said Gill.

'I don't want to,' I said. 'I'd rather stand.'

I wasn't sure why, but a curious line came into my head – *We'll do it together. We'll be standing when she meets us, by God we will.*

Gill interrupted with, 'I really think we should...'

'No. Just tell me.'

'We did the test.'

I nodded.

'There's no need to be too alarmed as this condition is manageable,' she said, as she must have done many times over to various worried parents. 'We tested Rose's blood and found an excessively high sugar content, over thirty-eight millimoles. I understand this will mean little to you right now, but, well, you'll understand it in time. And this reading means your daughter has insulin-dependent diabetes mellitus, or as we generally call it, Type 1 diabetes.'

'Diabetes?' I frowned. 'But ... she isn't fat. There's nothing on her.'

'Not all diabetes is weight-related and Type 1 is completely unrelated to lifestyle. No one really knows its cause. For whatever reason the body attacks the pancreas and it stops producing insulin. There are theories that it might be inherited, but we think it requires some sort of environmental trigger. Maybe an infection or virus or stress.'

'Inherited? But I don't think anyone ...'

'It's not *always* inherited.' She put a hand on my arm. 'Don't think too hard about the whys and hows. You'll drive yourself up the wall. Really this is a good thing to diagnose because it means Rose will be fine.'

'Diabetes,' I repeated, as though testing the strength of the word. Maybe if I said it enough it would make sense, sink in.

'Yes,' said Gill. 'It'll surprise you how fast she'll be herself again once we set up an insulin drip. By tomorrow she'll be alert, probably starving hungry. You'll be able to go home in a few days and give her the insulin yourself.'

'Insulin? What, all the time?'

'Yes, she'll need it for the rest of her life.'

'And how will she take this insulin at home? Pills? She's a bugger for not being able to swallow them. I have to buy liquid paracetamol.'

'No, not pills. Injections.'

'Injections?' I tried to imagine it and couldn't.

Instead I thought of when Rose went away with her grandma for a week and I had missed her smell. I still had Piglet, her favourite toy as an infant, which I'd kept in the vain hope of retaining that baby scent. But the fragrance had gone and it smelt like the inside of a stale box. I searched for remnants of other, still-smelly toys and rags. Eventually I resorted to Rose's pillowcase and there it was; the subtle essence of my child. Other kids smell alien, but our own babies produce a unique scent that we find irresistible. No sooner have they left the womb than they apologise for all the pain they've caused by seducing us with their odour.

I wondered if insulin wouldn't ruin Rose's sweet smell. I wanted Jake, realising it suddenly, like when you remember you've left a candle burning. It wasn't fair that I was alone, dealing with this. I feared sometimes that the longer he was away, the less I'd love him, that loneliness would replace my heart.

How would I do injections on my own? Jake would have to be told. Could he come home? Would they let him leave a warzone? I shook my head and refused to look at Gill.

'She can't have injections,' I said. 'She's stick thin, tiny. I can't put a needle into that baby skin.'

'Let's go into this cubicle, where it's more private.' Gill guided me and I let her, mental resistance to the news sapping all my physical strength. 'It will become part of life, I promise you.'

'But it won't be the same will it?'

'No, but I know many nine-year-olds who cope very well with the finger prick tests, injections and everything.'

'She shouldn't have to cope. She's a *baby*.'

'Let me get you a cup of tea. They'll get Rose settled on the ward and you can stay with her overnight if you want. A specialist diabetes nurse will come and explain it all to you in the morning.'

I surrendered to the news. No more words. No more arguing. A silent world again.

I let myself be taken to where Rose slept. I nodded as various consultants told me things I knew would matter tomorrow and a nurse asked if anyone could bring me a change of clothes.

And then it was just us again, in a sterile room with tan curtains that reminded me of school halls, and an empty handwash machine and a window that looked onto another identical room, except it was the opposite way around, like a mirror image. In that room an exhausted mother in a ridiculous stained dress and flour-white make-up didn't lean over the bed of a tiny black cat and smell its cheek. No one in that room felt overwhelming guilt and wanted to take the clock off the wall and wind it back so she could be a better mum.

I pulled up the plastic chair that would be bed for the night, put my head on Rose's tummy and held her free hand. The other one had a tube in it and a nametag about the wrist, like when she was born. I knew if she were merely sleeping she'd reach under her pillow, check her book was there.

But she didn't.

'I'll go and get one before you wake,' I promised. 'Whichever you've got under your pillow at home.' I paused. 'And you can read any of the books on my shelf. Well, maybe not the ones with the *really* bad words in. Look, we'll see. But just please *wake up* and you can read anything you want to.'

Eventually I fell asleep; but on the threshold of a troubled slumber, the image of the medal-wearing familiar stranger blowing out our pumpkin candle appeared in my head; and within the fug of exhaustion and confusion I realised what Rose had been saying as she collapsed on the kitchen tiles:

He'll get the candle.

2

THE PUMPKINS ARE SLEEPING

We are about 800 miles from land, so will try to make it.
Expect rescue anytime now.

K.C.

All through the night ghosts visited: pastel nurses in creased uniforms crept into our room and pricked Rose's finger end to harvest her blood, on the hour, every hour, over and over. The digits on their tiny machines meant nothing to me and the jargon on her chart could have been Russian for all I understood it.

I woke repeatedly at each of these disruptions, while my skinny cat remained unconscious. And then, before daylight washed over the rooftops like incoming tide, I woke fully. My neck was stiff and Rose's hand still curled inside mine.

Our pumpkin candle had haunted my half-dreams. How curious that I had imagined a stranger saying he would blow it out and then heard the same words from my fainting daughter's mouth. Was it possible that someone imaginary might extinguish a flame? What if it wasn't and I returned to a blackened building? How would I tell Jake that not only was

Rose diabetic but our house was gone?

I had to check.

Besides, I didn't want Rose waking up without a book. She loved them. It had been one of her first words; 'Book, book, want book, like book.' Jake had been delighted that our daughter craved literary sustenance over endless Disney movies. I'd suggested it was because I'd read aloud to her while pregnant because it was meant to encourage early language development. I hadn't wanted Rose to fail at school like I had. I'd also worried her interest might pass.

But she continued to prefer hearing stories read aloud to watching cartoons, nodding with excitement and trying to turn the pages as we went. The sentences I self-consciously pronounced must have evoked images that were better than an animated screen.

Now I whispered a true story in Rose's ear; 'I won't be long, I'll just put some more sensible clothes on, ring Dad, and bring your things.'

Then I told one of the nurses I'd be back soon and called a taxi.

Outside, the dark again whispered to me: Halloween's done, it said, the pumpkins are sleeping now, smell the whiff of dead leaves, of bonfires coming, of loose skin over fleshless bones, of goodbyes, changes. I could smell it all. And again the sea, on the wind, as though I were a ship moving through waves.

I thought I caught a hint of the brown-suited stranger's musky aftershave; I inhaled deeply and looked around for him. But I was alone; perhaps it was just my memory. The stranger really had reminded me of the grandfather I'd never met: Colin.

In the taxi I tried to remember more about him. I only knew flashes of drama, the medals given, the number of men dead, the bravery – sensational things fit for the blurb on a paperback. My dad used to say Colin never really recovered from his ordeal and all that kept him going afterwards were his three small children. This I now understood; this I now felt.

The taxi drove parallel to the River Humber, by the crumbling Lord Line Building, past rusted trawler boats, muddy waters, and the disused Sea Fish Industry Authority building at St Andrew's Dock. Long grass grew up around brick, like hands from the ocean reclaiming what was once theirs. These fish docks, years ago, were the busiest in Hull. Now they were abandoned, like those further east along the river, where merchant seamen once set sail in gleaming ships, where Colin would have departed long ago.

As the taxi left the river and we passed dying orange lanterns and discarded witch hats in front gardens, I tried to remember the stories about Colin, but they had died with my childhood. I could ask my dad or uncle or aunt for his full history but I worried it might make them sad.

I closed my eyes and tried to recall seeing Grandad Colin at the end of my bed years ago. Hadn't I smelt the sea then, too? Were those the high-temperature-fuelled hallucinations of a child who'd frequently had tonsillitis, or had I seen a ghost? Had I imagined the recurring sea breeze while worrying about Rose? Had I yesterday fantasised the somehow familiar brown-suited stranger?

Did trauma induce such imaginings?

But no, the man at the hospital had been too real. He'd

been *there*. I could still feel his chin whiskers scraping my cheek. He'd probably reminded me of Colin because I'd craved the comfort my visions had given me when I was tiny. Now, with my own child ill, I'd needed someone bigger, someone braver than myself.

The thought of her, alone at the hospital, turned my stomach over.

'Is this the street?' asked the taxi driver.

'Yes.' I was relieved. I could do what I needed and hurry back to Rose's bedside. 'My house is just past the lamppost.'

I leaned forward in my seat to check it was still there. April's overgrown hedge meant you had to be parked right in front of the door to see us. And there we were. Our home, not burned down, the house we'd bought ten years earlier because it was close enough to a main road and the local shops and schools, but safely tucked away at the end of a cul-de-sac.

I liked safe, hidden, private. Not having to make small talk with residents too often, being able to go to them if needed. Close but far. My love of privacy came from my father, a man who liked his own space; my mother's traits were weaker in me; but my occasional need for company and converse came from her, a social butterfly who flitted happily here and there.

'There you go.'

I gave the driver a generous tip because he'd not bothered me with unnecessary chat, and went inside.

I'd actually thought to lock the door after me earlier. Our pumpkin wasn't lit, the face we'd carved not visible in the darkened kitchen. I switched on the light and lifted its lid. The candle inside hadn't burned down all the way. It was hard to work out how long it must have burned after we left the house in a rush of muddy footprints and strange costumes. But this certainly didn't look like a candle that had had been alight for hours and hours, only dying when it ran out of wick – it had been extinguished. Had someone blown it out or had it flickered and faded in some errant breeze?

There was no way of knowing.

I went into the dining room. One of Rose's books stood on the table on its edge; triangular, like a tent. I missed our shared stories. She read privately now, to herself. I missed the perfume of her hair and the book pages, the discarded peel of her after-school orange.

Behind the table was the book nook, a place Rose had created and christened when she was five.

'How do you know the word nook?' I'd asked her, thinking it was an odd choice for a five-year-old.

'Mrs Atkinson at school told me,' she'd said. 'It was in this story about fairies and they had one. She said it was a cosy and nice place. You can make magic and stuff there. Plus book rhymes with nook.'

So we filled our book nook with two cinnamon-coloured cushions and a bookshelf donated by Rose's aunt Lily. Over the years our collection of books grew and grew. We picked them up in charity shops, at jumble sales, at book fairs and at Christmas. Most evenings Jake used to come home to us reclined in our squishy cushions, me reading, Rose in rapture.

'You're like two mice,' he'd say. 'Peace for me anyway.'

I sank into one of the cushions now. Though Rose rarely came here anymore, having naturally begun to enjoy TV shows more, I'd never had the heart to change it. Instead she kept books beneath her pillow, secret, selfish reads, each with a colourful marker like a flower growing from the words.

The night after Jake left I'd come here in the dark and cried a little. Now I did the same; I knew if I did I'd be able to call Jake without a fuss, be able go back to the hospital and greet Rose without burdening her, be able to do whatever diabetes dictated.

I buried my face in a cushion – even though I had no witness – and cried the way children do; greedily, loudly, unabashedly. When I was done I wiped my eyes with a corner of the artfully stained dress and realised I'd marked the cushion, as though I'd bled there. As though a pastel nurse had pricked my finger end to read its blood and spilt some.

I realised blood would soon be our life.

It was time to call Jake. I didn't want to. During the night I'd even considered letting him escape the upset. Why not tell him when he returned on his leave in two months? What could he do anyway, out there in a warzone? Might the news detract him from his duties, put him in danger?

But I knew him – I knew he'd want to know; *have* to know.

Our last call had been in the middle of October, out of the blue. He couldn't make promises about when he'd next ring – a sergeant in charge of a twenty-eight-man platoon in Kabul isn't able to nip off to the phone whenever he fancies. I knew this and accepted it, so I never tried to anticipate our next conversation. So when he did manage to get through, it was a pleasant surprise.

I got my welfare card from the drawer in the bathroom cabinet, where it was hidden beneath old cream bottles and vitamin packets; it was the most precious thing I owned right now, so I feared carrying it around or leaving it where burglars might search for valuables. All army wives are given them when husbands tour unreachable places. On this credit-card-sized slip is necessary emergency information, most importantly a helpline number so soldiers can be contacted in extreme circumstances.

This was an extreme circumstance.

I told the operator Jake's full name, rank and number so he could be alerted. She said it might be an hour until he called back so I asked if he'd ring my mobile and gave her the number.

Upstairs I finally changed out of my too-short nurse dress and washed my powdery face. Which clothes should I wear to learn how to inject my own child numerous times a day? What colour complemented blood? Festive green? Bleakest black? Perhaps I should pick my favourite dress with pink roses that I'd worn to a recent family christening, when Rose had said, 'There are tiny little me's all over it!' Or was a dress so cheerful making light of her diagnosis?

I put on leggings and a jumper, and went to Rose's room. Opening the door was like opening the lid on a favourite perfume bottle – its scent was familiar and uplifting and stimulated all my senses. She lived in chaos; papers and ribbons and socks and DVDs and stuffed toys and toothbrushes were scattered across the floor and surfaces. I'd long ago given up nagging and following her around with a bin bag. It seemed that, as in maths, where two negatives make a positive, two orderly parents make a messy child.

The bed was unmade; only one part was straight – its pillow, with two books beneath. Tornados have a clear, calm centre with low pressure; Rose's books were this centre. While she might happily drop clothes in her wake, discard paper without a thought, she never went to sleep without putting her latest reads beneath her head, as though the words might somehow penetrate her dreams.

I took them out. She was reading *War Horse* and *The Snow Goose*. Animals were her favourite characters.

'Animals are more interesting than people,' she once said. 'People do my head in. But animals always behave so much more better. They're never dickheads.'

To which I'd, of course, said, '*Language*,' and we'd argued about my swearing and how she was only copying me.

I needed to get back to the hospital. I put Rose's books in a bag with some snacks, a toothbrush, hairbrush and some of her clothes. Then I drove through the pre-dawn streets, no radio, no distraction, but no peace.

When my phone rang I didn't even look to see who it was. I pulled over by Rose's school and answered, my hand shaking.

'Are you okay?' asked Jake, no hello or other greeting. Usually we began gently, using affectionate nicknames and slightly shy from having not spoken in weeks.

'I'm fine,' I lied. 'It's not me, it's...'

'Rose? God, is she okay?'

'No. Yes. I mean – she will be.'

'Will be? What's happened?'

'She collapsed,' I said. 'It was all so crazy, so fast. She was...'

'What do you mean "collapsed"? Why? Where is she now?'
I understood Jake's panic, his need to demand answers. I'd been in that place only hours ago and so now I wanted to ease

his anxiety as Gill had mine.

'She's in the hospital,' I said, 'still unconscious, but they…'

'Where *are* you?' he demanded.

I could see him as clearly as I would if he'd been sitting in the passenger seat next to me – thick reddish hair grown out a little because he was home on leave, pale skin dotted with freckles, chin cut in half by a cleft, and eyes that studied me from beneath eyebrows too beautiful for a man. Eyes that I'd never been able to escape, frequently fought against, often surrendered to, and always looked at for security. I wished he was there.

'I'm in the car,' I said. 'I've been home to…'

'Home? Shouldn't you be with her?'

'I was – I am.' I tried to get him to understand. 'I had to get changed, get the card with your number on, get her some…'

'I told you to carry that card around in case there's an emergency and you need to call me!' His voice reached a pitch I'd only heard a few times before, once when Rose went missing in a department store and we found her after a frenzied twenty-minute search, trying on women's bras.

'I was afraid I'd lose it,' I said. 'Look, I'm driving back to the hospital right now; I only stopped to talk to you. I didn't want her to wake without her favourite books. Jake – she collapsed.'

'Why?'

'They said she has diabetes.' It felt like someone else said the words.

'What? I don't understand. How? I mean, she's *nine*.'

'It's not like that – there are two sorts apparently and hers is just random. It's no one's fault. Remember I told you a few weeks ago how she was thirsty a lot? I feel so bad that I didn't do anything then! I thought she was playing up. Missing you. I told you remember and you agreed and said she'd settle down.'

'I did, yes. But maybe if I'd been there I'd have known it was something more.'

'So you're saying *I* should've known?'

'No,' he said softly. 'I didn't mean that.'

'You did. And you're right. I'm terrible.'

'No, you're not.' He paused. 'Is she going to be okay? I just can't take it all in. What happens now?'

'Injections. Forever. But yes, they say she'll be right as rain in a few days.' I braced myself for a question I feared the answer to. 'So will they let you come home?'

Jake didn't speak. I imagined I heard gunfire, but it was only a truck backing up on the opposite side of the road.

'They *should* let me yes. I don't know how soon, I'll have to find out.'

'I'll cope until then,' I said, and added, perhaps more to convince myself, 'I *will*. I don't want you to worry; you have to stay safe. I'm sure I can manage this for a day or two until you're here. How hard can it be? They're going to show me how to do it all soon. I'll be fine. Rose will be fine. I promise. I'll look after our little pal.' We'd always affectionately called her this and as I said the nickname my throat closed up.

'I wish I was there for her,' said Jake.

'I know. But *I'm* here.'

'You need to get back to the hospital.'

'You want me to go?'

'I just want you to be with her, in case she wakes up,' he said. 'God, I feel so useless!'

'You're not. You're just doing what you signed up to do. Last week Rose had to do this project about who her hero is – she wrote about you. You keep yourself safe and I'll keep our little pal safe.'

When he didn't speak I knew all the words he wasn't saying.

'I'll get back to her,' I said.

'I'll ring as soon as I possibly can with news of when they might release me. You'll call the helpline if anything else happens, you promise?'

'Of course I will – but it won't.'

'I love you, Natalie.'

'Love you too.'

After hanging up I sat still for a moment. Sunlight began to slide its way along the roofs and trees, its fingers not yet quite long enough to touch my car. As natural light took over, the electric lamps died. Soon Rose would rely on injected insulin to do what was the natural job of her pancreas. How I wished I could give her mine.

I telephoned each of my parents. They'd separated when I was eleven, amicably, different natures dividing them like fields and forest. My mum lived on the Isle of Wight now with a man much younger, someone who lived life with the same vigour. My dad lived a bit closer, but his secluded nature sometimes made it seem as though he were as far away.

Each responded differently, but completely as I'd expected. Mum wailed and asked when she should come up, to which I insisted there was no need. Dad calmly asked practical questions and for facts about the nature of the illness. I gave them what they needed.

Then I drove back to the hospital.

⁓

Rose was still sleeping. A faint blush of red now coloured her cheeks. I'd wanted to call her Little Pink when she was born because the midwives had said what lovely skin she had. Quite rightly, Jake suggested she might be mocked at school, and so we settled on Rose.

I put her two books under the stiff hospital pillow and sat back in the chair. A nurse I'd not yet seen came in with one of the blood-reading devices.

'Oh, you're back.' She pricked Rose's finger end. This time my daughter jerked away. 'She'll be awake soon and she might not be herself – she'll be dead crabby. She'll want to eat everything in sight for days until her blood sugars stabilise.'

'When can we go home?' I asked.

'Usually it's after a few days,' she said. 'This morning Shelley, our diabetes nurse, will come and sit with you and explain everything fully. There's plenty of support, but she'll give you that information.'

'Thank you.' I suddenly realised that I too was hungry. When had I last eaten? I'd picked at Rose's chips yesterday lunchtime, finished her yoghurt.

As though she'd read my mind the nurse asked, 'Can I get you a cup of tea and some toast?'

'Oh, that would be wonderful.'

When she left I stood by the window and watched the

traffic build below. Nothing changed, not really. What happened in our small hospital room made no difference to the morning congestion; our frontline wasn't newsworthy, Rose's diabetes no headline.

I could see the river from here, the odd boat, the bridge. My breath clouded the glass and through its fog I thought I spotted the brown-suited familiar stranger strolling merrily past the ambulances. I wiped the condensation with my sleeve and looked more closely, banging my forehead on the window. I heard a whistle on his lips, that rich accent. Perhaps he was heading for the docks, for the sea. But it wasn't him – this man was blond and had a briefcase and umbrella.

I turned to go to the chair and as had happened yesterday when Gill tried to persuade me to sit down, a curious line came into my head: *You're going to be picked up, I tell you.* The room swayed like I was at sea. This must be exhaustion, I thought. I held on to the metal bed and shut my eyes a moment.

'They'll be picked up.'

I opened my eyes again. Rose was watching me, eyebrows frowny.

'Hey you,' I said softly. 'What was that you said?'

'What was what I said?' She sounded just like she did when I woke her too early on a weekend.

'Something about being picked up?'

She shrugged and I realised I was interrogating her. 'How do you feel?'

'Hungry,' she snapped.

I touched her damp forehead. 'You will be. The nurse is coming back in a minute and I saw a food trolley go past earlier.'

'What am I doing here?' she demanded. 'This bed is too hard.' She noticed the drip in her arm. 'What's this for?'

'Don't pull on it, you'll hurt yourself.' I tried to hold her free hand but she shook me off. 'It's putting some important medicine into you.'

'Why? What's wrong with me?'

I could only think of one word and she wouldn't understand it. I was rescued by the return of the nurse, holding a cup of tea and some toast and jam.

'Ah, you're awake,' she said to Rose. 'I bet you're hungry, eh? What do you think you'd like?'

'Don't care,' she said.

'Tell you what.' The nurse put my drink and food on the cabinet. 'I'll ask them to bring the trolley back so you can pick whatever you like. Okay?'

She disappeared again. I sat closer to Rose – her smell was off, alien, a mixture of sleepy child and sterile sheets.

'Look under your pillow,' I said.

She shrugged, ignored me.

'Go on, look. I put your books there, just how you like. I couldn't see a bookmark in any of them – sorry. Maybe it fell out? But I bet you'll remember where you were up to once you start reading.'

She shrugged again. 'Where's Dad?'

'He's away, remember. He'll be back just as soon as he can be.'

'But I want him now.'

'I know. I rang him and told him you're here. Even if he set off for home right now it'd take hours, even days, to get here. He's thinking of you.'

Rose still wouldn't look at me.

'Why don't you look at your books?' I pulled one from under the pillow but she didn't react. 'Well, you can read when you feel like it.'

Rose pushed my hand roughly and the novel flew across the room, falling like a parachute carrying life-saving supplies.

The nurse returned with a plate of toast and fruit and some milk, which she put next to my food before retrieving the book.

'*War Horse*? I saw the show in London,' she said. 'Have you seen it?'

Rose shuffled farther away from me, didn't answer. The nurse put a hand on my arm and whispered that she would be unreasonable like this for a few hours. She said we should wait until then before we explained everything to her.

But how would I ever tell Rose that the finger-prick tests and injections she'd soon endure while conscious would continue at home, forever? That what she might think was merely hospital procedure – medicine to make her better like Calpol – was in fact her new life. That if she didn't have it, she might die.

'Why don't you eat your toast and we'll look at *War Horse* together?' I said instead. 'Like we used to in the book nook.'

Rose shook her head. 'Get it away from me,' she cried. 'I don't want it. You think I'm stupid. Books won't make me feel okay. All the animals in them are dickheads – and you are too!'

My phone began ringing, demanding attention over Rose's outburst. I tried to calm her but had to take the call. It was Jake – as I left the room to speak to him, Rose's words followed me; their vowels and consonants clinging to my clothes like the sterile hospital odours.

'I won't be able to come home,' was all I fully heard from Jake. Then broken bits of explanation about how Rose was "in no danger" and her condition wasn't what they assessed as "life threatening" and so didn't "warrant compassionate leave." He'd be home in two months on his already arranged leave. I could hear how distressed he was about it but my own feelings of abandonment were stronger, and cruelly I hung up on him, regretting my haste immediately.

I went back into the room.

Rose sat, arms crossed, and as though to have the final word she said, 'I'm done with books.'

All the stories died that morning.

Until we found the one we'd always known.

3

FIND THE BOOK

Both as well as can be expected. Extra water and food keeping us going.

K.C.

Four nights I slept on a foldout bed next to Rose. It was too low for me to watch her sleep, whispering the curious, nonsensical language of dreams, but also hidden enough for me to use my phone to search secretly online for information about diabetes.

I was haunted by what I found. I heard whispered words like *kidney failure* and *heart failure* long after I'd turned my phone off. I heard *blindness* and *hypo* when being busily tutored in my imminent new care role by numerous professionals. I heard *risk of stroke* and *nerve damage* when trying to sleep.

Often during the night I left our little room and walked up and down the main stairs, over and over, until my knees hurt and my forehead sweated and my heart raced. I wasn't sure if I was running towards or away from something. I wanted to call out for help but had no name to call.

When I finally fell back asleep I dreamt I was on a boat.

It was small, perhaps only big enough for ten people, and it tipped and swayed with the waves' motion. Tins of something clanked together at one end, and a notebook or log or something else papery fluttered nearby. I touched the rough pages – it was too dark to see much so my fingers did the reading. Beside me, never waking, someone slept. No matter how I shook him and demanded, 'Why am I here? Who *are* you?' he never stirred.

I woke each morning to the smell of the sea, queasy with exhaustion, hoping Jake had rung back so I could apologise. No missed calls.

I drank strong coffee, and put on a smile for Rose, and was determined to learn how to care for her properly. Diabetes Nurse Shelley was my daytime mentor, coaching me in the use of finger-prick tests to read blood levels, and in how to prepare and give injections, and where on the body was best to administer them.

Having failed maths at school, I struggled with the numbers. The desired blood sugar reading for a diabetic is between four and ten, though this range varied depending on which website I read at night or which nurse answered my endless questions. Shelley said it would take time to get Rose down to such levels and that I shouldn't worry if her readings were still as high as fifteen for some weeks yet.

'Sadly,' Shelley said, 'these early days are hard because the pancreas occasionally adds its natural insulin to the insulin you inject.'

And then more numbers to baffle me – the dose of insulin. How to work that out? I learned that it depended on numerous factors; size of child, what has been or might be eaten, recent blood reading, and how many doses were being given each day.

I asked Shelley to give me a mnemonic, explaining that I did better with patterns, with words, with rhyme. When I was small I'd loved the quirky expressions my English teacher gave us to remember grammatical rules: I before E except after C, and when she told us to think of the apostrophe in *it's* and *she's* as a gravestone for the missing letter.

'You'll have to find your own way with that, pet,' Shelley told me. 'Diabetes is a condition where practice really does make perfect, to use a more helpful phrase. At home you'll fall naturally into your own routine. One day something will click – I promise you. But it'll take time.'

Time stretched before me, like darkness beyond the car headlights on a country lane. I knew there was plenty of travel looming but could only see the next few hours of it. At the end would be Jake's return, but between now and then it was just Rose and me. I longed for him to call. I knew he'd want to, that he'd have understood and forgiven my overreaction to his news. But his role as army sergeant in the middle of a warzone meant a quick visit to the nearest telephone whenever his wife had a tantrum wasn't warranted.

I'd already decided I couldn't go back to work, though for how long yet I wasn't sure. How long would it take to make sure Rose was okay?

I worked part time in our local theatre as an usher and loved that I got to see shows for free and watch the occasional rehearsal. Being in such a creative place made my heart warm, reminded me of how I'd felt long ago when I scribbled made-up stories in notepads. It never ceased to amaze me how a story could be brought to life by the actions, tone and voice of the actors, how lights and sound could recreate a scene from the past or realise one from the future. I would miss being there but knew the staff would understand.

My good friend Vonny looked after Rose when I was working. Vonny and I had known each other at school but being in different years meant our paths never really crossed and we only met properly at a prenatal group when we were pregnant at the same time, her with her son Robert and me with Rose. Then we'd found a gentle compatibility, a friend we could each turn to at any time.

She came to the hospital twice while Rose was there, bringing small gifts and making little fuss, as was her way, something Rose usually enjoyed. This time Rose took her presents but just nodded politely at Vonny's attentions, rather than making jokes and asking where Robert was.

Vonny would be a perfect carer for Rose with this new challenge, but I didn't want her to do it; I couldn't expect her – or anyone – to have to deal with injections. I wanted to leave work and be home all the time, whenever I was needed, so Rose never had to go to bed sad or wake up afraid.

In the hospital she ate everything the trolley provided and asked for more. I bought bananas and packs of crisps from the canteen on the second floor and watched her devour them without pausing for breath. Hunger replaced thirst and I was glad after the scales said she'd lost almost a stone in the preceding weeks. Her mood picked up when her appetite was satiated, then dropped when the nurse came in with the blood-testing meter. She clawed and hit us, threw and broke two devices, and called us dickheads.

One nurse offered her a Shrek annual to look at and Rose said, 'You must think I'm stupid – you want to stab me again!'

Shelley gave us a colourful book on diabetes, written for children and illustrated with simplistic pictures of too-happy kids self-injecting. Rose refused to look. She asked for her dad and continued to fight every finger prick and injection, and then cried into her elbow and wouldn't let me comfort her.

'Maybe it'll hurt less if you relax,' I said, feeling useless.

'You're supposed to be on my side!' she wailed. 'You're supposed to tell them I don't want it and make them stop. Why *don't* you?'

What could I say?

'Because you need insulin in your body now,' I tried.

'I'll swallow it then.' Hope made her touch my arm and let me sit closer on the bed. 'I'll swallow those little headache sweet things. I'll learn how, I *promise*, Mum.'

'It doesn't work like that,' I explained, relieved to be physically close to my daughter again, to be able to smell the yogurt she'd just eaten, breathe in her increasingly less familiar scent. 'When you swallow insulin it breaks down in your tummy before doing what it needs to.' I was surprised by how much I'd taken in over the course of my diabetes tuition.

Rose pulled from me again. She looked away to hide the fear in her eyes. But I saw it. Knew the reality that she was ill had begun to sink in. She didn't fight or kick when the nurse did the next blood test, she merely looked away as though none of it existed, and that made me the saddest of all.

On our penultimate day a dietitian told us about the best

foods for Rose. My daughter crossed one arm and with the other drew doodles of faces with mouths downward on a card her Aunt Lily had sent. I tried to take everything in, to hear this latest lesson over the angry scratch-scratch of her pen.

Not only was there a regimented routine of injection and finger-prick testing for us to look forward to, but Rose would have to avoid high-sugar foods and eat a portion of starch with each meal, as well as plenty of vegetables. Also we would have to maintain her sugar levels with regular snacks.

What would Christmas be like for her this year? Jake would be home after New Year and that might help her cope. But while others indulged there would be no treats for her; there would be injections with every meal, and a blood test before going downstairs to see if Santa had been. I decided I would forgo whatever food Rose had to miss, so she wasn't alone.

e

We settled in for what the nurse said could be our last night, Rose sulky in her pink cow onesie, me in clothes I'd worn for two days. We'd be disturbed in the dark at least three times for finger-prick testing so I wanted her asleep well before nine. She let me kiss her damp forehead and tuck the covers under her still-thin body. I slid *War Horse* back under the pillow in case she woke as hungry again for words as she was for snacks from the trolley. Her surrender to my attentions wasn't because she felt okay; it was resignation. Defeat. I wanted my fighter back even if that meant more battle.

On the pull-out bed I closed my eyes, exhausted.

'Tell him to stop pulling my covers,' Rose said, half asleep.

'Who?' I asked, sitting up.

But she'd gone, her chest falling and rising like the ocean.

I dreamt again that I was on a boat.

It was so small that if someone sat opposite me, our knees would have touched. My bones hurt like I'd been there a long time, and my lips cracked when I moved my mouth. Cold, salty spray showered my skin. Nearby, someone slept. I tugged on his shirt's coarse material but to no avail.

Eventually the rhythm of the sea and the swish-swish-swish of foam lulled me into lethargy. Can you sleep within sleep? I did – until roughened fingers tugged on my arm. He was silhouetted next to me, a shadow against grey.

'Who are you?' I asked.

'You know me,' he said.

And I did. Hadn't he come to my bed when I was small? Was it Grandad Colin? I'd never seen his face fully and I couldn't now. I realised how dark it was at sea when clouds suffocated the moon and stars. I wished for the moon; then I'd see. I wished for a star or two; then I'd know.

But I heard a voice saying, 'Mrs Scott' and knew real life beckoned. I resisted, reached for him, kept one toe in my dream.

'Why are you here?' I asked.

'Because you called for me.'

'Did I?'

'Find the book,' he said.

'What book?' I asked.

And then a nurse shook me awake, into light.

'The doctor's on his way.' She cut me free from my dream's

anchor and I drifted away. I resented her for severing the line. 'If he gives us the say- so, you should be able to go home,' she said.

The words terrified me. Home was a place no safer than an abandoned boat now. I wasn't sure I could do all the tests and injections there. Leaving the hospital with Rose, a box of diabetes paraphernalia, booklets and on-call numbers reminded me of when we'd taken her home from the hospital days after her birth and plonked her car seat in the middle of the living room and looked at one another in raw panic, saying, 'What the hell do we do now?'

But choice was not mine. Rose sat in the middle of her bed, face impassive. No joy at going home, no fear of what was ahead, no anything at all. A stain of orange juice circled the cow on her onesie pocket, like a protective halo. She shuffled back up the bed with her eyes closed, opening them only to stare out of the window.

'That's it?' I asked the nurse.

'That's it,' she said, and seemed to rethink. 'Of course you'll get all the support you need at home. You've got the hospital switchboard number too, yes? You're aware of hypo management?'

With Rose's blood sugars still so high we'd not experienced hypos yet but Shelley had warned me of low blood sugars resulting in moodiness, confusion, and eventual unconsciousness if not treated with glucose. It felt like if we conquered one part of diabetes, another challenge would surface.

'Shelley will visit you a couple of times in the next few weeks.' The nurse paused. 'I know how daunting it can be but it's very rare a diagnosed child returns to the hospital.'

I doubted there were any words she could have strung together that would lessen the weight of responsibility tightening every muscle in my neck. I should have said thank-you but was never very good at it. Instead, since action always distracts me, I got our things together and asked Rose to put on her day clothes.

War Horse fell from under the pillow when she got off the bed. She ignored it so I picked it up, instinctively dusting down the jacket and looking inside. There was an inscription – *Happy Christmas Rose, love Mum and Dad.* We bought her at least one book every Christmas and on birthdays; we also rewarded good marks at school with them, and chose a surprise one if we went away.

Find the book. My dream. *Find the book*, he'd said. Was *War Horse* the one I should seek? But we already had it, had never lost it. So which one was I supposed to look for?

Find the book.

But if I didn't know which one, how on earth would I know where to look?

4

EVERY STORY WRITTEN

One week over and no ship. Still hoping.

K.C.

Rose went missing six days after we got home.

Like a shadow at dawn, she slipped away while I slept. I'd been dreaming of the ocean again. This time the sun joined me, bathing my surroundings in sharp gold light, and I could finally see the vessel I'd drifted in night after night. It was a crude and weatherworn wooden lifeboat, perhaps twelve feet by eight. Masts at either end had greying sails attached, dangling forlorn in the windless air. The steering oar behind me was broken; without it navigation was impossible; and with the useless, threadbare sails, the travellers in this boat were at the mercy of the sea.

Except for me, it was empty. I wished for my ethereal companion and looked about for him, but there was nowhere to hide on this small craft. I stared out over the sea, rippling with jade and turquoise and amber, and then settled back against the wood and waited.

Water gently licked at the boat's edge; kiss, kiss, kiss. High now, the sun hypnotised me. I closed my eyes briefly and when I opened them again, after what seemed like forever, a flash of burnt orange caught me by surprise. On the opposite bench was a cushion. I recognised it at once – how many times had Rose sat on it, cross-legged, pages open, waiting for a story in the book nook?

But what was it doing here?

Wasn't I supposed to be looking for a book?

I might have slept on longer, and discovered who'd brought the cushion from home, but my phone vibrated on the bedside cabinet and pulled me away from the cruel sun, watery kisses and confusion.

'Hello,' I croaked, my throat parched.

How could a dream have such an effect? It felt like I hadn't had a drink in days, even though I'd had half a glass of water after doing Rose's finger-prick test at 3 a.m. Was this how Rose had felt?

'It's me,' a male voice said.

'Jake.' I sat up straight, dreams forgotten. 'Oh, Jake, I'm so sorry about how I was at the hos...'

'Forget about that,' he said, like I'd known he would. 'I know how that must have been for you and I've felt bad that I couldn't call sooner. Look, I might not have too long, so how are things? How's Rose?'

'She's...' I didn't know how to describe it.

The first three days back home Rose had ignored me, and the last three she had fought me as passionately as she'd previously disregarded me. At least in conflict I could see the child I knew before diabetes, the one who questioned everything I suggested and listened carefully to how I thought something should be done but then went and did it completely the opposite way.

Her middle name should've been Wilful, I'd often said to Jake, knowing the moment I'd finished that last syllable he'd say, *Just like you.*

Oh, she was headstrong. She challenged my patience. But this made her sweetness all the more potent. The times she'd stilled my hand from scrubbing a curry-stained pan or stolen my breath for a moment with some sensitive observation or compliment.

'She's...' I tried again.

'God, I feel so useless.' Jake's quiet words supressed what I knew was killing him. 'I can't even do any research on diabetes out here. I talked to a few of the lads – I *had* to – and one said his mum has it, but she lost her ... well, you don't want to know about that. Is Rose getting better? Is the insulin stuff working? Does she let you give her it?'

I nodded, said, 'Yes, we're doing the insulin.'

When she'd sat cross-legged on her bed the first morning at home, and held out a limp hand for finger pricking, I'd expected her to resist.

'You're okay with me doing it?' I'd asked, scared to pierce her tiny finger.

What if I did it wrong? How could I do properly what the nurses had been doing for years? I'd tried to think of anything except what I was about to inflict on her and my mind settled on the pumpkin still rotting on the kitchen work surface, its candle inside mysteriously dead. I saw the ridges and haphazard teeth and the crooked lid. Picturing it, I'd prepared the device, put the lancet in, clicked the lever back and held it clumsily, a student nurse trying to act like she's a pro. I knew that however scared I felt, Rose was the one truly enduring it.

When she gave no response to my question, I'd gently touched her cheek, tried to turn her to look at me. She'd acquiesced, but her eyes were dead.

'She was so compliant,' I told Jake.

'Well, isn't that good?'

'No,' I whispered. 'She wasn't *there*. For three days she just gave me her fingers ... let me inject her little legs. Oh, her legs – like two twigs. It was like some floppy, silly, obedient creature had replaced our daughter! But oh, she's back now.'

How suddenly Rose had changed from not there to absolutely there. On the fourth day at home she leapt out of bed and screamed when I approached her with the box of diabetes stuff. We'd circled the room, her the bull and me the bullfighter, her red nightie tempting me to tame her.

Catch me, her eyes said.

I did eventually, after verbal begging and persuading, after blackmail in the form of promised money and days out, after finally sitting on her tummy while trying to be kind, gentle, motherly.

Is a mother supposed to do such things? Should she physically force something on her child? Smother her child's protests, lose her own temper, and cause more pain? Forced flesh resists needle, resisted needle bites harder. But I had to put my guilt in the kitchen cupboard with the tins of beans so I could do what had to be done, and scream into a pillow later.

'You've no idea how strong she is,' I told Jake.

'Oh, I can imagine.' I heard a smile in the words and

my instinct was to berate him for being cruel, laughing at my difficulties, but I knew affection shaded the sentence. Suddenly I could smell him as though he'd sneaked up behind me. Clouds of his aftershave and deodorant and man skin enveloped me; loneliness joined it, threatening to suffocate me.

'She's never going to forgive me for forcing this on her,' I said.

'She will. She *knows* you have to.'

'I've already bruised her. I can't do it today, Jake!'

'You *can*,' he said. 'You're doing an amazing job. No one could do it like you. She was probably letting you because she trusts you.'

'I'm going to lose her.'

'Never,' he said.

But I already had. Whenever Rose thought I wasn't looking she glared at me, hazel irises aflame with rage and resistance, and with something I'd no name for but I feared was hatred. She'd scribbled all over the blood readings I had to record in a log book and growled when I said she was behaving like a three-year-old. She'd taken the insulin out of the fridge and binned it. She'd snapped the ends off lancets and cut up the repeat prescriptions before I'd even figured them out and eaten four snack bars instead of one.

Her pancreas was dying, and so was our relationship.

'Can I talk to her then?' asked Jake.

I looked at the bedside clock – how could it be nine? Rose should be awake. Even though I'd kept her off school a few days she had still woken promptly each day at seven-thirty, ready for battle.

'We've overslept.' I got up. 'I'll go and get her. Oh, I bet she'll be happy to wake up to a call from you. Might start the day a lot better.'

I headed across the landing to her room, collecting the dreaded diabetes box from the shelf by her door. In only five days it had become second nature to pick it up but I imagined it would be many months more until I didn't feel utterly sick with it in my hands.

'Listen, Jake, can I do her finger prick while she's talking to you? It might distract her.'

'Of course.' He seemed pleased to have a role in her care.

I opened her door but she wasn't there. The bed was empty; its covers were piled up like snow. Her pillow had fallen in what looked like haste, revealing the place where books used to be. I'd tried every night to tuck one back under her head and she'd say, 'Dickhead.' How could I punish her for such language – didn't I use it every day now?

'She's not here,' I said to Jake, confused.

'She'll be watching TV.'

'Maybe.' I pulled the covers back, looked underneath. I checked the wardrobe, then went onto the landing again, called, 'Rose! Come on – don't play about! Where are you hiding?'

'Don't panic, she'll be downstairs,' said Jake.

Before diabetes I'd not have panicked – I'd have known she'd be quietly reading in the book nook or lying on the floor in front of the TV. But the house was too quiet, my skin too prickled with goose bumps.

'Are you still there?' asked Jake.

'Yes.' I headed downstairs, looked in the dining room and

then the front room where the big TV is. Both empty. In the kitchen our pumpkin still mocked me, its sceptical eyes a reminder of Rose's yesterday. I'd bin it today. I had no idea why I'd left it so long. The candle; I'd keep the candle. My thoughts scattered. Unreasonable.

'Is she there?' asked Jake.

'No, she's not.' I opened the back door and looked at our long garden covered in gilt-edged leaves, conkers and dead twigs, surrounded by browning bushes and a fence that needed painting. 'Where the hell *is* she?'

'Calm down and think about it. She'll be somewhere. She's only nine – how far can she have gone?'

'But I don't know *when* she went missing,' I said. 'Could've been hours before I woke.' I paused. 'I'm supposed to be looking for a book, not our daughter.'

'What do you mean?'

I shook my head. 'No, nothing. I mislaid a book, that's all.'

Find the book. After that dream I'd half-heartedly browsed the shelf in the book nook, just in case, imagining something might jump out at me and give sensible meaning to the phrase that now haunted me. But nothing had and now *real* things were lost – Rose.

'I'm going to be sick,' I said.

'Look in the cupboards, places she might hide for a joke.'

I searched around the house while Jake continued to reassure me. 'Listen,' he said. 'She's never done anything like this before.'

'But you don't know her,' I said.

'Of course I do.' He was hurt.

'No, I mean you don't know her *now*. She isn't the same girl anymore.'

'For God's sake, she can't have changed completely in just a week. She's just a little girl and you talk like you hate her!'

'How can you *say* that?'

Jake didn't speak.

'You're not here,' I said. 'You don't know.'

'I can't help that,' he whispered.

'Yes, you can,' I said. 'You chose something that takes you away from us. No one made you go.' Jake's wordlessness, his apparent indifference, fired me further. 'It's not my fucking fault – it's *yours!*' And again I ended our call abruptly and threw my phone onto the table.

There was no time to feel bad about it – Rose was missing.

Where would she go? What did she like? I'd no clue anymore.

I ran outside, not caring that I was still wearing a sheer nighty. Rows of green wheelie bins on the path. Was it green bin day? I should put ours out. Not now, not now. Find Rose. *Find the book*. I ran up and down the path, up and down the street, up and down our path again.

'Rose!' I cried. 'Please, come out if you're there!'

April emerged from the overgrown bush that separates our gardens, a huge patchwork shopping bag over one arm and comfy shoes on her feet. She looked up and down at my see-through attire.

'Did you see Rose?' I begged her.

'Out here?' she asked.

'I don't know!' I wanted to sit on the cold path and put my head in my hands. 'Did she pass your window?'

'No, not that I noticed.'

'She's gone,' I cried.

'Oh dear. Shall I help look? Should I knock on Winnie's door?'

'Yes, yes, do that,' I begged. Rose often went to Winnie's house because she gave sweets out to the kids in the street. Now she'd have to miss out.

'I'll go look in the house again,' I said. 'Ring around her friends, the school.' My voice reached a crescendo. 'Should I call the police?'

'No, not yet, lovey.' April touched my arm. 'They won't bother unless it's been a few hours. Little 'uns tend to be just hiding somewhere or playing mischief. They always turn up, and Rose will. Let me knock on a few doors and then bring us some lemon biscuits.'

Rose wasn't a toddler, she was nine. She knew where we lived and how to cross a road and to avoid strangers. She knew our number so could call home. I decided I was going to buy her a basic mobile phone. I'd resisted until then, the old-fashioned part of me sure a nine-year-old didn't need one. But it was different now; she was ill – that was the only way to describe it. Her body was weaker than usual, her mind a mess, and her emotions in turmoil.

What if she was unconscious somewhere? What if she'd collapsed?

I was rooted to the spot.

April said, 'Look inside and let me check the street.' I'd explained to her a few days earlier about the diabetes. She'd looked upset and I was touched. She had grown-up daughters who didn't visit very often, grandchildren I knew she hardly saw, and a husband who'd died years earlier.

'The green bins,' I said, my mind a waterfall of worried thoughts.

I ran and opened every one, wincing at the rotten rubbish odour.

'Natalie!' cried April. 'Stop, lovey! She won't have gone in there!'

I kicked one over and went back inside, stood in the middle of the kitchen. At the cluttered table, I saw Rose yesterday, eating Coco Pops amidst my unwashed supper pots and piles of unread newspapers. I'd said as kindly as I could that she shouldn't be having those now, they were too sugary – Bran Flakes would be better. So she'd eaten them faster, *faster, faster*, until brown milk had dripped down her chin and chocolatey chips stuck to her cheek like fat beauty spots, and I'd pulled away the bowl. When she tried to escape before I'd got the injection, I grabbed her arm, too roughly, and she turned on me, said she'd ring 'socialist services'.

Who could blame her?

'Rose!' I screamed now.

I searched the house again, looking in the airing cupboard and my wardrobe. Then I called Hannah's mum, and Jade's. Both women said their daughters had gone off to school as usual, no sign of Rose, but that they'd ring me immediately if she turned up there. Hannah's mum paused and added, 'I'm so sorry to hear about Rose. I can't imagine what it's like for you.'

I called Rose's school, in case she'd woken and decided to head there without telling me, but the headmistress, Mrs White, assured me she'd not been registered that morning, and promised to call should she turn up.

'Rose!' I screamed again.

Find the book.

The words appeared in my head, like soldiers on the horizon, just as in the hospital when I'd gripped the bed end while hearing, *You're going to be picked up.* I didn't think these phrases: they marched into my head.

A knock on the front door and I rushed to it, heart expectant and arms ready for Rose. April stood on the step with a biscuit tin. She'd made an effort to apply blue mascara but most of it had clogged in the corner of her eye.

'Well?' I willed her to have good news.

'I couldn't find her.' She came into the hall, utilising my dilemma and gaining access to a house she'd previously tried to enter with promises of gossip and homemade wares.

'Shit.' I didn't think I could bear another minute of worry.

April followed me into the kitchen, sniffed at what I knew was the stench of old food and pursed her lips at the overflowing sink, as though my slovenliness was the cause of Rose's disappearance. I'd fallen into lazy habits, leaving pots in the sink for days and forgetting to turn taps off, so water flowed down kitchen cupboards. I had found Rose one afternoon watching my forgotten froth and whispering softly. I don't even think she could see the water and she'd barely responded when I moved her upstairs.

'Let's think where she might be,' said April, putting her tin on the table.

'She needs her insulin,' I said. 'She'll get ill without it.'

'When did she last have some?'

'After supper last night. She has four shots a day, with breakfast, lunch, tea and supper.'

'I'm sure it'll be okay for a few hours more.' April opened her tin. 'Now why don't you put the kettle on and I'll wash your pots and we can have a nice biscuit and think where else she'll be.'

'I can't sit around eating biscuits!' I cried. 'I've got to find her.'

'You should stay here in case she comes home,' said April. 'My Jenny went missing when she was about ten. I bit off most of my nails with worry. Then she walked in bold as you like, said she'd been "picking daisies with Mary in the next street." Rose will turn up.'

'It's not the same,' I snapped. 'Your daughter wasn't diabetic. What if she's hurt somewhere? What if she fell over and she's injured under a bush or something and it gets colder. She's not just any child.'

'I know,' said April. 'She's *your* child.'

'No, I mean she's vulnerable.'

April found a clean plate in my cupboard and put five biscuits on it. 'Let's wait ten minutes. She'll come home when she's hungry and she can have one of these. I put real lemon in them, you know.'

'She can't eat fucking biscuits!' I grabbed the plate, spilling the biscuits all over my gravy-stained work surface.

She barely blinked at my outburst. Suddenly I felt warmth towards her, bad for ruining her lemony bakes.

'Have you definitely checked everywhere?' she asked, practical, unmovable, solid: just what I needed.

'Yes,' I said.

'Cupboards? Wardrobes?'

'Yes.'

'Garden? Shed?'

'Yes.' I stopped. 'Well, not the shed.'

'Why not, lovey?'

'We never use it. It's just full of junk and spiders. Rose hates spiders. She'd never go in there and besides she can't reach the bolt.'

'Can't hurt to check,' said April.

She was right. So I walked the length of our skinny garden, gold leaves sticking to my slippers and breath smoky in the chill air. Our wooden shed hid behind a holly tree, as though embarrassed. Every winter Jake patched it up, hoping to get another year out of it. Wood overlapped wood, nails stuck out like bookmarks, and the roof sank at the back where wet leaves from April's oak tree had weighed it down over the years. I looked towards the house; April stood on the step.

One week over, still no ship.

'What?' I called.

'Didn't say anything, lovey,' she said.

I reached for the shed's bolt and realised it had been pulled back already; the door swung open easily with a little shove. It took a moment for my eyes to adjust to the dimness. Fustiness and the smell of doors-closed-too-long hit my nostrils first. Then I saw her – at the back, on a pile of old carpet. Rose. Curled up, shivering, dressed only in a yellow onesie. Relief rendered me briefly speechless.

I knelt down beside her. 'What on earth are you doing? You must be absolutely frozen, you silly girl.'

She elbowed me away. The whites of her eyes shone like a warning in the darkness. 'I'm all right!' she hissed. 'I'm just waiting.'

April called from the house, asked if all was well, and I shouted back that Rose was there, we'd just be a moment.

'What do you mean you're waiting?' I tried to help her up. 'It's past breakfast time. You must be starving.'

'No,' she insisted. 'I'm waiting for him! He told me to come here!'

'Who did?' I demanded.

I asked who, but didn't I already know?

'He comes to see me in the dark,' she whispered. 'He smells kind of ... you know, like the fish and chips at Hornsea? He said last night that he'd meet me in here, near the boxes.' She had pushed four cardboard boxes together as if to form a barricade on each side. But she'd let me in. I loved that she was talking to me again, so freely, so excitedly. I didn't care how cold it was. It was just us two, sharing stories once more, like in the book nook. 'You *know* him anyways so stop being silly. It's the man in the brown suit. He said he saw you at the hospital.'

I sat back on my heels. If I had imagined the familiar stranger – his whiskers against my cheek – then how was he inside Rose's head too?

'He might not come if *you*'re here,' Rose said, and the moment was over. She looked away, crossed her arms, difficult again.

I looked back at the shed door swinging back and forth on rusty hinges and realised something. 'How did you reach the bolt?'

'I didn't,' she said. 'He said he'd undo it for me.'

I shivered. Beyond the open door soft light fell hard; November's morning haze gave the grass a contrasting sharpness, its overgrown blades uneven, angry. I'd meant to cut it one last time in October; but winter had crept up on me like old age.

'Rose.' I grabbed her small hands. 'Your fingers are blue and you haven't eaten since yesterday. I'm sure the man in the brown suit would want you to come inside.'

'You think I'm stupid.'

I shook my head. 'Not at all.' I realised she had something hidden inside her onesie. It was book-shaped. I smiled. Was she going to start reading again?

'What's that?' I asked.

She crossed her arms over it, ignored me.

'Did you take that book I said you couldn't read?' I asked.

'You get all the best books,' she snapped.

'Give it to me.'

'No.'

'Now,' I demanded.

'He said you'd want it.'

'Who?'

I heard my phone ringing on the table and called to April to get it for me.

'Give me the book,' I said, sweeping away cobwebs that dangled by her hair, 'and I'll make you anything you want for breakfast.'

'Anything at all?'

'The book,' I said. My knees were damp from the rotten floor.

She pulled it out and handed it over with a scowl.

April shouted from the back doorstep. 'It's Jake on the phone!'

'Dad!' cried Rose, leaping to her feet.

This man was more important to her than the nameless one who appeared in the dark; she pushed me aside and raced back to the house. I called up the garden for April to let Rose tell her father she was okay.

Then I looked at the book.

It wasn't the one full of bad words.

Bound in leather as dark as rosewood, cracked like it'd been sitting too long in the sun, it was smooth but in my hands it felt as heavy as if it had contained every story written. Where had she found it?

One of the boxes was open. Dust and damp patches and stains covered the cardboard, like the land and seas on a map. I looked inside. On top were birthday cards bound with a rubber band. I opened one; my handwriting filled a page, each different-coloured letter bigger than the one before. I remembered how I'd felt I *must* fill in every bit of space when I was little. I rummaged further; found familiar photos of Christmas and school days, and strange items like an envelope of old stamps, a weatherworn wallet, and a lock of hair tied with parcel string.

I realised it was the box I'd been given when my grandma died seven years earlier. Too sad to look inside, I'd asked Jake to hide it somewhere, anywhere, I hadn't cared where.

I looked again at the book.

Two thick ribbons tied in multiple knots meant the pages were impossible to open. I fiddled a little, then gave up and turned it over carefully, like I'd just found a prize. The only thing differentiating the back from the front was in the bottom right corner – two inky initials: C.A.

Colin Armitage.

I smiled.

Find the book.

I knew I had.

5

LOST-AT-SEA DAUGHTER

One more week. Nothing seen.

K.C.

After Rose handed over the book I put it in my bedside table drawer, next to a photo of Jake in his uniform and some rosary beads my grandmother left me. During the night, after exhausting finger-prick tests, I would open the drawer and put one hand on the soft leather. In the dark, as though instinct would guide me, I began trying to tackle the knots.

There was no time during the day because after the morning in the shed, I lost Rose again.

She didn't leave the house this time, just me. She wouldn't acknowledge me for the dreaded finger-prick test but her hands spoke clearly; *I will not submit*, they said. She sat on them, refusing to let me pierce her finger ends. Again I cajoled. I whispered promises of pet rabbits and trips to theme parks. I pleaded, got angry, calmed down, said sorry, and then began all over again. My life was a series of circles, spinning faster, faster.

'Do you think I *want* to do this?' I said to Rose. 'I hate it too, but I *have* to do it. If we just do it quickly, then it's done.'

Somehow I managed. I pulled her hands from under her bottom as firmly as I dared without causing more bruises, and did what I had to. Prick, pain, blood. Harvest the crimson flow onto the strip. Read black numerical digits on the machine; usually still high enough to cause concern but dropping slowly, like a plane losing altitude. Then a meal or snack and an injection, the dose of insulin depending on how her blood sugar readings were doing.

You've found the book.

But Rose's logbook demanded my time too. It slowly filled with numbers; twelve-point-two, fourteen-point-three, seventeen, fifteen-point-four. We needed to achieve less than ten but Shelley assured us we were doing well. I'd decorated the logbook cover with a picture of Doctor Who, hoping it might make Rose smile, but she turned away.

On one of her routine visits Shelley said, 'No family finds a diabetes diagnosis easy and it must be especially hard that Rose's dad is away. Are your family nearby? Is there anyone who can come and stay, give you a break for a few days.'

Rose sat wordlessly between us.

I shook my head vigorously. 'My mum lives on the Isle of Wight and I don't want to disrupt her life when there's no need. I saw my dad last week, took Rose there for a few hours. I've got my friend Vonny. Jake rings when he can and he'll be home in about seven weeks. I don't need anyone else. We're *fine*.'

Shelley suggested Rose give us a moment. When she had stomped off, Shelley said, 'Have you thought about counselling, pet?'

'God, no. She's only nine. She'd be terrified. She'd *never* talk to a stranger.'

'I meant for you,' said Shelley.

'Me? Why would I need it?'

'Natalie, there's nothing wrong with admitting how hard this is. You're the only mum I've ever visited who didn't break down and cry.'

I felt it was a criticism. That she saw me as cold, emotionless. Why must I prove that I had feelings? Indignant, I said, 'I'll be sure to weep for you next time.'

Shelley closed her file. 'I didn't mean to . . . Look, it'll get easier, pet.'

'Don't tell me,' I sighed, 'but it'll get harder first?'

She left and I tried to rescue Rose with the only lifejacket in my possession; the man in the brown suit. In the shed her face had glowed when she'd talked about him, and we had somehow shared a curious communication with him.

So I asked, 'What did he say when he suggested you go to the shed?'

'Can't remember,' she shrugged.

'Was it in a dream?'

Another shrug.

'What did he look like? How did he talk?'

I was sure I saw light flash in Rose's eyes for a brief, hopeful moment, but it died as soon as it was born. Then she went upstairs and shut the bedroom door softly and stayed there until her next injection.

When I dragged Rose to the supermarket later I looked for the man in the brown suit myself – in windows, in faces, in bus passengers. Would I ever see him again the way I had at the hospital? Had Rose and I both conjured him up to come and rescue us, and now find we must save ourselves?

You've found the book.

I awaited the night, when my fingers continued to work at the ribbons.

Another day passed. Another prick, pain, blood, prick, pain, blood; another meal or snack eaten quietly while I forced cheery chitchat; another injection in a resistant too-thin thigh or tummy; bleak silence after silence after silence.

Only the dark was kind to me. At night, because she was half asleep, I managed to sneak in and do Rose's two nightly blood tests, before she realised and scratched me and cursed.

In between it all, there was a call from Jake: he mostly talked to Rose about going back to school. He was the only person she would open up to. Though envious that she found words for her dad, I loved hearing her description of why school was rubbish and she shouldn't have to go. If I closed my eyes and ignored the lancets on the kitchen worktop and the logbook on the table, it could almost be that we had gone back in time.

When I got five minutes with Jake, he said, 'She's quiet, isn't she?'

'Quiet? That was chatty compared with usual these days.'

Jake paused. 'You sound different too,' he said.

'I *am* different,' I said. 'It's all different, isn't it?'

'I wish I was home,' he said.

'So do I,' I admitted.

'Why don't you ask my mum to come and stay a while,' he suggested. 'You know she wouldn't mind.'

'I don't need anyone.' Jake's mum Krista was sweet, a

little bossy but well meaning. I didn't want her taking over. 'If someone helps me it's only delaying the inevitable – that there's just me. Just me and Rose. I'd rather face it straight away. Rip off the plaster fast.'

'Time will fly,' said Jake. 'I'll be back before you know it.'

When I hung up I felt sure for a moment that someone stood behind me. I spun about, expecting Rose. No one. Just a room full of things I had to do and emptiness I had to face.

You've found the book. The thought that later I would continue trying to unravel the knots to get inside it kept me going.

❧

Rose returned to school and I had no idea how she felt about it. Shelley educated the staff on Rose's needs and, having arranged to take three months off work, I went into school at lunchtime to do the necessary finger prick and injection.

We sat in the school office amongst grey files and boxes of footballs and lost PE kits. If a teacher entered, Rose gave me her hand, but never her gaze. Small heads bobbed past the sliding window, some jumping up to peer in and see what we were up to. I realised how different Rose must feel, having to think always about what she should or shouldn't eat, worrying about not-yet-experienced hypos and bruises and the new pink medical alert bracelet we'd bought.

One lunchtime I looked for her friends Jade and Hannah in the cloakroom. I wanted to ask how she seemed but Rose saw me first and found the voice she never gave me anymore. 'Mum, what are you *doing* here?'

'I was only going to ask your friends if you're okay,' I said, wearily. 'You never tell me anything and I'm just worried.'

'Mum, you can't,' she said, distressed. 'I don't tell them about diabetes.' She whispered the D word like something terrible would happen if it reached ears beyond ours. 'I don't want them to know.'

'They'll know,' I said softly, relishing our conversation, however fraught. 'Their mums probably told them.'

The potent smell of socks and plimsolls and floor polish made me feel as though I too were nine again. I recalled how important it was to fit in. How hard I'd tried to laugh at the jokes everyone else did and to do well at games.

'We don't talk about it.' Rose closed her eyes as though to make me disappear. 'We talk about stuff that I want to talk about. Stay away from my friends!'

'They *need* to know,' I said. 'They might have to help you someday – if you collapse or you have one of those hypos.'

'I wish you were dead!' she screamed, and ran back up the corridor.

For a moment, so did I. I turned and walked the long way back, not wanting to get home. The sea followed me. The smell was so powerful I wondered if I was losing my mind. Once home, without work or Jake or Rose to fuss over, I hardly knew what to do with myself.

I went upstairs to get the book.

Over seven nights I had patiently worked at the black ribbons; releasing each knot gave me the thrill of feeling closer to my prize. I couldn't bear to cut them. I felt that if such knots had been twisted into it over and over then I should have it not easily. I was supposed to work for it. When

I was small I'd often scribbled stories in those five-year diaries that had a tiny silver padlock. Then I'd lose the key and not be able to access the words that I'd strung together. Now I worked to find words that I was sure my grandad, Colin Armitage, had written.

Rose had eyed the brown book on the bedside table when we did her late blood test one evening. I watched her sneak another glance as I prepared the finger pricker. I smiled privately.

The next evening I made sure I spent a little longer fiddling with the ribbons, looking up to see if she was watching. Immediately she turned away. Perhaps it was good that something had piqued her interest. But I wasn't about to offer her, even let her look at what she found so intriguing; I didn't want the appeal to end too soon.

And so the book took on more weight; maybe Rose's interest would mean she settled. I shouldn't have felt so optimistic.

One morning, she left for school before we'd even done the injection. I lectured her about not having done homework, went into the dining room to get her maths book, came back, and she'd gone, leaving the door open and Bran Flakes strewn like soil on the table. I hurled the bowl at the wall. As abruptly as it came, my frustration went. It slid with the cereal pulp down our lilac wallpaper. I'd no energy to chase her, to go to the school, to do any of it anymore.

Like a weary soldier home from a long march, I slumped into a chair and put my head in my hands.

'Is it a bad time, pet?'

I jumped. Shelley stood in the open doorway. 'No,' I said.

'Yes. *No*. I thought you were coming on Wednesday?'

'It *is* Wednesday,' she said, coming into the kitchen.

'Is it?' I looked at the clock like that might help me. 'I lose track sometimes. I can stick to the injection schedule but days run away from me.'

'Can I sit down?'

'Yes.'

'Is Rose here?' she asked.

'She went to school without doing her injection.' I held my hand up, expecting a telling off. 'Yes, I know, I'm *trying*! I do everything the way I'm supposed to. It's been three weeks nearly and *still* she resists.'

'Shall I talk to her?' asked Shelley, gently.

'Look what happened last time!' Rose had sung 'Baa, Baa Black Sheep' while Shelley tried patiently to engage her, and I'd yelled that she was a rude madam.

'If it makes you feel any better, this behaviour is normal. Children her age who get diabetes often behave differently. She's likely depressed, anxious. With you, she'll get through it though, pet.' Shelley paused. 'What does she like?'

'What do you mean?' I asked.

'What does she enjoy? What hobbies does she have?'

I looked off towards the book nook in the dining room. The cushions spat dust now when you sat in them and the jackets of most of the books had faded from sitting too long in the same spot, like they had floated adrift in the sun.

'She used to love reading,' I said, softly. I'd was still trying to recapture her imagination, sneaking paperbacks under her sleeping head. In the morning they'd be upside down in the bin.

'Could you read together while you do her injection?'

'I've suggested that,' I sighed. 'She's not interested. And anyway she's not stupid – she knows it's just a ruse to get her to do what she doesn't want.'

'Is there anything at all that she loves?' asked Shelley. 'Anything, no matter how small or seemingly silly?'

For a moment I heard the sea swelling and falling, felt the tickle of its breeze about my bare ankles. Gentle – like the spray in my recent dreams – it swirled around my calves, climbed higher, caressed my knees, as familiar now to me as my own face. But this time it was just leaves near the back door being teased by the wind. I got up and closed it.

'There might be something,' I said. 'Some*one*.'

'Might they come and stay for a while, pet?'

I knew it would be impossible to explain to Shelley; I hardly understood it myself. So I just said, 'Yes, maybe.' Then we looked at Rose's logbook for a while, discussed upping each dose of insulin a tad, and she said she'd only come now if I requested it. Though her visits sometimes felt intrusive, as I waved her off I felt like I was being abandoned. No more hospital, no more nurses, no more help. Just us. Though I'd told Jake I wanted to face the injury under the plaster full on, I still felt sick.

You've found the book.

Now, with Rose's wishing-me-dead words in my head, I sat on the bed with it in both hands. I had thought about telling my dad we'd found it but wasn't sure how he'd feel. I'd even picked up the phone a few times, but then felt we were meant to read it first. So I wanted to keep it for us; just Rose and me. Maybe the mysterious book would make magic, reignite the gold sparks in her irises.

My grandad had died long before I was born, but I knew without question that inside these pages he would come to life again. I just had to untie the ribbons and free the words.

One knot – that was all.

One knot to undo and it would fall open.

I pulled on a silky ribbon and the pages parted; another tug and a faint, recognisable smell emanated from the sheets. Where had I smelt it before?

The two black ribbons dangled like the sails I'd seen in my dream. Though eager to begin, to open the book, I paused. Held it to my chest a moment. It was like when you wait a long time for a baby – you go through two days of labour and when you finally hold her you hardly know what to do.

I opened the leathery cover to the first page. It was yellowed and the ink upon it had faded to ash grey. Looped words filled the space – graceful, level, high reaching – as though the writer had chewed his pen-end and thought carefully about what to record. They looked like the neat sentences of someone over the worst, someone looking back.

Am home. But home is not quite like it was before. Because I am not the same. Am home.

The opening lines. I whispered them aloud, and then read no more. It was enough for now. Instead, I flicked gently through the pages. The draught lifted my hair from my face. A muddle of entries flashed past my eyes, in different pen colours, scribbles and ink stains, changes in flow.

Inside the front cover, stuck to the page with threadbare tape, were two buttons. One was small and brown, the other brass. I touched the dent they made in the material but didn't free them.

What did these tiny things mean? Why had they been kept?

In the back I found more – newspaper cuttings from 1943, official letters addressed to my grandma, an invitation to Buckingham Palace, a scrap of paper with dates on, and one photograph.

I put the book down and looked at the black-and-white picture – it was the clearest image I'd ever seen of Grandad Colin. He stood by a flowering bush, the variety of which I couldn't say without colour, and he wore a thick tie and had his hair slicked to the left and the start of a smile that hadn't quite reached his eyes. He wore a suit. I didn't need a colour picture to know its shade. The photograph confirmed all that I'd thought.

Am home. But home is not quite like it was before. Because I am not the same. Am home.

Grandad Colin was the man in the brown suit.

He was the man who'd reassured me at the hospital.

He was the man who'd invited Rose to the shed.

It was no surprise at all. I had called him the stranger in the brown suit, but he wasn't. He was my grandfather.

And I sensed him then, looking over my shoulder, sad also, knowing my pain. Knowing, somehow, that he was here for me. For us.

6

A FAIR RATE OF EXCHANGE

I don't think they are looking for us.

K.C.

'Find something Rose loves,' Shelley had said.

So we did. We began trading blood for words. Rose would endure the pain of finger pricking and injections in exchange for a story. But when we made the pact I wondered if my stolen-from-newspapers-and-brown-diary words would be a fair price? Would they distract from finger prick after pierced thigh after finger prick after pierced arm after finger prick after pierced stomach?

Would it be enough?

This I often asked of myself when we began our swap. This I wondered each time Rose came into the book nook with her box of lancets and vials of insulin, ready to draw blood, to cut, to read and record numbers in a log like those kept at sea, to hear my story. A logbook full of dates and volumes of liquid is the dullest of stories and I had to make it interesting. So I dropped syllables into its endless ocean.

We first made our blood for words pact when Rose crept

into my room three nights after I'd opened Colin's diary. I didn't mind that she woke me with a brusque shove. While I'd always responded gruffly to such disturbances in the past, now I was glad she'd come to me.

But I wasn't glad for long.

'I've come to just tell you something,' she said, carefully and seriously.

In the darkness her voice reminded me of the wind when it picked up and dropped the worn tarpaulin on the shed roof. Some words fell so softly I had to fill the space with what made sense; others plummeted.

'I've decided I'm not doing it anymore,' she said. 'I've thought and thought about it and I'm not having diabetes any more. I've done it for more than a month and that's enough. I'm sure my pancreas can fix itself. Harry Potter would be able fix himself without bloody injections. So I'm not doing it. Don't care if I go totally all unconscious again. I'm just going to go and lie in bed from now on and that's it. Stay there and wait for my long-forever sleep.'

In the blackness I listened. As my eyes got accustomed to it, her silhouette became more defined, as though she'd not been real earlier and now was. I didn't move. I could feel the lump of Grandad Colin's diary under my pillow, kept safe the way Rose used to cherish her books.

'Goodnight, mum,' Rose said.

I couldn't speak. I knew if I let her go back to her bed, I might never get her out of it. She began to head for the door.

Do something, my mind screamed.

Then, in the dark, Rose stopped and said, 'Will you say bye to Dad for me?'

'The thing is,' – I tried to stop my voice breaking, glad of night's camouflage – 'how will I be able to tell you about the man in the brown suit if you go to sleep forever? Don't you want to know who he is?'

Silence. I waited for her to speak. What more did I have to say? What lifeline did I have to keep her? I'd played the only card I had straight away, like a novice. If she expressed no interest what else did I have to offer?

I touched the book. I'd read more the previous evening. Childhood memories had returned. I'd let them wash over me, fill my pores, hydrate me.

Eventually she said, 'You could just tell me about him now.'

'It's way too long to explain in minutes,' I said.

'If we start right now we might be done by tomorrow night.'

I was throwing her a lifeline and then pulling it away. But I had to make it more appealing. Hide my pain and pretend I didn't mind if she wanted to grab hold of it or not.

So I said, 'Rose, I'm going back to sleep, and so are you. And when we get up in the morning, I'm going to tell you the greatest story you can imagine. About the man in the brown suit. It could take weeks, even months. But *only* if you let me do your finger pricks and injections. Let me do them and I'll give you a story way better than *War Horse* or *Harry Potter*.' I paused. 'Because it's true.' She didn't say a word so I continued. 'We can get up a bit earlier and you can do your blood in the book nook. It's entirely up to you. You have a big think about it. Go on – go back to bed now.'

Breath held, I waited. Then I heard the soft swish as she

opened my door again and the sound of her bare feet going across the landing and then the closing of her bedroom door. I had no idea if she'd departed with plans to meet me in the book nook or if she still intended to lie down in her bed forever.

I could not get her words out of my head – *Will you say bye to Dad for me?* I'd never tell Jake she'd said that. Never. It would kill him deader than any landmine or gun could.

I tried desperately to sleep. I wanted to escape Rose's death wish, wanted to drift on the sea again. How could an abandoned lifeboat hold more appeal than my own home?

I did dream of the boat and this time I wasn't alone. Other shadows crowded into its limited space. The lack of moonlight equalised them; they shuffled for the best spot in a craft designed for half their number and they sang softly until sleep washed whispers away, a mixture of accents and tones and depth.

One sang the loudest.

Grandad Colin.

He sang a song I felt I'd heard before. Then the other shadows added their notes. They told stories. Mouths I knew must be cracked and bleeding didn't talk of that place beyond the makeshift lifeboat; they didn't say 'home'. Home was too painful. They told made-up stories to escape. Lies bounce best on ocean waves; pretence gives more comfort than truth. And in the dark we're all the same; no one is more hungry or happy or needy or worthy or injured than the next person.

Then I was alone. Just the sea and me. I knew as I bobbed about on the boat that I'd wake soon, and I desperately clung to its edge. I wanted to hold onto Grandad Colin. Wanted to shout him to come back.

෧

I woke the next morning and remembered my grandmother taking me for fish at this fancy restaurant and telling me Grandad Colin hadn't talked much about what had happened to him. That he'd taken his thoughts to the grave, leaving only physical mementoes, medals and photos, official letters and locks of hair. Had she even known there was a diary? Had the leathery book been overlooked by everyone until now? Had it been waiting for us?

Today I had to tell a story.

I wasn't sure I could.

When the clock digits changed to 7:00 – the perfect blood sugar reading – I got up and went on to the landing. The distance to Rose's door seemed longer, like the horizon moving away the closer you get.

Would she want to start our trade? Could the story I'd promised shrink her bruises? Could it ease the constant cycle of changing injection sites to cause least damage, cushion the cut of finger end?

I opened her bedroom door, inhaled sleep and glue and wax crayon. The bed was empty but neatly made, each pillow symmetrical with the duvet. What did it mean? She was never tidy.

Where was she?

Downstairs I went, afraid of what I'd find, dreading an empty house and open back door. I sneaked into the kitchen, the hallway, the dining room. There in the book nook, cross-legged on a cinnamon cushion with the diabetes box on her knee and a scowl on her face, sat Rose.

'If this story is rubbish,' she said. 'I'm going back to bed.'

I nodded – the joy and relief at her being there suffocated all words.

'It'd better be more good than...' Rose stopped to think. 'Than *Charlotte's Web* and all the Harry Potter books. Something I can look forward to. Not boring and with really proper chapters.'

I hid my panic with a calm nod.

'So who's the man that whispers to me all the time?'

The weight of responsibility stopped me midway across the dining room. What if I couldn't tell the story? What if I didn't do it justice? Paint it well? Find the right words or put them together in a way that Rose loved? I'd written stories on notepads until I was perhaps fifteen, and still often woke with ideas in my head and lovely lines on my tongue, but I was no writer.

And I'd have to speak this story, put together the collectanea of things I'd read in newspaper cuttings and Colin's diary recollections and my own imaginings. And all on the spot.

'Well,' said Rose. 'Who is he?'

'Let me get your cereal and some milk first,' I said. 'Then we won't have to stop. We'll do your blood reading in the book nook and you can eat your breakfast here too and have an injection without interrupting the story.'

'What about school?' demanded Rose, still scowly.

'What do you mean?'

'When you do my injection at dinnertime – what then?'

'Oh.' I thought about it. 'Maybe I could read a few lines from the diary then?'

'What diary?'

'The brown book by my bed. The book you found in the shed,' I said. 'It's his – the man in the brown suit.'

Rose stared up and to her right. I'd once read somewhere that when we remember we look to the right as we try and recall. If we're asked to imagine something, to invent or create, we look left. Left to lie, right to recall.

'He got a diary to match his jacket,' she said, more to herself than to me.

'I suppose he did,' I said.

I went quickly to the kitchen and got the packet of Bran Flakes and a bowl and spoon and some milk before Rose changed her mind and crept back off to bed. I sat on the cushion opposite her with everything we needed, and put the strip in the blood machine with nervous fingers.

Hands behind her back, Rose said, 'So who is he?'

She wanted this story – I could tell – but the price for hearing it was high. I held my hand out to take hers and she looked at it but not at me.

'I promise I'll tell you if you let me do your blood,' I said.

It seemed an age until she held her arm out straight in front, like children did in the days when schoolteachers rapped their fingers with a ruler for bad behaviour. I was going to hurt her too. I had no choice. But I could take us somewhere else; we could escape to the ocean.

'He's your great grandfather,' I said, selecting a finger that didn't look too sore. 'My grandad, my dad's dad. And his name was Colin.'

I decided to try and start gently. Wasn't that how great stories began? I pricked Rose's finger end and she scratched me.

Quickly I tried to find words that would soothe. I said, 'Colin's story started about a thousand miles off the coast of Africa, near a place called Ascension Island, on 19th March 1943. This small volcanic island was a safe haven for mariners and named so because it was discovered on Ascension Day. That was when the resurrected Jesus was taken up to heaven and everyone...'

'No bible stuff,' snapped Rose. 'We do enough at school! Tell me the adventurey stuff or I'm going upstairs.'

'It kind of fits in with the story,' I said.

Her blood read nine-point-four and I was pleased. I poured milk on the cereal and handed it to her.

'I'm supposed to try and make it as good as a proper book remember,' I said. 'With the descriptions and interesting stuff. If I'm going to be as a good as JK Rowling I've got to do the build-up and all that haven't I? That's the part you loved when you were little and we read together. You'd bounce about and get excited at the start.'

'Bet I didn't.' She noisily ate her Bran Flakes.

'So it all began in the middle of the night when an Italian navy submarine torpedoed the ship carrying Colin – he was a merchant seaman and had been for a while. There have been arguments about whether the submarine even was Italian; one seaman said that Germans surfaced after the sinking and they machine-gunned some of the men in the water. Of course, there must have been a great deal of panic so I imagine...'

'This isn't a build-up,' said Rose, spitting milk. 'This is an info dump.'

'A what?'

'Info dump. At school Miss said you should scatter your information through the story like bits of bread. You know like in "Hansel and Gretel". Otherwise readers get really bored. You're supposed to hook your reader with action first, not lots of crappy tell-y bits.'

'Oh.' I wasn't sure how to go on. 'Do you want to know about Colin's ship?'

'Suppose.'

'Okay, she was called the SS *Lulworth Hill*, a cargo ship travelling from Cape Town back to England. She was carrying rum and sugar from the West Indies, and probably explosive material too, which might be why they sailed separately from a convoy. She was attacked in the middle of the night and sank in just one and a half minutes while most of the crew were asleep. She split right in two when she sank. Each part landed in the seabed miles from the other.'

'You sound like one of those newsreaders,' said Rose.

I knew I was saying all the things I'd memorised from the newspaper articles, afraid to let go and wander off the factual path in case I lost my way. How did actors in the theatre find the character? I'd watched rehearsals at work; I should be able to do this.

I took the insulin pen from the box and measured the correct dose. Rose got up and my heart sank. But she put her empty bowl on the table and came back; her face was still unreadable, a blank page waiting for paragraphs.

'What did Colin do when the ship sank?' she asked.

What had he done? How must he have felt? What must it have been like?

I closed my eyes. *Let it in*, I thought. *Let him in. You know this story.* Rose tugged my arm roughly. She pulled up her nightie, revealed a small area of skinny thigh so I could inject her. Now *she* closed her eyes.

'I'll tell you,' I said.

As I began to tell her the story of Colin, we no longer sat in the book nook. The early sun no longer landed gently like an appeasing mother's hand on our heads; orange cushions no longer supported our bodies; Rose no longer argued and scowled and frowned.

And I no longer struggled to find the right words, to find the character. When I spoke I was Colin and the verses came easily, like the lyrics to a song I'd never forgotten. I spoke for him, and I could smell salt and oil and fire, and the ship rocked and tipped and rolled, and we were there.

7

ABANDON SHIP

Proceed independently for homeport at all speed.

K.C.

Once upon a time there was a ship called the SS *Lulworth Hill*. She was a very smart ship and she was on her way back to England, across the South Atlantic Sea. World War II had started four years earlier, on Colin's seventeenth birthday, and many men had been lost fighting all over the world. Now though, as the *Lulworth Hill* made her way steadily across the sea, the allies were beginning to defeat the Germans.

One sunny afternoon in March all the men were hard at work, painting and cleaning the decks. This is the tradition on a ship that's on its way home. Colin polished the rails until they looked like silver, and he whistled happily. The men had always called him the Merry Whistler. 'Give us a tune,' they would say on quiet days. And if he was in a jolly mood Colin would reward them with a bright melody. But if they caught him on a grumpy day, they would regret asking, and the air would be filled with an angry tune.

Today's song was *Whistle While You Work*.

Whistle, whistle, whistle.

When the crew finished cleaning the ship that afternoon they were worn out. They sat on the deck with cigarettes and mugs of tea. Colin mended his shirt, and enjoyed the cool of the evening and the crew's chatter. Being only nine degrees from the equator meant it was very hot all day, so they counted the minutes until the sun sank. Spirits were high tonight because they were heading back to Hull and travelling at twelve knots meant it would only take a week.

Proceed independently for homeport at all speed, the Captain had ordered.

In the glow of the setting sun, the men began to talk about loved ones waiting at home. They poked fun at a young lad who said there would be a letters from film star Lana Turner awaiting him.

Then they all sang a song about the white cliffs of Dover.

Colin's parents were anxious for his return. He felt he travelled too much to find a girl. He had been all over the world, seen New York and much of Africa. He knew really that blaming travel was an excuse since so many of the other men had managed to find love.

Colin liked single life. He was happy as he was. The Merry Whistler.

He looked towards the horizon and wondered what his parents were doing. His mum had probably made tea hours ago and washed the pots by now. What day was it? Friday. Maybe they'd had fish. Or maybe strict war rationing meant just bread and jam. Food stamps were needed in England to buy meats, canned milk, cheese, butter and all tinned foods.

Colin could picture his dad smoking a pipe and reading

the paper. Maybe he was seeing things too prettily. Life would be different there now. The war had changed even small things.

At seven-thirty a ship gunner cried, 'Torpedo on the starboard beam!' The shout broke into Colin's happy thoughts.

A torpedo is a bomb that swims under water. All seamen are terrified of them. Never had the men finished a tea break so fast. Cups and biscuits scattered all over the deck. Men cursed and screamed and crashed into one another. Colin remained calm. He watched the torpedo speed past and gulped relief.

But they were not safe yet.

An enemy submarine surfaced two hundred yards away. The *Lulworth Hill* gunners took their positions and fired three shots, but missed. The sub disappeared in a fizz of bubble and foam. The Captain ordered more speed. Colin dressed more warmly and waited for orders by his lifeboat station.

He looked in the boat and tried to imagine living on it for a few days. What would it be like?

At ten o'clock the submarine surfaced four miles away. It was much faster than the ship so there was nothing they could do but wait to see what happened. The Captain told them to get some rest. *Sleep in your life jackets*, he ordered. Six men went on lookout, and the rest retired to their cabins.

In his room Colin wrote a letter to his mother. Writing always comforted him. He liked seeing the neat sentences after a hard day. And most days at sea were hard.

Colin was responsible for maintaining and repairing equipment. He kept deck areas right, and also did his fair share of lookout duty. He managed the cargo gear and the machinery, and he took care of lifesaving equipment. He loved being at sea. He took pride in everything he did.

In his letter Colin told his mother about the torpedo and how the men had irritated him with their silly behaviour. He knew he'd be home before she received the note, but still he wrote and wrote and wrote.

The last word was his name.

Then – surprisingly – he slept. Until he was thrown from his bunk when an explosion rocked the ship. He staggered to his feet. Then a second blast threw him against the wall. There was no time to waste. He had to get out, now.

On deck it was chaos.

'We're going to die!' someone screamed.

'Need to get out! Need to get out!' yelled another.

There was grey smoke from the explosion and the sound of screeching metal as the ship strained.

'God, help me!' came another cry.

Men Colin had treated like family, who had enjoyed cups of tea last night, had changed in an instant. Through boiling steam, they yelled and attacked one another. Some had put on their best suits while others were dressed in warm layers with a life jacket on top. Some curled up on the deck floor and didn't move.

Colin's cabin mate was a Birmingham boy who often drank rather too much rum. He now ran about in just a vest and underpants. Then he climbed over the railings and leapt into the sea. Colin didn't know if he'd never see him again.

But he knew he must abandon ship.

Get out, get out, get out, he thought.

Seeing angry torrents of water just thirty feet below, he knew a second's delay could be fatal. He ran desperately to his lifeboat station, but the boat-deck there was under water.

Through smoky mists came shrill cries for help. Shouts of 'Jump, for God's sake jump!' guided Colin along the railing. He didn't call out. He just looked for escape.

Get out, get out, get out, he thought.

Colin reached the front of the ship, the bow. Opposite, the stern had disappeared into the sea. He heard another boom of fire and knew the ship would not last much longer. Smoke and oil smells filled the air. Waves rolled and roared. Men ran about the now sloping deck.

So little time had passed since the first torpedo that the propellers were still spinning, half in and half out of the water.

'Don't stand there gawping – jump!'

Colin didn't know where the voice came from. Someone was crying nearby, but he couldn't see them. Probably one of the very young lads. Some were only seventeen and away from home for the first time.

Get out, get out, get out, he thought.

So Colin stopped gawping and he jumped.

He wrapped his arms around his chest, shut his eyes tightly and straightened his legs so he'd hit the water easily. As he plummeted through darkness he realised he might not survive. No one would go on after him. He'd be forgotten. One of many men lost at sea. He always gave solid advice and a shove in the arm when his friends felt down. Now he wished someone might do that to him.

I'm just going to go and lie in bed from now on and that's it.

Where did the words come from?

Stay there and wait for my long-forever sleep.

What sleep? There would be no sleep now. What strange words. They must just be the rush of cold air. The approaching sound of surging water.

An icy blast forced the words from him.

Colin opened his eyes. In the bubbles he saw the letters in the note he'd written to his mum earlier. He saw pages drowning. Down, down, down he went. Deeper, darker, kicking hard, trying to surface. Turbulence pulled him.

When the SS *Lulworth Hill* sank she was greedy. She took those aboard and many who had jumped free. Turbulence happens when a ship sinks. It makes those who've escaped think they're being sucked down too. But it's just the water whirling. It soon stops. So if a seaman fights hard enough he will surface.

Colin did fight hard. He thought his lungs would give out. He had sucked them flat by the desperate need to breathe. Then, just when he was in danger of taking in water, he shot violently to the surface.

Gasping and coughing, Colin tried to stay afloat. Then he remembered his life jacket and allowed it to support him. The water circled wildly about, a mix of salt and sticky fuel oil.

Many cries of 'Help me!' pierced the night. Sound increases when it travels over water so Colin couldn't tell if they were near or far.

'Over here!' he cried. 'Ahoy there! Over here!'

It was hard to see through the wreckage and surf and mists. Bits of wood and boxes and bottles drifted past. Colin knew provisions would be needed to survive. Every box could carry them, but he couldn't hold onto any. He bobbed about like a bit of twig caught in a river whirlpool.

Again he called, 'Anyone there! Ahoy there! Over here!' The effort made him retch.

Then he realised the turbulence was fading. His fight to swim grew easier. The SS *Lulworth Hill* must have gone.

Sadness stopped Colin's vigorous paddling. Gone. The grand ship, only three years old, destroyed in minutes and heading for the ocean floor. A sinking ship is not only greedy but also heartless. She doesn't care what she takes. Some say the sea doesn't care, but ships care less. On board were men and gifts from various ports and photos and rum and sugar and memories.

Colin suddenly had a vivid memory. He saw First Officer Scown's little girl, Wendy, waving the ship off. She had been allowed aboard and had jumped with excitement at the flush toilets. Not many people had such a thing. How long ago that seemed now.

Colin mentally punched himself.

Right, the ship's gone, he thought. *Don't dwell on it. Get on with you.*

He swam backwards for speed. He hoped to find something to climb onto. Someone to share his search. It was best to swim away from the oil, but he hated leaving where others might be.

The voices died.

The stars overhead twinkled so cheerily they seemed laugh at Colin. *Where are you going, young man*, they smiled. *How will you survive, alone down there, cold and tired and hundreds of miles from land?*

He wouldn't think about the dangers. He wouldn't think about the sharks that swam in these waters. Or if he would find some sort of boat. Or how long he'd last without fresh water and food. Or how hard it would be on his own.

Was he too far away from where the ship had sunk to hope for a lifeboat? How long had he been swimming? All Colin knew was aching legs, stomach muscles resisting the oil he'd swallowed, and the sting of salty water

Then he knew pain – suddenly in the back of his head.

What the devil?

Colin felt about in the dimness. It was some sort of boat. Maybe one of the smaller boats the *Lulworth Hill* had carried. Relief warmed Colin's bones. Now he could escape the ocean, search for provisions and find others.

The life jacket made climbing aboard a struggle. So he undid the straps and threw it in first. Then he grabbed some rope and pulled himself in too.

The exertion left Colin sprawled on his back, panting. He was overjoyed to be on a solid surface again. When he'd caught his breath, he looked about. Listened. All was silent, except for the sea. The wind got up and made his shirt flap, so he put the life jacket back on and tied it tightly.

Was he the only one left?

The *Lulworth Hill* had left Hull with fifty-seven men aboard. Surely she couldn't have taken them all to the ocean floor with her?

Colin's brother Stan had been lost at sea two years ago when his ship, the *Trevarrack* was torpedoed and sank southwest of Cape Clear. A third officer at only twenty, Stan was one of forty-five that went down. Colin's mum rarely spoke of it, but he knew she grieved deeply each time he left for the ocean. She cried when his older brother Alf, a ship Captain, left to sail too.

But both of them chose the sea for their life, a ship for their home, a cabin for their bedroom.

Now Colin's home had gone.

'Ahoy there!' he called through cupped hands. 'Anybody out there?' His voice died on the wind. 'Ahoy there! Someone, *anyone!*'

It seemed there wasn't. There was nothing to do but wait. Nothing to do but watch the stars and try not to think about what morning might bring.

Despite being cold and wet, Colin's eyes grew heavy. He curled up in the middle of the lifeboat. He wished he had a letter to write. He wondered if his parents were warm in bed. He imagined what Stan must have gone through. Was it better to have gone down with the ship?

Maybe Colin would sleep. Just for a moment. Then he would shout for the others again. Then he would look at the provisions.

Then he would fight.

8

NOBODIES, FLOATING ON OUR BOAT

Unfortunately, no survivors have been reported, but should we receive any news, we will immediately communicate with you.

I stopped talking. Really it had felt like reading, even without a book in front of me. Or recalling maybe. I looked at Rose. During the story I'd glanced at her, but just briefly, for fear of breaking the spell that sparked her eyes with gold and slackened her mouth like an old hammock. November sun had warmed her face; a strand of red-blonde hair had fallen from its clip; next-door's ebony cat had perched on the windowsill and stared at us.

But Rose hadn't noticed any of it.

Now she realised I'd stopped speaking, the magic died in a stormy, scowly puff. She looked around and seemed surprised to be in the book nook and not far out on an ocean. Reality clamped her lips tight again. She roughly pushed the loose strand of hair aside and squinted at me through the pathetic light.

'That can't be it,' she said. 'It was only two minutes long.'

The clock defied her; twenty minutes had slipped by like mast rope through a sailor's hands. Rose's quick change from contented, glowing child to scowling brat with flat eyebrows reminded me of an interview I'd watched once. Marilyn Monroe's friend had described how she 'became Marilyn as though a light switch had been flicked on'. Something mystical happened and her body lengthened, her voice changed, her skin lit up. With Rose, a light switch had been flicked off.

'Did you enjoy it?' I asked. 'That's why it felt quick.'

Stubbornly, she shrugged. 'Suppose, yes. But you can't do *once a bloody time* at the beginning again.'

'*Language.*'

'You're telling it to me like I'm a baby.'

'I'm not.' I was hurt. 'I'm just trying to do it the way you'll like it.'

'No, you're doing it the way you *think* I should have it!' She kicked at the bottom row of books. 'You're talking down to me. Just tell me the real story. I'm in the top English group, remember.'

'But...' Had I imagined the magic?

'It got a bit better at the end. I've got more questions than answers. It's not fair – I can't just go to school with them all messy in my head!'

'Surely the best stories leave you feeling that way,' I said. 'Remember you asked me things for weeks after we did the Narnia books.'

'Is Colin going to be totally on his own forever now?' she demanded. 'You *have* to tell me or I won't concentrate at school.'

'You'll be fine – it just means you have something to look forward to,' I paused. 'Did it make your injection hurt a bit less?'

'No,' she snapped, knocking over her empty cereal bowl, spilling the remains of milk on the cushion. 'I want more and that might make it not hurt. Tell me if Colin finds any of his friends. Does he see any sharks? What will he eat? Why did...'

'Rose,' I said, making great effort to be patient. 'We can find out tonight at tea time. It's not *that* long to wait. Remember our agreement? I said I'd tell you everything about him if you stop messing around for blood tests and injections.'

'I never agreed.' She stood, arms crossed, eyes narrowed to slits. 'I never actually said anything, remember?'

'When you were sitting here this morning, I took that as your consent.'

'I'm not going to school.'

'Oh, you are,' I said.

Where had the magic gone? How could words that had soothed and silenced her so much be forgotten this quickly? Be so harshly criticised? Was it going to be worth conjuring up paragraphs again if she fought so hard in between? How would I tell the story right? Without it I feared another visit in the night, another ghostly daughter telling me she wanted to fade away, another white face asking me to say goodbye to her dad.

'I don't like school,' she said.

'You *love* school.'

'Not anymore,' she said.

'Why not?'

'Doesn't matter.' Her voice was tiny now; the fight died.

'It matters to me,' I said softly. 'Tell me why you ...'

'I'm going to get ready for school,' she said, and headed towards the stairs.

'But I thought you...'

She had gone. I stood in the book nook with the box of diabetes paraphernalia in my hand and the weight of failure in my head. Rose might have harshly critiqued my first attempt at telling this story, but I had felt amazing when I brought Colin to life. Something odd happened that I couldn't explain; what I'd read and what I imagined merged like two paint shades on a palette. Maybe this was how the actors I'd watched at work pulled it together?

I went upstairs and stood at Rose's bedroom door, watched her put books into her glittery Hello Kitty bag.

'Don't forget the glucose tablets, just in case,' I said.

She'd not yet experienced the dreaded hypo. The nurse had explained how blood sugar levels of less than four make a diabetic dizzy, hungry, sweaty, and unable to concentrate. How this needs treating immediately with glucose. Now Rose's blood sugars were slowly coming down to a more normal level, the risk of one grew.

I feared it happening at school and no one noticing, least of all Rose, who might not even realise what was going on. I found myself watching her for every sign, over-analysing every sudden tantrum, every yawn and expression of feeling odd.

'I've got them,' snapped Rose.

'And put your medical bracelet on.'

'I have.'

'And remember your new phone.' I'd bought her one, just in case.

'Can't you talk about anything else?'

I didn't know what to say. Was there anything else right now?

So I went downstairs and sat at the table and listened to her activities. Only nine and she was more independent and contrary than any other child I knew. Perhaps there was one similar. I saw myself aged ten, listening while the lady next door explained how I should pick the garden flowers by cutting at an angle, so they lived longer. I saw myself nod politely and then wrench up roses with bare hands.

How would I have coped with diabetes? Would I have listened to the things adults suggested? Taken the pain without tantrum?

When Rose left to meet her friends on the corner, with no word of goodbye or glance my way, I sat for a long time at the table, staring at nothing. The house felt cold, even though the heating had just gone off. I rubbed my arms to warm them. I'd never felt so alone. I felt if I opened the door nothing else would exist, that the road and lawns would have been sucked into some void, leaving only me.

I put my head on my arms and closed my eyes. When I looked up there was a candle on the table, its flame flapping like a tiny orange butterfly. Not just any candle – the one I'd removed from the pumpkin.

He'll get the candle, Rose had said.

I looked around. Who'd put it there? Was Rose home?

Somewhere in the house was whistling; a merry tune I sort of recognised. Perhaps the window cleaner had turned up a week early. I looked outside. No one. Besides, the sound was too close and clear to belong to anyone beyond the walls. I went into the hallway, looked upstairs.

'Is it you?' I called. What was I saying? Who did I mean?

The whistling stopped. I listened. Radiators clicked, still

emptying. The clock by the small window marked my wait.

'Colin?'

I began up the stairs but the phone stopped me. I opened my eyes. Saw the kitchen. The table. No candle. I'd fallen asleep in the chair. How long had I been out? The phone continued ringing.

I picked it up. 'Hello, Mrs Scott? It's Mrs White.' Rose's headmistress. 'I'm afraid there's been an *incident*. Can you come into school?'

'An incident? Is Rose okay?' Visions of hypos and unconsciousness made me close my eyes.

'Yes, she's fine.'

'Is it a hypo? Did she ...'

'No, nothing like that.'

'You can't just ring and tell me vaguely that there's been an incident when a child has diabetes!' I cried. 'I'll imagine the worst.'

'I'm sorry,' said Mrs White, in the least apologetic voice possible. 'I assure you Rose is physically fine but she's locked herself in one of the toilet cubicles and she won't come out. She also stole some food from the canteen, and she pushed another child and injured him.'

'*Stole* is rather a strong word,' I said. 'We pay for school dinners so it's hardly theft. I'll come straight there.'

It took ten minutes to reach the school gates, another five to get through the office's strict security, and a further two to find myself standing outside the toilets with Mrs White and her assistant head teacher, a long-haired man who looked about fifteen. Further up the corridor a group of twenty of so children had gathered, giggling and gossiping and gawping.

'I must first explain that we *have* tried to reason with Rose,' said Mrs White. She wore large tortoiseshell glasses that gripped her nose, and she closed her eyes briefly at the conclusion of each sentence she spoke. 'We're not in the habit of breaking down school doors, especially with a child on the other side. So there's no way to get to her. Mr Copeland and I have tried all manner of reasoning but I'm afraid she shouts obscenities at us.' Here Mrs White closed her eyes for an extra second or two. 'Bradley Jones from 5M sustained a rather nasty bruise when Rose pushed him against a table.'

'Can I just talk to my daughter?' I asked.

Mrs White nodded her assent and followed me into the school toilets. The overuse of bleach made me gag. Soap dispensers were covered in blue liquid and one of the sinks was blocked and full of dirty water. The door to the last cubicle was shut. I knocked gently upon it.

'Rose? It's me. Are you okay?'

'I'm ace,' she said. 'I'm just eating chocolate flapjack.'

'Flapjack?' I supressed a smile, despite knowing it would send her blood sugars rocketing.

'That's what she took from the canteen,' said Mrs White. '*Eight* of them.'

'Send me the bill then,' I snapped. Then more softly so Rose wouldn't hear, 'Could you leave us? I'll try and coax her out.' How on earth did I think I could manage that? My daughter rarely did anything I asked at the moment.

'Very well,' said Mrs White. 'Then bring her to my office please.'

Then once more it was just us – divided by a door. I perched on one of the unblocked sinks and sighed. How to piece together my words? What to say to make her come out? How had I created a story earlier and yet now had nothing?

'Why did you take the flapjacks?' I asked eventually.

No answer.

'Mrs White isn't here,' I said.

'Bran Flakes are shit,' said Rose. 'You made me have them this morning and every bastard morning. I wanted something nice.'

'Rose, please! You can't talk like that. You're *nine*. What would your dad say?'

'He's not here,' she said.

No, he wasn't. How would things be different if he were? Would I be doing better? Would Rose be eating stolen flapjack in the school toilet if Jake were home to help us?

'*I'm* here,' I said.

'*You* swear like that all the time.'

'Why did you hurt that boy?' I asked.

'Don't change the subject.'

'Rose, you can't hurt people.'

No answer again. I feared I'd have to suggest to Mrs White that the caretaker remove the screws and take off the door. How long would that take? What if she did this again? I looked at the mould-stained ceiling as though the answers might be written in the dirt. Eventually Rose spoke.

'Bradley called me a freak,' she said quietly. 'He said I'm going to die cos I'm so thin I'm like a skellington. He's been saying it loads. He gets his friends to say it too. So I pushed him over. And I took the flapjacks cos I was totally starving. I wasn't nicking them! They all went so mental that I ran in here.'

Tears tickled the corners of my eyes. Rage fired my heart. I wanted to grab the boy who'd called her a freak and shake him hard. He must have been the reason she said earlier that she didn't like school.

All parents see their own children as the innocent ones, as perfect. Not me. I knew Rose's flaws as well as I knew my own. But knowing them enlightened me; it shone a light more clearly on the dark parts of her nature. I'd punished her many times for over-ebullience at school that led to cheeking teachers. She'd once sat in her room for hours after swearing at next-door's cat. But this time she had merely responded to being bullied, only taken food because her poor body dictated she should.

'I promise I'll explain it all to Mrs White,' I said. 'Why didn't you tell me about this Bradley? I could have come in and sorted it out. You don't have to push me away all the time. Why do you always fight me when we're on the same side?'

No answer.

'Shall I go and talk to Mrs White and come back for you?'

After a moment the sound of sliding latch bounced off the tiles and the door opened a crack. Rose peered out, her thin face smudged with chocolate flapjack. It was like I viewed her with new eyes. I saw how emaciated she still was, how lank her hair, how dark the lines beneath her eyes.

When Jake had been away for months and came home, I often saw new things in his features – new lines, new freckles, new whiskers, new life. Whatever absence does to the heart, it does more to the eyes. It opens them. It was as though Rose had been gone months too and now I saw her. Really saw her; what she was going through, her bravery, her flawed beauty.

My love bubbled to the surface. I felt sure she'd feel it too and held out arms for her to fall into. But she wiped her mouth and blew her hair off her face and said, 'Mum, Mrs White hates me. She's going to kill me.'

'We'll see,' I said. 'Come on, let's go and sort this out. You do know your blood sugars will be high at lunchtime?'

'Doesn't matter. You said I get to look at Grandad Colin's diary.'

I had forgotten it, neglected our lunchtime pact. 'It's at home,' I said. 'I left in such a rush. We'll worry about that later.'

'But you promised,' she pouted. The bell sounded; feet scurried past the door, shook the tiles beneath us. 'You can't like say things and then ...'

'For God's sake, let's just see Mrs White first.' I guided her firmly out of the toilets. 'You'll have to say sorry to the boy if they want you to,' I said, adding quickly when she reacted with a scowl, 'but I'll make sure they know what he's been saying to you first.'

Children swarmed past us, heading for whichever classroom or hall they were supposed to attend. Mrs White opened her office door and ushered us inside, expression grim, glasses clinging on. We sat, separated from her by an orderly desk where files had been placed on one side of the computer screen and a keyboard on the other. I used to be that tidy; I used to keep my house beautifully clean.

'Rose is sorry for hurting the child – Bradley, isn't it?' I said. 'But I would like you to know that he's been bullying her since she came back to school, saying some rather vile and upsetting things. Obviously if he's sorry we can put it behind us and move on.'

Next to me, Rose fidgeted and picked her nose, looking everywhere but at Mrs White.

'I'm sure you'll understand that I cannot permit vigilantism in my school,' said Mrs White. 'Rose should have come to one of her teachers and we could have dealt with Bradley in an appropriate manner. Taking the law into her own hands and using violence is not the answer.'

'I understand that,' I said, trying to keep my voice even. 'But children don't always have the courage to speak up when being bullied. She only reacted so angrily because he said she's going to die. Can't you have a little compassion and see that Rose has recently been diagnosed with a serious medical condition and is still coming to terms with it?'

'Yes, I'm aware of that,' said Mrs White. 'All of my staff have been understanding and helpful with this, as have I. But I cannot excuse violence, nor, of course, the theft.'

'Oh, for God's sake,' I snapped. Rose stopped fidgeting. 'You're going to call it theft? I pay for her school lunches! She just had it a bit early. Not to be condoned, I agree, but diabetes can make you hungry at random moments.'

'Didn't Rose have snacks with her?' asked Mrs White.

I looked at Rose. She nodded, said softly, 'I ate them all at playtime.'

'Look,' I said. 'The diabetes nurse told us Rose will be hungry for weeks while her body gets back to normal. She can't help wanting to eat. It's not just like when you or I feel hungry.'

Mrs White closed her eyes before speaking and clasped hands in front of her on the desk as if to prevent them from strangling me. 'I understand all of this, I do. But I cannot bend the rules for one child and not for another. Violence and theft are serious issues. So I have no choice but to suspend Rose from school for a week. I ask that you take her home now. Extra work will be forwarded to you.'

'That's it?' I was stunned; it was all I could think to say.

'It might do Rose good,' said her head teacher. 'She can recover fully at home, take some time to deal with her new situation, and then come back to school feeling a lot better.'

'She already had time off,' I said. 'What if I want her *here*? It's better for her to be with friends than sitting at home thinking about diabetes?'

'Clearly she needs *more* time away,' said Mrs White.

'Oh, don't make out now that you're doing this to be kind,' I snapped.

'My only concern is for my pupils,' she insisted.

I stood up. 'Right, if that's it, we shall be on our way.' I helped Rose up. 'I will be taking this to someone higher than you, I can assure you of that. I'm not sure of your policy on disability but I doubt it allows discrimination. Rose will return when your school learns a little sensitivity in handling a child with a very serious medical condition. You'll be hearing from me.'

With as much dignity as I could manage, I guided Rose out of the office and closed the door softly, before marching her down the corridor to the exit. She fidgeted out of my grip and bounced alongside me, asking over and over if she had now left school forever. I shook my head, more to loosen my anger than to negate Rose. Thank God Jake probably wouldn't be ringing anytime soon; he'd only called a week ago so it might be a fortnight or more until the next time. How on earth would I tell him that she'd now been excluded from school?

No – I'd taken her out of school. Removed her because they didn't understand the implications of diabetes. Made a stand against it. No. No that wasn't it at all, and I knew it. I had taken the frustration at what was going on in my *own* life and rolled it into a ball and thrown it at the school? Was I excusing Rose too easily or standing up for her?

In the car I sat a moment. I wanted so badly to hit the steering wheel and shout *fuck* over and over, but I resisted. Rose always took the seat next to me when Jake was away, promoted to my other half. She watched me; emotion flickered behind her gilded irises. Was it admiration? Surprise? Confusion?

'You *really* told Mrs White off!' she grinned.

'Look,' I said. 'I'm not excusing that you pushed a boy over – that wasn't nice. And I can't condone you locking yourself in that toilet and causing a scene. So don't think I'm happy about it. But I do think the school are being overly harsh.'

Once home Rose skipped about the place. My scene with Mrs White seemed to have lightened everything. Would it last? Had I done the right thing? How would this affect Rose's education, her future?

At lunchtime she brought Colin's diary to me, holding it reverently with her thin fingers. 'You promised,' she said.

'We need to read your blood then,' I said.

Her eyes clouded over. That part of the bargain had been forgotten in the excitement and I felt terrible reminding her that this wasn't merely the fun sharing of a fairy tale.

She brought the diabetes box and I followed her to the book nook. Grey clouds had swallowed the sun, and the corner was gloomy. On opposite cushions we faced each other. I prepared the finger pricker, and she opened and closed her fist. I'd read that this makes blood circulate more freely, so it flows better.

Neither of us spoke.

I pierced her fingertip; she cried out. Quickly I opened a random page and read the neat handwriting there; we'd not agreed to select words that way but it felt somehow right, somehow fated, and Rose didn't argue.

I used to see my mother at night sometimes. In the dark I'd look at the shadowy heaps – the other lads, what was left of them – and wonder if they longed for their mothers too. The younger ones cried out for them. Only eighteen some, so no wonder. I used to wonder if her name came from my mouth when I slept. Might've been embarrassed if I'd had the energy. Grown men aren't supposed to want their mums, are they? Not a great lunk like me anyway. I still saw myself that way – big lunk. But I knew from looking around me during the day that I couldn't be. Used to see my own physique in the other lads' skinny frames. They were my mirrors. Horrible mirrors they were. Horrible, horrible.

'Don't stop,' said Rose, when I did.

'You need to eat something.' I closed the diary carefully, my heart swollen with sadness. Perhaps I didn't have the easier side of our trade after all. Sharing this story might break me. 'Eat now and we'll do your injection.'

'Let me look at the book,' she said, reaching out. 'How far in was this bit? What happened just before? Where was ...'

'No, let's wait. Let's do it one bit at a time. Like we said.'

'I never agreed to do it like that,' she cried. 'All out of order and stupid.'

'Don't you think it's a good idea?' I held the diary to my chest. 'Random. Like when you throw a dice. I'll tell you the big story in the right order as it only works that way, but maybe at lunchtime when we look at Colin's own words we should let the pages open. Like maybe he's picking them.'

Rose considered it. I could tell she pretended to think long and hard so I'd know it was actually an awful idea I'd had and that she was very gracious to permit it. She nodded then and looked at the diabetes box.

'So another page with my injection?' she urged.

I agreed. She remained in the book nook while I made ham sandwiches. I wondered who I would most long for if I were lost at sea. As though reading my mind, Rose called, 'I reckon people only want their mums cos they grew in their tummies. But anyone can love you. You don't have to be born out of them or in the same family. What about friends?'

'Friends are important,' I said. 'Some people reckon they're the family you choose – which I kind of like.'

I sat cross-legged on the opposite cushion with her sandwiches.

'I'm ready,' Rose said, offering up her thigh. White flesh was marked with bruises; some fresh, some older, all small, like a dot-to-dot puzzle not yet solved. And I had no choice but to add another. After pushing the milky insulin into her skin, I grabbed the diary.

'Just any page?' I asked, making sure.

'Any page,' she said.

I let one fall open and read aloud; like a backing singer

Rose repeated the odd word in a whispery echo after it had emerged from my mouth.

The sea is full of life. You're not really alone out there. If animals could talk you'd never want for conversation. We saw turtles and dolphins and whales – and of course the dreaded sharks. We saw shoals of fish so colourful you'd think you'd finally lost your mind and imagined them. I remember these great silver fish – maybe a foot in length – that liked to follow the raft. They stayed in our boat's shadow, so maybe they liked our shade. Maybe they thought we in our strange vessel might offer protection from the bigger fish. Sometimes when I felt really rotten I wanted to shout at them that there was no point – we couldn't help them or ourselves. We were just nobodies, floating on our boat, waiting for death.

When I stopped, Rose said, 'I told you animals are the best characters' and then she disappeared upstairs.

We moved the rest of the afternoon as though to catch the other out. I hovered by her bedroom door, hoping she'd come out and ask what we might do together. When I went downstairs to make a cup of tea or answer the phone, she scurried along the landing to the toilet and then back to the sanctuary of her room. I didn't like to knock in case it irritated her further.

How was I going to fill the days ahead between telling Colin's story? Rose would *have* to go back to school. This was harder than being on my own, knowing my daughter occupied the same space and chose anything but my company. If she was at school I could at least pretend our relationship was how it had been before diabetes.

When we returned to the book nook at teatime, the morning's playful and bouncy mood was gone. Rose didn't bring the diabetes box and she sat on a different cushion to the one she'd occupied earlier, as though to tell me not to get complacent, to show that I wasn't in charge of her. Once again she was the floppy, dead-eyed creature who had replaced my daughter.

I brought a plate of beef casserole to eat where we sat and then read her blood. She sucked her finger, scowling. The machine said her blood sugar was fifteen-point-nine so I injected her arm this time, and she ate her tea.

'The story then,' she demanded.

'Okay, so ... well, once upon a ...'

'What did I say about that?' Rose pushed her plate away. 'I won't eat if you say once upon a time.'

'Okay ... um, well, Colin wasn't alone for long,' I said.

'Really?' Rose's eyes shone. 'Who's coming? Who's he found?'

'Let's go and find out,' I said.

Then, just like that morning, I tried to make magic. From somewhere I found the story, and I tried to share it how Rose wanted.

We returned to the lifeboat, to the dark. And the diabetes box and the needles and Rose's bleeding finger and bruised skin floated away, and the sound of the ocean swelled and rose around us, and Colin whistled, and I knew the words.

A SKY FULL OF STARS

Many went down with ship.

K.C.

When Colin woke he thought perhaps he'd died. All he saw was a sky full of stars and he couldn't be sure he wasn't up there with them, heavenly. Then he felt the hard surface of the boat against his back and the cold spray of sea. An acute and sudden depression gripped his chest. He shook his head. He'd fight. So he sat up and looked about.

Still night. A half-moon emerged from the clouds as though making sure he was still there. *I am*, Colin thought. He wasn't sure if the thought came as relief or as regret. Any joy at surviving this far was dampened by the knowledge that it was no feat, that greater tests lay ahead.

After a while a sound different to the monotonous swish of the ocean rose over it. At first Colin thought he'd imagined it. Then he spotted a dark shape, perhaps ten yards from the boat. It moved, slowly, closer. A shark? Colin shrank back. No, the clumsy movement was too human.

'Ahoy there!' he called, joy making him tremble. 'Can

you hear me? Say something if you can! I can hardly see you! Hello there! Are you deaf?'

The shape came closer.

'Hold on,' called Colin. 'Just hold on.' He searched desperately in the blackness for oars and finding none he paddled with his hands, trying to close the distance between the boat and the shape as quickly as possible. By some luck, waves pushed the shape against the raft and Colin reached down to haul it in.

'Do something to help, chum,' he urged.

It took an age to get the dead weight into the vessel and when it was finally aboard Colin panted with labour. Then he rolled the shape over and peered into a familiar face. It was Kenneth Cooke, the ship's carpenter.

'It's you, Chippy.' It was the affectionate nickname the crew had often used. 'Thank God.'

Now safe, Ken passed out. Colin wrapped his body around his mate to warm and revive him. He rubbed his hands and feet, and encircled his chest with his arms to share what little body heat he had.

Ken had been aboard the *Lulworth Hill* since her voyage began in Hull. Though not particularly close, the two men had mutual respect for one another, and Colin could not have wished for a more sturdy and reliable man to have as companion and fellow passenger now.

'Thank God,' he repeated. 'I thought I might be on me own for the long haul. I imagined a very lonely fight, chum.'

Colin began to whistle. His melancholy song pierced the night. It must have roused Ken for he stirred, shook his head and murmured something unintelligible.

'Am I ever glad to see you,' said Colin.

'Oh, I am too,' rasped Ken.

'I thought the current was gonna take you the other way.'

'Colin Armitage?' Ken sat up with effort. 'I thought it was you, lad. Couldn't be happier to see you. Good to hear a Hull accent.' He paused, looked out across the black ocean. 'Did it really happen?'

'It did,' said Colin softly.

'Have you seen anyone else?'

'Not since she sank.'

'I jumped off the bow – how about you?'

'Same,' said Colin. 'We must've been minutes apart.'

Ken sat up straight suddenly. 'I saw the enemy sub that sunk us,' he cried, as though remembering.

'You did?' Colin frowned.

'Yes.' Ken spoke grimly. 'I was in the water with the ship's gunner, name of Hull funnily enough. There were three red lights flickering, so we swam towards them. I thought I was delirious. Then a white light blinded me. Thought I'd met my maker, I tell you. But it was a sub. Not one of ours. German. Oh, my heart sank. But I thought, well, better than nowt. And I scrambled aboard.' Ken paused, shivering violently.

Colin huddled closer to him, said, 'Come on, Chippy, rest now. Talking's exhausting you.'

Ken shrugged him off, cried angrily, 'No, let me! I might not remember it all tomorrow. These men came out and Gunner Hull got taken inside. The Captain spotted me. He spoke good English and asked lots of questions; what cargo were we carrying, how many crew, what was my rank. I answered truthfully. What was the point in not? He said

Gunner Hull was a soldier and they'd taken him prisoner. But I was a civilian and I should die.'

'Are you sure?' asked Colin. 'It was a *German* ship?

'Of course I'm sure. And so he went inside. I heard the diesels start up and I knew they would submerge again, with me and other chaps still on board. I hung on as long as I could. One poor chap got cut in half by the propellers.' Ken covered his ears and face in agony. 'I'll hear his scream as long as I live.'

He paused and Colin opened his mouth to offer some sort of comfort but Ken pushed him off and continued. 'Then I was in the water again, exhausted. Heard the screams of those around me, injured, calling about sharks. I swam and swam and eventually there you were. Was I glad? So how did *you* get here?'

Colin recounted his story. 'This beauty,' he concluded, touching the boat's edge, 'almost knocked me out. Like she'd been waiting to pick me up.'

'Sometimes the sea takes, sometimes it delivers.' Ken settled against the wood, spent now.

Colin did the same, said, 'Aye.'

They leaned against one another again. Excitement gave way to exhaustion. Joy at discovering one another settled into weary acceptance. They would think about maps and plans and food and water and rescue and finding others tomorrow. Neither said this; it was an unspoken oath.

The moon ended her shift and the horizon shimmered with gold promise. Lulled by the boat's gentle motion, the two men slept on and off. Only when the sun's warmth touched Colin's face did he wake. How glad he was for the light. How different the sea looked now rippled with green and turquoise and ochre in the morning glow. On the ship he'd never got this close to it. Thirst and hunger abated a little with dawn's hope.

Perhaps they'd find others today.

Now he could fully see the boat that had been his saviour in the dark. She was about twelve foot by eight, had two masts – one at either end – and a steering oar at the back. Benches lined the edges, and two crossed the middle. Her sides were slab with a flat foredeck, while the well was deep and protected by canvas dodgers. He had polished and painted these crafts many times but never really believed one would become his home.

Colin wondered how she had come to be floating so far from the ship. How had she come to be at all? He guessed that some lifeboats had been freed before the *Lulworth Hill* sank. Or he could have swum in circles last night for all he knew and ended up near where he began.

Ken woke then, sat up and licked dry lips. 'Anything to drink, lad?'

Colin shoved him roughly. 'Shake a leg and let's see what's what.' He was afraid of how little they might find but didn't say so.

'I know there's food and water on here cos I've checked every week for three months,' said Ken. 'She's a good boat, you know.'

'I know,' said Colin. 'How do you reckon she got here?'

'What do you mean?'

'I didn't think they managed to release any lifeboats.'

'One or two,' said Ken. 'Not sure if anyone was in 'em though.'

They rummaged around, pulled out tins and boxes from

beneath the seats and piled them up in the middle. There appeared to be plenty of water, a good few Horlicks tablets, some Bovril squares, lots of ship-issue biscuits, and chocolate too. There were two tins of distress flares and three smoke floats, which might be even bigger lifesavers.

Colin saw then the familiar inscription painted on the gunnel: *To carry twelve men.* He knew that most of them had room for a dozen while some small ones held six.

'Seems there's plenty of grub,' he said.

'Depends how long we're on here,' said Ken ruefully.

'Aye,' said Colin. 'And how many others we pick up.'

They looked at one another, grim and knowing. The more survivors, the better. But with more men came more appetites. More thirst. More needs. Provisions wouldn't go very far amongst ten or more men.

Ken eyed a water tin. 'Should we have a drink now?'

The thought of it made Colin dreadfully thirsty but he wondered if they shouldn't wait. Who knew how long it might be before they were picked up or saw land?

As though hearing his concerns, Ken said, 'We'll wait; let's get through today.'

They packed away the tins and sat at opposite ends of the craft, moods bleak again with the knowledge of how desperate their situation was. Both were more than able seaman but they longed for their captain to take charge.

Colin thought of whistling but his parched throat hurt too much. He stared out over the ocean, mesmerised by its swirling currents and harsh rhythm. Just when he found a pattern in the waves, they changed. The ocean seduced and promised – and then tricked.

To the east Colin saw something moving. He stood and shaded his eyes and stared harder. Two black shadows, waving. Two men standing, somehow, out in the middle of the sea.

'There's two blokes!' he cried. 'Look, Ken!'

Ken joined him. '*Ahoy there*! Can you hear us? They're waving; I think they see us too. Can we get to them do you think?'

Colin squinted. 'They're too far. It's just a plank they're on. Maybe a hatch cover. They'll drift if we don't get there.'

'Try the steering oar!' cried Ken.

'I am, I am!' Colin grabbed it and tried to manoeuvre the boat, but it wouldn't budge.

'The wind might guide us if we're lucky,' said Ken.

'There's no bloody wind! The sails are barely moving.'

Ken shoved Colin, impatient. 'Let me try.'

'You won't do it,' snapped Colin. 'It's useless!'

Ken pulled on it, swearing with frustration.

Colin called out to the far away men, hoping to give comfort. 'Ahoy there! Can you hear us! Can you row towards us?'

He was sure they had grown smaller.

'Damned thing!' Ken abandoned the steering oar and tried paddling with his hands. Colin joined him and they worked frantically in unison. But the two men grew smaller and smaller. Ken flopped down on the wooden floor, exhausted, but Colin continued waving and calling out.

'Stop it will you?' snapped Ken. 'We can't steer this thing and the current's taking them the other way.'

'But we can't just do nowt.'

'There's nowt to be done!'

'I won't give up.' Colin watched the two shadows fade.

'Fight's pointless. They're bloody gone.'

Reluctantly, Colin sat next to Ken. 'How long will they survive on that plank?

'Not long,' said Ken. 'Sharks will get 'em.'

'I can't bear to think of it. Christ, I hate sharks.'

'Every seaman hates sharks.'

Colin put his head in his hands. Would it be the sharks? Or the sun? Or would they drown after they could no longer stand up? He shouldn't let it torment him. What was the point when it couldn't be changed?

Dejected, the two men lolled against the boat edge. The sun rose higher in a cloudless sky. Its heat was unbearable in the absence of water or a mug of tea. Three dolphins swam past but they didn't notice. Colin closed his eyes and tried not to think of his mother receiving news that the ship had sunk, its crew presumed dead. Would she believe it? Or would she somehow know otherwise and sense him here, alive on a lifeboat? Would Colin's father console her or insist hope was futile? They would think of Stan, that much was true. Colin reproached himself for being glum. What was the good in it? Whining was soft; he had to be tough.

After a time he looked at his watch, laughed mirthlessly. 'How stupid. It's stopped of course.'

Kenneth looked at his. 'Mine too,' he said. 'At 3.40. Must've been the moment she sank.'

Colin unfastened his and laid it on the boat edge; Kenneth did also. Neither had the heart to dispose of them, useless as they were. Time would now be guessed by the sun's position. By their hunger.

'We should dry our shirts while the sun's strong,' Colin said after a moment.

'Good thinking, lad.'

They took off them off and lay them on the deck.

'Not too long or we'll burn,' said Ken.

'Reckon they'll dry in minutes,' said Colin 'We could cook an egg on the deck. I could just eat a nice juicy egg. Lightly cooked, with a mug of tea. Lovely.'

Kenneth groaned. 'Don't, lad.'

They leaned back, closed their eyes, and soaked up the sun's rays a moment. Colin opened his after a while, not sure what had made him do so, and looked straight at a boat on the horizon.

He jumped up, cried, 'Look Chippy, to the west! Do you see – a small boat.'

Ken joined him. 'One of ours! The current's sending it this way!'

Colin waved, called joyfully, 'Ahoy there! Ahoy there!'

Ken waved too. 'How many aboard?'

'I don't know – a few, I reckon.'

Ken looked to the sails. 'The wind's got up – it's taking us towards them.'

'They're using the oar.' Colin shaded his eyes to view better. 'Steering this way. They're going to make it!'

The glittering blue gap between the two vessels grew smaller.

'I see Weekes!' cried Colin. He was the engineer's mate, a young and likeable man with a jovial disposition, known for practical jokes. When mood was grim aboard the *Lulworth Hill* and thoughts of home weighed heavy, he could be relied on to lighten the load. 'Thank God for Weekes. We need a chap like him.'

'And I think there's Platten and Young Fowler!' cried Ken.

They whooped their joy, and the crew in the second boat echoed the sentiment. As it approached, the three men aboard were grinning broadly.

'We thought it was gonna be just us!' cried Weekes. 'Thank God for you pair of bastards!'

Colin hauled him aboard and slapped him on the back. 'And the same to you,' he said.

Though they made jokes, each man was relieved to have found the others. Weekes, Platten and Fowler came aboard. They tied the smaller second boat to the first; it would serve as a storage space.

'You see anyone else?' asked Ken.

'Just you,' said Young Fowler, sinking into the boat's well. He was a young cabin boy and looked barely fifteen.

'Might still be more,' said Colin, hopeful.

There were. Throughout the day more men joined them, making fourteen in total, all confined to a space designed for a dozen. Some were picked up from the sea during the afternoon, barely alive. Some were found clinging to another slowly sinking craft. All were cold and scared but able to find the strength to come aboard. All were greeted with joy, despite each of them meaning less water per man, less food, less room.

And then, as though they'd followed in the wake of the rescued men, tins of water and milk tablets and Bovril floated past too and were quickly retrieved.

By nightfall they knew the chance of finding anyone else was slim. The small crew was all that was left of the fifty-seven men who'd left Cape Town weeks earlier on the SS *Lulworth Hill*. Wordlessly they settled down to sleep, heads resting on one another's shoulders, not enough room to lie down.

And so the first day on the raft ended as it had begun; more crowded but still with a sky full of stars.

10

SMALL THINGS

Have been expecting to be rescued today but no luck.
Not a thing seen.

K.C.

After a day of stories Rose slept soundly. But she asked endless questions before climbing into bed. Was it okay if she liked Colin and Ken best because she'd met them first, just as she'd met Hannah and Jade first at infant school and so stuck with them since then? How old was Colin? How soon would he be saved? And was she really not at school tomorrow?

I responded as best I could. I said, yes, I supposed it was fine to like them best; Colin was twenty-one; and yes, she had to stay home. The rescue question I said I wouldn't answer.

'In a good story rescue never comes quickly' was all I said.

At this she seemed to suddenly remember I was the enemy, the one who cut her finger ends and injected her flesh, and she turned the other way and pulled the duvet up over her head.

'You're still making the story easy,' she said. 'But I'm glad you said bastards.'

'Well, it's how the men would have spoken.'

'Keep it like that,' she said.

Silence again.

'Do you want to read one of your books again?' I asked her.

From under the covers I made out, 'Won't be about Grandad Colin.'

I supposed the fictional tales Rose had once enjoyed might now pale in comparison. I'd hoped to reignite her love of books while getting her to have injections but maybe I'd done the opposite. Still I suggested she put *War Horse* beneath her pillow just in case, but she grunted and I was dismissed.

I'd upheld my side of the bargain; I'd tried to be the storyteller, attempted to make magic, perhaps distracted her from diabetes.

As I headed to the door she lifted her head and said, 'Anyway, I can just ask *him* when he's rescued'

I frowned. 'Who?'

'Grandad Colin,' she said. 'He'll tell me.'

'How will you ...'

But Rose had disappeared again. She faked a snoring sound, which made me smile. In her deepest slumber she never snored; she sometimes shouted and occasionally flapped her arms about but otherwise her night habits were gentle, quiet, childlike.

'Remember when he told you to go to the shed?' I'd tried asking her about that day often and she'd remained mute. '*How* did he tell you?'

Rose ignored me, continued fake snoring.

'You said he came to see you in the dark. Did you mean when you were awake or maybe in your dreams?'

No answer.

'Because I think I used to see him when I was little,' I said. 'And he came to talk to me when you were at the hospital. He sat with me while I waited. I didn't know it was Colin then. I still don't really know if I imagined it all.'

The fake snoring stopped but the shape beneath the duvet didn't move.

'I guess somehow he's here,' I said.

I think Rose fell asleep then.

I went back to my room but didn't turn any lights on; I always saw better in the dark. After the day's storytelling I was wide-awake, buzzing the way an actor must after a sell-out play. Suddenly, and despite my dread at mentioning Rose's suspension, I longed to share it with Jake. I wished I could tell him I was more hopeful about coping until his return because I'd found something Rose was interested in. My heart sank; it would likely be weeks until he rang.

It occurred to me with sudden clarity that Jake must feel like Colin had on his boat. Surrounded by a platoon of men who'd no doubt now be firm friends, Jake must still miss home and at times feel alone in that strange land. While his tour of Afghanistan was supposed to last six months, there was always a chance that this could change. Like Colin, he'd never know when rescue might occur. Orders from high up didn't care about feelings, about homesickness or about wives having temper tantrums. Colin had endured sharks and ruthless heat and not enough water; landmines and gunfire were Jake's daily dangers, what might prevent him making it home.

In comparison, it was easy for me. At least I could escape if I wanted. I could walk to the countryside, visit my dad, call my mum, get a book from the library, or have coffee with Vonny.

I remembered the first time Jake went away – six years before, to the Falklands. Then I'd done all those things. Vonny had taken me and Rose, then only three, to stay at her mum's villa in Tenerife. We'd sunbathed and caught colourful fish in rock pools and browsed quaint markets for gifts. I'd felt guilty that Jake was working while I had fun. I'd argued when he rang. I'd sworn that it was his fault he was away. I'd thoughtlessly rebuffed his suggestions of having someone stay with me, and I'd hung up on him twice.

In the dark, I realised with sudden light that being here with diabetes was not as bad as being away from it. I could conquer it face to face. Jake had to worry and wonder without the reassurance of seeing efforts take effect. I should make sure he returned to sanctuary after battle, to a strong woman after wounded men. To safety.

Get a grip, I thought. *Your house is a disgusting mess, woman. You haven't washed your hair in four days. Pull yourself together. Fight better. Fight like Colin had to, like Jake does every day. Like your daughter is.*

I tidied the house. What example was I setting Rose by being so lazy while expecting her to manage diabetes? I washed pots that had been soaking since Monday. I picked up damp towels and three piles of dirty laundry and put them in the washer. I watered limp plants, polished dust-caked furniture, emptied bins, threw out newspapers and discarded food wrappers, mopped kitchen tiles, and vacuumed. It felt good; I was purged.

In the book nook I fluffed up the cinnamon cushions and dusted the shelf top and books. On the floor was Colin's diary. I picked it up, sat in a cushion and sniffed the old pages. It was hard now to remember exactly the details of his face in the hospital. I'd not taken as much notice as I should have. Hindsight made me wish I'd listened more closely to all he'd said, studied him harder.

The writing inside his diary took me back to my childhood scribbled notes; I used to find comfort in jotting down thoughts. It was as though they somehow took better shape. A love of words had come down the generations, like a river through various countries; from Colin and his secret diary, to my father, an occasional songwriter, to my childhood scribbles, to Rose with her love of books.

I let a page fall open and Colin spoke to me, answered a question I didn't even know I'd posed.

You think there's weakness in it but I learned out there on the sea that asking for help is fine. I asked God for all manner of things while I tried to sleep to the sound of ailing men and angry ocean. I asked Him for things I knew He'd never be able to deliver and then cursed Him for proving me right. Wasn't even sure I really believed? Never had before and today I'm even less sure. John Arnold told us, Ask and Ye Shall Receive. *I realised maybe the asking was wrong. Ask for what you might receive and then you will. Drove me half mad thinking about it. So I asked for small things – small things a simple man might deserve. And looking back now, I suppose He delivered.*

I've always found it hard to ask for help. In our family we keep our problems to ourselves. We just get on with things. Jake is a private man too. But did I want Rose to grow up feeling she had to battle alone? Was it really so bad to admit when you're not coping?

Hadn't I cried out for help when Rose collapsed?

A man at war doesn't fight alone – he has his comrades. A

man lost at sea doesn't survive without surrendering to the help of his crew. So I decided I'd call Shelley tomorrow and ask her to speak to Mrs White about Rose's unfair dismissal. Shelley knew diabetes and would defend her better than I could.

Ask and Ye Shall Receive.

I put the diary on the bookshelf and considered it a moment; I wondered again should I perhaps tell my dad about our discovery. Was it fair to keep it for just Rose and me? But I absolutely knew two things – one, that my dad would be happy we had the book; and two, Grandad Colin had guided us to it for a reason.

e~

The following morning I called Shelley and told her what had happened at school. She listened, interjecting occasionally with a sympathetic 'eh, pet'.

'I'm sure I'm overreacting,' I admitted. 'I'm being too protective, making excuses. I want to protect Rose, but I can't permit bad behaviour. I'm a strict mum but this wasn't *like* her – she's never pushed anyone or taken food.'

'Absolutely,' said Shelley. 'She's still in the very early days of coping with the changes that diabetes brings, not just to her body but to her physiological state. She's anxious, depressed. I'll speak to them today. Rose shouldn't have been dismissed. No one is excusing anything. I'm sure an explanation to the parent of the other boy would be enough. Leave it with me, pet.' She paused. 'How are things other than that?'

It was a hard question to answer.

'There's a local support group,' said Shelley. 'A group of

parents with children who have Type 1. Lovely people. I can give you their number.'

Though I'd realised that there was nothing wrong with asking for help, a support group wasn't me. Sitting with strangers, discussing my intimate worries, it made me nervous. I could read stories on the internet if I needed them but I wasn't comfortable sharing mine.

And anyway, we had Colin's.

'Remember you asked if there was anything Rose loved?' I said. 'Well, we found it – a story. Something she's really enjoying. It hasn't stopped her dislike of injections, I doubt anything can ever do that, but we haven't missed any since that morning you were here.'

'Wonderful,' said Shelley. 'There's a girl I see whose mum sings songs as she injects her. Ever so funny. She does opera and all sorts. Everyone finds something. Well, I'll get onto the school. Leave it with me and I'll call you when I have any news.'

I was so indescribably grateful, but when I hung up realised I'd not said thank you.

Mid-morning, April came by with an apple pie, still warm. She wore her usual shoes that favoured practicality over style. She'd not bothered us since the shed incident. I let her in and she put the treat on the table and looked around, obviously admiring my now sparklingly clean kitchen.

'I always do a spot of housework when I need to clear my head, lovey' she said. 'How's young Rose? Ah, she's here. Not at school?'

Rose came downstairs, empty cup in hand. I'd not seen her since breakfast. If I entered her room she responded to my friendly chat with basic replies, neither ignoring me nor interested.

'I'm off all week,' she told April.

'Ah, there're lots of bugs around. Best to take it easy.'

'No, I got into trouble and they chucked me out.'

'Rose,' I snapped. 'I'm sure April hasn't got time for all that. Do you want another drink? Something else?'

'Natalie's just trying to get rid of me,' Rose said to April.

'Stop calling me that,' I said. This was a new annoying habit she'd developed.

'I have to go now anyway, run a few errands,' said my nosy but harmless neighbour. 'I made the apple pie without sugar so you can have some too, Rose.'

'That's very thoughtful,' I said. 'Now say thank you, Rose.'

'Thank you Rose,' said my unruly daughter, and she bounded up the stairs again.

'She's a real character,' smiled April. I could tell she was itching to know what had happened at school but good manners preventing her asking.

'Oh, she's a character okay. Listen, it was very kind of you to make the pie. She can have a piece after tea.' I remembered how thoughtful April had been when Rose went missing. I should thank her but was so useless at it. Felt like it was an admission of weakness. Of needing help. Silly, but true.

'Well, I'll get back to my jobs,' she said. 'May I have the pie dish back after you're done, lovey? I made Winnie a chicken pie last month and she never did give me the dish back, so I'm one short.'

'Of course.' I went with April to the door, watched her walk to the end of our path. I still couldn't thank her. What a hypocrite I was, insisting Rose say it, chiding her into good manners as most parents do.

'April,' I called.

She stopped, eyebrows arched in query.

'I ... I'll make some sugar-free custard maybe for the pie.'

'Perfect, lovey,' she said, and disappeared.

Rose and I drifted through the rest of the day, floating on a sea of not knowing what to do without school's anchor. We only found land in the book nook for our blood and words exchange. There dust particles danced around us in the winter sun. Rose gave up the fight, stopped calling me Natalie and surrendered to our history.

Colin's story continued. Breakfast, lunch, tea and supper divided the chapters. His random diary entries merged with my whirlpool of words.

Just over a month of diabetes and already I held the finger-pricker and lancet as though I'd been doing it for years. Doing each many times a day, every day, meant no time to falter, no chance to forget. My hands mimicked this action at arbitrary moments; twist, click, test, press. Twist, click, test, press. I'd wake in the night with my fingers wrapped around an imaginary insulin pen.

Every mealtime, prick, pain, blood-reading. And again, prick, pain, blood-reading. Only the numbers differed; ten-point-seven, eight-point-six, eighteen-point-three. Then one hand squeezing her flesh, while the other injected. Over and over and over. Repetition can be a comfort. In difficult times you resort to habit. But this was one I'd never enjoy.

Before Rose scoffed thick custard and a slice of apple pie at teatime, I measured insulin and pumped it into her thigh, a favourite spot where pain is concerned. Then I read the roll call of the fourteen men on the lifeboat for the second time;

I'd listed them that morning too. Then I'd described their various injuries, broken ribs and feet, cut heads and burnt skin. I'd told her how disheartening it was for them to watch a boat two of the men had arrived on sink, taking precious rations before they could do anything.

'The roll call's like the school register,' Rose had said then. 'Yes miss, no miss.'

'How can you say no miss if you're absent,' I'd laughed.

'So tell me all their names again,' she said now, 'even though I'll have forgotten again by tomorrow.'

I did; I listed them, every one. They were:

Basil Scown, First Officer,
Unnamed Second Engineer,
Platten, Chief Steward,
John Arnold, Apprentice,
King, Apprentice,
Kenneth Cooke, Carpenter,
Colin Armitage, Able Seaman,
Davies, Able Seaman,
Weekes, Engineer's mate,
Fowler, Cabin Boy,
Stewart, Cabin Boy,
Bamford, Army Gunner,
Bott, Army Gunner,
Leak, Army Gunner.

That morning I'd told Rose they had seen five vicious-looking, white-bellied sharks as soon as they were all aboard the lifeboat. Though not too large at four feet long, the men knew what sharp teeth they possessed and were relieved to be safely - for now - aboard Colin's lifeboat. They made no attempts that day to move the boat because Officer Scown said they'd managed to get an SOS signal out before the ship went down and if it had been heard by any nearby vessels they should hang around a while and keep a lookout.

'Like in that film *Jaws*,' said Rose, of the sharks.

'I suppose,' I said.

'They're the only animals I don't much like.'

'Neither did they,' I said.

At lunchtime I'd opened Colin's diary and read the letter that had been sent home to his family from the owners of the SS *Lulworth Hill* weeks after the ship went down.

Mrs R Armitage,
East Yorkshire.

Dear Madam,

We deeply regret to inform you that the vessel on which your son was serving is gravely overdue and we are now advised by the Admiralty that she must be presumed lost by enemy action on the 18th of March. Unfortunately no survivors have been reported, but should we receive any news, we will immediately communicate with you.

The directors and staff of this company wish to express to you their sympathy and understanding during this period of anxiety.

Yours faithfully,
The Counties Ship Management Company Ltd.

Colin described next to it tremendous feelings of sadness that his mother had received it. He wrote that had he known of its existence while on the lifeboat he might not have gone on, and certainly would have felt guilt at causing his mum grief she had already endured when Stan was lost at sea.

Now I tried to go on with the story. I feared not doing it right. I had been faltering at certain words, trying to find one that Rose would understand but also not berate me for patronising her. How did the professional writers that she so loved keep their readers hooked? I supposed it was because they knew the audience was out there, in the dark, waiting for words, for escape. They knew that audience trusted their ability.

But my small audience of one was critical.

'Okay,' I began, 'so the sun came up very gently on ...'

'Don't baby me!'

'I'm not. The sun *would* have been gentle in a morning.'

'Okay,' she sighed.

'The sun rose on day two ...'

'Are we definitely done with day one?' asked Rose.

'Yes,' I said. 'Not much happened really, apart from the men getting acquainted. They were tired, remember. Too tired to make proper plans yet. Relieved just to be out of the water, I imagine. To have found one another.'

Rose nodded, patiently, and said, 'Now Colin. What about him?'

And so I told her.

11

MAYBE TODAY A SHIP

We have fourteen men on two rafts.

K.C.

Dawn on the second day and Colin grudgingly opened his eyes. He knew before he came fully conscious where he was. The boat's persistent motion, his damp clothes after a night of spray, and the smell of salt meant no escape, not even in dreams. He had woken over and over to the crew's cries of *mum* and *help us*. Perhaps today would bring rescue.

He said softly to himself, 'Maybe today a ship.'

Ken close by asked gruffly, 'What's that, lad?'

'We *must* keep watch all the time, Chippy.'

'We are. Officer Scown ordered it.'

'I know,' said Colin. 'But I'm watching even when I'm not on duty. We all should. Can't rely on the younger ones.'

At sunset the previous night Officer Scown had suggested the men try and sleep, setting a rota of two on watch for four hours. Looking out for a ship round the clock, he said, was their most likely hope of rescue so far from land. But four hours proved too long for the men to stay awake. With nothing but black sky and sea, the sameness lulled them into lethargy.

'Aye,' said Ken now. 'Some of the young 'uns are barely eighteen. This is their first voyage. We'll need to look out for them as much as for a ship.'

'Look lively,' said Colin. 'Some of 'em are stirring.'

It was a sorry-looking lot of men they beheld as the sun lit a new day; violent water and explosions had torn clothes. Barely recognisable faces were black with fuel oil, and many were already severely sunburnt by the mixture of salt and sun. But, despite an uncomfortable night where they couldn't lie down in unison due to lack of space, most woke quite cheerful.

'Where's room service?' demanded Weekes.

'Shocking quarters they've given us on here.' Colin continued the joke. 'I mean to complain to the highest powers.'

'Right, shake a leg,' ordered Officer Scown, to exaggerated groans.

Last night he'd suggested they not issue food or water until dawn. 'We're not feeling too bad yet, lads,' he'd said, 'and we may have a long way to go. Also, I've still to assess rations.' Quietly he'd admitted to Colin and Ken that he was afraid to look at what they had, both from Colin's lifeboat and in the things they'd picked up from the sea through the first day.

'Tomorrow,' he'd said. 'When we know what's what.'

Scown had been the fourth survivor Ken and Colin found; he was swimming so weakly when they spotted him that they had known he was mere hours from death. He was a great seaman, a strong leader, a man who'd long earned his position as the ships' first officer. Though weak for his first hours aboard the lifeboat, and unable to issue orders, he'd recovered enough by evening to take charge of the fourteen men.

Now, with everyone awake, Scown said he'd decided that since no one had the energy for a longer watch, it would just be a two-hour shift. 'The gunners Bott, Leak and Bamford will only do days. They're not accustomed like we are to night duty. Any objections?' He paused as though bracing himself. 'Right, let's see what rations we've got.'

The men had endured over thirty-six hours without so much as a drop of water, during which time much effort had been made rowing, tying the two rafts together, and constantly bailing water out of the boat's well. Due to excess weight, a slight dip meant seawater pooled quickly at their feet, rotting all it touched.

Hunger gnawed at Colin's stomach. He imagined it as a living creature with teeth as sharp as blades and bloodshot eyes. Thirst hurt more; it fattened his tongue, dried out his lips, and thickened his blood.

'A drink,' he heard Young Fowler say softly. 'Oh, for a drink.'

Officer Scown ordered Platten, the ship's steward, to put together a list of what they had. At twenty-six, Platten had been a seaman for five years. Though a slightly built man with wiry arms and legs, he was incredibly strong, a father to twin girls at home. Stoically, he set about his assigned task.

Scown found a damp pencil in his pocket and asked who had paper. Most did but naturally it had been soaked to pulp by this point. Young John Arnold came forward with his bible. The seventeen-year-old was an apprentice from the south of England, and fervently religious. Many had mocked and bullied him for quoting from holy text so frequently. Now he held the book out with thin fingers – it too was soggy mush. But inside was a protected picture of the Virgin Mary.

Gratefully, Officer Scown took the card from its cover and let it dry for a few minutes in the sun. The men closed in and watched as though they might be witness to some spiritual vision. Colin was never sure what he believed. He supposed he believed in what he saw, what he could touch. But it was not lost on him that the Holy Mother had remained unaffected by the elements.

When the picture had dried Officer Scown drew a small-scale chart from memory, marking their last observed position on the angle formed by the lines of nine degrees south and nine degrees west of Greenwich. Like an artist, he sketched deftly, eyes narrowed, tongue slightly protruding.

'I reckon we're about ninety-five miles from the ship's last definite position,' he said. 'That puts us here.' He marked a large X. 'Which means Ascension Island is our nearest land. But we'll never make it there – too hard to find. So our best hope is to find the coast of Africa.'

'What about Pernambuco?' asked Colin. 'Couldn't we pick up the southeast trades? Aren't we right in the shipping lanes?'

The officer shook his head. 'If we were a few more degrees south, maybe. No, the nearest mainland is Cape Palmas on the border of Liberia. Strong currents sweeping up the shores of Africa might bring us in line with the Europe-bound traffic. So that's where we hope to reach – Africa.'

Bamford, one of the gunners, asked the question everyone

dreaded knowing the answer to: 'And how long will that take us?'

'I estimate thirty days,' said Officer Scown.

The words settled heavily on the crew. Thirty days. Four weeks. A month. Scown could have said forever and Colin doubted the men would feel more hopeless. Was it better not knowing?

No, survival at sea was about planning.

'So that's what we'll set the rations for – thirty days,' said Scown. 'Any objections? If you have, make them now.' Platten had totted up what food and water there was and quietly spoke with the officer. Grim-faced, Scown then addressed the men. 'Right then, daily rations will be as follows – one biscuit, one ounce of Bovril, four Horlicks milk tablets, and three squares of chocolate. Water will be two ounces per man, three times daily.'

No one spoke. Even the sea seemed to listen, calm for a moment, its many colours merging into sparkling gold. Colin cut off thoughts beyond two days ahead. He was unable to imagine his hunger on so small an amount of food and so little water. Looking around at the craggy faces of his mates, he could see in their eyes the same fear. But it had to be. Much as the craving was there, they couldn't eat more heartily for fear of how long rescue might be in coming.

'Now,' said Scown, 'there are men on board with more serious injuries. The Second has nasty wounds on both feet and Davies has broken ribs. I suggest they're allowed a few extra rations. Any objections?'

There were none.

The Second was an engineer, a quiet, morose man who

had never made any close friends, and therefore no one on the lifeboat ever knew his name; everyone called him the Second or occasionally the commonly used nickname, chum. Extremely good at his job, he was well respected. He met the constant pain his injured feet must have caused with silence, never grumbling or asking for help. Being thrown by the constant movement of the raft caused those injured or most severely sunburnt to cry out as they hit wood or each other. But not the Second.

'Right, we'll have breakfast,' said Scown. 'Platten will issue it.'

'About time,' joked Weekes. 'Make mine three eggs.'

Scown held up a plastic cup. 'This'll measure the water,' he said. 'It's marked with ounces so no man will get more or less than another. And this spoon will measure out the Bovril.'

Food was eaten and water consumed, with no joy. It hardly took the edge off Colin's hunger. So small a meal only served to remind him how much he needed.

'I'd give anything for a nice cuppa now,' joked Weekes. Colin knew he was trying to lessen their misery but many swore.

'Aye, milky and sweet,' continued Ken.

'No, strong, a good brew,' insisted Platten.

'Oh, for a ciggie,' said Leak, one of the gunners. 'Why can't them rations include cigs?'

'Stop will you,' snapped Bott. 'Just stop it!'

His words worked; the men fell quiet again and resumed their positions about the boat. Time passed slowly, as it does when nothing changes. The sun kept up her persistent baking temperature. Only six men at a time could shelter under the canvas awning, so they took turns escaping the heat, panting unanimously.

Mid-morning during his lookout shift Weekes leapt from his position on the foredeck and cried out. Colin expected a ship on the horizon and when it didn't materialise he very much wanted to punch Weekes.

'Another boat!' cried Weekes. 'One of ours. Down wind, to port. Look there. Low in the water, mind. I reckon it's slowly sinking.'

'How far do you think it is?' asked Ken.

'Maybe a few hundred yards,' said Officer Scown.

'Reckon we can get to it,' wondered Colin. 'Might we use our smaller raft?' Two men had slept on it last night to make more room on the bigger boat but it could easily be untied again.

'Reckon there'll be anyone on it?' asked Young Arnold.

'Maybe,' said Scown, 'but it's what else is aboard that I'm thinking of.'

Extra rations might mean the difference between life and death. Though this was not spoken, they all knew it. Officer Scown asked for volunteers to go out to it and Ken, Weekes and Colin offered.

In unison they rowed the smaller boat for ten minutes and retrieved what felt like an abundance of tins. Exhaustion set in halfway back and they had to encourage one another to keep going. Weekes joked about lemonade waiting in the luxury quarters and received a hearty slap or two. Back at the lifeboat the men patted them on the back for the gifts they brought.

'No need to open these to see what they are,' said Platten.

'I know these tins alright, biscuits most of them, and water the rest.'

'They'll cover unforeseeable events,' said Officer Scown. 'And as extra for those most injured.'

Colin, Ken and Weekes were spent and rested briefly, flopping like marooned fish on the deck. Platten and Bamford tied the small raft to the big one. Though the smaller boat could be rowed easily, the big craft was entirely unnavigable. Throughout the day everyone tried a hand with the broken steering oar but to no avail; the sails took them where the wind chose.

Colin hated that they were ruled by the elements and must go where they were taken. He liked to take charge. At least when it came to his turn for lookout duty he had something of substance to occupy him.

Young Fowler, the cabin boy, joined him. Officer Scown teamed more experienced men with the younger lads. Colin and Fowler took positions on the foredeck, one concentrating on the south, the other the north, each occasionally looking east and west.

Astern of the boat half a dozen dolphins followed in their wake, darting left and right, seeking prey. Shoals of flying fish shot out of the water, followed by streaks of silver lightning as the dolphins sought lunch. Colin knew that sea lore hailed dolphins as a symbol of protection. There were many tales of them helping those in peril at sea, but he reckoned these creatures were just after a good meal.

'I should like a piece of fish very much,' said Young Fowler, his pale face a picture of desperate longing.

'Ken told me last night that he's going to make some sort

of spear,' said Colin. 'He hopes to catch us something. I think all of us would like to sink out teeth into a meaty morsel, lad.'

'Do you think we'll get picked up?' asked Young Fowler.

'We have to think so don't we, lad, or else what's the point in going on?'

'But what do *you* think?'

Colin realised that though he was only maybe three years older than the boy, Fowler thought the gap was much bigger. The blunt truth came to his lips; *God only knew*. But he bit the words down. Better to give the lad a meaty morsel of hope. 'I think there's a very good chance of it,' he said.

Young Fowler seemed happy with this; he settled back and spoke little for the rest of their watch. Colin whistled gently, unaware he was doing so until Weekes spoke up.

'For God's sake, make it a cheery one – we're not at a funeral.'

With a grin, Colin whistled a ridiculously upbeat melody. Some of the men joined in, though it must have hurt their throats, until the entire crew were following Colin's lead. Like a band of soldiers marching merrily home from war, they whistled, the tune rising and falling like the endless ocean. When the song died, the silence was somehow louder.

Officer Scown broke it. 'Right, let's check the flare tins.'

Platten dragged them from under a bench. 'Water's got in 'em,' he said.

'Better dry them out, just in case,' said Scown. 'Our lives may depend on it. You'd better make a list of what we've got in the firework line even if you keep it in your head.'

There were twenty-four Port Flare Type Red Distress Flares and three smoke-floats.

'Take charge of them, Platten,' ordered Scown. 'See that one is always handy. Men on watch will, upon seeing a vessel of any description, set off a flare without awaiting orders. Understood?'

Colin eyed the flares and imagined grabbing one at the sight of a ship on the horizon. How quickly could he let it off? Would they still work after having been damp? No point dwelling on it. They'd find out when the event arose.

With the sun at its highest point, some of the men stripped off and dried their damp clothing on the deck. Their grey garments looked like squares of faded paper awaiting words. Colin thought again about the last letter he'd written his mother when he was still aboard the *Lulworth Hill*. He wished for a notepad. Wished he could reassure her there was hope, he was alive, not gone like Stan.

Food and water were, of course, what all the men craved most. But sitting to record his thoughts at the end of the day, losing everything in the act of doing so, had been heaven. It somehow put the hours to rest.

Colin settled back for the last ten minutes of their lookout, but Young Fowler grabbed his arm and pointed wordlessly astern.

'Shark,' he said softly, as though the creature might hear and attack.

A triangular fin approached the boat, cutting through the water with expert precision, a metal blade pulled towards their magnet. Once it reached the craft, the shark circled slowly as though assessing what was to be had. Perhaps fifteen feet long, his hefty body was scarred. One wound cut his face almost in two, like a forward slash dividing lines of poetry.

One of the lads – Colin was never sure who – cried out *Scarface*. And so he was named. They would see him often. He became as constant a companion as the sea and sky and thirst.

This time Scarface merely circled the boat and swam back off in the direction he'd arrived. Silence fell upon the crew at his departure.

Colin knew their inner questions must echo his. What had stopped him attacking? Maybe their number? He was sure the creature would return. He'd heard of cases of sharks attacking boats up to ten yards in length, much bigger than theirs. But it wasn't common. Humans are not preferred prey for sharks but that didn't mean they were safe.

'Right, next lookout,' announced Officer Scown. 'Ken and John, you're up.'

Colin retired from his duty wishing he could continue. Looking for a ship was all he wanted to do. Even with men on shift, he scanned the horizon, only stopping when Officer Scown announced the evening meal. Platten measured the rations and they ate. Despite the day's cruel heat, the roughness of their salty clothes and the small portions, the men chatted contentedly afterwards as though it was a tea break aboard the *Lulworth Hill*.

'I wonder how long it'll be before we get another cig,' said Leak, one of the gunners. He'd lost his dentures when the ship sank and the words whistled and vibrated against his bare gums.

'Who knows?' said Stewart. He'd been stark naked save for his life jacket when Ken and Colin fished him out of the water yesterday. The men had ribbed him for it since, laughing as they shared spare clothes with him.

'I think we'll be picked up,' said Weekes.

'The *Lulworth Hill* was an unlucky ship,' said Bott.

'I'll not have you talk about her that way.' Officer Scown held up a hand. 'She was a *fine* ship. One of the best I sailed in. No ship could have outdone that U-boat, I tell you.'

Most nodded an agreement, some adding that they had enjoyed every moment aboard her. They talked of happy days going about their duties while heading home. Behind them the sun began its descent, snatching Colin's good mood and taking it down too.

Two days and no ship. He had to imagine day three would bring one or else he'd not want to wake in the morning.

Ken had fashioned a good spear and in the evening's softer light he jabbed viciously at the water, while the crew encouraged him with hearty cries of, 'Go on, lad!' But he caught nothing and gave up after ten minutes, the fatigue at engaging in such a simple act too much now.

Ken, like Colin, preferred to keep occupied. He tore pieces of material from the sail and began a log, writing as follows:

Sunk 19th March by U-boat. Time 3.40am. Two torpedoes hit nos. 1 and 2 holds. Ship sunk in 1 and a half minutes. Many went down with ship. We have 14 men on two rafts. We are about 800 miles from land, so will try to make it. Expect rescue anytime now.

Darkness suffocated the boat, put out the day and hushed words. The moon's absence balanced them. Black shadows they all became, none older or younger or hungrier or less injured than the next man.

After a while Ken said to John Arnold, 'Say a prayer, lad,' arousing crude insults.

'What harm in it?' demanded Ken. 'I could use some peaceful words to calm my mind.'

'God can't help us now,' said Bott.

'Maybe not,' said Platten, 'but maybe it'll help us help ourselves.'

'Aye, let him say something,' said Colin.

And so a peace settled again over the crew and Young Arnold recited a bible passage from memory. *And God said, let the waters bring forth abundantly the moving creature that hath life. And God created great whales and every living creature that moveth. God saw that it was good. And God blessed them, saying, be fruitful and multiply and fill the waters in the seas.*

Then Arnold asked God to receive those who had perished on the *Lulworth Hill* and to bless those who had survived and help them find their way home again. Murmurs of *Amen* concluded his words, and then twelve men groaned and turned over and tried to find a comfortable spot.

Scown and King began their night lookout shift. Colin tried to sleep, squashed hard between Ken and Davies, whose broken ribs caused him to cry out constantly. Scown had tried to bind his chest with trousers but it can't have lessened his suffering much.

The sea got up quite a storm and pushed and pulled at their boat, like a tired parent rocking a sleepless baby too hard. Colin dozed fitfully.

Curious visions punctuated brief moments of sleep. A place he'd not seen before but that felt somehow familiar. Not home, but somewhere homely. A place with books, ones he'd never beheld before. Their spines were more colourful than the royal blue and burgundy ones in the ship's library. He longed to look at one but, as is the way with dreams, he found his hands stupid and clumsy.

Then Colin realised he wasn't alone. Someone came for the books. Someone turned, perhaps aware of him. He tried desperately to hang on to the dream but it dissolved, the way Bovril tablets do in boiling water. Colin woke with words in his mouth, with names, questions, desperate appeals.

'What's that, lad?' said Ken, his voice muffled.

'I ... she...' He realised he had no idea. 'Just a dream.'

'Go back to sleep,' said his chum. 'You're on shift at dawn.'

But Colin didn't sleep again. When shreds of orange peel announced day three on the horizon, he was relieved to begin another lookout. It was like the act of watching for a ship encouraged one to arrive. If he turned away, even for a moment, it might pass by unseen.

Hold on, hold on, just hold on, he thought. *Maybe a ship, maybe a ship, maybe today a ship.*

12

COLOURS LIKE THOSE AT SEA

Men getting downhearted.

K.C.

December arrived quietly. Like a wintry tooth fairy, she sneaked in and put frosty days under my pillow. I only realised when I tore a page from the Cute Animals calendar Rose had picked, revealing puppies in Santa hats. What had happened to November? She had passed on a choppy sea of needles and numbers and insulin measurements and battles with Rose and school problems.

It was the month I had become a storyteller. I had tried to choose the right language for a nine-year-old, and insulted my clever daughter. Then I'd worried that I was summarising too much, giving little background, painting in broad strokes, repeating descriptions previously used.

But somehow I took us to the ocean.

Now my private, frenzied reading of Grandad Colin's diary, newspaper articles and letters, along with Rose's sharp, probing questions and a rise in confidence that my words were helping her, meant I looked forward to finding out about him. I think Rose did too, secretly. She might fight and ignore and call me Natalie to irritate the rest of the time, but in the book nook she was mine.

During her forced time at home our story-sharing fell into a comfortable routine. I called it story-sharing that week because her questions after each chapter proved how much she'd listened, taken in, enjoyed; this participation meant she contributed to my putting paragraphs together and inspired future prose.

We split the ocean days in three; one day on the raft we made last through breakfast, tea and supper. Then at lunchtime we let Colin's diary pages fall open and took turns reading aloud. His words rose and fell in the sunlit book nook corner. His thoughts of those difficult days were a mix of comical memories and sad observations and confused conclusions.

On Tuesday, from a page marked sixteen in faint pencil, Rose read aloud, slowly and carefully.

There were some funny moments – not too many, it has to be said, but a few scattered through the darker times. It must be hard for anyone to imagine it, but we found humour in silly inconsequential things, like when we'd all taken our shoes off to dry them a bit and then didn't know which ones belonged to whom. We were all trying them on and remarking over the good feel of the better ones, as though we had just been paid and were in a shoe shop on Anlaby Road. One of the lads said he wasn't even sure if his own feet were actually his. It doesn't sound that funny now. Sounds silly. But we laughed. It might have been the last time we did.

Rose giggled too, a melody of undulating notes. How I'd missed the sound.

I smiled, said, 'Even when things are hard people can always laugh. It does actually make you feel better, you know.'

'Mrs Kemp never thinks so when we laugh in *her* lessons,' said Rose.

'That's not a time for silliness,' I chided.

'It is when Jade's drawn something rude on the desk,' said Rose.

I wanted our giggly sharing to last but too soon Rose wandered back to her bedroom until our next story chapter.

At teatime I told her about day three on the lifeboat, describing their discussion of how to eat the very hard ship-issue biscuits without breaking their teeth. Parched throats meant they could barely swallow the hateful things. Leak, who had of course lost his dentures, sobbed as he tried to eat one. They smashed one with a boot heel, then wrapped another in cloth and banged it against the boat edge.

'Who invented such a nasty biscuit?' asked Rose.

In the end Stewart the cabin boy suggested they soak it in a very small amount of seawater. It worked. But Colin longed for something moist to eat. He watched with the others as Ken continued to jab his spear at the water, some mocking cruelly when he failed to catch anything. Colin felt despair at Ken's failure, wanted to shake his friend by the now thin scruff of his neck and scream his misery at him. But he didn't.

After the chapter Rose asked, 'I can't remember exactly who's who. Good stories shouldn't just chuck totally loads of characters at you all at once.'

'I had to cos they all arrived that way,' I said.

Then we talked about the crew, trying to imagine exactly what each of them looked like.

'It's easy to recall the unusual ones,' I said.

'Like John Arnold cos he does all that bible stuff,' she said. 'I see him as kind of skinny and with a squeaky voice.'

I nodded. 'I remember the injured ones most. Like Davies with his broken ribs and the Second with bad feet. I can't imagine their pain.'

'But that Second is boring,' snapped Rose. 'I like Weekes cos he's a joker. He'd be real good fun. I'd want him on my boat.' She paused. 'Grandad Colin is the best though,' she said, softly.

'Yes,' I agreed. 'But they were all special to someone, remember.'

'They're not all going to get home are they?'

'We'll find out,' I said.

'They're not. I know it.' Rose switched off then. Like Marilyn Monroe assuming her famous persona, Rose stripped off her bright, interested coat and revealed the familiar alien beneath. She disappeared to her bedroom and I sat for a while in the book nook, clinging to the remnants of our words.

It felt at times like the ocean was more real than my everyday life. I remembered the way I'd written stories as a child, how I'd always picked words that matched (as I'd called it) so that when they were all in a row I could quite literally see them bounce. Now they didn't just bounce, they jumped into life.

On Wednesday, from page twenty-five of Colin's diary, I read another segment.

I miss the colours. Now I've been home a few weeks I can't picture them anymore. There are no colours like that here. I don't miss much else. I don't talk about it to anyone. It hurts. My throat closes up like

*it did on the boat. I just write it here. There are no colours like those
at sea. I can write colour names like cobalt and teal and cerulean
and turquoise but none of those terms do any justice to what I saw.*

'I saw colours like that when I fell down,' said Rose.

'When you fell down where?' I asked, concerned.

'In the kitchen, silly. When we went to the hospital. When
I was feeling like all weird, I saw these crazy colours. They
weren't blue though, more reds and orange.'

'That's because you weren't well,' I said, sadly.

'Like Grandad Colin.'

'Yes, like him I suppose.'

She opened the diary again, at the front. 'What do you
think these buttons mean?' she asked me, stroking them.
'Why did Colin stick them in here?'

'Who knows,' I said.

'Which do you like best? I like the gold cos it's so pretty.'

I put my hand over hers, expecting to be pushed away. But
for a moment she kept it there. 'I like the brown one,' I said.

'Why? It's totally boring.'

'Maybe that's why,' I said. 'It looks so small and
insignificant. But what if it's a big part of the story?'

On Thursday, due to her first low blood sugar reading
– three-point-nine – Rose ate some fried chicken before her
teatime injection instead of after it. It wasn't dangerously low
and she'd had no hypo symptoms but I knew she must eat first.
I fussed a little, reread my manual, but Rose wrinkled her nose
at me and said it was fine; she was just hungrier than usual.

So I told her about day four on the lifeboat.

One of the hardest things as time went on, aside from
the increasing thirst and hunger, was the boredom. The

abundance of time and nothing to do except look for a ship and think was torture. And thinking was no good because home occupied so much of Colin's mind. He dreamt of his mother's living room at night, and while lolling about on the deck in the daytime. He could almost put out a hand and run it along the walnut cabinet, sniff the air, smell his mother's stew simmering, see dust dancing by the net curtain and a glimpse of the garden beyond.

In the afternoon Ken tried again to catch a fish and after ten minutes of effort realised with joy that he'd plunged his weapon into the side of a wriggling blue creature. The crew whooped with delight as he raised it from the water. Hungry hands reached out to pull it in and the fish – perhaps sensing it was his last chance – writhed ferociously, freed itself from the spike and swam away.

This time no one mocked Ken. No one had any words, any heart. Colin returned to his spot under the canvas. He didn't speak for the rest of the day. None of them did. Even John Arnold's now daily prayer was said with little hope or enthusiasm and night fell on a desolate crew.

'Poor Grandad,' said Rose afterwards.

'I know,' I said, emotion high in my throat.

She pushed a last piece of chicken around her plate. 'I feel bad that I can eat this.'

'You need to,' I said.

'Wish I could somehow take it to him on the boat.'

'You'd have to travel seventy years backwards,' I said. I found it profound that while Colin had dreamed of home, we told stories about the sea and escaped there.

'I bet *I* could do that,' Rose said softly.

Our week at home continued. Shelley did what she had promised during our phone conversation; she went into school and sat with Mrs White for an hour and explained how Rose's unstable blood sugars could result in changes in behaviour, in severe and sudden hunger, and in mood swings.

'I tried to make it clear,' Shelley told me, 'that this didn't mean they should overlook bad behaviour because obviously there may be times when Rose has genuinely done something she shouldn't ...'

'Of course,' I interrupted, knowing my daughter well.

'But if, say, during a hypo she did things she normally wouldn't, they should look on it with a bit of compassion. I explained more specifically all the signs of hypo so they know to encourage her to drink some Lucozade.'

'I did explain all this when Rose went back to school after the diagnosis,' I said, exhausted by it.

'Look, pet,' said Shelley. 'We may have to explain it a few times more. And then she'll go to high school and you'll have to do it all again. It's a complex condition and there's lots of misinformation out there. But you're doing everything right. You really are.'

'Doesn't always feel like I am,' I said. I was glad Colin's diary entry had made me reach out to Shelley, but I still found it difficult to thank her, to admit I had needed help.

'Remember you can ring me anytime,' said Shelley.

Mrs White called me on Wednesday and said that if Rose really wanted to return to school the next day, she could. But I suggested perhaps we would take this time to master Rose's condition even further and the headmistress agreed that it might be helpful to all of us. She never apologised but

I didn't mind. That she had called was enough, and I never found apologies easy either.

But I'd lied a little when I said I'd kept Rose home to master the diabetes. Yes, I supposed that was the reason, but really I wanted her with me. Even in her difficult mood, with a foreign-to-me-at-times personality, her presence stopped me feeling so utterly alone.

It was almost two weeks since I'd spoken to Jake. When he'd been gone this long I often found it hard to picture him, perhaps the way Colin had forgotten the sea's colours. I'd think of specific moments during our relationship to recapture him. But his face was always hazy, like when photographers blur faces of interviewees to keep their identities secret.

I remembered the first time I knew Jake and I were really going to be together. I closed my eyes and saw the memory clearly.

We'd only known each other a few weeks. He lived with his grandfather then and I lived alone, twenty miles separating us. Funnily enough, it was December, like now. Snow had fallen heavily, blanketing everything in fresh white, and we were looking forward to Christmas.

Jake had always stayed at my place on a Wednesday and Saturday. But this was a Friday. I'd finished work, eaten tea, had a bath and decided to go to bed early. As I turned out the lights, there came a soft knock on the back door. Nervously I'd opened it with the safety chain attached. There stood Jake, covered in snow, his thick coat disguised by the flakes and his red hair so wet it looked black. His bike stood by the shed.

'What...' I wasn't sure how to finish the sentence. I found a question. 'Did we plan something tonight and I've forgotten?'

'No,' he said, smiling.

'What is it? Is everything okay?'

'Fine,' he said. 'Honest.'

'Do you want to come in?'

He shook his head, sending snowflakes scattering like white confetti. 'No, I can't stop. I was in the bath. Hopefully it'll still be warm.'

'In the bath?' I couldn't help but laugh. 'So you got out and came here?'

'I had to tell you something.' Now Jake looked serious.

'I'm worried,' I admitted, wrapping my dressing gown more tightly about my body. I'd had a hard time starting a relationship with Jake. Hurt previously by a man who'd ended things by simply leaving, with no word, letter or phone call, I'd built a protective barrier around myself. So I began to think Jake had come to break it off, that I'd done something to cause it. Perhaps it was my coolness or my stubborn nature. I supposed that at least he had come to tell me and not decided to slink off into the night and disappear without trace.

I prepared to fight. I planned my response; that I didn't care (I did) and I didn't want him anyway (I did) and I'd cope on my own again (I would but with a heavier heart this time).

'It's nothing bad,' Jake said, tenderly touching my arm. 'No, I just ... well, I was in the bath, like I said. Just lying there and thinking. And I realised something. I mean it came to me so clearly and I was so excited that I had to come and tell you.'

'What?' I still thought he was going to end it.

'That I love you,' said Jake.

'Oh.' It was all that came out. My fears fell away like melting snow.

'That's all.' He retrieved his bike and climbed on.

'That's all?' I repeated dumbly.

'Yes.' He grinned. 'I just had to tell you. So you knew. I hope you don't mind? And I don't want you to say anything back to me. I didn't tell you for that, I just thought ... well, you should know. I'm really happy.'

And then he rode off into the night, leaving me cold and warm and speechless and full of silent words. I closed the door and stood in the dark, my safe place.

Now when I worried that his absence would kill my love I thought of that night. I'd told Rose the story before she was ill and she'd said it was like one of those princess stories (which she'd never liked) but much nicer because it was real and Dad sounded cool.

And so it came to Friday, the end of Rose's week off, and we reached day five on the lifeboat. At breakfast Rose came to the book nook with her diabetes box and half a bottle of water. Nothing changed in our story corner, only the shape of the cinnamon cushions after we'd sat in them. The many books remained on the shelves, still ignored by Rose.

'Are you thirsty?' I asked, concerned.

'No,' she said. 'I just want it with me.'

'Oh.' I looked at it, felt guilt at remembering when Rose told me she was thirsty over and over, and I'd suggested she carry one around.

As I prepared the finger-pricker, she asked, 'Do you think the rocking boat would have been nice at night? I do. I wish my bed rocked.'

'Sadly, the bouncing boat just hurt their burnt skin and broken bones.'

I knelt at her feet to prick her finger end. She barely flinched now, just squeezed her eyes shut. Her blood read nine-point-two so I prepared the injection and continued the story.

'The men slept very little,' I said. 'Was it any wonder? Imagine being starving hungry and desperately thirsty, and sleeping half sitting up on a cramped wooden floor?'

'You're asking *me*?' Rose shook her head, held up the water bottle. 'You forget I *know* what it's like to be that thirsty! It's totally crap. And I told you that bed at the hospital was too hard.'

'Of course. I'm sorry.'

'I used to dream about big jugs of icy water,' she said. 'I used to get up in the night and drink your Fanta. But it didn't work. Nothing did. I was so so so thirsty. Would Colin have felt like that?'

'Yes, like that,' I said. So softly, *yes, like that*.

'Fanta must be like how seawater is,' said Rose. 'Just makes you want more but not feel no better.'

'*Any* better,' I corrected gently.

I'd explained yesterday how drinking seawater was lethal; that the excess salt made you urinate more than the water gained from drinking it, so increasing dehydration. 'Like the sugar in my blood making me wee so much,' Rose had said, excited that she understood.

'So how long would I live on a boat like that?' she asked now. 'Like without my insulin and stuff?'

There were various answers, none of them optimistic. In as little as twenty-four hours diabetic ketoacidosis would occur without insulin. Vomitting would follow, then dehydration, breathlessness, and confusion. Coma would eventually result. It might take hours, days, even weeks with the little food that the men on Grandad Colin's boat had. But – as with all humans – the lack of water would be most dangerous, leaving Rose's blood even thicker with sugars.

I wouldn't sing the lines that answered her question. I wouldn't give my daughter *that* hopeless story.

'Tell me,' she insisted.

'But we don't *need* to know,' I said. 'You're never going to be in such a situation. Now, let's do your injection and we can get on with the chapter.'

'You don't know that I won't end up there.'

She was right; I didn't. But I couldn't spend my life imagining such scenarios. I felt sick now at the thought of her wasting away again, lost at sea. This week the colour had returned to her cheeks. She was the Little Pink that we'd almost called her when she was born. I wasn't sure if it was her body returning to a more normal state or that she so loved Colin's story.

Was he bringing her back to life as much as the insulin?

'You're a coward then, Natalie,' said Rose.

'Stop calling me that,' I snapped. 'I'm not Natalie, I'm your *mum*.' I paused. 'I suppose, I am a coward. I'm not as brave as you, but I'm trying. Now the injection and then your Bran Flakes.'

She looked away, her beautiful hazel irises dull as December evenings, her freckles like scattered red glitter.

'Come on,' I said, 'you know we have to.'

Rose had to always eat a meal rich in starch and fibre, then and tomorrow and forever, or she would not last. Every day

I'd have to urge her to eat. Even when she didn't feel like it, even when she was ill. A sickness bug might mean a hospital stay again. But I wouldn't think about that. I had to shrug off worries and open myself up to Colin's story again.

'Tell me then,' she snapped. 'Which day are we up to now?'

'You know it's day five,' I said.

'Just checking *you* bloody know,' she said.

'*Language*.'

'*Story*.'

'I imagine,' I said, 'that day five felt like the hundredth.'

I pushed Rose's skirt up, gently squeezed her flesh and administered the injection, avoiding bruises. They're curious, often appearing long after pinprick. Yellow the old ones, purple newer. We had to watch out for a more serious issue; lumps under the skin caused by having to have many pricked into the same spot.

'Natalie, the story,' urged my daughter.

I hadn't the energy to berate her again.

'When Colin woke that day,' I said, 'he felt utterly wretched, certain he couldn't go on much longer. His tongue was swollen fat in his mouth with dehydration. It made it difficult at times to talk. Salt-water boils covered his arms and legs. But staying asleep was never an option...'

Once again I closed my eyes. I sank into the cushion and let the words wash over me. I saw the colours of the sea the way Colin had tried to describe – divine gold, vibrant green, purest blue.

And we were transported back to the lifeboat.

Back to the sea.

13

LOOKING FOR THE WRONG THING

Expect rescue anytime now.

K.C.

There was a game Colin played on the lifeboat to pass time. When looking back months later, he realised it had also prevented him jumping overboard. This game involved finishing a task or counting a certain number of things, and praying the reward was a ship on the horizon. So, if he managed to count sixteen blue fish while on lookout duty, say, a ship would arrive by lunchtime. Or if he saw a solitary dolphin, he'd see a ship at teatime. Or when it was his turn to hand out rations he'd decide that if he got it done without a single grumble from any of the crew, a ship would certainly arrive in minutes.

Each time Colin lost, he fought the desire to give in. Instead he decided he'd just been looking for the wrong thing. It wasn't meant to be a dolphin but a shark. It was supposed to be eight *black* fish not sixteen *blue* ones. And the men always moaned so a day they didn't definitely meant salvation.

In the absence of a notepad, the game replaced letter writing. It kept Colin's thoughts in order, made him look forward. So he never stopped playing. Just one ship and he'd have won.

Sunrise on the fifth day and he whispered his game's title – *Maybe today a ship*. But he was afraid to open his eyes and actually look. Nearby Ken muttered something and turned over, sleep still protecting him from reality. Colin never had the heart to wake a sleeping man from his temporary escape.

Last night, when his lookout duty ended, his partner, Officer Scown had told him to wake King for duty. The lad had looked so peaceful that Colin couldn't do it. He chose to leave King sleep longer, yet hours earlier he'd thumped Young Fowler for spilling valuable water drops on the deck. Being on the lifeboat made the men both kind and cruel. Fatigue and dehydration drove the punch; regret filled the gap afterwards. Fowler – who reminded Colin of his brother Eric – rubbed his thin arm and turned away. Colin tried to say something but it stuck in his throat with the pieces of hard biscuit.

'I'll do lookout for another hour,' Colin had told Scown last night in the dark. 'Let's leave King. I don't think I'll sleep anyway. I'm not tired.'

He felt wretched about Fowler. Also the boat had been particularly violent all night, rocking back and forth, splashing the men with water and pushing them into each other. Shrill screams dotted the black like gunfire as wood hit bones and rough material chafed bare skin. It was a miracle King had slept at all and Colin couldn't disturb him.

Scown had looked at Platten, somehow also sleeping, and

said he'd do another hour too. So he and Colin remained on the foredeck until the soft sameness lulled them to lethargy and they *had* to wake the other men.

Now Ken stirred, muttering something about a decent cuppa. Colin opened his eyes. Far on the horizon he spotted something almost as welcome as a ship – a fat grey cloud, puffy no doubt with water. Just the thought of crystal liquid falling into his open mouth and waiting cup made him breathe harder. During the days the sky was mostly cloudless. It was the kind of weather those back home would celebrate, encourage them to run back inside to get deckchairs and jugs of lemonade. Here they longed desperately for rain.

'See that, lad,' Colin said to Ken.

'What?'

'That cloud. Think it'll come this way?'

'Don't get your hopes up, chum.'

'Never know.' Colin willed it to float their way, deciding if it moved west they'd see a ship later.

Officer Scown ordered that Platten 'serve the grub' but it wasn't met with the cheerful cries of yesterday. Apart from what was essential – like 'pass the cup' or 'you're up next' – conversation was subdued. Swollen tongues and parched throats made it too painful. Growing hopelessness meant no words were worth hurting that much for. But once the meagre breakfast had been consumed the men perked up enough to make half-hearted conversation.

Colin studied his seawater-soaked biscuit. 'It's not nearly enough, Chippy,' he said.

'Barely enough for a small child,' said Ken.

'We'll not last, you know.' Colin looked at the mouthful

of liquid in his tin cup. 'Not on this amount of water.'

'Shhh, lad.' Ken shoved his mate, but less roughly than they had been doing days earlier. 'Don't let the younger ones hear you. They look to us, you know. And morale is bloody low this past twenty-four hours. It's only been five days and they think we're doomed. Didn't you hear them last night?' He softly mimicked their words. 'We've had it, we've had it. We'll never be picked up.'

'Five days,' said Colin. 'Can you believe it? Feels like so many more. No wonder they feel desperate. It's the Second I feel for.'

They both looked to the spot under the awning where the Second Engineer lolled, his face rubicund, beard salt-caked, eyes yellow, chest sunken and feet rotten. Gangrene was eating the flesh away and the smell was pungent, sweet yet sour. Still he bore it well, never emitting more than a grunt.

'He won't eat,' said Ken. 'There's nowt anyone can do to make him. I know – I've tried. Sat with him yesterday and held the cup to his lips but the bloody fool refused. Not sure if he's delirious.'

'That's why we've got to believe a ship's coming,' said Colin. 'It makes us get up, lad, makes us eat.'

'Them young 'uns don't think so today.'

Ken looked over at Arnold, Fowler and King, their thin shoulders hunched over as though to protect what little bit of hope remained in their hearts.

'Do you?' asked Colin.

'Do I what?'

'Think a ship'll come?'

Ken didn't reply. He studied his roughened, cracked hands, turning them over as though looking for something in particular. Then he picked up the spear he always kept close by as if this was his answer.

'Do you *believe*?' repeated Colin.

'What does it matter to you?' snapped Ken. 'Whether I do or not won't bring a ship, will it, lad? Won't change a thing. But keeping this spear sharp and doing a bit of fishing every day, that'll maybe keep us alive. Believing isn't enough unless you *do* something.'

'I know that,' said Colin, hoarsely. 'That's why I keep looking out. It's the doing of it that keeps me going. I have to get home. *Have* to. Stan never did ... I *must*.'

'Stan?'

'My brother,' said Colin softly. 'Never came home from sea.'

'I'm sorry.' There was nothing else to say.

Breakfast done, the day dragged on, its hot sun oblivious to the misery of the crew below. The morose monotony was broken only by inadequate meals, lookout shift change, swapping for a sheltered spot under the canvas, and a dark cloud that had promised rain but passed over without bearing a drop. Colin watched it disappear. He pursed his lips to whistle – unaware he'd even done so – but nothing emerged.

'Give us a tune,' croaked Davies. Five days of coping with broken ribs had left the seaman too weak to move. The others took rations to him at each meal and helped him to the foredeck when he insisted on lookout duty.

'What?' Colin frowned.

'You were about to whistle.'

'Was I?' He pursed his lips again and tried. Nothing. 'Nowt there,' he said. 'My throat's too dried up, lad.'

Just after noon, when the sun bore down most unbearably, the gunners – Leak, Bott and Bamford – began complaining. It was understandable. The three weren't true seamen like the others, having had less than six months' ocean experience and being accustomed to working on farms and the city street. On top of that, all of their clothing was now so rough and caked in salt, it was an agony to wear, and seawater boils covered any skin exposed to the elements. Tempers flared when bodies collided and swearing regularly coloured the air.

But the gunners' negative words had a huge impact on the younger lads, many of whom held their heads in their hands and moaned.

'We'll never find land, you know,' said Bott. 'Not on this thing. It's bloody useless. We're just drifting aimlessly. Going nowhere.'

'We'll not get picked up either,' said Leak. 'We've not seen one ship in five days! What does that tell us? There aren't any bloody ships. What's the point in looking out? Might as well curl up and die.'

'We'll all die on here, I tell you,' Bamford wailed.

'Stop it,' sobbed Fowler. 'Weekes told me we'll be picked up.'

'What does he know?' demanded Bott. 'He's a bloody joker that one. He's teasing you, lad!'

Before Weekes could intervene, Officer Scown did. 'Right, that's it,' he snapped. 'We've no room for moaning minnies on here!' He swept his arm over the smaller second boat. 'If I hear any of you buggers talking nonsense, I'll put you aboard *this* boat, give you some rations, and untie it and set you adrift. Do you hear me? And you can go to hell.'

He didn't raise his voice – likely he was unable – but something in his tone shushed the grumblers. Silence fell on the rowdy crew. And it was at that moment that a large, juicy flying fish chose to land with a delicious plop on the deck. For a stunned moment, no one moved. They watched it wriggle and flap, its silver skin sparkling like slimy sugar in the sun.

Then Ken cried, 'Grab him, lads!' and all hands came to life.

'Fetch the knife,' ordered Scown.

Platten smashed its head against the deck and then divided it into fourteen bloody portions, while watering mouths hung open in anticipation. Once shared, it wasn't quite large enough to make a hearty meal but it was moist and fresh. Platten passed the small pieces around.

Young John Arnold shook his head, said, 'Give mine to the Second. I think he could do with it more than me.'

Most had already eaten their piece, sucking vigorously on every bit of bone.

'Are you sure?' asked Officer Scown.

'He'll not take it,' said Ken, quietly.

'He's not even eaten his own,' said Weekes, sucking blood from his fingers. 'Look, he's dropped it. Might as well give it to someone.'

The Second had barely acknowledged the fish's arrival. He sprawled against a bench, his rotten feet in the constant puddle of water that pooled there.

Arnold knelt by him and said, 'You need to eat else you'll

not get better. I've prayed each night for God to cleanse your feet. Here, please let me help you.'

Other men joined in the encouragement, chorusing his appeals with cries of, 'Go on, chum, it'll do you good', but the Second refused to eat. His eyes were dead and his thin mouth was clamped shut like two pages in a discarded book.

'May as well eat your piece, lad.' Ken touched Arnold's shoulder. 'I'll give the Second's piece to Davies, if no one objects?'

Young Arnold ate but without the passion the other men had.

When they were all finished with their surprise morsels Ken nudged Colin, said, 'I'm gonna do a bit of fishing again. Was a real bit of luck that fish landing on deck, but I mean to *make* us some luck from now on.'

Colin watched his mate take position; Ken knelt close to the edge, in what must have been a painful stance, so he could best reach a catch. Holding aloft the spear, his eyes never left the water. Some of the crew joined in, crying out at the sight of fish. Colin quietly played his game – if Ken caught one fish a ship would show by teatime, two and it would be in minutes.

He thought about Ken's words earlier, that it was no good just believing something would happen, you had to actually do something about it. So he did something too. He held onto Ken's shirt so he could lean even farther out, and cried, 'There, Chippy, see that black one!' along with the others.

Scarface put in an appearance after a while, two of his friends on either side. They swam alongside the boat, causing the crew to shrink back and move to the middle. After only minutes, the creatures disappeared beneath the waves.

'I'd like to catch me one of them.' Ken resumed his position, spear held aloft again.

'Be hard to get the bugger aboard,' said Colin.

'You know the old superstition, don't you?' Ken said quietly to Colin. 'A shark follows a vessel when they know death will visit.'

'Now who's despondent?'

'It's true.'

'Maybe.' Colin considered it. 'But if that's true, then dolphins mean protection and there've been plenty of 'em.'

He watched bubbles froth at the bow, spiralling and whirling as though dancing to a song he couldn't hear. As if to prove him right, two dolphins surfaced just ahead. They leapt from the water in perfect unison, their sleek, grey bodies adorned with crystal dots. However low he felt, Colin never ceased to be awed by their beauty, by their clicking sounds bouncing off the water, by how they enjoyed play like small children, nudging and chasing one another.

'Sharks'll eat anything, you know,' he said to Ken. 'Nowt they won't tackle. When I was in Sydney they caught one with a broken bloody chair inside it. Half a horse inside another and enough bones to feed a dog!'

'I could eat a horse right now,' said Ken. 'Could eat anything. Could eat you.'

'Wouldn't taste good, mate.'

'But a drink – oh, for a drink.' Ken groaned.

'Don't. Just don't.'

As though reminded of how little he'd eaten and drank, Ken put down the spear. 'Enough for today,' he said. 'More tomorrow.'

Colin had lost another game.

In the evening, after another small meal revived them briefly, the men talked not just of home, but of love; of sweethearts, of fiancés, of wives, of girls they liked, girls they hoped to court, girls on the silver screen. Love revived more than their tiny cup of water. Even just imagining it irrigated the crew's hopes of getting home. Platten had his wife and twins waiting there, Scown a wife and six-year-old daughter Wendy, and Ken had a girl, Kathleen, who had joined the Women's Auxiliary Air Force and was in the Orkneys.

Colin didn't have a girl but he liked listening to the others chat. Between their words he kept hearing the soft clacking of brass against teeth. Earlier, Scown had suggested sucking on a button to combat the endless thirst. He told the story of an old friend, who had sucked on a small stone, while in the desert, which kept the mouth from getting dry. Many of the lads had torn one from a cuff or collar and eagerly put it in their mouths. Colin's was brown; he ripped it from his breast pocket. It helped a little, reducing his thirst by retaining what little moisture he had in his mouth. From then on he kept it to hand, in his worn top pocket, or nestled beneath his tongue.

'My Kath's probably just knocked off work,' said Ken. 'She might have got my last letter today. I hope so. She won't be worried, at least. We're not even missing yet.'

'How come?' asked Bamford.

'It's a few days until the *Lulworth Hill* would have arrived in England,' said Officer Scown.

'So they won't even be looking,' moaned Leak.

'Don't start that again. We got the SOS out. Let's keep

talk on pleasantries, shall we? Who's waiting for you, Leak? A lovely lassie?'

Colin wondered if being needed back home gave one greater incentive to survive. He had no dependents, no family responsibilities, no wife and no children. Colin desperately wished that his mother would not have to relive the grief of losing a child, and having no body to bury.

She had five sons, Colin, Alf, Gordon, Stan and Eric. Though she would no doubt mourn Colin's absence and feel as she had when Stan was missing, she had support. She was a strong woman. As an army sergeant major's wife she was often alone; son Alf was in the merchant navy with Colin, Gordon was in the royal navy, and Eric the army. The Armitages had a long history of service, going back to Colin's great, great grandfather, who served in the navy under Nelson.

Even without being needed back home, Colin missed it desperately. He didn't speak of it as easily as some of the others, preferring not to appear overly sentimental. He'd never been given to emotional outbursts, perhaps even been brutal on the ship when a man cried with loneliness. But being on the lifeboat with nothing to do but think left Colin vulnerable to the same longings as the crew.

In the growing dark, he relived childhood days with his brothers. Out hunting for brambles and sticks, and adventures in the woods surrounding their Yorkshire village. Arguing over who got first dibs on a swing they'd made from metal pipes and rope. Squabbling over who got the biggest slice of apple pie their mother had packed for them. Jumping into the stream when they'd been told not to and coming back long after sunset. Colin could smell the apple pie, the woods, the brambles, so sharply that he opened his eyes expecting to see food and his brothers. He saw only the deteriorating black shapes of his ocean brothers.

Stan's voice had always risen above those of his other siblings – 'Catch me, Colin, I bet you can't! I can run faster than the wind! Faster than fire!' Colin missed him acutely yet felt somehow closer to him on the ocean. This was where he'd passed. They were together here.

'You're not saying much, Armitage,' said Weekes. 'We're on lookout in a few hours. You gonna keep me awake or bore me to sleep?'

'What's that, lad? I'll shove you over the edge – *that* should keep you awake.'

'It's pretty black tonight.' Colin could barely make Weekes out as he spoke. 'Must be a new moon. Gonna be hard to stay awake. At least we could smoke a few ciggies on the ship night shifts.'

'There was tea and all,' moaned Stewart.

'How about a prayer, John?' This time Ken's request met no argument; the men were glad of a bedtime story, of words they didn't have to think up, of something to lull them into oblivion.

Softly, Young Arnold recited a passage; his tremulous voice all that existed in the dark.

Glorious and gracious God, who dwellest in heaven but beholdest all things below, look down we beseech thee, and hear us calling out of the depth of misery, out of the jaws of this death, which is now ready to swallow us up. Save us Lord or else we perish. Send thy word of command to rebuke the raging winds and the roaring sea, that we are delivered from this distress and may live to serve thee and glorify thy Name all the days of our life.

Colin settled down in a spot between Ken and Weekes, knowing what sleep he might find would be brief, and he'd soon be shoved awake for lookout duty. He wondered where Fowler lay. He wanted to make some gesture to show his regret for the thump yesterday, but darkness shrouded them all.

When he fell into a fitful slumber, Colin dreamed again of books; a rainbow of books: green, gold, blue, turquoise, all the colours of the sea. Among them was a brown one, the colour of his best suit hanging in the wardrobe at home. Colin wanted to pick it up but his dream fingers wouldn't work.

Then he was no longer alone.

Someone came for the brown book. Someone turned, perhaps as aware of his presence as he was of hers. She – he realised it was a *she* – picked up the book and held it to her chest. Colin tried to speak, to ask who she was, to ask her to tell everyone he was at sea, and their ship had sunk.

But the harder he tried the fainter she grew, and the book and the girl disappeared, and Ken was shoving him, saying, 'Go back to sleep, lad, you're hallucinating, there's no girl here, it's just us, just us, just us.'

14

WISH-WISH-WISH.

Looking for a ship every day and night by keeping one-hour watches. May God help us.

K.C.

The morning Rose returned to school she locked her bedroom door by pushing the bed up against it, and I lost my temper. Just over five weeks of diabetes, of arguing with her, of being on my own, built up like ice in a broken fridge and shattered in a chilling explosion of language and threats.

I woke feeling morose anyway because it was Jake's birthday and he wasn't home to celebrate it. The day would mean nothing to the army. Those in his platoon might pat him on the back and sing a few lines of 'Happy Birthday' but he'd not be permitted a call home and I couldn't be sure the card I'd sent last week would have arrived to let him know I missed him.

We always put up the Christmas decorations on his birthday (the seventh of December) and I promised Rose we'd do it after school, so she'd gone to bed last night in a cheerful mood, saying I couldn't put Mary or Joseph in the mini wooden stable because she liked to.

'You always do them wrong,' she said.

I got out of bed, soft dread ever present at the thought of more finger pricking and fight. Last night I'd hardly slept. I'd read a news article about a diabetic girl who had died in her sleep; her blood sugars had dropped so low, she simply stopped breathing. So now, on top of the midnight blood test, I was up and down in the dark, watching Rose, checking she was still breathing.

I collected the diabetes box and went across the landing. Rose's door wouldn't budge. I knocked, panicked.

'Rose!' I cried, imagining her unconscious on the other side. 'Answer me, please, or I'll have to call an ambulance!'

'I'm fine,' she said.

'Why won't the door open?'

'Because the bed's there,' she said.

'Why on earth? Move it now and let me in.'

'No. Because you'll make me go to school.'

'You're damned right I will.' I knocked harder. 'Open it *now*.'

'*Language*, Natalie,' she said.

'Stop with the Natalie!' I tried to breathe slowly, stop the blood racing through my body, think of a way to cajole her. But hadn't I done all that? Hadn't I pleaded and promised and persuaded for weeks? Hadn't I been patient and done my best? I was tired. Beyond tired.

'If you don't move the bed now I'll smash this door up,' I said. 'Don't think I won't because I will. I'll get your dad's hammer and I'll smash it up and you'll be going to school.'

No answer. I'd either scared her or she was still refusing to budge. But I had no way of knowing. When I'd made the threat, it was empty; I'd expected her to open the door. Now, I'd finally had enough. I went downstairs, searched roughly through the kitchen drawers until I found Jake's wooden mallet. On the landing I passed it from hand to hand, assessing the damage it might do.

'Have you moved the bed?' I demanded.

'Nope,' she said.

'Are you going to?'

'Nope.' She didn't think I'd do it.

'Stay clear of the door because I'm coming in.' I paused; was I really going to smash it down? 'Where are you?'

'Near the window.' She sounded unsure, like she didn't know me. Good. Let her be shocked. Let her see *me* have a tantrum for a change.

'Stay away from the door.' I raised the mallet. All the frustrations of recent weeks came down against the door with it. Smash, crack. And again and again and again. The flimsy wood splintered and broke. I could see Rose through the ragged gap by her strawberry curtains, mouth open, eyes two large plates, looking very small. Sweat coated my forehead.

'Stop,' she cried. 'I'll move the bed.' She abandoned her corner and pulled it clumsily into the middle of the room. I opened the shattered door, went in, and dropped the mallet with a clunk by her bin. She backed away.

I kicked her bin over.

Furious, I said, 'If you ever pull a stunt like that again, I'll call Dad's emergency number and tell him that he shouldn't bother coming home again. Do you hear me? Because I will.' Rose didn't look at me. 'Don't you ever stop to think that maybe I hate all this as much as you? I *know* you have to endure the injections, that's why I've tried so *fucking* hard to do everything I can think of to make it as painless as possible. But this behaviour stops now. Right now! I can't help you if you don't let me. You have to *let* me. I want my daughter back!' My voice reached a crescendo, and then softened. 'Do you hear me? I don't like *you*. I don't know who *you* are – I like Rose. You smell like her and you look like her, but you're not her.' I stopped to get my breath. Rose hadn't moved an inch. 'Right, we're going to read your blood and do your injection without Colin this morning. I haven't the energy for it. And then get your things together because you're going to school. Understood?'

Rose didn't argue or say *language* or call me Natalie. I followed her downstairs. My anger dissipated as quickly as it had flared at the sight of her spindly legs beneath a purple polka dot nightie. How could I have frightened her like that? Been so violent, spoken so brutally?

I pricked her fingertip; as it bled onto the machine's strip I saw a thousand future readings, a thousand days of bloodshed, of numbers, of pain. Even if we conquered this disease, it would never be over. Rose would take it into her teenage years, into adulthood, parenthood, old age.

And I couldn't even keep my temper in check.

While she ate her Bran Flakes quietly at the table, I washed the pots so she'd not see my tears. They fell into the bowl, bursting bubbles. She put her empty dish next to me and I turned to try and say sorry, but she'd gone back upstairs. Footsteps above; back and forth from bed to wardrobe to bed to drawers, pad, pad, pad. Packing for school. No arguing. I'd won the battle but feared I'd lost her for good.

When she went out of the door, silent as Santa Claus, I called after her, 'I'll come in to school at lunchtime with Colin's diary, okay?' and watched her disappear around the hedge.

To occupy myself until then I rang Vonny. We chatted for half an hour but I didn't mention my outburst that morning. I couldn't, I was afraid she'd think me terrible. The words *I want my daughter back, I don't like you* followed me as I walked around the house with the phone. I tried to drown them out with trivialities; I talked about where we might go on holiday next year and the Christmas shopping and what I might buy Jake. But Vonny wasn't stupid; she knew me better.

'What's wrong?' she asked.

'I'm fine,' I lied. 'Just tired.'

'You're not *you*,' she said. 'The bounce has gone out of your voice. Do you want me to come over after work?'

'I'm okay. We're putting the decorations up tonight so that'll be nice. Rose is happy about it. We always do it on Jake's birthday.'

'It's today? No wonder you're sad. Must be horrible not having him there.'

Far more horrible, I realised, to endure the anniversary of your birth on a lifeboat in the middle of the ocean, as one of Colin's crew had.

'Is Rose okay?' asked Vonny. 'Feels like I haven't seen her in ages.'

You wouldn't know her now, I thought.

'She's putting weight on,' I said. 'She takes the injections better now.' What more could I say? I longed for lunchtime so I could maybe apologise; I dreaded it in case it the words wouldn't come.

When I put the phone down, it rang again immediately. My boss Sarah asked how things were. I knew she probably needed to know when I was planning to return to work, but she didn't ask. I was missed, she said. Everyone was thinking of me. Was there anything I needed? I needed so many things. Like Colin had in his diary – *ask and ye shall receive* – I asked only for a small thing. I asked Sarah if I might ring her in another few weeks, once Rose didn't need me quite as much.

When I hung up I went upstairs to get the decorations from the loft and saw the broken door. Its top panel looked like a row of broken shark teeth. I'd have to replace it before Jake returned. He'd seen me lose my temper before, smash plates and swear at inanimate objects that wouldn't work. But the knowledge that his wife had taken a hammer to a door with her child on the other side might be too much to take. What kind of person did such a thing? I'd have to tell him. But I'd do it when he was home and I'd made everything right again with Rose.

I carried two boxes of decorations into the living room and realised we didn't have a tree. Last year our silver one had died. The threadbare six-foot twig had been passed down from Jake's great granny and had served us well, if a little pitifully, throughout our marriage. Every year I'd squint as Jake plugged it in, say, 'Surely this time it'll blow up.' Last year it had, with a smoky stench. Rose had jumped up and squealed. Jake and I had laughed hard.

That was a lifetime ago.

I'd have to buy another – a new tree *and* a new door. I spent the morning unhappily browsing online for a door that would match the others, and for a tree gaudy enough to please Rose. Before I knew it, lunchtime had come and I got together the diabetes paraphernalia and Colin's diary and drove to school.

It was trying to snow. I hoped it would; it always reminded me of Jake's surprise visit on his bike. Tiny flakes fluttered across the windscreen like the white feathers Rose often caught and wished upon. She sometimes said the swish-swish-swish of the windscreen wipers sounded like wish-wish-wish.

Did she still wish?

Mrs White met me in the school corridor with a pile of folders, holding the hand of a boy covered in yellow paint. The last time I'd been there was to persuade Rose to open a toilet door. How had I succeeded then but not this morning? I seemed to be getting worse at my management of things, not better. Mrs White was warmer with me and didn't even mention the suspension.

'Rose is in the staff room waiting for you,' she said. 'You can use my office while I go for lunch.'

In the staff room Rose sat alone, Hello Kitty rucksack in her lap and a tiny smudge of ink streaking her left cheek like a tick after the right answer. One sock had fallen down and wrinkled around her ankle; the other clung victoriously to her knee. She stared at the floor and hummed a melody I didn't know. The enormous room dwarfed her.

I waited for her reaction upon seeing me. My heart hung on it. But at that moment a dinner bell rang and I flinched when children filled the corridor and so I missed Rose standing up and coming to the door.

'Are we going to the cloakroom?' she asked. It was where we'd done previous injections when a room wasn't available.

'Mrs White said we can use her office while she's at lunch.'

We walked to it, Rose swinging her bag, shy somehow, coy. It was difficult to assess her expression so I tried small talk, asked about PE and what she'd done at playtime and got a couple of agreeable answers. Once in the office, I locked the door and got out the lancets, insulin, blood meter, and Colin's diary. On the table the book looked out of place, like a prop from a period drama abandoned on the set of a contemporary play.

'I'm gonna sit on Mrs White's chair,' said Rose. 'See what it's like to be boss of the whole school.' She jumped into the leather seat and twirled it around a few times, her hair dancing flames. Just like the old Rose. 'This is cool,' she said. 'I'd make a great headmistress, wouldn't I?'

When she stopped spinning I knelt at her feet and she offered her hand. More than ever I didn't want to cut her finger end. Like Grandad Colin, I often played the wish exchange game; I'd imagine that if I saw three birds on the washing line Rose's blood sugars would be perfect, or if the bin men came ten minutes earlier than usual I'd find a book under her pillow again.

Now I held her finger softly between mine, wanting to kiss its pink tip before clicking the pricker against it, wanting to utter a million apologies. But I was afraid to speak. I was afraid to break the spell and stop her being an agreeable Rose who answered my questions (if a little reservedly) and swung on chairs with abandon.

'Go on then,' she urged.

'Should we open the diary now?'

'No, *after* my injection,' she said, 'because *I* want to read it this time.'

'You do? Okay.'

We did her blood – seven-point-six – and I injected her tummy (Rose's least preferred place). Then, between mouthfuls of cheese sandwich, in a careful, reverent voice, she read from another randomly opened page.

I have never forgiven myself for hurting Young Fowler. But I did worse. I can write now all the excuses. I can record that it was a particularly bad day, following a particularly bad night, but they were all bad, all enough to drive a man to do things he might later regret, things that might later wake him in the dark and have him lying there trying to ignore his demons. I do not now know for sure which day it was – it could have been the fifteenth or the twentieth. We were weak. I was weak. But some of the men began singing, 'Two Dead Men and a Bottle of Rum', over and over and over. It drove me half mad. It was King and then Bott. Bott sang it and sang it, his eyes wild, and I couldn't stand it. I punched him, right in the face. He stopped at once. I don't think he'd even known he was singing. But he stopped. He didn't sing again. Yes, I can write now the excuses, but they do not lessen my anguish. They do not help me sleep. And it's much too late to say sorry.

When Rose finished reading, the last line hung in the air between us. The faraway sounds of chairs scraping on floor and a whistle in the playground hauled us back to reality again. I wanted to say sorry; sorry I'd scared her and behaved like a bratty child, sorry I'd said the F-word when she didn't deserve it, sorry I'd been stupid and cruel.

But Rose spoke first.

'I get why Grandad Colin got so mad,' she said. 'When you feel that tired you always act mean to the ones you like most. I just wish he didn't feel so bad afterwards. Cos he really wasn't.'

Was she talking about my behaviour too? Was she explaining how it had been for her, and excusing me for breaking the door?

'Yes,' I said, softly. 'And the ones you like most always understand.'

Rose opened her crisps and ate noisily. 'Remember when I snapped all the needles up and put the insulin in the bin? Well, I was just trying not to smash the door up. Cos that's what I *really* wanted to do.' She paused. 'Grandad Colin didn't have a door to smash.'

'Neither do you now,' I said.

Rose looked at me with a smile in her eyes but not yet her mouth. I pursed my lips and tried not to smile first. It was a game we used to play called *First to Laugh Loses*. This time I didn't care who lost and I smiled before she did.

'I shouldn't have lost my temper,' I admitted.

'No,' she said. 'You're meant to set an example. I wasn't scared though.'

'No, of course.'

'I wasn't!' she cried.

A soft knock on the door interrupted us; Mrs White wanted her office and it was time for Rose to go back to class.

I walked her so far before we parted at the main doors.

'You know when you get my new door, Mum,' she said. 'Can I have a pink one with my name on it?'

'We'll see,' I said.

I watched her walk to the classroom, trailing her bag along the dusty tiles, dawdling like time didn't exist. It was only when I was in the car and had started the engine that I realised she'd called me Mum again. It gave me hope that we might get through.

A few days later I ordered a new white door to match the others; curiously, when it arrived it was unpainted pine with a tinge of pink, as though it had maybe been in the sun in a factory somewhere. I couldn't be bothered to complain or to gloss it and anyway Rose rather liked it. We even got a sparkly name plaque. So, somehow, she got her wish.

When she got home from school that evening Rose was grumpy about her homework, a project about motorways. I loved how ordinary her problem was, that it had nothing to do with needles, and that she shared it with me.

'Motorways?' I asked. 'I think I'd be put out too.'

'Five hundred words,' she said. 'Like I haven't got better words to think about?'

At the teatime injection I told her about when a shark rammed into Colin's boat. Another flying fish had landed on the deck – big enough for quite a meal this time – and after cutting it up Ken had licked blood from the blade and then thoughtlessly dipped it into the ocean to wash it. Within moments the stream of blood enticed an eight-foot shark to seek prey. A powerful flick of his tail sent the boat sideways a good fathom.

'What's a fathom?' asked Rose.

'It's an old imperial measurement,' I said. 'About two metres.'

'So why not just say two metres?'

'That's the word they would've used,' I said. 'Just trying to make it more authentic. You wanted me to do it properly.'

'If you say so.'

'Voice is everything in a story, don't you think?'

I continued telling her how quickly the men had grabbed oars from the second raft and so were ready when the shark butted his great heft at the boat again. Weakness meant their blows were only enough to scare him. He came at the raft again and again and again, then dove beneath, came up under the bow and knocked several planks adrift. Instinctively, Ken grabbed his spear and jabbed at whatever he could reach – it must have hit a tender spot because the brute swam off as quickly as he'd arrived.

Rose cheered and cried, 'Go Ken! Spike that shark!'

Story and injection done, I opened the boxes on the table and took out strings of gold tinsel and garlands of fake holly. Rose danced around, clapping her hands, excited about Christmas. She took out wind-up reindeer and Santa snow globes, and oohed over them as though she'd never seen them before. Every year we added a new ornament; the garish trinkets were testament to the length of our marriage, each shiny bauble or singing snowman tribute to another year survived.

'What about the tree?' she asked.

'I couldn't find a good one online,' I said. 'We'll get one at the weekend.'

'Can I decorate it?'

Jake usually did. 'Of course,' I said.

Christmas might get us through until he returned. Rose wrapped a string of multi-coloured lights around the shelves in the book nook and plugged them in.

'Did you ever meet Grandad Colin properly?' she asked,

holding her hands up near the tiny bulbs so they glowed red and green and purple.

'What do you mean properly?' I unravelled another string.

'Like when he was alive. Not the way we've seen him. Cos you seem to know him as well as you know me and Dad.'

'No,' I said. 'Sadly he died long before I came along. Even my dad was only three. But I do think memories get passed on genetically and relive somehow in our DNA.'

I may have only read about Grandad Colin – had fleeting glances of him as a child – but I smelt his presence between the black printed paragraphs. The same smell he'd had at the hospital that night.

'I know he survives the lifeboat,' said Rose, thoughtfully. She knelt now before the lights and let them flash near her cheek, as though being blessed. 'You said he didn't have no children back at home. So like...'

'Any children, Rose. *Any* children.'

'So anyways Grandad Colin *has* to get back to England or he'll never meet a girl and fall in love and have babies. Me and you wouldn't even be doing this if he doesn't get back. So when you tell me the story I'm like whispering in my head, *You must live, Grandad Colin, you must or I'll disappear.*'

She looked at me, her eyes a million years old.

'When's Dad home?'

She asked softly, perhaps still hearing the echo of my unkind words earlier. *I'll call the emergency number and tell your dad that he shouldn't bother coming home again.* I would forever regret saying it.

'Just after New Year,' I said. 'It'll soon come – you break up from school in two weeks and then it'll be Christmas and then...'

'Won't be the same without Dad,' she said.

'No, it won't. But we'll make it special.'

'I won't be able to have a Selection Box or mince pies, will I?'

I wasn't sure so I gave her another story; one I hoped also came from truth. 'You'll have everything. I won't let diabetes change a thing.' I paused, wondering if she'd now answer the question I'd asked a few times. 'You know when Grandad Colin told you to go to the shed? How did he tell you?'

'He was at the end of my bed,' said Rose, her face blue then orange then yellow, as though her emotions were now electricity powered. 'Not right close cos I think he didn't want to scare me. He doesn't know I don't get scared, *ever*. He wasn't there like proper real people neither. Like if I'd blinked he'd have disappeared. I wasn't dreaming cos I could smell him. Like when my shoes have been in the cupboard too long, except nicer than that. He talked but like it was in my head. Said there was something in the shed that had been there a long time and he'd meet me there. I said I couldn't get in the door cos the lock's too high and he said he'd do it.' She paused, sad. 'Then he didn't come.'

'But we found the diary,' I said.

'He doesn't come as much now,' she said. 'In the night, I mean.'

'Maybe that's because he's here in the book nook with us instead.'

'Maybe.' Rose got his diary from the shelf where we'd begun keeping it – between *Harry Potter* and *The Lion, the Witch and the Wardrobe* – and took his picture from the back.

I joined her and we looked at it together, three generations quiet in the glow of festive lights.

The phone rang and reluctantly I returned to reality. It was Shelley. She asked how things were and reminded me about our first visit to the children's diabetes clinic the following week. I hadn't forgotten; it was circled in red on the calendar.

'I want to suggest something,' she said. 'Something you can both aim for, pet. We can discuss it fully at the appointment but I want to run it by you first.'

'Why do I think I won't like it?' I looked back at Rose, sprinkling white confetti on our windowsills to mimic snow.

'It's been six weeks since Rose was diagnosed. I'd say a good few weeks of you managing very nicely. Well, we do like to encourage youngsters to start sharing the responsibility of their diabetes as soon as we can. It gives them a bit more freedom. Means you don't have to always be there with them.'

'I *like* being with her,' I said, 'and we've just got into a routine that works.'

'I know. I'm not suggesting she suddenly has to do everything – not at all – just that she helps more, pet. Like maybe she measures the insulin or prepares the finger pricker.'

'Can't she be a child a bit longer?' I said the words to myself more than to Shelley. 'Can't she have a mum do it for her? She's only nine.'

'I know,' said Shelley, kindly. 'But you do her no favours in the long term if you don't let her *try*. Maybe I can drop off some pamphlets that'll hel...'

'Bloody pamphlets – all theory and patronising suggestions.'

'Is it a bad time? I can ring back, pet.'

'No, it's actually a good time,' I said.

I had no desire to upset things again with the suggestion that Rose start doing her own injections.

'I don't know if she's ready,' I said.

'I'll talk to her at the clinic,' said Shelley. 'See what she says.'

'If you must.' I hung up, dreading the clinic even more now.

Instead, I turned my thoughts to the suppertime story. Colin's adventure had become the highlight of my day. I sometimes wondered who I was really telling the story for. Rose brought her box of needles, eager too, and I measured and prepared the devices. Ten bubbles spoilt the smooth span of insulin, like barnacles beneath a boat; Rose's blood read ten-point-ten; we were at day ten on the boat.

Every now and again she had asked for extra chapters between pinpricks, promising she could endure pain without words if this ended the story sooner, but I always said, 'No, let's wait. Let's remain true to our trade.'

She had waited well and now I tried to recall the diary pages and newspaper clippings I'd browsed last night. I opened my heart to Colin's voice while the facts filled my head. I had to make the story right for Rose while honouring our history. But most of all I wanted us to join him, relive it, understand it.

'It's getting better,' said Rose. 'No more *once upon a time* or simple words or talking to me like a baby.'

I smiled.

'Day ten,' I said. 'And still no rain.'

'Not a drop?'

'No, not a drop. Officer Scown has put Ken in charge now

beca...'

'Why not Grandad Colin?' demanded Rose.

'Well, I don't know,' I said. Should I have made something up? No, I was honest and admitted I wasn't sure. 'Maybe Ken was more able, or maybe he offered to. But anyway Scown was in quite a bad way by this time so he couldn't lead. His lips were so fat he couldn't talk, his skin blistered, tongue blackened, and his headache never ending. Of course, they were *all* in a bad way, but he'd deteriorated faster. He was a good ten years older than most of them and these things matter in such circumstances. So just before morning, Ken and Grandad Colin were on lookout and Colin must've fallen asleep because when he woke ... where was Ken?'

'What? Ken's gone?' Rose cried. 'No!'

15

FOURTEEN SCARECROWS IN A ROW

Things look bad.

K.C.

A curious dream filled Colin's guilty lookout duty sleep. In it a young girl with hair like sunlit straw tiptoed over the sleeping men, knelt down by his ear and whispered, 'You must live, you *must* or I'll disappear.' He reached out to see if she was real or just a thirst-induced ghost and woke when his elbow hit the gunnel, miserable upon remembering where he was.

Nearby, the thin shapes made a pitiful sight. On the horizon grew the faint promise of another day.

But where was Ken? Hadn't they been sharing the watch?

'Chippy?' The word escaped his parched throat.

Had he also fallen asleep mid-lookout? It was getting hard now to stay awake for two hours at a time, to scan the darkness for ships' lights on the horizon with eyes dry and fed up of the endless nothing. Colin crawled through sleeping bodies and lifted heads to check for Ken. Some men continued napping, others swore at this rude awakening.

None was Ken.

Colin looked under the benches and near the diminishing supplies, fearing something more sinister than sleep. What if Ken had chosen an escape route one or two of the crew had discussed in recent days? In weak moments, between the paltry meals, some said they might leap overboard and wait there for sweet oblivion, whether by shark or drowning. Some even tried and were pulled back by their mates, arguing and begging to be let go.

'Ken!' called Colin. 'Where in the hell are you?'

At this, a head popped up over the stern. It was Ken, wet hair accentuating his skull and making him appear skeletal. 'I'm here!' he cried.

'What the hell, mate?' Colin went to the boat edge. 'Thought I'd lost you! Gave me such a bloody fright. What the devil are you doing in the water? Are you stupid, lad, there's sharks about. You weren't...?'

'You dozed off,' said Ken. 'I needed to keep awake and fancied a dip. Imagined it'd feel good on my skin – and it does, so good. But I'm tired now. Can you help me?'

Colin hooked an arm under Ken's and tried to haul him in, alarmed by how little strength he had. On the *Lulworth Hill* he'd been renowned for his ability to pull the winch in twice as fast as any other man, for his prowess when cranking the windlass. Now he trembled at the slightest exertion, even though he knew Ken was considerably lighter than he had been at the start of their time on the lifeboat.

'Didn't you think?' he snapped at Ken. 'We've no muscle now. We're like bloody kittens. Can't go lugging weights around.'

He tried again and failed. Ken gripped the boat and tried to hoist himself aboard and failed also. Dawn's ginger streaks scratched farther across the sky. In its radiance Colin thought he saw a large black shape in the water, half a mile away.

'What?' Ken asked, following his gaze.

'Nowt. Let's just get you in.'

They struggled vigorously and finally Colin heaved Ken back into the boat. Utterly spent, they lolled on the deck for a long time before speaking again.

'What did you see out there?' Ken glistened in the morning light.

'Can't be sure.' Colin sat up, surveyed the sea. 'But it's better off you're out of the water. Bloody fool. You could've drowned while I was asleep.' He paused. 'Is that what you wanted?'

Ken shoved him. 'Not ready to meet my maker yet.' But the over-zealous response had Colin concerned. What had possessed him to go over when it was so risky, such a stupid thing to do? 'It was *your* fault,' snapped Ken. 'You're about as much use as a chocolate fireguard dozing off and leaving me!'

'I never got any sleep yesterday,' said Colin.

Officer Scown had been ranting much of the day and night, cursing the Germans and their ships. Leak and King had begun openly drinking seawater, having done it on the quiet for days, and were often delirious and quite violent towards anyone who intervened. It was difficult for a man to stop once he started drinking. So Ken – after having been given command – ordered that anyone caught doing so would be lectured and denied extra rations. It seemed to have little effect. Those addicted to drinking it cared little for such threats.

'Maybe today a ship,' said Colin softly.

'You say it every bloody morning.'

'Arnold says prayers every night. Guess this is mine.'

Men began to stir so Ken ordered breakfast. Platten – face drawn, shoulders two sharp nubs – issued the scanty portions. It was water that was most wanted. They'd have sacrificed biscuits and Bovril tablets for more of it. In frenzy, both Davies and Fowler reached for the same cup, almost knocking it from Platten's hand. Then Bamford cried out that he needed more, had to have more, someone pass him the tin or he'd stab them all there and then.

'Take it easy!' cried Ken. 'Get a bloody grip, lads. You can't waste precious water like that. Rations is rations and ignoring them'll be the death of us all. Do you hear me?'

'Who says *you* get to decide!' It was Weekes. Gone was pretence at being cheerful; his jokes had dried up like the last bit of a puddle on an August day.

'I say we drink *more* water and to hell with it!' King joined in the rebellion.

'Who's going to stop us?' cried Bott.

'Look, you all agreed for Ken to take over,' said Colin. Weakly, he stood between Ken and the growing mutiny. 'So let him do it. What he's saying is true and you all know it.'

Yesterday Officer Scown had asked each survivor if they agreed to Ken's charge, and upon receiving unanimous assent he simply said, 'Right men, you've agreed Cooke shall lead you and it's up to you to do what he says in every matter.' The effort of talking had left Scown unable even to support his own head and they made sure he spent more time under the awning, out of the sun's cruel blast.

'Ranting at me does no good,' said Ken now. 'What's decided is decided. Go rant at the sea, at the sky, at God. You'll thank me for sticking to rations when it's tomorrow and there's still summat to bloody drink!'

He took the cup from Platten, asking first if Colin wanted it, and only drinking when his chum shook his head. He tried to go slowly but was unable, licking his lips and trying to make every bit of liquid last. Then he passed it to Colin, who drank greedily before pressing the cool mug to his forehead.

The rest of breakfast was consumed in glum silence, with no one voicing further opposition. Sunrise painted the ocean in all its morning colours, shades that most eyes now viewed with indifference and would one day forget. The chill of evening gave way once again to unbearable heat. The water's reflection doubled the strength of the sun, hurting sore eyes further. Men often discussed which they dreaded more, the evening's bone-numbing bite or the day's suffocating heat – an answer was never quite agreed upon.

'Right, Leak and Stewart are on lookout,' said Ken. It should have been the Second but he was in such a state that he wasn't capable of duty. His feet were as black as funeral apparel, propped up on empty tins. 'I'm going to lessen the watch to just an hour,' Ken added. 'Most of you look exhausted after two.'

No one argued with this. Such physical decline meant two hours of concentration was too much and an efficient lookout was the only hope of spotting and being picked up by a ship. Colin knew his falling asleep earlier had pushed the decision and felt bad that he'd left Ken to shoulder the lookout burden alone.

He still felt terrible for thumping Fowler and had offered the boy an extra bit of his chocolate. He'd said he'd take over lookout when Fowler wilted, and offered his button to suck on when the boy lost his. But none of this appeased Colin's pain. Guilt and anger flowed faster than hope on the lifeboat; optimism took effort, while rage had a life all its own.

'I'm going to do a bit of fishing,' said Ken.

'I'll see if the Second needs anything,' said Colin.

'Let me,' said Young Arnold. 'He calmed down yesterday when I prayed with him.'

'I'll sit with Officer Scown,' said King.

There was little else for anyone to do. Meals and lookout were the only duties. Those still able helped others move around or tended injuries; those in a worse state dozed on and off, waking to cry out obscenities.

An appearance by Scarface mid-morning united the lethargic and alert into action and had the crew huddled together on the centre of the deck, waiting for him to attack or leave, spear and tins raised to fight if needed. Today they were lucky; it was the latter.

Time passed slowly otherwise. A huge whale swam by so close that they fancied they could smell its blood. It was pure torture. Unrippled sea and small swells meant a motionless boat, in which the heat gathered like flies on a corpse. Around lunchtime Bott, King and Leak began swigging seawater with wild abandon, shoving away those who tried to intervene. Young Fowler held his head in his hands and moaned while Weekes feebly warned them about the order not to.

'Knock it off, lads!' cried Ken, throwing down his spear. 'It's no example to set the younger ones!' He tried to pull

King back from the edge and was thrown onto the deck, surprised by the man's strength. Desperation pumped up even the weakest muscles.

Ken stood again and gripped one of the masts to appear strong, show his authority. 'Christ, if it's not enough living without water, I have to watch you doing that.' His voice was ragged and dry. 'We've got to keep bloody strong. *You* lose it and we *all* lose it!'

'Sit down, Chippy,' said Colin from his seat by the foredeck. 'No good you getting wound up.'

'Let me be,' cried Ken. 'If I want to rant, I will. You lot can't stop, why should I? I tell you, I curse that torpedo. I curse the men who designed it, the miners that built it, the officers and crew, and all their families.'

Colin approached his chum. 'Ken, come on, it's too hot. Not worth it.'

'Get off me – can't a man speak? I'm tired of trying to keep morale up. Tired of making the decisions. You can all bloody get on with it. Drink your seawater, finish the provisions, jump overboard. Why should I stop you?' He paused, breathing hard, then said more softly, 'It's Sunday today, you know. They'll all be praying for us back home. Praying for our wretched souls. But what good's that if you don't help yourselves?'

He flopped down, finally spent. Colin wasn't sure whether to go and sit with him or let him rest. He decided upon the latter. He doubted there was anything he could say to appease Ken's despair. It was hard now to get a grip of his own. Perhaps feeling bad for Ken – or maybe just having had their fill of seawater for the day – Bott, King and Leak abandoned their frenzied drinking. They returned to various positions on the lifeboat, barely aware of the men around them.

'You're doing well, lad,' said Colin to Young Fowler.

The boy still held his head in bony hands. 'I'm not,' he moaned.

'You *are*. It's easier to give in and drink that water. I think of it all the time, of how cold it might be on my throat.' Colin gulped; without any moisture it was agony. 'Keep at it. Follow Ken's orders. He means well for us all. So does Officer Scown. He's seen us through this far.'

'I want to go home.' He said it so quietly that Colin took a few seconds to work out the words.

'We all do,' said Colin.

'I can't be here.'

'You can. You'll *have* to, lad, else you'll not get back. If you want to go home you've got to keep at it. If you give in, you'll never see England again. So keep away from the seawater and make sure you eat your meals.'

'Want to see my mum again.'

'You will,' said Colin, because he had to.

Fowler didn't respond. Colin left him. He'd said all he could.

Now he couldn't stop thinking about his own mother. He closed his eyes and saw her abundant figure, her safe curves, her kind eyes; he smelt the cold cream she wore, the lavender perfume for special occasions; he heard her voice, patient and no nonsense. How could he see her so well when his mind was so exhausted? He wondered about his recurring dream. Maybe the young girl Colin had seen was his mother as a child? It would explain the familiarity, the feeling of comfort.

With no sisters or girlfriend it could only be her.

Now there was no lookout duty until evening and nothing else to do, so he curled up and tried to sleep, to return home, to see the girl.

At about three o'clock two dolphins chased a school of flying fish past the stern and four landed aboard. It was the finest harvest they had yet collected. Platten cut them into generous portions and passed the bloody morsels around.

The effect of the extra meal was immediate and lasted hours. Colin felt invigorated by the juicy piece and spent a good fifteen minutes sucking every bit of blood from the bone. Followed with the regular portion of water and some chocolate chunks, the men felt they had eaten like kings. They sat in the dying sun, enjoying the brief hour when the temperature was neither too hot nor too cold but perfect on the face. Gentle conversation even got up.

'When I get home I'm gonna go to our local and gonna buy me a pack of cigarettes and a pint of lemonade,' said Weekes, the joker once more.

The *when I get home* sentence had begun many a chat, but usually only after a meal or some sleep.

'Lemonade,' spat Davies. 'You a fairy?'

'He's right,' said Stewart, softly. 'I might never take another beer. Doesn't quench thirst like a cold soft drink – or water.'

'You'll not be thirsty when you're home,' argued Davies. 'There'll be an abundance of water. Might be rations but plenty to drink. You'll forget all this when you've been back a week. You'll forget us.'

'Oh, for the rations at home,' groaned Fowler. 'At least there's butter. A bit of bread, an egg, some milk. A day's ration there I'd swap for a week's here.'

Many nodded. 'I'd not turn down a beer,' said Platten. 'Sugar in it. Be good.'

Drinks often dominated any conversation that took place, painful though it was.

'Twenty days,' said Fowler, bleakly.

'What you on about, lad?' It was King.

'Officer Scown said thirty days to the African coast.'

Scown had barely acknowledged the conversation and seemed contented with rocking back and forth, eyes half-closed.

'It's day ten,' said Fowler. 'So we're maybe a third of the way there.'

'It was only a guess,' said King. 'Could be wrong.'

'If he *is* wrong, we're doomed.'

'How so?'

'Well, we've rationed for thirty days.' Fowler looked around at his companions. 'If it's longer – what then?'

'Let's not get ahead of ourselves,' said Ken, holding up a hand. 'We've a bit extra for such emergencies and we've had a few fish land on deck, remember. I might yet catch something myself.'

'Might not,' snapped Bott.

'There are lots of mights and might-nots,' said Colin. 'Best we talk only of the mights, eh, lads? Setting a target of thirty days gave us something to aim for.'

'So it could be a lie?' demanded King.

'Not a lie,' said Colin. 'An estimate. A bloody good one too.'

'Without summat to aim for, we flounder,' said Ken. 'So

let's be thankful for it. Now, Arnold, how about a prayer? I'm sure we could all use some of your good words.'

No one argued and Arnold nodded, dipped his head and spoke softly.

Lord God, ruler of land and ocean, bless those at sea. Be with them in fair weather and foul, in danger or distress. Strengthen them when weary, lift them up when down and comfort them when far from their loved ones. In this life, bring them safely to shore and, in the life to come, welcome them to your kingdom. For Jesus Christ's sake, Amen.

A chorus of Amens echoed Arnold's. Whatever their beliefs, the evening prayer had become a part of daily life on the boat, as much as the battle with thirst, the boredom, the arguing, lookout and sleep. That evening, after much encouragement, Colin even managed to whistle. The Merry Whistler licked his parched lips and blew a cheery tune. It floated over the weary heads of the crew, over the softly undulating water, over the horizon to where ships might wait.

But it would be his last tune on the boat – he vowed inwardly that he would only whistle again when he saw home.

Night fell. Colin was on lookout with Ken from ten. They hadn't spoken since Ken's outburst. No one had bothered him much all day, leaving him to sullenly stare out to sea, spear held limp by his side. He'd tied a rope around the remaining water tins and attached it to his ankle, in fear of someone delirious stealing them. No one had argued about his obvious mistrust. Now Ken and Colin sat back to back, watching the water.

'I lost it,' admitted Ken.

'We've all done it,' said Colin.

'But I'm supposed to be in charge.'

'None of us are immune. We're human.'

'Scown put his faith in me.'

'And rightly so,' said Colin, glancing over at where the officer lay, muttering into his chest. 'Bott, Leak and King have settled now. You're keeping order. Spirits are up after that catch.'

'But what about if we all lose it? What then? What about if there's no one to stop it? What if I lose my mind for good?'

'Can't think too much,' said Colin, patience wearing thin. If he'd had the strength he'd have shaken his chum. 'Can't beat yourself up about it. Get a grip, lad.' He paused. 'Let's agree now.'

'Agree what?'

'When you start ranting, I'll knock you over – and you do the same to me.'

Ken grimaced and Colin realised he was trying to smile. 'Let's suck our buttons.' Ken reached into his pocket. Frowning, he felt about his body, looked around by his feet. 'Must've dropped it,' he said.

'Here,' said Colin. 'Share mine.'

They took turns sucking on it during their hour lookout, sharing the tiny brown button like schoolboys with a last peppermint sweet. When Platten and Fowler took over, they nestled between the snoring shadows and tried to sleep.

Colin hoped to see the girl with sunlit straw hair; she hadn't turned up for his daytime nap but maybe now she'd whisper in his ear. Instead his dreams were filled with jugs of water he could never reach, glistening pools of liquid that disappeared when he got to them.

So it was some relief when he woke to Ken shouting, 'It's raining! Wake up, lads, it's raining I tell you!'

Colin sat up. Sure enough spatters of mist-fine rain hit his face in the darkness. No further coaxing was needed for those able to spring to life and shape the canvas awning into a pointed spout aimed at an empty water tin. But joy gave way to torment. It only rained long enough to coat the raft and canvas with a thin film of moisture. Sobs burst out from the younger men; the expectation and resulting disappointment was too much. Colin wanted to scream out, *what more can we take?*

But he bit it back. He wouldn't lose it.

'Wait,' said a voice in the blackness. It was Bott, the gunner who had never wanted to leave his farming job. 'Something we could try. I've seen animals do it after a frost. Licking tree trunks and things. I've seen foxes and deer do it when they're thirsty. Why not?' He put his tongue on the moist rim of the raft. "Good. A bit salty, but good.'

And so the men knelt, as though praying, and licked whatever dampness remained. The fourteen scarecrows in a row, with feet either bare, black or adorned in salt-caked shoes, their smacking lips piercing the night, made a funny sight.

But no one laughed.

16

NOT DARKEST BEFORE DAWN

Both still as well as can be expected.

K.C.

Christmas is only truly Christmas when you're a child; when you believe the story, the cartoons, the songs, the magic. The minute you know the truth it dies. You stop listening for Santa on the stairs with your eyes squeezed tightly shut in case he knows you're awake. You stop leaving out a carrot for Rudolph and the other reindeer. You stop trying to be good.

I stopped believing when I saw my mum carrying a new bike into our back room the Christmas Eve I was seven. I'd woken from a nightmare and tiptoed nervously across the landing in case Santa caught me being naughty. Even at that age I'd not sought comfort from my parents. I'm not sure whether it was down to nature or nurture but then as now I rarely asked for help.

Carrying a cup of water back to bed I heard a commotion downstairs and looked over the bannister. My mum had a red bike bedecked in a silver bow. It all clicked into place – Santa had never been and he'd never come again. I didn't know for sure if Rose still believed. She was only nine, yet she was sharp; too sharp. She loved books – or at least she used to – but she knew what was a story and what was real.

Days after putting up the decorations we found a half-price gold tree and hung sparkly baubles all over. I asked if she'd like to go and see Santa at our local garden centre.

'Not bothered,' she said.

'You always go,' I reminded her.

'I'm older now,' she said.

'We're *all* older.'

'Depends if I get a present.'

'There's always a gift,' I said.

'Maybe.'

'You enjoyed decorating the tree,' I said.

I wondered if she carried on pretending to believe in him for me. Maybe she thought I liked the Santa game; that I liked recreating the magic. Last year she'd hugged him tightly when he came to the school party. She told him she'd tried hard not to swear at next-door's cat so he'd come on Christmas Eve. This year she was excited for the Big Day, as she called it, and enjoyed sitting near the lights each evening for Colin's story. But I wasn't sure she *really* believed in Santa.

Had diabetes made her more cynical? Was it because Jake was away? Maybe she *wanted* to believe but was afraid. Had her faith in happiness shattered when she got diagnosed? I should ask her but feared she would close up again, and I couldn't risk that.

One evening after our teatime lifeboat chapter she joined me on the sofa for a festive episode of 'Deal or No Deal', and we laughed at the ostentatious costumes. Since my door-smashing episode she had left her room to occasionally sit with me, something she'd often done before diabetes. She still gave brusque responses to my suggestions and slammed doors, but we seemed to have reached a stalemate in our battle.

'Can I get a pink Santa hat for the school party?' she asked.

'Of course.' I was pleased at her enthusiasm. 'Do you need a full costume?'

'No, we just have to make a hat. But I can't be bothered. You can just buy me one – I've seen the one I want.'

I couldn't ask whether she believed in Santa; I didn't want the answer. Couldn't face it in absolute black and white. So perhaps I *was* clinging to her youth. Perhaps I couldn't accept the loss of her innocence along with the loss of her health. Even if she did believe, Christmas wouldn't be the same now.

'What will I do at the party?' she asked. 'Can I have cakes or just boring sandwiches?'

'If it's at lunchtime it won't matter,' I said. 'You'll just have your injection and maybe a bit extra insulin.'

'It's in the afternoon,' she said. 'Last lesson. You didn't answer my question – can I have cakes?'

'I'll ask Shelley when we go to the clinic. I'm sure there'll be a way around it. Don't worry, I'll make sure you get to have cake.'

'I'd deal,' she said.

'What?'

She motioned to the TV. 'Sixteen thousand is a good offer.' We often played along to 'Deal or No Deal', me cautious and dealing early in the game, Rose more of a risk taker. Today we swapped roles; I gambled and lost.

'I could invent a cure for diabetes with that much money,' she said when the contestant won ten thousand.

I couldn't tell her that millions of pounds of research hadn't even come close yet. Instead I shuffled closer, hoping to sniff her sweet cheek, maybe get a hug. But she got up and went to her room.

When I tucked her into bed that night she asked from beneath the heap of covers, 'How did you know the bit about me?'

'What bit about you?' I wondered if she was half-asleep, dream talking.

'When you said in the story that I went to the boat and whispered in Grandad Colin's ear.'

'Did I say that?' I had to think about it. Often when I was finished telling the story I could not recall my exact words. All that would remain was my fast-beating heart, Rose's rapt face, and fragmented images of the men on the boat.

'Yes,' she said. 'How did you know?'

'I don't know. I don't even remember saying it. Why?'

'Because I've never told you about it,' she said.

'Told me what?'

'That I've been to the boat.' Her voice was so muffled that I knelt down by the bed. 'Only twice,' she said. Sleep began to steal her words. 'I was just ... tired ... thinking about it ... and I saw ... the boat ... him ... Grandad...'

She drifted away.

I stayed for a while, staring at her slightly pink door illuminated by the light from my room. Would she tell me what she meant tomorrow? But Rose often said things as she fell asleep and then had no recollection of them in the morning.

More than ever I felt the story was bigger than a device to help Rose through diabetes. I wasn't missing Jake as much this week. When had I stopped counting the days in my diary until his leave? I realised it was just over three weeks since he'd last rung so there might be a phone call anytime. Usually this had me restless, but the story was helping me forget real life as much as it was Rose.

In the morning I reminded Rose we were going to the diabetes clinic, anticipating arguments. I hid my nerves with a joke about wearing my lucky socks so it would go fine. But Rose just shrugged, took her diabetes box to the book nook, and switched on the lights so the depressing December morning twinkled.

With the blood test and injection I told her about when Ken confessed to Colin that he'd seen Christ in John Arnold's face. It had disturbed him. Arnold's gaunt cheeks and skinless forehead haunted him. But he was sure he saw someone else in those listless features. Death maybe? And then he realised it was Jesus; Jesus in his dying moment. Colin reassured Ken that the association was only because Arnold led the evening prayer, and believed most fervently in God. But afterwards Colin couldn't speak to John Arnold without seeing the Lord too.

'If you *really* believe in God then he exists, doesn't he?' said Rose.

I shrugged. 'I suppose, yes.'

'Do you?'

'I don't *not* believe,' I said.

'A bit like me with Santa,' she said.

I smiled. 'Well, whether or not you believe, I'm sure he'll

leave you a few presents on Christmas Day.'

'He'd better.'

'Okay, school. I'll pick you up at lunchtime for the clinic appointment.'

She got ready without fuss and I watched her disappear around the hedge; every time she left a part of me aged, like an apple left too long in a bowl. The sweet faith in me soured. I feared a phone call from a teacher or from a stranger who'd found Rose unconscious and seen the medical bracelet and our number on it. I feared the sound of an ambulance. But I had to close the door and get on with my day, bite the apple and all its bruises.

I collected Rose just before lunch, our appointment in half an hour. Mrs White asked to speak with me and took me into her office like an unruly nine-year-old. I dreaded another locked door incident, punishment, though I could hardly complain after my recent behaviour.

'Rose hasn't done anything,' she was quick to say. 'I wanted to tell you personally in case you heard it via playground gossip. Our stand-in PE teacher – Mrs Brompton – came to me with concerns over the bruises on Rose's legs. Obviously we all look out for such things. But she hadn't been made aware then of Rose's diabetes and so didn't know that her injections cause this and not ... well, not anything more alarming. She knows now. I just didn't want you to hear about it and not know that we've since educated her.'

I was grateful she'd been more sensitive this time but sad when I imagined ignorant eyes thinking Rose's bruises were the result of abuse. Sunny holidays spent in bikinis would now likely draw narrowed, suspicious eyes from other tourists, frowns asking who had hurt this poor, skinny kid. Who could blame them? At times her thighs did look like someone had hurt her.

'It's the Christmas party on Friday,' said Mrs White. 'Can Rose eat with the others or would you rather she ...'

'Was separated?' I finished, always on the defence.

'No, would you rather send in some sugar-free foods?'

'No, I want her to have everything the other children do. I'll ask at the clinic about extra insulin and come into school if needed.'

Mrs White seemed pleased – perhaps at my willingness to help, perhaps at my having got past her rash suspension of my daughter.

Rose was waiting in the corridor, one shoelace undone and fingernails filthy.

In the car I asked her, 'Do you want to do your blood and eat lunch in the car park or in the hospital waiting room?'

'But what about Colin's diary?'

'I brought it.'

'In the car,' she said. 'Won't be the same at someplace we don't know.' She was nervous now and trying to hide it by speaking in a more singsong voice. I wanted to squeeze her tightly but knew she'd rebuff it. 'I know,' she said. 'Park by the river. That's right near the hospital. I'd like to look out at the ships.'

'You won't see many,' I said.

'You only need one,' she said softly.

So I parked by the old docks and Rose scanned the brown water for ships while I got out the lancets and blood meter. It was trying to snow again so I left the engine on – cold fingers produce less blood.

'What's that big one down there?' Rose asked, pointing farther along the river.

'That's the ferry,' I said. 'It goes to Belgium.'

We pricked her finger end and the machine read six-point-eight. Rose's sugar levels were getting better all the time. Our hard work had begun to pay off.

'The diary,' she said, sucking her finger end.

'Does it hurt still?' I asked.

'Of course,' she snapped. 'It never won't, will it? Like if someone kept hitting you with a stick, would it get better the more they did it?'

She was right; suffering continuously never made it hurt less. You just adapted to it, perhaps learned to handle it better. I let Colin's diary fall open and read aloud while Rose ate the cheese wrap I'd prepared.

I keep thinking of this proverb that says it's darkest before dawn. It's one of those sayings that's supposed to lift you, make you believe that when things get very, very bad all will soon be well. I don't think it is darkest before sunrise. It wasn't out there on the sea. It was darkest when the sun had disappeared for the day. When light first went – that's when it was darkest. Once we got past that nightly hour, our eyes grew accustomed to the blackness. I suppose I'm saying that proverbs should at least come from a bit of truth or else what hope do they offer? Help doesn't always arrive when you're at your worst, and trying to believe this only caused me great anguish on the lifeboat. I remember a night when it started to rain but stopped after minutes. We licked the canvas, desperate for any moisture. I thought then that things couldn't get much worse, that surely dawn would bring a ship now. I was wrong. When a ship didn't materialise I began to fear for all of us. But most of all I feared giving in to my fear and losing the only thing that kept me going – hope.

I closed Colin's diary and let his words float on the simmering warmth the car heater pumped into our space.

'Me and Dad watched this survival show once,' said Rose, softly. 'There was this man who was at sea for two weeks all totally by himself and he said that surviving doesn't have anything to do with how strong you are, like, in your body but how strong you are in your head.'

'It's probably true,' I said, thinking of Rose's slight size. 'No good being fit if you make a bad decision, I suppose.' I paused. 'We'd better go to the hospital or we'll be late.'

'Are they going to do anything horrible to me at the clinic?' Rose sounded about five.

'No,' I reassured her. 'Just a finger prick test like the one we do – and I think your weight and height.'

'Promise?' she asked.

'Promise,' I said.

We drove to the hospital. I realised the last time she'd been here was at diagnosis, so she probably viewed the ugly grey building with distrustful eyes. I hated it too; except for seeing Colin there. Inside we went, Rose gripping my hand for the first time since I could remember, me chatting about what we might do at the weekend, just like the old days.

The paediatric department was decorated appropriately; stuffed dragons and fat owls hung from the ceiling, bright bookshelves lined two walls, children's paintings and information posters overlapped as though fighting for first place, and stacks of toys sat on a mat in the corner. Not wanting to be lumped in with the tots, Rose sat next to me, nose turned up at the infantile offerings. She was in that difficult no-child's-land; too old for picture books and games but not quite old enough to sit still without some sort of entertainment.

A nurse called us into a room after ten minutes and Rose was weighed and measured. She'd grown a full inch and put back on all but three pounds of the weight she'd lost. I couldn't help but think that as Colin lost weight, Rose gained, as though he gave it to her.

'Perfect,' said the nurse. 'She's going to be tall, isn't she?'

'Am I?' asked Rose as we waited for Shelley to call us next.

'Your dad's tall, so likely you will be.'

'Tall is good.' She paused. 'Was Grandad Colin tall?'

'I don't think so. But we're all getting taller, with evolution.'

Shelley called us then and took us into a small room where she pricked Rose's finger end; Rose looked helpless and I knew it was because she was accustomed to Colin's story helping her through it. Then Shelley explained how the blood would go into a big machine and we'd get what was called an HbA1c number, which gave a picture of Rose's blood sugar levels in previous weeks, more accurately than our blood meter. It would take a few minutes so she took us in to Doctor Grey's office to chat while we awaited the results.

Doctor Grey was everything you'd hope a paediatric doctor might be – rotund, rosy-cheeked, white-bearded, blue-eyed, like he'd just stepped out of a cheerful children's story. But I knew it wouldn't fool Rose.

He asked us about our routine and how she felt about everything, to which she just said okay. Whatever Doctor Grey or Shelley asked, this was her response; okay, okay, okay.

'Rose,' I said. 'If you don't answer with more detail, how can they help?'

Soon they're going to suggest something you really won't like, I thought. *Doing injections yourself.*

'Do you want to get a cup of tea?' Shelley asked me, clearly hoping I'd leave the room. Did she think Rose would reveal an agreeable face once I left?

But I stepped into the corridor anyway – then hovered near the door to listen. She was my daughter and I wanted to know what was being said in my absence.

'Are you curious about maybe trying to read your blood yourself?' Shelley asked her.

'Not bothered,' said Rose.

'How about just preparing the pen so your mum can do it, pet?'

'Not bothered.'

A pause. 'Have you slept over at a friend's house since you got diagnosed?'

'Don't know.'

'You must know.'

No answer.

'Would you like to be able to sleep over with friends like a big girl? No one wants their mum there *all* the time do they, pet? If you just started with something small like making up the pen or recording your blood sugars in the log, I think you'd quite like it. You're a clever girl. Then you could work up to maybe even doing your own finger pricking. Does that sound exciting?'

'You don't have to talk to me like I'm five,' said Rose.

'No, of course.' Shelley paused again, perhaps wondering

how to get it right. 'Shall I be frank then?' she eventually asked.

'Yes,' said Rose, and I smiled.

'Okay, I'll let you into a secret – I don't think your mum *wants* to let you do them. Of course it's natural that she takes care of you. That's what mums are like – they care, don't they? But the sooner you have a go at things, the sooner you'll have control of your diabetes, and that means more freedom – freedom to sleep over at your friends' houses again or go away on school trips. The longer you leave it, the harder it will be.'

No response. I felt a bit sorry for Shelley. She'd been so helpful and I knew better than anyone how Rose could push buttons.

'Would you like some nice pamphlets on h...'

'No thank you,' said Rose. 'If I decide to do it, I'll just do it. Don't need a stupid pamphlet thing.'

'Okay.' Another silence. 'Your mum tells me there's a story she's been reading to help with injections. Do you want to tell me about that?'

'It's totally amazing,' said Rose. Now Shelley had her. 'And it's totally true. About our Grandad Colin who was dead brave. His ship sank and he had to live on this lifeboat.'

I decided it was time for me to return.

'We were just talking about your book, pet,' Shelley said to me.

'It's not a book,' said Rose. 'It's out of Mum's head. She does use Grandad Colin's diary and some newspapers, but she puts it all together.'

I nodded, proud. 'We do it a few times a day.'

'Each time you do injections?' asked Shelley.

I nodded. Shelley's expression faltered a little but before I could question it, another nurse bought in the results of the big blood test – Rose's HbA1c number was 10 percent, which Doctor Grey explained was good progress. The aim was to get closer to 6%, which he was sure we'd achieve at our next clinic appointment in three months.

As we left, Shelley held me back a moment. 'Wait for me at the reception desk,' I told Rose.

'I think it's great that you're sharing this story, pet,' she said. 'But I'm just a little concerned that there will come a time when she'll have to do injections without such distraction. You don't want the story to become a crutch. Something she finds hard to give up.'

Indignant, I said, 'But *you* suggested finding something she loved.'

'I did but I meant perhaps for a week or two.' She touched my arm. 'Listen, I *know* how hard it is, how you must get tired of us health professionals suggesting things. We can't possibly know what it's like for you. I just think you should try *sometimes* without the story. See how it goes.'

'We'll see.' It's the answer we often give to children when they nag for something. When I said it to Rose she always grumbled that really I meant no. Did I mean no to Shelley? I wasn't sure. I just knew how much I looked forward to our time in the book nook. To the smell of Rose's warm forehead, the small pulse of her breath in the soft skin of her neck, the blinking orange and red and pink lights, and the words that calmed and lifted and united us.

When we got home the telephone was ringing, and I asked
Rose to get it while I put the shopping we'd picked up en
route away.

'It's Dad!' she cried, and I closed my eyes and held a tin of
beans to my chest. Now he'd called I suddenly missed him,
felt joyful.

I unpacked, hearing only Rose's side of the conversation.
'Yes, yes, we're fine! Yes, we've been to the clinic. No, totally
boring. Mum's been telling me this ace story. No, Dad, a
proper true one. About her grandad – he's called Colin. Yes,
he was lost at sea in the war and they don't have much to eat
and only like a tiny bit to drink and these sharks keep tr... No,
she's been telling me it out of her head. Yes, she is. If you get
home soon maybe you'll hear some? When are you coming –
is it long now? But I can't wait until then.' She paused. 'No,
I don't want to talk about it. No, Dad. It makes me too sad. I
said *no*.' Pause. 'Okay, I'll get her.'

Rose brought the phone to me.

'Jake,' I said.

'Natalie.' His voice was warm, rich with happiness and
misery at the same time.

'How are you?' I asked.

'Tired,' he admitted. 'You?'

'Same, but let's not talk about that. Tell me what you've
been doing? Did you get my birthday card? Are you excited to
come home? Only three weeks!'

He told me about some of the local Afghan women he'd

met that day and about his platoon's main project, helping rebuild a local school. I closed my eyes and he could have been lying next to me, whispering the words in my ear. His stories soothed me, simply because they were his; he could have described how he'd built a bomb and I'd be happy.

'Rose won't tell me about her injections,' he said, and I opened my eyes again. 'Is she okay? She only wanted to talk about this story you're telling her. What made you choose it?'

'Remember the box I got when my grandma died?' I asked him. 'She found my grandad's diary in it. Did I ever mention him... that he survived his ship sinking? Well, he recorded his thoughts in this diary after coming home from sea.' I wasn't sure Jake would understand the strange experiences we'd had, seeing Colin, feeling him around us, having him lead us to his book. So I stuck with the facts. 'I've been reading the newspaper cuttings about him too and putting it all together and then telling Rose the story to get her to have injections. It's the only thing that's worked. She loves it.'

'Isn't it a bit dark for a nine-year-old?'

'I don't think so.' I was disappointed in Jake's reaction. 'I tell her it in a *hopeful* way. There are some beautiful parts and I don't linger over the suffering too much. When things start to get really dark I'll temper it with nicer things. Or maybe not – she keeps telling me off for making it too babyish.' I paused. 'She *should* know the story – it's her ancestry.'

'You wouldn't let her buy *The Book Thief* because you thought it would be too much because it was sad and now you're telling her a story about sharks and starving men. How's that supposed to help her cope?'

'It just is,' I snapped. 'She counts the minutes between

our chapters. She doesn't fight her finger prick or run away from injections.'

'And what about when it's finished?'

'We're not even halfway yet so there's plenty to go.'

'But what about when it is?'

'Then we find something else,' I snapped.

Shelley wanted us to do injections without it sometimes and now Jake seemed against it. I'd worried about telling him that Rose had been in trouble at school and that I'd broken her door, but I never thought our story would bother him.

'I don't mean to be negative,' he said more gently. 'No disrespect to your grandad and what he went through. It's just that I feel protective of my daughter – she's only nine and she's been ill.'

'So who better than her to understand such a story?' I demanded.

'I don't like to think of the two of you cooped up alone, getting morbid. Isn't it bad enough that I'm *here*? Don't you think I keep some of the atrocities I've seen from you to protect *you*? It's hell, Natalie. I saw one of our men die last week. Barely even a man. He was only nineteen, been out here two weeks. Routine patrol and he walked over an IED.' I knew this was an Improvised Explosive Device – a bomb like a landmine but made from whatever materials are handy. 'Lost both legs. And I was with him.' Jake paused; he edited his story for me just as I did for Rose.

I wasn't sure what to say, found only, 'I'm sorry. That's horrible. His poor parents.'

'Real life is hard enough,' he said.

'I know,' I said. 'I can't imagine what you do there.'

'Sometimes it's better not to know.'

'But you can always tell me.' I said. 'Never keep it in because you don't want to worry or scare me. I'm tougher than that.'

'Can't you tell Rose a nice made-up story?' he asked me.

'She doesn't want a nice made-up story,' I said, softly. 'She wants *this* one.'

We hung up with exchanges of affection and promises of exclusive thoughts, but the shadow of disagreement darkened our goodbyes. Rose skipped about, happy to have spoken to her father, excited about story time. When I'd made our barbeque chicken, I took her portion to the book nook. Rose was already sitting cross-legged on her cushion, as is good story-time tradition.

When I held her finger end ready to draw blood I asked, 'Do you want a more festive story tonight?'

She frowned, pulled her hand away. 'What do you mean?'

'Perhaps we should do something more Christmassy.'

'You mean about elves and stuff? No, thank you.' She put her hand behind her back and all the dread I'd felt weeks earlier about getting her to do this returned.

'One day Grandad Colin's story will finish,' I said softly.

'I know *that*,' she snapped. 'All stories end. But you can't just stop in the middle.'

'Will you be okay when it does end?

'Yes, cos I'll know what happens!'

'You'll still do your injections?'

Rose paused. 'Yes. Cos I'll forever have this story in my head.' She slowly held out her hand again. 'So day fifteen – what else happened?'

I hadn't wanted to read a Christmas story either, not really. It wasn't that we didn't believe in Santa or God, only that we didn't *not* believe. With Grandad Colin it was simple - we knew absolutely that he had existed. And by sharing his story he never died; he lived on in my words, in Rose's captivated face, in the sparkle of the lights, in the darkness, in the ocean, in the sky, forever.

17

HE'LL GET THE CANDLE.

One more week. Nothing seen. Where is our navy?
K.C.

Day fifteen on the lifeboat and dawn meant searching one another's faces for signs of life. It was a morning ritual that no one spoke of but everyone did. Colin assessed each man by his eyes; the face might give cause for concern, with sunken cheeks and cracked lips, but if the eyes still focused, still fought to face the day, then there was hope.

The Second was in a pitifully weak state, his foot causing great pain. To Colin he hadn't existed for a long time beyond his colourless irises. Young Fowler had in recent days also grown so weak that he barely left his position, and Colin was concerned that his eyes too had dimmed forever. Feeling guilty over punching the lad, he had tried often to engage with him, asking what he'd like to do with the rest of his life once he got home. But Fowler never answered.

Day fifteen also brought a birthday.

Resting his tired eyes after studying the men, Colin heard soft sobbing that stopped and started with the flapping masts. He opened his eyes and saw Ken go to John Arnold and sit with him. They bowed heads as though praying together. After a while Ken put a hand on the boy's shoulder and Colin heard him say, 'Don't give in.' Then he ordered Platten to issue breakfast and to make sure Arnold got a little extra today.

'It's his birthday,' Ken told Colin as the water came around.

For those too weak to hold the tin cup a hand often helped. Those helpful hands also fought viciously when someone tried to take their tiny portion.

'Eighteen years old,' said Ken. 'Imagine that? Eighteen and suffering like no man ever should. We can't even sing him a song. No one has the energy.'

Colin shook his head. 'What can you say? Happy birthday? Nowt happy about it.' He looked across the sunlit water, at the glinting waves winking like an evil character in a fairy tale. 'Who'd think such a beautiful view could mean such pain? That such colours could hurt so terribly.'

Ken studied him, then said, 'You never said it this morning, chum.'

'Said what?'

'Maybe today a ship.'

'Didn't I?'

Colin was sure he'd thought it, even if the words hadn't reached his lips. Or had he? Had he been too busy searching for death in his mates' weathered faces? Too busy trying to shake off nightmares in which Death stalked the boat in a hooded black cloak, poking and prodding men as though deciding which one to take. Colin always cried out to warn them and scare Death, but his parched, bloody lips stuck together as though stitched up.

'No, you didn't,' insisted Ken.

'Maybe it's someone else's turn to say it.'

Colin turned away and ate his sea-water-moistened biscuit in silence. They'd all had little sleep. Some nights were better than others. Sometimes the boat stilled slightly and the spray ceased its severe onslaught, but even then the hard, wooden deck and cold dark meant little comfort. Last night Scown had woken everyone with his high-pitched screaming, angry words hurled into the darkness, some making sense, some senseless.

Yesterday he had asked Ken for the knife.

Afterwards Ken told Colin he'd demanded to know why he wanted it.

Officer Scown had said, 'That's my business.'

Trying to maintain his recently granted authority, Ken had insisted Scown stop talking rubbish. He said they could still be picked up any day, which only incited Scown further. He lashed out with surprising strength, grabbing Ken's waist and pockets, searching for the weapon. All Ken could do was push him off roughly and watch as the man cried like a child.

Scown had spent the rest of yesterday afternoon ranting and cursing. His rage was understandable. As a man ten years older than the others, who had spent twenty hours in the water before being picked up, he'd done well to keep order for so long. Colin very much admired him.

Many of the crew ranted back at Scown and Colin feared there would be mutiny – such rage is contagious, especially among men so hungry, thirsty and tired. But fortunately

Officer Scown ran out of steam for an hour and this broke the growing panic.

Now he lolled in the boat's well, neither awake nor asleep, refusing his breakfast and ignoring everyone. So when he sat upright at around ten, perked up and called Ken over, Colin anticipated another outburst and braced himself to mediate. But the two men talked so quietly that he left them to it and tried to concentrate enough to watch the horizon for ships.

Watch duty had become so hard on the men that it now occurred as and when someone felt able. If a man was up to it, he offered. If no one spoke, they left their rescue to fate. Stewart had done an hour during the night with Platten, and Colin had shared a shift with King, though the man had kept saying there were lights, dozens of them, so very pretty, until Colin told him to knock it off.

Mid-morning Officer Scown beckoned Colin, bid him with a weak nod to move close so he could speak hoarsely in his ear. It made sense that the officer would call Ken – he was in charge now – but Colin wondered what he could possibly want with him. He expected demands for the knife.

But different words scraped from Scown's throat, like fingernails on sandpaper. 'I spoke with Cooke earlier,' he said. 'Gave him a message for my good wife back in Willerby – I know Cooke's not far from there. You too.' So this was why Colin had been chosen: geography. 'I haven't the energy or the heart to repeat that message to you,' said Scown. 'But I want you to make sure Cooke tells you it so that you can tell my wife if he doesn't.'

'I think you'll be able to tell your wife yourself, sir,' said Colin.

'No. I'm done,' he said. 'I know I won't last much longer so you have to promise me you'll get that message off him.' His calm talk contrasted so harshly with the wild ranting of previous days that Colin wondered if Scown even remembered those words.

'Don't talk rubbish, man!' Colin said. All formality dissipated – this wasn't the ship's first officer now but a man who needed a vigorous shake and Colin would give it if needed.

'I know how I feel,' Scown said, so quietly that Colin took a moment to digest the words. Then he looked right at Colin, the effort of lifting his head causing a film of moisture to coat his brow. His eyes had lost all radiance, as though it was needed elsewhere in his ravaged body, and this Colin knew to be more hopeless than his words. 'Promise me you'll talk to Cooke. I'll not know any peace until you promise it.' He gripped Colin's hand with such surprising strength that Colin nodded, agreed.

Then, as though all was now well and he had permission to surrender, Scown closed his eyes and slept. Colin waited a moment, fearing more than sleep, but the officer's chest moved ever so slightly, up and down, up and down.

He approached Ken on the foredeck.

'I don't think Scown will get upset again,' Colin said.

'What did he say to you?' asked Ken.

'Not much.'

'I thought he was gonna beg for his knife,' said Ken. 'But he said he could feel deep down that he's not gonna live much longer. Said he's made peace with it.'

'The man's delirious.'

'Except he isn't, is he? He's calm.'

Colin had to agree.

'He gave me a private message for his wife,' said Ken. 'I need to …'

Though he'd promised the officer he'd learn it, Colin shook his head. 'I don't want to hear it.'

'No, lad, you must. I have the signet ring his wife gave him too.' Ken opened his palm. Two broken pieces sparkled within, gold half-moons. 'He wants me to take it to her,' he explained. 'Some of the lads helped me cut it off with the jack-knife cos his finger's so swollen and burnt. He reckons I'm gonna make it.' He looked at Colin. 'You too, chum.'

'No,' insisted Colin. 'That message is private. Just for his wife.'

'But what if I *don't* make it? I think you will, lad, so I need to tell you. I'd like you to look after the ring bits for me. I'm so stupid I've lost all my buttons. Keep pulling 'em off, then I lose 'em. You'll take care of the ring pieces well, I know.'

'Keep the thing.' Colin pushed him away, not sure why he was angry. Perhaps it was that their officer had resigned. Given in. Anger came from the fear that Colin too might surrender one day. No, he'd go on fighting. 'The man needs to fight and give that message to his wife himself.'

'He's not as young as you or me,' said Ken.

'Then we up his rations!'

'Just let me tell you hi…'

'Keep it!'

Ken appeared to realise it was no good arguing further. He put the gold pieces in his pocket and resumed watching the water for fish, spear held close despite not having had any luck with it yet. Colin had to admire the man for never giving up; Ken had the spear and Colin had his game. But there were only so many times he could count sharks, hoping the fourth would bring a ship, and not lose hope altogether when it failed to happen.

Just before lunch, Scarface made an appearance.

He tracked the lifeboat most days now, seemed to be assessing the crew with his cold, steely eyes. Sometimes a friend joined him; occasionally they bumped into the stern as though warning those aboard that they were waiting. Waiting until they were too weak to fight them off. This time the appearance of grey sharks was silver-lined because they caused three more fish to land in the boat's well.

'Grab them!' cried Ken, and those most able sprang to life.

Weekes held one down, Young Arnold another and Platten the third. Ken found the knife – he'd kept it close by after yesterday's events – and cut the brawny creatures into fourteen wonderful pieces, so fast that Colin imagined a heart still beating when he ate it. The scraps were consumed in joyful silence, with much licking of blood and sucking of bone.

'Happy birthday, lad,' Ken said to John Arnold.

'It's your birthday?' chorused Davies weakly.

'Why didn't you say?' asked Weekes, slightly energised by the meal. 'I'd have made you a cake and covered it in cream icing.'

Young Arnold managed a smile; it creased his face, threatened to tear the papery skin that barely clung to flesh. Colin couldn't look at him without seeing Christ – without fearing that his own face now looked ten years older too.

'You know what, lads,' said Ken thoughtfully. 'These fish are a different species to them that jumped aboard last week. Bigger, more colourful, different fins.'

'So?' demanded Bott. Since giving in to drinking seawater on and off most days he had become belligerent and argumentative. Maybe he gained some sustenance from doing it because he, King, Leak and Stewart (who indulged the most) seemed to be fitter than Scown, Fowler and the Second who hadn't.

'It must mean we've made progress,' said Ken. 'Different fish. We must be in new waters. Maybe we're closer to land.'

'Do you really think so?' It was Fowler, barely audible. Platten had helped him eat his fish. Blood now stained his chin like raspberry juice.

'Wouldn't say it if I didn't.'

'Doesn't mean we're nearer the coast,' argued Leak. 'Only that we've moved. We could be drifting farther out to sea.'

'What the hell's the point in saying that?' demanded Colin. 'I should come over there and thump you one.'

'Just try it,' said Leak. 'I'll break your bloody arm.'

But their words were far stronger than their bodies now and neither man attacked the other. While they argued, no one noticed that Officer Scown had crawled towards the foredeck and begun to climb over the edge.

Ken spotted him first, cried, 'Scown! Grab him!'

Colin and Platten went for his legs; Ken pulled an arm so roughly he feared he had dislocated it. But Scown's scream was merely one of rage at not succeeding in his suicide mission. He collapsed on the deck, red-faced and cursing, finally sobbing again.

'What the hell are you thinking?' asked Platten, panting with exertion.

'You fool!' cried Ken. 'Scaring us all like that.'

'Is he though?' asked Colin, softly.

'Yes, he is. Now they'll all be at it and we'll have to watch him all the time.'

Ken ordered that whoever was on lookout had to also keep an eye on Scown and give the alarm should he try and jump overboard again.

'Should've let him go,' said Colin quietly. 'I reckon he doesn't want to burden us. He's an officer through and through. Without the energy to fulfil his duty I reckon he'd rather go. Should've just let him if he so wishes.'

'What, and let everyone follow?' Ken shook his head.

'If they do, they do. Who are we to stop them?'

'It's what you *do*,' snapped Ken. 'They're our friends.'

'So shouldn't we let them choose their own fate?'

'Isn't the will to survive stronger than the will to jump?'

'Clearly not,' said Colin.

'But it *has* to be.'

'With so little water ... barely a mouthful ... how can the will go on?'

'It *has* to,' insisted Ken.

'It's been two weeks,' said Colin.

'I know.'

'What if it's another two?'

Ken wouldn't look at Colin. 'Then we survive another two,' he said.

'And you think we can? On portions like these? On lucky bits of fish?'

'What other option do we have?' demanded Ken.

Colin nodded. 'No, you're right. We sink or swim. We give in or go on.'

'I intend to swim, chum.'

'So do I.'

The rest of the day passed relatively peacefully. Scown made no more attempts to abandon the boat. A gentle breeze got up that cooled the simmering heat and kissed hot skin. The sun did not hurt it quite so much now, having toughened it into leathery resilience. But dry throats still ached for liquid, any liquid – blood, water, rain, and of course seawater, which some continued to consume. Heads pounded from dehydration, bellies rumbled angrily for food.

The evening meal was eaten without conversation and Arnold's customary prayer followed, the men devouring it as much as they had the fish earlier. Colin realised that comfort found at home in wives, girlfriends or mothers was now sought in the almighty Father.

It was a simple prayer that night, one that came from Young Arnold himself, one that concluded with fourteen faint Amens.

Dear Lord, look down on us here with mercy. See how much we need you, how very much we long to find our way home, how very desperate we are for your kindness in helping us get there.

Ken took the evening's first lookout with an unhappy Leak at his side. He kept awake for the first twenty minutes by writing in the log, which was now a piece of torn sail covered in neat dates and facts. When there was anything to report, Ken recorded it. No matter how burnt his fingers, he made sure everything that mattered made it to the improvised log.

This he did for the duration of his time on the lifeboat.

Colin tried to find a comfortable sleeping position in the boat's well. With less meat on his bones now, and more bruises and cracks and cuts, sleeping proved agony. But while thirst caused insomnia, hunger meant exhaustion – and so he eventually slept, with an arm reaching out above his head as though clinging to hope.

Dreams came gently that night. No vicious Death-filled nightmares. Colin found himself in a house, one different to any he'd seen before. It was a kitchen where the surfaces gleamed metallic, shinier than a ship's polished railings. The oven top was silver as a new shilling; nothing like the stone one his mother cooked stew on and cleaned daily. In the alien beauty was chaos; crockery had been abandoned on the table, shoes were piled high in a corner and muddy footprints marked the floor tiles. It was as though whoever lived there had left in haste.

On the counter sat a pumpkin.

When Colin was young he'd carved out a turnip at Halloween because it was all they could afford; one between the five of them. This pumpkin was fat and rich orange. A candle still burned inside, illuminating disjointed eyes and teeth so the face leered at him with fiery life. Someone must have forgotten to blow it out.

'He'll get the candle.'

The words came from nowhere, sweet and hopeful. Colin looked for the speaker. No one there. He was alone in this foreign yet familiar and welcoming kitchen. Perhaps he should blow the candle out. Perhaps whoever had departed in haste would be grateful he had.

In one quick puff he extinguished the flame. On the lifeboat he blew into Bott's ear, causing him to stir and cry out for his mum.

Neither woke fully.

In the ocean, on both sides of the boat, sharks followed.

18

OUR OWN SPECIAL GUEST

Extra water and food keeping us going.

K.C.

It was a week until Christmas and no one wanted us to be alone. My mum rang from the Isle of Wight three times, reminding us we'd be welcome to go there for a few days. She'd first suggested it weeks ago and I said I'd think it over. But I knew now where I wanted to be – home.

On recent mornings I'd felt happier than in weeks. When I crossed the landing, the diabetes box didn't feel quite as heavy in my hand. I'd open Rose's hint-of-pink door and she'd be sitting on her bed edge waiting and we'd go down to the book nook as though it was all we'd ever done.

But my mum wasn't having any of it.

'It'll be just you and Rose, all alone,' she said, aghast at the idea. 'There'll be loads of us down here. George will cook turkey and our friends Carol and Jim are coming over and you can ...'

'Mum, we're fine,' I insisted. 'Rose wants to be here. I do have friends as well you know.' I was defensive; I'd always chosen friends carefully, preferring a few special ones to hordes of acquaintances. 'I'll invite people over if I need to.'

'I don't like to think of you both there alone when Jake's away. It doesn't seem right. Christmas is about being with your family.'

She didn't know we'd be sharing it with family. How could I explain that we had our own special guest? That Rose's great grandfather Colin was with us four times a day. Mum had said the word *alone* numerous times, yet I didn't feel like we were. There was no point telling her.

'Look,' I insisted. 'You're kind, but Jake will be home just after New Year and I'd like to be here if he rings on Christmas Day. I'll feel somehow farther away from him down there.'

'That's silly,' laughed my mum. 'He couldn't be further away than in Afghanistan, so what does it matter if you're down here or up there?'

'I feel closer to him at home.' I did. He was everywhere here – in pictures, in the TV unit he'd built, in the pile of boating magazines at the bottom of the wardrobe, reminding me of his watery sailing dreams. 'Can't you see that?'

She acquiesced and said I had to do what I must but that she'd worry over Christmas. We parted with promises of a spring visit. My dad rang that evening suggesting in his customary don't-mind-either-way manner that we could go there for Christmas lunch if we felt inclined. Vonny then texted, saying her home was open if we needed, and my boss Sarah left a message saying they were having a get-together the night before Christmas Eve and everyone hoped I'd go.

They all understood that Rose and I had our own simple plans; a small chicken, our favourite vegetables, minty potatoes, Doctor Who crackers and a sugar-free sponge because neither of us liked Christmas pudding.

Even April knocked on the door late morning with a fruity Christmas cake ('sugar-free,' she smiled) and offered her services. Frosted air left her mouth like magic dust. She was elated that she'd been invited to her daughter Jenny's home at Christmas but said if we needed anything before then we should just knock.

'I'm not interfering,' she said quietly, as though others might be trying to learn our doorstep secrets. 'But it's a tough season to be on your own, lovey. I know – I've been there. My Gerald was often away on the rigs. It's all about family and couples and ... well, you can feel the odd one out, can't you?'

'I'm not odd,' I said. 'I've got Rose.'

'She's only nine. You can't look to her for companionship or support. It's not her responsibility to be your friend is it, lovey?'

'Of course not,' I snapped.

'I didn't mean that quite the way it sounded. I'm just trying to watch out for you both. Look, anyway, I hope you enjoy the cake. I got a bit carried away with the brandy so maybe just a small bit for Rose?'

'Thank you.'

The words surprised me; they came out so easily. It was a thank-you for helping me find Rose weeks earlier, and for the sugar-free apple pie she'd made then, and for not asking why Rose had been in trouble at school. I said it spontaneously, the way we try and get our children to and never can. The way it happens when we're suddenly overcome with gratitude.

'It was nothing, lovey,' April said, both belittling and

elevating my simple sentence. She disappeared around our hedge.

People were kind with their cakes and offers, but they didn't know that Rose and I weren't alone. Fourteen men joined us each day. I laughed when I imagined telling my mum we'd be sharing the season with a gang of young seamen. Sometimes I'd wash the pots and hear their voices in the gush of water; or during a shower the rush of bubbles merged with the ocean's melody and Colin whistling.

There was a week until the big day and still all the last-minute Christmas jobs to do, cards I'd forgotten to send that might not make it their destination now and items to take to the charity shop.

On the last Saturday before Christmas Rose and I headed into town for some final gifts. I'd already bought her stocking-fillers and wrapped them weeks ago and hidden them in the airing cupboard. Her main gift, a sewing machine so she could make bags and other knickknacks out of scraps, was under my bed. But I needed to buy April a little something for being kind and had forgotten to get a box of chocolates for Rose's teacher.

'Can we go to McDonald's for dinner?' asked Rose as I finally found a parking spot in the main shopping centre.

'Maybe,' I said. 'It'll be packed. I just want to buy what we need and go home. The queues will be down the street.'

'You're no fun,' she pouted.

'Anyway,' I said, 'I don't reckon Colin's diary will sound right in MacDonald's. Do you?'

'You brought it?'

'Of course. In case.'

She smiled. 'People might look at us a bit crazy.'

Eating out could be difficult; nervous about doing her blood test and injection where others were, Rose always insisted we squeeze into a toilet cubicle. Hardly ideal, but few places had anywhere else to do it. On the rare occasions we'd done it at our table because the toilets weren't suitable, it never failed to surprise me how much people stared. No attempt was made to hide mild revulsion or blatant curiosity. Once a woman leaned over and asked if we should be doing such a thing in public, to which it had taken all my strength not to say sarcastically that normally my daughter did heroin in a derelict house.

'We could read a page in our heads for once.' Rose got out of the car. 'Together so we're getting the same bit at the same time, like loud reading.'

We were at day nineteen on the boat already. Where had the time gone? While it flew for us, I imagined it was quite the opposite for the men at sea. So little had happened since day fifteen that each chapter now was like an old-fashioned record playing again and again, crackling with dust and scratches. Meals merged into one, sleep and waking had no pattern, with the men hardly knowing if they were conscious or out. The sun rose and fell. And between this only monotony, agony, thirst and no ship.

Rose pursed her lips. 'But it might not be the same if we read the diary in our heads. Like does a spell work if you don't say it out loud?'

I locked the car door and fastened her coat; within five minutes she had unfastened it again. We weaved through crowds of shoppers who banged us with bulging bags. I tried to hold Rose's hand but she roughly pulled free.

'Have you got your medical bracelet on?' I asked, eternally afraid of losing her and having something happen in my absence.

'Yes, Natalie.'

'Don't start with that again,' I sighed. 'Have you got your phone?'

'Yes, Na– *Mum*.'

I decided I could get all I needed in one store; Rose nagged to go a shop she liked because she had five pounds to spend and insisted that was the only place she'd be able to afford anything. I said we'd maybe go later and her fierce glare indicated she didn't believe me. Looking back afterwards, I can say it all started there. Not with the undoing of coat buttons or the rejection of my hand but with her scowl after the amiable conversation in the car.

While I tried to look at flowered make-up bags for April, Rose huffed and puffed and said she was so bored she could die. I suggested she sit on a chair near the changing rooms so I'd get done faster and we could maybe go to McDonald's after all. With a grunt she flopped into it and I wandered the aisles looking for April's thank-you gift. Lost in choices – and some half-price earrings I liked – I forgot for a moment that Rose was even with me.

Then a commotion drew my attention to the changing room area. Above the reindeer jumpers and yuletide scarves, a row of heads bowed, watching an event unfold. One or two faces turned to scan the store. I realised who they wanted – me. Dropping the purple earrings, I ran to the crowd, dreading what I knew awaited me.

On the floor, Rose glared at the shoppers. She'd overturned a rail full of fake fur and they surrounded her, covering the ground as though she'd prepared a bed to collapse in. When an old woman with blue hair bent to ask kindly where her mum was, Rose threw a fur at her.

I pushed through the throng, said, 'She's my daughter, please let me past,' and knelt down and tried to calm her.

'Fuck you,' Rose spat, eyes wild and skin shimmering with damp.

Disapproving murmurs surged through the crowd the way surf does from the wave machine at our local swimming pool. It must be a hypo. I'd only read about the symptoms – the clammy flesh and pale skin and extreme stroppiness – but nothing could prepare me for the reality of it. For how it changed a person. This wasn't my child.

'She's diabetic,' I told the crowd, 'She's having a hypo. Can't you give us some space?'

I'd have to do a blood test, make sure of it. Had I brought Coke to treat it? I surely couldn't have forgotten today. Every time I left the house with Rose now I did the checklist in my head: glucose tablets, Coke, snack, blood meter, lancets, emergency GlucaGen pen.

Talking gently to Rose, who barely registered my words and babbled in nonsensical language, I searched for the plastic purse I kept her implements in. Thank God, it was there, with a small bottle of Coke.

It must have been almost eleven – we'd missed her ten o'clock snack. What number had she been at breakfast? Four-point-four. Not a hypo, but low. No wonder she'd crashed – an empty tummy and busy shopping and a distracted mum.

I'd just begun to feel more confident. Now I fell apart.

'Can I help?' asked the blue-haired woman kindly.

'No.' I opened the plastic purse. 'I have to do her blood.'

I reached for Rose's hand but she snatched it back and shook her head, skin ashen. Her eyes lolled back into her head, like marbles rolling in a child's hand. There was no way I'd be able to prick her finger. I'd have to presume this was a hypo and treat it. I unscrewed the Coke bottle and held it to her lips. Rose spat it out and said, 'fuck off fuck off fuck off,' over and over.

What if I couldn't get the sugar inside her? Unconsciousness? I couldn't face that again. She'd have to have it, one way or another.

'Let me help.' The blue-haired woman took the bottle.

So I gripped Rose's face, turned her towards me and spoke firmly, 'Drink it. You have to drink it.' Then the woman tipped the sugary liquid to Rose's mouth and I held her face as still as I could while she swore at me. But the Coke trickled into her mouth. She swallowed between words. I imagined the sugar reviving, sparking like electricity, regenerating.

Having lost interest, the crowds dispersed. Once we'd got the Coke into Rose and her swearing slowly gave way to less angry get-off-me's, the blue-haired woman went to find a store manager. I helped Rose back into the chair and knelt before her.

'Look at me.' I held her face. 'Look right in my eyes.'

The clouds across her irises dispersed, allowing those hazel flecks to shine again. I thought of Colin assessing eyes for life. Hers were reawakening; the sugar was taking effect. I found the diary in my bag.

'It's just us,' I said. 'Just us and Grandad Colin.'

And there in the middle of a busy department store at Christmas time I read a random diary page. It occurred to me, in the midst of the drama and panic, that it was a miracle we'd never opened it in the same place twice. Surely the law of averages determined we should have done. Surely when a page had been opened already it creased in a way that made it likely to fall open again.

But no, always chance. Always a new story.

Be glad it's not you. That's what Ken said to me each time it happened. Be glad it's not you. He said once, 'I fear I'll not go on if it's you, chum.' So I said, 'Don't talk that way.' I used to shout at him to get angry! Fight, Ken! Anger sustains, sadness doesn't. Sadness drains. I'm angry! Angry that I'm here, back home, and I can still hear Bott's screams and Scown's ranting. I'm angry that they're louder than the silence of this room. I'm home and still that places haunts me. I think when you've fought so hard to survive it can be harder not to have that battle any more. What do you do when life is easier? What do you fill it with?

I paused when Rose smiled weakly at me, even through such sad diary words.

'I don't know yet,' she said.

'Know what?' I asked.

'What we'll do with when we get to the end of the story. I'm not scared though cos I'll know the end.'

The blue-haired woman returned with a bag of cookies she'd bought and a burly store manager. He took us into a back room where Rose ate a couple of biscuits in peace. I stroked her hair, meeting no resistance now. She looked exhausted though, like she'd run a marathon.

'I was there,' Rose said.

'Where?' I asked.

'On the boat.' She munched noisily. 'I could hear you talking but it was like you were the dream and the boat was the real.'

'You couldn't see me?' I asked.

'No, just the boat. I lay next to Colin but I don't think he saw me. He was sleeping. He looked thin and hairy. So I whispered and he moved a bit. I said, "No, don't wake up. Stay asleep." And then I said, "Dream about nice things and you won't be sad. But it's okay to be sad cos that's part of being brave. I just can't remember the other part right now." Then I looked around the boat. I wasn't feeling all weird like when you made me sit near the changing rooms. I was totally strong. Stronger than they are. But there weren't fourteen – someone was missing.'

I was so relieved to have her back that I hardly took in the account. Pink coloured her cheeks. Perhaps she'd had a vivid dream induced by the hypo. But hadn't she said last week that she'd been to the boat. I'd asked her again about it but she'd shrugged and started talking about her motorway homework.

'Do you feel okay now?' I touched her forehead.

'Yes, I feel good.'

'Do you remember what you said?' I asked. 'While you were on the floor.'

'I was on the floor?'

'You don't remember that?'

Rose looked genuinely surprised.

'What's the last thing you do recall?' I asked.

She thought about it. 'You told me to sit on the chair and went to look at something.'

I hadn't the heart to tell her how she'd acted – she might be embarrassed and scared about it happening again.

'The next thing I saw,' she said, 'was you reading Colin's diary out to me.'

'It's my fault,' I said. 'I completely forgot to make sure you had a snack and then I went off and left you.'

I'd never do it again. In a rush of guilt I thought of Jake's words, his concerns that Colin's story was too much for Rose. Real life is hard enough, he'd said. He was right. It was. I was never going to get this diabetes right. I thought of Shelley's suggestion that the story was a crutch. Maybe the weight of it had contributed to Rose's hypo. Perhaps it was time to stop after all. Was it fair to continue reading a tale of dying men to a child recently almost unconscious?

I knew what was coming. Last night I'd skimmed newspaper cuttings and glanced at a letter Colin had sent to his mother once he was well enough. Could Rose handle day nineteen? Should I assess her bravery each day and miss a chapter if needed? Was it fair to exchange blood for pain in our trade?

'Don't look so gloomy,' said Rose, clearly buzzing with sugar. 'It's Christmas soon. Can we go to McDonald's? *Please* can we?'

I took her. I watched her devour a burger and slurp juice, determined I'd never stop watching her again. By the time we got home I was so exhausted from my constant watching that I could have gone to bed for the night then. Rose ran to her room and I went to mine. There I fell asleep for an hour, knew nothing, not a dream, not a sound, not a word.

When I woke the house was quiet. It was almost four and in the December evening's half-light my bedroom appeared as depressed as I felt. Teatime, injection time and story time. For the first time in ages I wasn't sure I could do it. Rose had had the hypo but I felt low. Still, I went to get the diabetes box.

It wasn't there. Neither was Rose. The hint-of-pink door opened onto an empty room with a floor covered in cut-up Christmas cards and glitter. I panicked, ran downstairs.

There in the book nook, illuminated by the rainbow of lights, I found both Rose and the box. She was cross-legged on her cushion, and had prepared her finger pricker.

'I'm keeping the box in my room now,' she said.

'Why?' I sat opposite.

'I want to be responsible for it. It *is* mine.' She held it out. 'It's nearly empty by the way.' Unlike on the lifeboat, our dwindling supplies could easily be ordered from the doctor and replaced.

'I'll look after it,' I insisted. 'You shouldn't have to. I need t...'

'Mum, I know you like to *think* you have to, but I'm old enough.'

'I know that. But...'

'What?'

'I'm your mum.'

'Colin kept going because of his mum and she wasn't there, remember.'

'I'm not going anywhere,' I said softly. Perhaps she was worried I'd go to another country like her dad? Who knew how children thought?

'I know that!' she snapped. 'I'm just going to have a go at doing stuff!'

'Are we still doing the story?'

'Of course.' She looked at the finger pricker, anxiety dimming her eyes. 'Maybe you do it now and I will next time. But if I do, I'll still need a chapter.'

I took Rose's hand in mine. Before diabetes I'd felt sad that I never got to hold it now she was nine and said handholding was babyish. This was the only gift diabetes gave – being able to have her delicate fingers in mine again. I pierced the skin. Nothing. Some days blood wouldn't flow, no matter how we tried. Rose bore it well when we tried again. But on the third attempt I cried inwardly. How much should a child go through?

'It's okay,' she said. 'Being sad is how you start to be brave. I'll do it.'

'No, you shouldn't have to.'

Before I could stop her, she grabbed the finger pricker and clicked it into her flesh. Red gushed from the end and she squealed, 'Ow, ow, ow.' I harvested the blood and she sucked her finger.

'Are you okay?'

'Yes,' she insisted. 'Just do the story.'

'Were you really on the boat?' I asked, before we set off.

'Yes,' she said. 'So don't try and protect me. Tell me it exactly how it is.'

Rose would know if I deviated from the truth and doing so to cushion her wouldn't be fair to either of us. We had begun; we would continue.

19

THEY DIED THAT YOU MIGHT LIVE.

Scown. Mate.

K.C.

Maybe today a ship.

This prayer woke Colin on the nineteenth day. He wasn't even sure if he'd said it or if it was merely the ocean singing her eternal song. He imagined the swish-swish-swish must be how mermaids sounded when they sang so beautifully that men leapt to certain death, just to get closer to the music.

'I think you could be right, chum.' It was Ken, at his feet.

So Colin must've said it aloud. He hardly believed there'd be a ship that morning though. Hardly wanted to open his cracked eyelids and look yet again upon the misery of his mates. Upon the now salt-caked lifeboat and the sparkling sea with its far away, ever empty horizon.

How many more mornings could he stand to see this? How long before the ocean's song seduced and he too jumped?

'I don't feel so bad today,' said Ken. 'Wasn't the night calm? What a relief to not have endless stinging spray. First time I think I really slept. Done me good, lad.' He paused.

'How about you?'

'Not sure.'

Colin realised he must have slept a little because he'd dreamed. His sleep escapades were sometimes more real than daily existence on the boat. Certainly he preferred them. Last night he'd returned to the strange silver kitchen. Beyond the polished surfaces – in which he saw his face how it was before the ocean – was another room, one with a shelf from which he longed to pull the colourful books. Next to it sat the girl with hair like sunlit straw.

Remembering it, Colin eagerly told Ken the details. 'I dreamt about that young lass again. I don't know her yet but she's so familiar to me. You know when you get déjà vu – it's like that. She looked sad. Had this box on her knee – don't know what it was, like. Couldn't see. But she didn't seem to like it very much. She was making something. Something that looked like an ink pen and had all sorts of attachments. Then she looked right at me and said something dead strange. She said, "I'll have to do it myself one day." What does it mean, Ken?'

'Means you're stark raving mad, Armitage.' Ken shook his head. 'Only joking, lad. Who knows what such dreams mean? I think we have 'em more vividly out here cos we've so little else to do. And God, to have something to talk about – something that isn't home or rations or ships.'

'You're a bit more chipper today,' Colin said. 'I've been worried about you.'

'Wouldn't call it chipper.'

'We're still all here to face another day.' Colin wasn't sure if he said the words in relief or with dread.

The other men began to stir, twelve skeletons wearing tattered garments and agonised expressions. Colin knew he must look how they did. Never a vain man, he knew he'd been called a good-looking chap, if in a rough, coarse kind of way. He had dark eyes that looked into a person with unnerving directness, open, warm, honest. He wondered how he'd look if he ever got off the boat. Would his hair regain its colour? He'd noticed in others that the sun had bleached the blackest hair grey. Would his mother recognise him? Would he find a sweetheart looking this way? What did any of it matter if he couldn't last until a ship?

'I bet most lads slept better with the calm,' said Ken.

'Doubt it,' said Colin. 'Not with all the noise.'

Most of the crew had called out in the night, more than usual, their discordant lyrics at odds with the sea's soft symphony.

'Never heard it,' said Ken.

'Lucky you. I thought Bott was gonna kill someone. Officer Scown tried to go over but he's so weak now that Weekes only had to put a hand out to stop him.' Colin paused. 'I didn't know whether to...'

'What, lad?'

'You know ... just let him go.'

'Soon there'll be no one with the strength to stop him.'

Ken tried to stand and when his legs gave out he refused to look at Colin, perhaps embarrassed at his increasing weakness. He half crawled, half staggered to the rations, announcing that breakfast was up.

Few bucked up at this declaration now. Tongues stuck like gangrene to teeth and to the roofs of mouths. The men were so parched that the ounce of water issued barely went past their throats, leaving bodies desperately dehydrated, heads fried, and blood syrupy. Colin hated how thick and foul-tasting his saliva was. How tight his face felt as his skin shrivelled.

He knew those unable to drink – like Scown and the Second, who refused – would have ceased generating saliva at all, the tongue hardening until it swung on the still-soft root like a tiny wrecking ball.

That morning they let John Arnold say a prayer. Then Bott, Leak, Stewart and King began their daily drinking of seawater, a habit Ken had given up railing against. It was hard enough finding the strength to issue rations, choosing men still well enough for lookout, and making sure no one jumped overboard.

Three days earlier Ken had screamed at them. 'You lot drinking seawater – knock it off! It'll do you no good. Christ, as if it's not enough living without much water, I have to watch you lot! We've got to look out for each other. Keep strong! *You* lose it and we *all* bloody lose it. Damn you all to hell!'

It had made no difference and now Ken ignored them.

Colin approached Officer Scown. The man lay in the well, his head propped up with a life jacket. He wore a hat Weekes had made from a trouser leg. His breathing was so shallow that at first Colin paused, afraid to approach, until Scown muttered some desperate plea into his chest.

'Should we give him water?' Colin asked Ken. 'He refused breakfast. We ought to make him take some.'

Colin held Scown's head with two hands while Ken

measured two ounces into the cup and put it to the officer's lips. Colin imagined the water reviving, sparking like electricity, regenerating. But most trickled down his chin.

'For God's sake, *drink*,' Colin urged.

'Some must've gone down,' said Ken. 'Nowt more we can do. Most can't swallow anymore. What's the point in issuing meals? And them buggers drinking seawater – to hell with them. Let 'em drown in it.'

Desperate to keep Ken's mood up Colin said, 'Come on, Chippy, you don't mean it. The only thing that keeps us going is a meal. We live the day by it. Even if there were nowt left to eat we'd make the pretence of preparing it just to ... just to go on.'

'But would we?'

Ken returned to his place at the stern, spear in hand. He hadn't caught a single thing. Colin had consoled him by saying that he'd not won his game either, the one where counting a certain number of fish or clouds or stars resulted in a ship. Ken had insisted he'd succeed first.

Mid-afternoon Officer Scown sat up, appeared lucid. He smiled at those around him and began idle conversation. Perhaps he had taken in some of the water earlier or maybe covering his head had reduced the effects of the sun. Ken glanced at the crew and was answered by a row of nodding heads. So he measured another two ounces and helped the officer drink it.

'You're a good crew,' Scown said. 'As good a crowd as I've ever sailed with. No, *better* I tell you. I thank God for it. One bad character could easily have been the death of us all.'

'You're a good man too,' said Platten. The small, strong

father of twin girls had skin so dry now that his eyes appeared like two raisins in dark dough. 'You've been a splendid officer, sir.'

He had. Sober habits and strict discipline meant Scown had been highly regarded and respected by all aboard the SS *Lulworth Hill*. His orders always came sharp, and he never watched them executed, showing confidence in the crew.

During his time on the lifeboat, he often spoke proudly of his daughter Wendy back home. However, he rarely mentioned the bike he'd bought for her in Africa, intended to be a seventh birthday gift. It had gone down with the ship. Nor did he speak of the tiny knitting needles and wool she had gifted him before he set sail – to keep him busy, she had said. The loss of these items upset Scown greatly.

That the men were upset about items lost didn't mean that they didn't care for men lost, rather it was perhaps easier to think only of bikes and knitting needles forever on the ocean floor.

Scown raised the empty cup. 'I thank you all for keeping a good ship.'

'To you, sir,' said Young Fowler, weakly.

'To you,' chorused the crew.

'To my daughter,' Scown said softly. 'My wife.'

Colin joined in but felt he watched from a distance. All day he'd felt like he wasn't part of the crew. Like he was hearing them through cotton wool. Through gauzy fabric. At times his heart pounded so fast that his head spun. When he raised his arm with an imaginary cup to salute Scown, and his weatherworn sleeve slipped down, he was shocked at the visible bones and absent veins.

This isn't my body, he thought. *I don't want to live in it.*

'Maybe now he'll sleep peacefully,' said Ken, making Colin jump.

Scown lowered himself onto his back and a smile fluttered about his lips, a butterfly that danced only a moment and flew off. Stewart sat next to him. Colin hadn't the energy to leave his spot on the bench and he watched Stewart take Scown's hand and lean close as though to listen to his heart.

'I see Mum,' whispered Scown. 'There's Mum.'

Suddenly the young cabin boy screamed and began beating Scown about the head with his fists. Platten pulled him free and slapped him, breaking his hysteria. Tears replaced the violence.

'He's dead,' sobbed Stewart. 'Mr Scown's dead, I tell you.'

Ken approached the officer and knelt before him. Colin followed. Scown's mouth hung open, showing the remnants of six or so malted milk tablets. He'd not had the saliva to dissolve them. Ken tried to shut his lips, afford him some dignity. Platten lifted Scown's lids to reveal eyes devoid of life. John Arnold gently unbuttoned the officer's shirt as though opening an unwanted gift and put an ear to his sunken chest. One glance at the men spoke a hundred words.

He began to pray.

'Not Scown,' sobbed Stewart.

No one moved or uttered a sound for an hour. A heavy blanket of shock settled on the crew, suffocating all words, muffling all movement. It seemed impossible that one of them had gone. Even though Scown had been ill, some still in their delirium thought he might be sleeping and wake for rations at tea.

Colin was haunted by Scown's final words: *I see Mum, there's Mum.* He knew the other lads – what was left of them, what was still human – longed for their mothers. Most cried out 'Mum!' as they slept. Colin wondered if he did.

Sometimes he walked around his mother's back room in his dreams, as though he was actually there. Maybe he was. But if so, why wasn't *she* there? If he *had* called out for her, why hadn't she responded? A mother was the first person to hold you at birth – it made sense that she might come at the end. Who would hold Colin if he passed here?

He wouldn't pass here – that was all there was to it.

When it came to evening rations, Platten nudged Ken and pointed to Scown and then looked out to sea. Colin thought about Scarface. An hour earlier he'd followed the boat like he was tethered to it. Did he know? Had he smelt death?

'We can't,' said Ken, softly.

'We've got to put him to sea.' Platten gripped Ken's arm. "We can't keep him on here, Cooke. You know it.'

Ken looked pained. "We can't let him go, not yet. It wouldn't be decent. I'll not give the order.'

Colin understood – it was too final.

Platten spoke more harshly. 'It might not be decent if we don't. He's flesh and blood, and there are thirteen starving men on board.' He paused. 'You *must* give the order.'

Ken looked around at the crew. 'Right, lads,' he said softly. 'Let's, with dignity, move our officer.' He looked at Colin and Platten. They needed no instruction. The three men tried to lift Officer Scown. Wasted as he was, it proved impossible. They simply hadn't the strength.

'The canvas,' said Ken.

Gently, they rolled Scown into a section of it and positioned him on the gunnel while Arnold said a few words in prayer.

'We commit his body to the deep, looking for the resurrection of the body and the life of the world to come, through our Lord Jesus Christ, who at his coming shall change our body that it may be like his glorious body. In accordance with the mighty working. Amen.'

As the young boy finished his words, Platten and Colin freed Scown; Ken held fast, unable to let the officer go. Scown's shirt ripped and Ken was left with it in his hand as the body slipped into the water so quietly it was like he'd never been there at all. Colin put a hand on Ken's shoulder. Ken showed him the cloth with a brass button still attached and put it in his pocket and patted it.

'Won't be the same without him,' he said.

In the dying light afterwards rations were issued with even less enthusiasm than usual. Colin could barely swallow his Bovril tablet, even though his belly cried out for food. He hadn't looked at the sea since they'd cast Scown into it; he knew Scarface would be there with his friends but couldn't think about what they might be doing with the officer's body deep below the surface.

Ken took the brass button from his pocket and turned it over in his palm, like it might cast a spell. In the fading day it was all that shone. 'They died that you might live,' he said.

'What's that, chum?' asked Colin.

'I don't quite know.' Ken looked baffled. 'I thought I heard Scown say it. Just now. I really did. I can't get it out of my head. Did you hear it?'

'No.' Though he hadn't, Colin didn't dismiss Ken's words. He knew how real such voices and sights could be. The girl with sunlit straw hair had appeared to him as true as any of the crew.

'What does it mean?' wondered Ken.

'What does any of it mean?'

Without warning, Ken sat up. Seemingly strengthened, he got his spear, ordered Platten to fetch some line, and tied the brass button tightly to the end.

'Right,' he said to Colin. 'You drag this through the water, keeping it within my reach. Understand? The sharks will be attracted to the gold colour – you'll see. We shall have one. Oh, I'll catch us one.'

Caught up in Ken's infectious enthusiasm, Colin took the line and leaned over the boat edge to dangle it in the water. Those strong enough joined them, urging Ken to be ready with his spear. Before long a young shark emerged from the depths. The flashing yellow must have been like a mermaid song beckoning him.

Bott gripped the boat edge, muttering, 'Come on, come on, come on.'

With a swift movement Ken stabbed the creature, piercing its side, disabling it. How fiercely it wriggled and squirmed to escape, all snapping teeth and thrashing tail. But these were desperate men, driven by hunger, and Ken, Bott and Platten held fast and heaved the shark aboard.

What a fine supper he made. Being big, he was enough to serve each of the now thirteen men a steak-sized piece, and perfectly moist. Blood was drained into a tin and shared around as a drink and as lip balm. The meal did much to lift them, even with Scown gone. The stronger ones made sure the Second got plenty of sustenance, though he barely seemed to recognise his mates now. Perhaps Scown's refusal to take water near the end compelled them to make sure others in a bad state did. Whatever the reason, Leak and Bamford sat with the Second until they felt sure he'd consumed enough blood.

'I'll take the first watch,' said Ken. 'Who's with me?'

Despite the nutritious meal, Colin still felt weak. Like his body existed but his head was elsewhere – or perhaps the other way around. None of it felt right. He didn't think he could stare at the horizon in search of a ship that didn't materialise without joining Scown.

'I'll watch for an hour,' said Weekes. 'If you've got a ciggie we can share.' Jokes had been rare recently, but he got a few smiles.

'I win,' Ken said to Colin, in joy rather than with one-upmanship.

'You do?' Colin's lips glistened bloody red like he'd taken wine as communion.

'The catch,' said Ken. 'Thanks to Officer Scown.'

'To Officer Scown,' a few of the men chorused again.

'Told you I'd succeed first.' Ken paused, maybe realising that if Colin won they all would. 'Now it's your turn. I've done what I set out to do.'

Colin turned away, the weight of the game he'd created dragging him from the others. Fight gone, he found a solitary spot under the canvas and surrendered to sleep. There he dreamt of the girl with hair and eyes that gleamed as brightly as the sea. It was a vision so powerful it followed him into dawn and consciousness.

This time she came to the boat.

She smelt clean amidst the rotten stench of gangrene and decaying wood; she glowed like an angel. She leaned down by his ear and said, 'No, don't wake up. Stay asleep. Dream about nice things and you won't be sad. But it's okay to be sad cos that's part of being brave – I just can't remember the other part right now.'

Colin didn't want to wake unless it meant he was home or in the silver kitchen or in the place with all the books.

When he opened his eyes on another day in hell, the girl had gone. But her words lingered, ebbing and flowing with the sea.

It's okay to be sad cos that's part of being brave – I just can't remember the other part right now.

Ken recorded his own words on a torn sail that formed another page in the on-going log.

SS Lulworth Hill – *Deaths – Scown. Mate. 4.30pm. 6th April.*

20

HOW TO BE BRAVE

Expect rescue anytime now.

K.C.

Midnight on Christmas Eve and wine had made me melancholy; the sweet tang that initially brought song and smiles and silliness had died, leaving me tearful. Sparkling wine is like insulin; if consumed in small doses it lifts, but too much leaves a person low afterwards. My bubbles had burst.

I put my half-empty glass on the table near the remains of the buffet I'd excitedly prepared earlier for the friends I'd invited over. My thoughts turned to Jake. I missed him. What he'd said the last time we spoke – about Rose and I being cooped up alone and getting morbid over Colin's story – was haunting me.

Now that school was finished for Christmas I also grew concerned that Rose might feel isolated, home with me all the time. So I'd let her invite Hannah and Jade for a sleepover last night. Maybe my mum's concerns and April's words had influenced me too, and I decided Rose should be a child, that foolery and fun should flood the house again.

She'd loved sleeping on the blow-up bed with her friends, watching *Doctor Who*, telling ghost stories, being allowed to stay up until midnight and have sugary popcorn for once.

'We won't tell Shelley,' I said, away from Hannah and Jade, 'and if your blood's a little high in the morning, it's just one time.'

In the middle of the night I'd looked in on them all, breathing in comradely unison, three fluffy heads sticking out of the green camping duvet like flowers in a spring bed.

Since the hypo at the shops I'd been watching Rose constantly, analysing every colour change, every mood swing, every word use. I'd told Shelley about it and she said I'd always remember the first one. They would catch me out again but I'd never again feel quite so helpless. A bit like when your heart breaks the first time; that's it, it's broken.

I was exhausted from watching her all the time, but witnessing Rose's joy at a simple sleepover had lifted me and I'd decided to have my own little party.

Rose and I left out cake for Santa. Then Vonny, her friend Jane, and my boss Sarah came for festive drinks. We cracked open bottles of Prosecco and played music and ate April's cake and talked about men, holidays, childhood and life. For a while I forgot blood tests and lifeboats and needles and hunger; I felt thirty-five again instead of three hundred.

But now, hours later, I sat in the grim afterglow of buzzing Christmas lights, sausage roll crumbs and empty bottles, and thought about Jake.

I remembered our early, childfree days, times when we only had to think of ourselves. I worried that he would come home to a woman he didn't recognise. To someone who only slept for an hour at night before waking to go and check Rose, then do her midnight blood test. Someone who paced the house, worrying about hypos, jumping at every phone call, old while she was still young.

'Mum?' Rose stood in the doorway, hair tousled and eyes red like she'd rubbed them. She came into the living room, squinting at the light.

'What are you doing up?' I went and touched her forehead but she swiped my hand away. 'Are you okay? Do you feel low?'

'Just can't sleep.'

Rose fingered leftover sausage rolls and cheese bites, perhaps imagining how it could feed the lifeboat crew for a whole day. I hated food waste now. I'd recently become obsessed with portion size, not only to keep Rose's blood sugars stable but because I'd imagine how long each uneaten morsel might sustain Colin. I couldn't discard pieces of chicken or potato without guilt.

And I'd never spill a drop of water. I followed Rose around the house with her cups of it, checking the bath didn't overfill, using half the amount I usually did for washing pots.

'Did our noise keep you up?' I asked. 'Sorry we got a bit loud. They've gone now. I'm about to go to bed.'

'It wasn't you,' said Rose. 'Though you were very silly singing Lady Gaga like that. You shouldn't sing, Natalie. *Ever*.' She paused. 'I can't sleep cos I keep thinking about Colin – about all of them. I can hear them crying out on the boat when I close my eyes. I can hear Fowler.'

On the twenty-second day, which we'd shared on Monday, Young Fowler had woken unable to move. He sat with his back against the mast, incapable of eating breakfast but eager for his water ration when it came. I'd wanted to gloss over his end, make pretty the pain, and did so by telling Rose that when he passed away in the afternoon the men were surprised. But Rose had interrupted my flow and insisted I tell her how it had really happened.

Being pulled out of the story made me more factual and I listed the events preceding his death, how he had spoken only when approached by Colin, who asked if Fowler needed anything.

What could he have done if the boy had asked for water? Food? His mother? Instead Fowler said, 'Just sleep. Let me sleep. I'm so very tired. No pain now – just need sleep.' Afraid of what the boy really yearned, Colin encouraged him to share lookout duty in the late afternoon and they sat back to back against the mast, too weak now to be without its support.

Colin fell asleep, even in this awkward position, and when he woke the crew were standing around Fowler. He had passed; his eyes were open, watching for a ship that never came. Colin could not accept his death and gripped the boy's limp arm until Ken prised him away. He'd been such a cheerful creature, hardly grumbling. And Colin had punched him.

Now he'd never make it up to him.

The wasted body was cast into the sea with a prayer. I didn't tell Rose how the men likely covered their ears to the swirl of waters as sharks tore him apart; I told her he sunk to the bottom, like the ship, like Scown, where there was only peace.

Now Rose said, 'They're all starting to die, aren't they?' She squashed a handful of the cake Vonny had left on her plate. 'If only we could go to the boat with all this food. Don't seem fair that we have all this and you don't even want it. And I can't have it, can I?'

'*Doesn't*,' I corrected. 'I'll cover it up and we can have some tomorrow.' I paused. 'Maybe we should take a break from the story if it's keeping you awake.'

'No! You can't stop now.' She wiped the crumbs from her hands in a violent motion and held my waist, eyes pleading. 'It's like totally inside me. You'll ruin everything if you stop! Why do you keep saying it?'

'I don't mean we should stop altogether.' I put my hands over hers and she let go. 'I just mean we could take a break and carry on again after Christmas.'

'What's Christmas got to do with it?'

'We're supposed to be happy, aren't we?'

'I won't be if you stop.' Rose sat on a cushion in the book nook. 'Anyway we have to finish before Dad gets back.'

'Do we?' I joined her, in the flickering lights.

'You don't get it,' she said, miserably. 'When he's back you won't be bothered about it. You'll have him again. You won't need me or Colin.'

Did Rose really think I'd abandon her when he returned?

'I'd never do that,' I said. 'If we're not done by then, we can come to the book nook like this and I'll tell Dad he has to keep out, it's our time.'

Rose shook her head. 'If you stop now, you've broken your promise. You said if I gave you my blood you'd give me a better story than *Harry Potter* or *War Horse*. I've done my bit.

Have you forgot? Just because I get a bit sad about Fowler dying doesn't mean we stop. Why do people think you have to avoid that stuff? You have to know how to be sad to know how to be happy and if you know both of those things you'll know how to be brave.'

I had no words. My beautiful, wilful daughter had said them all.

'Also,' she added, 'I want to be able to do my own injections and stuff when Dad gets back and I can only do that with the story.'

Since her first clumsy attempt at finger pricking last week, she'd been preparing it but letting me draw blood. The same with her injection; she'd screw on the lancet and measure the dose while I'd push the needle into her flesh.

'There's no pressure,' I said. 'You don't need to do any more than you are. Dad will be overjoyed at how you're coping with it all. He won't expect you to be able to do it yourself.' I paused. 'He'll be as proud as I am.'

Rose looked at the clock and her eyes grew like saucers. 'It's Christmas Day,' she said, suddenly a child again. 'Can I open some presents?'

'Santa hasn't been yet,' I said, thinking of the bag of gifts I'd yet to carry down and put under the tree.

'Why don't you just get my pressies from the airing cupboard and let me have one?'

'Rose!' I laughed, unable not to. 'Not until morning. Come on, we should go to bed or we'll both be shattered.'

She got Colin's diary from the bookshelf. 'Can't we just do one page? It's Christmas Day. If you won't let me have a pressie, read me a bit.'

I sighed. 'Okay, a tiny bit. But that's all. It's bedtime and Santa won't come if you're awake.'

'If you say so.'

I sat next to Rose and without words we agreed that she let a page fall open. Again, I found it startling that we opened it in a spot I'd not shared with Rose, on a page that spoke so perfectly to us in that moment. I might have questioned the miracle of this in more everyday circumstances, but something happened when we held this diary, and I doubted I could ever fully explain it. I'd been reading it myself, privately, along with letters, newspaper pages, and the photocopies of Ken's sail scrap log. But the diary was magic when I shared it with Rose.

My first Christmas being home and Mum went to extra trouble. She had been saving housekeeping money for months to give us a veritable feast of choices. We got a good fire going and it crackled and spat while we ate. All I could smell though was the sweet, tart satsumas in the bowl on the cabinet. Oh, how we'd have devoured those at sea. We left a chair empty for our Stan, as we have done the last two years. None of us said anything about it – just like last year – and no one sat in the seat either. I couldn't stop thinking that there might have been two empty chairs for my mother to fill with her memories. But I'd made it. I've always found Christmas to be rather melancholy but that one I quite found the jolliest. Curious, really. I expected the cheer to grate on me. But the tot of sherry and seeing my brothers together – even Stan really, in spirit – had me quite grateful for my lot.

'Poor Stan,' said Rose. 'Lots of people died in that war didn't they?'

I yawned, stroked her hair. 'Come on – it's bedtime.'

'Would you keep my chair out if I died?'

'Don't say that.' I shook my head at the thought.

'But would you?' she demanded.

'Bedtime!'

I made sure Rose was tucked in and stood on the landing for ten minutes until I was sure she'd fallen asleep. Then I took her bag of gifts down and put them under the tree. When I got into bed I expected to lie awake for a long time but exhaustion had her way.

The next I knew was my phone ringing on the bedside table. It was so early that the heating hadn't even kicked in and daylight would be an hour yet. A first Christmas morning with Rose still asleep; a first Christmas morning with Jake not there; a first Christmas morning with injections to be done.

I picked up the phone, croaked, 'Hello' into it.

'Happy Christmas, Natalie.' It was Jake.

I smiled. 'Happy Christmas.' Now it felt special. 'What a lovely surprise.'

'They've let us all make quick calls home.' He sounded distant, strained. 'Sorry to wake you early but I knew Rose would be up. Is she there? I bet she's opened half her presents already. Did she like the sewing machine?'

'She's not awake,' I said. 'She was up late and had a sleepover the other night so I bet she's tired.'

'Is she okay though?'

'Yes, she's fine.'

'Injections okay?'

'They don't bother her so much now.' I thought about telling him of Rose's pledge to be able to self-administer for his return, but didn't. 'So it's just us for once. How are you?' I hadn't stopped thinking about the young soldier who'd died with Jake at his side, not unlike Young Fowler passing on a final lookout with Colin. 'You don't have to edit anything,' I said softly. 'Tell me how you *really* are.'

'I'm sad not to be there today,' he admitted.

'Me too.'

'But we'll have a hundred more Christmases,' he said.

'A *hundred?*' I smiled. 'How long do you plan on living?'

'Forever,' he said.

'You'd better,' I told him, never forgetting the dangerous place he was in.

'Natalie, I've some news you won't like.'

I closed my eyes as though this would shut out sounds too.

'I hate to tell you – it's about my R and R. I don't think I'll be home in January.'

I sat up in bed. 'What?'

'I *might* make it, I just can't say for sure. It just might not be January now. You know I can't talk in detail about these things but some of our helicopters are being tasked elsewhere and...'

'I don't *want* the details,' I said, deflated.

'You know there's nothing I can do.'

'I know.' I tried not to be sulky or difficult. It was so much harder for him. At least I was home with our daughter at Christmas. 'It isn't your fault. When will you know for sure?'

His silence answered me. 'I have to go,' he said. 'Please kiss Rose for me. And remember, I *will* be home, soon.'

When he hung up I sat for a long time, trying not to cry. I hadn't in a long time; I bottled up tears whenever Rose was around, not believing a child should be saddled with adult trouble. So much that I wondered if I'd forgotten how.

Now I remembered.

I buried my face in Jake's pillow, his smell both comfort and hurt, and cried as I had that morning after the hospital. Though I'd washed the bedding since he'd been gone, I'd left his pillowcase alone, and his memory lingered there, only just. I barely noticed that Rose had come in until the bed gave under her slight frame and she was patting my head, awkward but well meaning. I had to stop and get a grip, or I'd alarm her. But I was a broken tap, gushing salty water.

'It's Christmas,' said Rose.

I couldn't say that her dad wouldn't be home yet. I couldn't say that I didn't even know when it might be or that sometimes I was terrified he'd be killed and never get home at all. I couldn't say that I wasn't sure I could get up and do the things I must. I couldn't speak.

'Is it cos I called you a coward?' she asked. 'That day I was grumpy. I didn't mean it, you know.'

The bed moved again and her feet pitter-pattered to the landing and back. I tried to breathe. To get up. To be a mother. The bed gave again at Rose's return and I heard lancets rolling around in the diabetes box, like stones on a beach.

'Let me make you better,' she said, putting her finger pricker together.

'No,' I said.

I was the storyteller; I was the magician.

'Let me do the words,' she said, and pricked her finger end.

Blood flowed, thick and rich. She caught it in the strip.

'It's only fair I do some story,' she said. 'Listen to this. I went on the lifeboat again last night. I snuggled down between the sleepy men and stroked Grandad Colin's hair and whispered right in his ear how proud I am of him. Just the way you said it to me last night. I always know who he is, even in the dark. He just smells right. Even though he looks like a scarecrow now, all hairy and ragged, he still smells like us. I said I'd think of a story to stop his nightmares and make the wooden floor more softer. It's dead uncomfortable. Not even a sheet. I said I bet he misses spider webs in rain. And butterflies. And birds. He used to go bird spotting with his dad. On the ocean a bird means land and safety, you know.'

Rose patted my head, gentler now.

'I said, *If you don't live I'll disappear, Grandad. Can I call you Grandad? You're really my Great Grandad, but I like Grandad better. If you don't live, Grandad, I won't be able to come back and stroke your hair. I'll just dissolve like a salty ghost.* So then I got a bit of the canvas logbook and drew us all in there; you and me and Dad. I wrote above it that I was learning how to be brave, and he was making it a lot easier. I wonder if he'll find it? This morning when I woke I thought of him and Ken having their tiny bit of water and horrid dry biscuit and milk tablet with the others. I saw them looking out at sea for sharks and dolphins and birds and a ship.'

Rose showed me her blood meter; she was six-point-two.

My tears dried and I touched her face. 'Let's get breakfast,' I said.

'Can I have chocolate cos it's Christmas Day? I don't care about my blood sugars today. Go on, go on!' She was a child again and so I easily slipped back into my role as mum.

'We'll see,' I said.

'That means no. Oh, *please*! Can I open some pressies before I eat?'

'We'll see,' I said.

She danced around the bedroom. 'Two *we'll see's* means a yes! It's the law!' On our way downstairs she said, 'I'm going to do my blood test from now on. And I'm going to help you do the story too. We can take turns. Think how good it'll be if I do it?'

'No, you don't ha...'

'I want to – I can't wait!'

'But I'm supposed t...' I tried.

'You've got to learn to share,' she said.

So no more trading her blood for my words. No more blood friends forever. What kind of exchange was it going to be if Rose did so much of the work, bringing the blood *and* the words?

I'd kidded myself all along that the trade was to help her but I realised it had been for me too. So I could keep her for myself. But she didn't belong to me; she belonged to the sea and the sky and the past and her future.

And I had to let her go.

21

STITCHING TRUTH AND MEMORY

But we have greater hopes now.

K.C.

Before Rose learned to read – and long before we created the book nook – I used to read stories to her at bedtime like most parents do for their pre-schoolers. She once asked me, 'How do words in books know where to go and who to be friends with?' I can't remember how I answered, but her question comes to me every time I read my newest paperback. How carefully did the author think about which words they put together?

Rose and I ate our Christmas dinner at four so she could have her teatime injection just after. I carefully served us a medium portion, not wanting to waste the slightest bit. We hadn't been to the lifeboat yet; she'd been wrapped up in opening gifts and testing out her new sewing machine on scraps of material and watching festive cartoons and pulling all the crackers in the box, one after another. I was glad. She should be a child on Christmas Day and I didn't want to break the spell with talk of hunger and thirst and insulin.

Watching her fashion a small purse from an old pillowcase, I forgot how upset I'd been earlier. How unhappy I was that Jake would be away for longer. I just enjoyed Rose's creative activities. While she pinned bits of ribbon to silk and chose a brown button from the many coloured ones and slowly stitched, her cheeks coloured pink. Now that she'd regained most of her weight, she looked a picture of health. I think she actually forgot about diabetes for a magical moment.

But she hadn't forgotten about helping with the story.

I found a radio station playing old-fashioned hymns and began washing the pots while Rose finished her purse. The swish of soapy water and the sound of *Silent Night* had me for a moment at sea, so acutely that I smelt salt in the bubbles, heard soft groans, felt a hand grip my arm, and heard Colin asking how long now.

'Let's go to the book nook then.' It was Rose's hand on my arm. I looked at the clock – suppertime, already.

'Did you get the diabetes box?' I dried my hands.

'Of course. It's my turn to do it.' Rose bounced off.

I followed her and sat on the cushion opposite where she'd flopped. 'You mean your blood?' I asked.

'Yes – *and* the story.'

'How will you know what happens?'

'Same way you do, silly,' she said. 'I've seen the diary. Then some of it just comes, doesn't it? I just get inside Grandad Colin's head somehow. And you forget he tells me bits in my sleep.'

'And your injection?' I asked. 'You want to do one?' I knew I should be happy she'd come on so well, that she'd adapted to and accepted her condition, but I was terrified still to relinquish my care.

'I've let you do them today because I didn't want you to be sad,' she said, though I knew she'd been nervous, building up to it.

I had prepared and done the blood test and injection at breakfast, lunch and Christmas dinner, not mentioning that she'd said she wanted to and hoping that maybe she'd changed her mind. I saw her watching carefully, assessing how I twisted the dial and made sure there were no air bubbles.

'I'm doing this one,' she said now. 'No more being a baby.'

'You're not a baby.'

'Anyway we can do everything together, can't we? Two together is the best. Isn't there that saying – two heads are better than one? Like when you can't think of the right word for something and Dad says it. I can do that too, you know.' She paused, then said, 'Wish Dad had rung when I was awake.'

'It was only a quick call,' I told her. 'He said he was sorry he couldn't be here with you and hoped you liked the sewing machine.' I still couldn't tell her he might not be home as soon as she thought.

'I did.' She glanced over at it on the table, surrounded by gaudy offcuts, buttons and thread. I knew she had missed Jake today. Every now and again she had gone to stare at his photographs on the living room wall, whispering things to him that I'd never know.

'Did you still enjoy Christmas?' I asked, thinking how different it must have been to other years. She had diabetes now, her dad was away, and Santa no longer existed.

'It was special,' she said.

There was a knock on the door and I left Rose to go and open it. A gang of teenagers wearing scruffy Santa hats and brand new trainers shuffled close together in the glare of my hallway light and began singing *Silent Night*. I couldn't help but smile. Their voices did not harmonise but grated and contrasted like sand and stones. I counted the teens; twelve, like those remaining on the lifeboat. For their bravery, I handed over five pounds.

I returned to the book nook.

Rose was hunched over, saying, 'Bloody dickhead.'

'Language!' I said. Then, 'What are you doing?'

'Trying to do my blood.' She showed me her finger.

'You should've waited for me.' I sat next to her, realised she was close to tears. 'What is it?'

'It just won't come – my blood. I've dried up! Like the men on the boat!'

Laughing gently, I said, 'No, you haven't. Are your hands cold? Is that it? Let me warm them up.'

'No,' she snapped. 'They're warm. I totally did everything I should. I made the finger pricker and wriggled my fingers and pricked my skin three times. Where's my blood?'

'Let's wait and then *I'll* try.'

'I don't want you to help me!'

'Everyone's allowed help sometimes, even adults. Why don't we do some story and that'll maybe help?'

Was I doing everything Shelley had said we shouldn't and using the story as a crutch? What were we going to do if something didn't work next time and Rose got distressed again, but the story was over? Should I try something else? What else was there?

Rose pulled her hand away from me and sat on it, the way she had weeks earlier when refusing to do the test. 'Don't worry, I'm going to do it,' she said, reading my mind. 'I'm just making them warm.'

'I know you want to do the story but shall I start?' I asked her.

'Where are we up to?'

'Day twenty-four.'

'Do we have long to go?' Rose asked.

'How long is a piece of string?'

'Don't be annoying!'

'Okay,' I said. 'How do you think day twenty-four begins?'

'Like all the others,' she said. 'But worse.'

'I'll begin then – and you join in.'

And so we returned to the lifeboat, stitching truth and genetic memory and imaginings together like I had at the start. Except now Rose helped and our story was a collective work.

Between Christmas Day and New Year we visited the sea many times. We floated on book pages and syllables. Sometimes Rose brought her latest fabric creation to the book nook and she attached sequins and buttons to bits of velvet or cotton while we joined our words in a similar fashion. We too added our shiny vision to the story's fabric – Colin's diary.

The child who had once asked, 'How do words in books know where to go?' now found out.

22

GRANDAD

Still hoping.

K.C.

Grandad.

'What's that you say now?'

Had the question come from Ken or one of the other semi-comatose shapes? Was it morning yet or did Colin imagine strings of vermilion light spreading across the water like burnt fingers, stealing the dream he so wanted to hold on to.

Grandad.

Had he spoken the word?

'You keep saying it, chum.' It was Ken. He rolled over with an agonised moan and glared at Colin. Ken's ghostly face, with salted beard and bloodshot eyes, was a cruel mirror; Colin knew how bad he must look now. 'Your grandad's not bloody here,' said Ken. 'Just us twelve.'

'No, not *my* grandfather.' Colin couldn't sit up; the simple act took such effort now that most men waited a good while after waking. 'No, I think *I'm* one. That's what she said. "Grandad".'

'Jesus Christ, Armitage. Please tell me you've not been at the seawater an' all. Am I going to have to bloody lash you down too for going mad?'

Ken motioned towards King, who they had tied to the mast with rope yesterday after his thrashing around in the boat's well put everyone in danger. Hours of guzzling seawater had left the man insane, ranting about escaping the ship, the Germans, the sharks.

'No, I haven't. Not a drop. The girl in my dream called me Grandad. Remember, I told you about her? She actually said *Great* Grandad. But then Grandad.' Colin pulled himself slowly up, the scratchy cotton shirt torture on skin. He felt about for the canvas log and studied the words there. 'I'm not hallucinating. It was too real for that. She was *here*, I tell you.'

Was he saying this? Did he believe it? Every day their bodies worsened but Colin's mind tried to cling to hope, to routine, to dreams. This one, however, had been more. In it the girl had drawn some sort of picture in the log and written words alongside it. Was he willing them to be there? Instead there were only Ken's neatly and patiently written recordings of their ordeal.

'I don't know about owt no more,' said Ken. 'I only know I should order rations. I should try and stop the buggers that guzzle seawater. And I know we should still be watching for a ship.'

One-hour lookout duty had been abandoned yesterday. None of the crew disputed it, but Colin had asked Ken – as they retired with the sun – why he'd not announced who was on shift.

'They can't bloody do it, lad,' he said.

'But someone *has* to,' Colin insisted.

'How? Most of 'em can barely keep awake long enough now. Me, you, Platten and Weekes are about the only ones that can move, and we're exhausted. Can *you* do it tonight? I know I bloody can't.'

Ken was right; how could eyes as dry as desert sand keep open longer than half an hour when the sun never gave up her watch and the salty spray never died? How could minds beyond exhaustion concentrate on an endless, unchanging horizon that never gave a ship?

Colin had vowed at the start that he would watch, even when not on duty, afraid that if his eyes left the sea for a moment a ship would sail past, unseen. Now – while Ken and Platten issued the meagre morning water ration – he tried hard to keep an eye on the ocean, which only lulled with its motion, cruelly causing sleep when he so needed to be alert.

He whispered, *Maybe today a ship, maybe today a ship, maybe today a ship.*

He banged his head on the boat edge when his eyelids drooped, just to stay awake.

e⌒

'Instead they watched each other,' said Rose. 'Like how you watch me to check I'm okay all the time. Annoying. And like when we play *Who's Going To Laugh First* except it was *Who's Going To Sleep Forever First*. Scown and Fowler have gone, and they're all very sad. Colin wishes he could have patted Fowler's head and said sorry in proper words, but men didn't do that stuff then, did they? Death sits next to them all the time. He's like a real man, you know. And he's not always a dickhead. Dickhead isn't swearing, Mum! Anyway you said I couldn't read *The Book Thief* – but I did. I hid it under the wardrobe and got it out when you turned off the light and read it with my torch. Death's a real person in that too. On the boat he whispered good night without promising Colin would wake in the morning. He stood right behind John Arnold when he prayed. But by day twenty-four Arnold's lips were so cracked that Ken said he'd take over prayers for a bit. He had to make one up cos he wasn't dead religious or anything. He said, "Dear Lord, please guide to us a ship tomorrow. We need your help, Lord, if ever men were in need of it. Amen." It was nice. And all the men said Amen. Colin tried hard all day to search for a ship. He sat on the foredeck and sometimes Ken sat with him. They talked about what it might actually be like if a ship came. How soft the blankets would be and how nice the food and how good the beds and how warm the nights. But most of all how much water there'd be. How much water they would drink. It took lots and lots of being good not to just jump into the sea and drink it all up. I don't know how they didn't. I know all about thirst too and it's really horrible. I remember having butterflies in my tummy all the time and a fuzzy head and my throat being all tight. I think I'd have stolen water from anyone on that boat – even you, Mum. I'm sorry to say that but I would have. I would.'

ℯ

'When darkness fell at the end of day twenty-four, the twelve men could not have distinguished that day from those before it. The sun had crossed the sky; Scarface had made an appearance or two; water had been measured and devoured by all; food had been winced at and consumed by some; the boat had gently rocked; Ken had tried to catch a fish while Platten dangled Scown's brass button; a ship had not been sighted.

Colin prayed for change – any change would be something. Change broke routine, lifted hearts. Sameness destroyed them. It came just before midnight when a great splash woke him from a dreamless slumber. Ken's eyes shone yellow in the darkness. 'Did you hear it too?' he asked.

'What was it?' wondered Colin.

'Scarface?' Ken sat up, alert. 'Wake the lads. Get my spear! Man the boat!'

He woke one or two of the crew and they half-heartedly peered over the edge. When no sharks surfaced they cursed being woken and returned eagerly to their sleep spots.

'I definitely heard it,' hissed Ken, confused.

Colin crawled about the boat. In the moonlight he found the mast and only rope. No King.

'He's gone,' he cried. 'King! Must've managed somehow to get free of the lashing. That splash must've been him, Chippy.'

Ken slumped down with his spear. 'May God have mercy on him.'

'Amen,' whispered Colin.

'Jesus Christ.'

What else was to be said? Another man gone. Just eleven left. Would morning bring another absence? What could Colin do except lie down and wait for another day. Dreading a return to dreamless sleep he thought, *Can you hear me? Girl who called me Grandad, wherever you are. Because I'm not sure I'm gonna make it. Can you hear me? I'm sorry but I'm not sure I'm gonna make it.*

In the morning Death had not taken anyone else but there was little joy in this fact. When it came to early rations, Platten no longer had the strength to give them out alone and both Colin and Ken helped. John Arnold was so ill that he insisted someone else eat his portion. He said it was a waste when he would not be around for much longer.

'Don't bloody talk that way,' snapped Ken.

Colin knew he had the same fondness for the boy that he'd felt towards Fowler, that he was merely trying to break him out of his miserable mood.

'Ken,' croaked the lad. 'May I pray?'

Colin watched his chum swallow hard and bend down to Young Arnold. Whatever the prayer was, Colin didn't hear. It was their moment. Colin went to the foredeck and played his game of six fish for one ship. As always, he lost.

After a while Ken put a hand on his shoulder, said softly, 'He's gone.' His eyes were so full of grief that Colin had no clue what to say; so he said nothing.

'He passed in my arms,' said Ken. 'I was so useless. Just held him and let him go. He said, "I'm going to die." No fear in his voice. Then he said, "I've been talking to God. Some of you are going to be saved, and I think you'll be among them." And he gave me a message for his mum and dad that I must deliver.' Ken put his face in his hands. 'So many messages to be given. Such responsibility. You have to hear it, lad, in case I don't make it.'

'You *will* make it,' said Colin.

'I still have to give you Scown's message for his wife. What if I take these messages to my grave? You owe it to our men to hear me.'

Colin's fist found Ken's jaw before he even realised he'd moved. Stunned, Ken backed away. 'Don't you fucking realise?' cried Colin. 'If I let you tell me then you'll have less reason to go on! If you're the only one who knows them, you *have* to survive! Don't you see? I don't want you to die, you bastard.' Colin slumped exhausted to the floor. 'I don't want to do this without you. I can't do it without you! And I have to do it. I have to get back. My mother ... Stan ... I *have* to.'

Ken nodded; he understood. He sat with his spear a while and let Colin doze under the canvas. Now there were ten men, only four had to endure the noon sun while six sheltered beneath the awning's protection. The Second – with his gangrenous injuries – held a permanent position there, propped up by someone's life jacket and fed water by whomever was nearest at mealtime.

Leak, Bott and Bamford crawled out intermittently to cup seawater with their hands and drink heartily. No one cared about it now; whatever damage was done by days of doing so was likely irreversible.

In the evening a great blue fish fell prey to Ken's spear, as though it were a parting gift from Young Arnold. The generous portion lifted spirits and those who were still able to talk did so, softly, of what those back home were doing, of the men now gone, of days on the SS *Lulworth Hill*, which seemed a hundred years ago.

'I'm going to start the watch again,' said Ken. 'I never

should have let it stop. If any man feels able, then shout up. If not, I'll go first.'

'You need a hand?' asked Colin, much revived by his fish morsel.

'Always,' said Ken.

And the two friends took the first lookout.

 ✎

'Death is black and mean, isn't he?' said Rose. 'But when he comes for people who're poorly then he's nice, right? He should wear yellow then. Like when he came for the Second on day twenty-six. He was kind then because that poor man hurt lots but never whined. I think Colin was relieved. One good thing about there being less of them was they got more to eat. I bet they felt mean about being glad of eating more in case it meant they were glad their friends had gone. But they weren't. They missed their friends. I miss Dad. But it's a different missing, isn't it? Because I'll see him again. They must've been scared of ending up all on their own. Imagine being the last one to die, Mum. How horrible would that be? No, I don't want to stop! Why do you always say that? I watched this film once with Dad about some men lost at sea and it was all really happy and lots of singing and laughing, and I got dead cross and told Dad it was all wrong. Because after days and days you'd get sad. You'd fight and argue with each other. Like us. I hate books and films that lie like that. I *know* Grandad Colin suffered. It makes me very sad. But I don't want anyone to lie to me, because that makes me even more sadder.'

e⁓

I remember when Bamford passed away, God rest his soul. I remember it only because it was so forgettable. I do not say that with rude disregard or disrespect for the man – Bamford was an amiable young chap. I say it because by then we were immune to death. He was the sixth to die and we had quite literally run out of care. The shock when Scown died, and then Young Fowler, and Arnold, meant we had so little feeling left as time went on. It was the twenty-ninth day when Bamford passed and we hardly prayed when we put his body to sea. Now I am shocked by it. I think of him on the SS Lulworth Hill, once when we sat on a tea break and he told me about a girl he liked in his village and how he was too shy to tell her he liked her. I was coarse with him and told him to seize life by the shoulders. So I had a drink for him one night in our local when I'd been home a while. One beer. For Bamford. To say, we did care. We were just young and tired and thirsty and hungry, and we wanted to go home.

e⁓

Colin woke hopeful on day thirty – it was the day Officer Scown had predicted they might reach land. As though in the same mood, the ocean appeared remarkably calm. Her waves lapped affectionately at the boat. Perhaps foolishly, Colin dipped a hand in the water and let it caress him, before Platten woke and told him to get his bloody fingers away from the sharks.

'Maybe today land,' Colin said to Ken, as they poured a few more ounces of water. Every time the cup came around the men tried to savour it, to slowly sip and relish each precious drop. But it proved impossible and they glugged it in two or three too-brief mouthfuls.

'Land?' asked Ken. 'What about your ship?'

'It's day thirty.'

'So?'

'Day *thirty*.' Colin repeated it, knowing Ken would realise.

He did but his reaction was one of indifference. 'Just another day,' he said. 'No more chance today of a ship or land than there was yesterday or the day before or will be tomorrow or the next day.'

The previous night Ken had caught a large ray, a beautiful creature that fought hard to escape the spear. They shared and devoured him desperately, licking and sucking every bit of flesh. Afterwards – revived as though they'd had a few brandies – Ken had been optimistic, saying that if they caught more fish they could well last until they reached land or sighted a ship, whichever came first. Colin, in a slump then, had wanted to say that when the water ran out it wouldn't matter how many fish they caught. But he'd stopped himself.

Now Colin felt hopeful and Ken dismissed him. So went their relationship aboard the lifeboat; when one man gave up, the other pushed ahead.

Day thirty wore on with mind-numbing tedium. Colin was determined he'd be the first to see that hazy hint of land. He lay on the foredeck, drifting in and out of sleep, where brutal dreams offered a ship that was only clouds, and consciousness gave the girl with Titian hair, who urged him on and called him Grandad.

When the sun had reached her cruel heights and all were

sprawled in the bottom of the boat, Bott suddenly leapt to his feet, shrieking maniacally. For a brief, wonderful moment Colin thought he had sighted land.

But with superhuman strength Bott grabbed the two nearest men – Weekes and Leak – and jumped overboard. The whole thing happened so fast and yet unfolded sluggishly before Colin's fatigued eyes. He saw it like slowed-down film footage; like the time he'd gone to the picture house with his brother Eric and the film broke.

'Grab them!' yelled Ken, rushing to the boat edge.

Colin and Platten joined him, calling at those who had barely moved, 'Men overboard! Men overboard!'

Sharks had already closed in. By some fluke Leak floated near the boat and was hauled back in. He was so stunned that Colin felt he wasn't even sure what had happened.

Platten stood, put a foot on the edge, ready to go. Colin did too.

'It's suicide.' Ken stopped them. 'They're too far to reach. There's nothing you can do now!'

'But we have to ...' Platten appeared not to know what they had to do.

A shark flashed through the water like the sub that had taken the *Lulworth Hill* down and attacked Weekes. His scream ripped through them all. Bott was flailing about madly and had managed to keep them off, but now the grey shapes closed in. Ken turned away and covered his ears, his face a picture of misery and guilt. Platten and Colin did too, the three of them like the *See No Evil, Hear No Evil* monkeys. But nothing blocked out those final screams or the wild whirling water.

Afterwards they offered Leak a drink, but he pushed them off, swore and curled up to sleep.

'We should've...' Colin wasn't sure what he meant to say.

'Should've what?' cried Ken. 'Bloody jumped too? We did what we had to do! If we'd saved them, how could we have closed any wounds? They'd have bled to death in minutes, lad. We had to let them die or die ourselves, so we did what we did and only God knows if it was the right thing.'

'Weekes was trying so hard,' said Colin, angry. 'He just said to me last night that he really thought he might get home. Bott had no right to take him like that. Jump if you must but don't take others with you. The bastard.' He paused. 'What can we tell their families?'

'We lie,' said Ken. 'Say they died peacefully, a mate at their side.'

Colin nodded. 'What good would the truth do?'

Platten said, 'If I don't make it I want you to tell my twin girls that ...' He stopped, hand gripping his lapel. 'However I go I want you not to dwell on that, but to tell them they were in my thoughts at all times. And tell my wife – tell her she made me very happy.'

There were only six of them now. Leak and Davies were semi-conscious but Stewart joined in the conversation. 'Tell my mum,' the young lad said, with effort. 'Tell her I did my best.'

Ken looked at Colin. 'Well?'

'Well, what?'

'What should we tell your family if ... you know?'

'I'll tell them myself,' he snapped, and went to the foredeck to look for land.

By dark he gave up. No land or ship appeared on the thirtieth day. He cursed Scown for giving them false hope, cursed Bott for taking the cheerful Weekes overboard, and cursed himself for letting any of it happen.

In the morning Leak died, his tongue by then so black and swollen that he choked to death. It was another name added to the many now in the death log, leaving just five men, all wondering who might be next.'

e~

'I just can't imagine watching all your friends die like that,' said Rose. 'Fourteen is half my class so like if I was on a boat with the girls from 5F I'd have to watch them die one after another. But I'd be first wouldn't I? Cos I'd have no insulin. No, I want to say it! That's how it would happen. Might be good to go first. Not watch all your friends die. By day thirty-three Grandad Colin had lost eleven friends. I know he liked some better than others. I definitely do. Like at school Rebecca Hartley is totally annoying but I'd be sad if she died. Anyway, by the end of day thirty-three there was just Colin, Ken and Platten. A whole month – that's such a long time to live on a small boat and look at the same stuff every day. I've had diabetes two months now and that seems like millions of years already. I reckon when you do the same thing over and over it makes time drag. Don't you? And they don't even know how long they've got to go, do they?'

e~

I received today a letter from the Ministry of Information, which I have filed with all other correspondences relating to the sinking of the SS Lulworth Hill. It read, in part, as follows – 'I would like to stress the importance of your giving your account entirely in your own way, and would ask you, therefore, to regard these (enclosed) notes as nothing more than sketchy suggestions. There will be many points, which will benefit by being illustrated by your own reminiscences. I hope to have the opportunity of arranging for you to visit one or more of our factories in the near future, and will communicate with you on this point a little later.' I think in relaying the facts of what happened, as I have had to do on numerous occasions and to a variety of organisations, the true story gets lost. But I am happier with the facts. I dwell too much on the reasons and they drive me half mad. I think it would make a good story. I think maybe somebody one day might tell it far better than I ever could. They might find more poetry and meaning and artistry in it than I.

૯

'On day thirty-four the heat reached its most intolerable intensity yet. It was the end of April now and the sun's rays scorched everything below. The only solace was that the awning provided ample shelter for the tiny party.

Beneath it, the three remaining men formed a triangle as though trying to fill the boat in the absence of the others. Platten was the weakest now and slumped against a mast with his chin on his chest. Colin wanted desperately to go and watch for a ship but the heat that day rendered them all immobile.

Ken called a conference, which merely meant he announced – without moving – that they should talk about rations now they were just three.

'What does each man think of an ounce of extra water?' he asked, his words a dry rasp.

Platten looked up. 'Is there enough left?'

'Now we're three I think we've got another week's worth. Food too, though biscuits are low.'

'Shouldn't we try and make rations last ten more days?' asked Platten.

'What does it matter?' said Colin. 'What's the use of trying to make the rations last longer than we can? Food's no good to a dead man. Nor is water. If we're not picked up soon, we shall be dead. I'm sure of that, yes. Let's take a chance on it and up the rations quite a bit, Chippy.'

Ken drew up a new list, determining they could now have two ounces of Bovril, six malted milk tablets, and four squares of chocolate. Biscuits could not be increased as they were running out. No one cared much for them anyway. Ken's examination of the water situation raised hopes a little; having been so careful with the stuff meant they still had a good few tins of it.

'I think,' said Ken, 'that we're safe to set water rations at three ounces, three times a day. What do you think? This seem fair?'

It sounded heavenly. 'I won't argue with that,' said Platten.

'Nor I,' said Colin.

As it was midday Ken issued the water and Colin studied his slightly fuller cup with thirsty eyes. It was hard to know how to best use the water; dry lips longed for its moisture, baked throats craved lubrication, blood screamed for liquid, and fried brains cried for relief. But thirst dictated Colin down it as quickly as possible.

'What about the grub?' he said. 'Since we've decided to go rash with the supplies, how about starting now with a meal?'

They ate their Bovril Pemmican and milk tablets in silence.

'I think,' said Ken, 'with today's oppressive heat, that we should rest until the sun goes down and resume lookout with the cool of the evening.'

Who could argue? The act of talking and issuing rations had drained them and even Colin had no heart for watch duty. While they dozed, Scarface tailed the boat, maybe waiting for another body to be released to the sea, maybe weighing up how he might overturn the vessel, or maybe he somehow knew who was going to survive and he wanted to be there at the end too.

&

I remember waking on the thirty-fifth day to Ken shaking Platten roughly. It is the most vivid day I can recall, apart from one other. It is the one that I think of most often, apart from one other. I shouted at Ken to give over and when he did, Platten fell with a heavy thud. The man had died. We were stunned, even after the eleven deaths we had witnessed by then. It was not only that he had been so well the day before, but that now we were just two. We clasped hands, I remember. We looked at one another for a long time, hardly believing it. It had begun with Ken and I, and now we thought it might end with us two. We were so very sad for Platten – he'd been a grand chap. His quiet personality had done a lot for the crew and he'd been known as Fair Play Platten aboard the SS Lulworth Hill.

We tried hard to give him a dignified and worthy send-off, but our sapped strength meant we had to kick him overboard and then sit and listen to the sharks tearing him apart. I wonder now how we survived so long and the other men did not. Over and over I think of it. Ken and I were not any bigger or stronger or better or fitter than the other men. We did not pray any harder or believe any more than they did or do any more. We were not more worthy. It does not seem fair. But I realised out on the ocean that fair doesn't come into it. There is nothing fair about any of it. Fair is something we men have invented to try and make sense of it all. But there is no sense. There is only what you do.

e

'So there was just two of them,' said Rose. 'It always was really, wasn't it? Just like us. You always need two, you know. One of you to be sad and one of you to be happy, and then you'll both be brave together.'

23

NEW YEAR, NEW BOOK

We think our speed about twenty miles a day. If we can stick it
out we should make land. I think we can, with God with us.

K.C.

I've always liked New Year's Day so much more than New Year's Eve. You get to start all over again. You're bursting with hope, like a new term at school when you decide to write neatly in your blank exercise book and not make any mistakes or rush homework.

New Year's Eve is an ending, the full stop that concludes a book. New Year's Day, the new book. That year I was glad to say goodbye to it and knew I'd not look back with particular fondness. This one will be better, I told myself. That was my self-promise: hopeful, non-specific, just better.

Rose and I spent it quietly. A quick visit to my dad, a few hours with Vonny, a brief look around the sales at more remnants for Rose to stitch, and then back home for an evening of TV, roast beef, story time and watching the fireworks from my bedroom window.

At midnight flashes of fire lit the sky above our shed,

scattering gold dust and ice-white stars, boom, pop, boom, pop.

'Is that what a flare looks like?' asked Rose, nose up against the glass.

'You mean at sea? I'm not sure. It'd have to be bright though, wouldn't it? To be seen from afar.'

'Everything to do with danger is totally bright,' she said. 'Lighthouses and police sirens and those red warning signs in movies when the bad guys have set bombs off.' She paused, her breath smoking the glass. 'Will Dad have fireworks?'

'Not sure.'

'How many sleeps until he's back?' she asked.

'Maybe, um, nine or ten.'

'Maybe?' demanded Rose.

'It just might not be exactly the day he said. Because of the army and how long the journey is. It'll be soon. That's all you need to know.'

Soon wasn't a lie, it was the story she needed. Or was it the one I needed? Weeks ago I'd threatened that I'd tell Jake how badly Rose had behaved and make sure he didn't come home again. Now it felt like I was being punished for my behaviour that day, for breaking up the door.

'Tomorrow I'm going to do *two* of my injections,' she said. 'Cos I don't want you coming into school at lunchtime when I'm back next week, and I want to go on the Year Five trip to Whitby in summer and I'll look like a total idiot if I have to have my mum come too!'

'Please don't call yourself an idiot,' I sighed. 'And even if it isn't me, someone will always have to watch you when you do everything. In case you measure the wrong dose or you're low and can't hold it.'

I should have felt glad at her huge efforts toward independence. But part of me died. Let her go, said my head; I can't, said my heart.

In the last week she had done five injections, with difficulty. The angle was different when self-injecting as opposed to having someone else do it. I was able to go straight into the flesh, clean, in and out. She had to bend her arm while squeezing a small bit of tummy flesh with her other hand and pressing the pen lever at the same time. At times she panicked and pulled the needle out before the full insulin dose was released, meaning her blood sugars rose. Or she couldn't press the lever at the same time and had to start again, meaning more bruises. It would never be easy, no matter how old she got or how long she had diabetes. Each time I offered to take over Rose shoved me away, determined to conquer it.

'Don't suffocate me,' she yelled. 'Stop watching me all the time. You're putting me off.'

'You should be glad,' she said now. 'You can go back to work and stuff. You must be bored being at home. I would be if I was stuck in all the time like a little rat in a box.'

An emerald firework splattered across the sky like sparkly grass cuttings spat from a lawnmower. Rose was right. It was time to think about going back to work. I'd soon be totally redundant from my role as storyteller, blood reader and injector – and what then?

I glanced at the clock on my bedside table: twelve fifteen. 'Bedtime now,' I said. 'You've seen in the New Year.'

'Did you make a wish?' she asked as I tucked her in.

'Not really,' I admitted. 'More of a self-promise. Did you?'

'Yes, but I can't tell you or it won't come true.'

I went to kiss her forehead but she wrinkled her nose and turned away, a child one minute, a mystery the next.

'How will I be able to do Colin's diary at lunchtime if I don't come into school anymore?' I asked her.

'Mum, the story's going to be over by then,' she said, exasperated, as if I should have known. And I did, I just didn't want to think about it yet. I had worried how she would cope when it finished, but I'd never really thought about how I'd feel – until now.

When I pulled away something fell from under the pillow – a book. It was *The Lion, the Witch and the Wardrobe*. I remembered how desperate I'd been at the hospital to get her to take one.

'You're reading again,' I said, pleased.

'Not yet.' I could tell she was half-asleep. 'I put it there ready.'

'Ready?'

'For when Grandad Colin's story is over.'

'That could be another week,' I said. 'We're still only at day thirty-nine.'

'I'm ... just ... getting ... prepared...' she said, the words separated by sleepiness.

I put the book back under her pillow, sniffed her hair. It was all warmth and sleep and faint coconut shampoo. I turned out the light. In my bedroom I watched the dying fireworks and wondered why I wasn't elated. I'd done it. *We'd* done it. *She* had done it.

Rose had not only accepted her blood tests and injections but she had done some herself. And now at last the little girl whose first words were 'book, book, want book' was returning to her beloved stories.

I'd called Shelley a few days ago and told her about Rose's first self-administered injection. 'You must be overjoyed,' she'd said to me.

So why wasn't I?

The year had been a tough one but tomorrow, I self-promised, would be better. I looked at my phone, knowing I wouldn't have missed a call from Jake, but hoping anyway. There were Happy New Year texts from my mum and encouraging words and offers of help from Vonny.

Perhaps Jake still being away was why the fireworks hadn't made me clap my hands and jump the way Rose had earlier. And, of course, we hadn't finished Colin's story yet. I knew we were coming up to the most difficult chapters and I feared their effect on Rose. Might his worst suffering undo all that we'd achieved? It had helped so far but now came the greatest test of his life.

I closed the curtains and crawled into bed.

\~

In the morning we woke late and I made eggs and bacon and we took them into the book nook. Rose switched on the fairy lights, said, 'Can we keep these here? I like them so much.'

'They're Christmas lights,' I said. 'I'll be taking them down tomorrow.'

'They could be lights for lots of reasons,' she snapped. 'Reading lights. Summer lights. Just lights, like, in general.'

'We'll see,' I said, and she mimicked my words with a

scowl. 'Let's do an injection and you can have your bacon. Right – day thirty-nine.' I paused because we still shared the story sometimes. 'Shall I begin or shall you?'

She shrugged, sulky, so I began.

~

The only real event that lifeboat day was a horrid one: the biscuits ran out. Rose argued that Colin hated the things and so was glad they had gone. I agreed but explained that they were the only food of any substance. That the chocolate and milk tablets and Bovril would hardly keep a cat alive. As much as the hard texture had tortured their dry mouths and swollen tongues, Ken and Colin knew that without them they'd be considerably weaker.

But it was water they wanted most and longing for it filled every moment of the day, waking or asleep.

Rose pushed her egg around the plate. 'I'd not eat for days if I could take my food to the lifeboat,' she said. 'All those Selection Boxes in the cupboard and I have to wait for a hypo to have them – such a waste!'

'I know,' I said softly.

At lunchtime we let Colin's diary fall open to reveal a short passage, words written in blue amongst black like water against night sky. Had his pen run out? Had he added these thoughts long after the others or had he purposely recorded them in such a way that they stood out?

I read them carefully; sure that was how he'd want them to be voiced.

I think when I have filled this book I will dispose of it. I should not like to think of anyone else reading my laborious thoughts, my confessions, or about my mistakes. Recording these things has helped me make sense of what happened though I don't suppose it should matter very much to anyone when I'm no longer here. I'm just an average man who experienced something quite extraordinary.

'I wonder why he didn't get rid of it?' asked Rose.

I closed the book. 'I don't suppose any of us know when we're going to die, do we? Maybe he intended to throw it away and...'

'Never did,' she finished, softly. 'I'm so glad, or we'd never have had it.'

'He wanted us to have it remember.'

'Yes.'

'He told me to find it; then he led you to it, in the shed.'

Rose paused, and then said, 'And now he doesn't come as much. In the night, I mean.'

'Maybe he doesn't need to,' I said. 'We know him so well now, don't we?'

At teatime we reached day forty. Rose prepared the injection, correctly measuring the dose, testing it, and gripping her tummy's small bit of flesh, ready to pierce the skin.

'Not so rough,' I guided. 'You don't want to bruise even more.'

'I know, I know!' she snapped. 'You start the chapter, I'm concentrating.'

'Okay, day forty began like all the others in many ways,' I said. 'The sun began her daily ascent, the sky was as cloudless as ...'

'Is Ken going to live too?' asked Rose. 'I *need* to know, Mum.'

'I thought you knew the story as well as me.'

'I do. Grandad Colin's part anyway.'

'Haven't you read the newspaper cuttings?' I asked her.

'No, they're boring,' she said, wrinkling her nose.

'What about the last pages of the diary?'

'Can't read *that* fast.'

'You'll have to wait and see then,' I said. 'Shall I go on?'

The question needed no answer. I went on. We went on.
As did the ocean.

THE BEAUTY OF ESCAPE

Still two of us left, but we are getting very weak, can't stand up now.

K.C.

A curious noise woke Colin. No sounds were curious now – the sea's infinite rhythm swished all day and all night, over and over and over. So did the wind when it got up. Aside from nature's tune, the repetitive creak-creak-creak of the weatherworn boat and their occasional words, there was little to break the tedium. Colin longed for the unusual. He prayed many times for a new melody. His prayer for change had been answered only once when a great splash in the night had announced King's suicide leap overboard.

Not that, that that, he willed, thinking of Ken beside him.

But the curious noise was not watery, more a kind of caw-caw-caw sound. It pulled Colin from a mish-mash of dreams, in which his mother poured great jugs of water into their tin bath and the sunlit-haired girl clapped her hands at amber flashes in an inky sky and books fell violently from a shelf. Caw-caw-caw interrupted the swilling and clapping and thudding.

'Hear that?' he croaked.

Only Ken would understand his question. Parched vocal tracts meant the pitch and volume of their voices had deteriorated, but since the decline had taken time and happened in the sole company of the other, each man understood his companion as if they communicated by telepathy.

Ken didn't move though.

'Hear that?' Colin repeated with effort.

Ken still didn't move. He was curled up in the same position he'd assumed last night after evening rations and a half-hearted prayer. Colin was afraid to turn his chum over. Afraid not to.

Yesterday they had begun sipping seawater. Now, Colin could hardly believe they had done it. The one thing he knew might be their undoing. What had possessed them? They had only sipped a little, each punching the other if he got carried away. No verbal agreement was ever made about doing so; maybe the two men had been together so long now that they knew each other as well as they knew themselves. Often, they did other things in synchrony. Colin would take out his button to suck at exactly the same moment Ken did. Ken would begin a sentence that Colin mirrored simultaneously. Both would cry out during a dream, their anguish colouring the dark.

Now, after yesterday's foray into seawater drinking, Colin felt awfully thirsty. Drier than he had in all the forty days so far. It was a huge mistake. They should not have given in to the cold, abundant, inviting seduction of the ocean. How could they have forgotten what it had done to Leak and King?

And now Ken wasn't moving.

'Ken,' croaked Colin. 'Chippy?'

Last night's prayer had been a disjointed collection of pledges, to each other, to God, to their future. 'Chum, promise me...' Ken had begun.

'What?' Even breathing was an effort now and Colin had wondered if Platten died so suddenly simply because he hadn't the energy to do so.

'Promise ... you'll still ... be ... here ... when I wake,' Ken had said.

It was something they feared more than rations running out; waking up and being the only one left. Often, when they dozed during the day, Colin thought, *I'll sleep when Ken wakes. It'll comfort him to see me sitting here when he comes round.* But then he could never manage it and would wake, his face cooking in the sun, and his tongue as fat as a feather pillow in his mouth.

'I'll ... I'll try to be ... here...' Colin had said last night, mindful of his ability to keep such a promise now. He knew Ken just needed to hear it. But had hearing that and gulping seawater yesterday been all he'd needed to let go? Had he gone as Platten had, well one minute, dead the next?

Colin still hadn't the heart to shove Ken and find out the truth.

Sometimes they clung together, made desperate oaths; sometimes they felt nothing, not for each other, not for themselves. The previous morning they had glared at one another from opposite ends of the boat. Their hearts dried up with their minds and bodies. Ken cursed Colin for rescuing him that first day, said he should have left him in the ocean so he'd not be suffering now. Colin called Ken a bastard, said he was a useless friend and a coward of a man. An hour later they wordlessly ate rations and fell asleep muttering further insults. By evening, in the calmer cool of twilight, they could barely remember their hatred and prayed together as fervently as children in Sunday school.

'You've been a good friend,' Colin said now, to Ken's inert body. In the dawning sun it was bathed in holy light. 'I couldn't have asked for a better friend.'

It hurt so much to talk that he resorted to merely moving his mouth, playing his old *If I See Three Fish Then a Ship* game and imagining he could actually hear the words. *If I hear that sound again I'll get up, if I hear caw-caw-caw I'll see to Ken, if I don't I'll wait here and see what God does with me.*

Colin must have dozed off because the next he knew was a shove and Ken's gaunt face looming over him.

'Am I dreaming?' he croaked. 'Are we both goners?'

'Shake a leg, you fool,' said Ken. 'We've got company.'

'Huh?' Colin pulled himself up, his bones cracking and scraping without the cushion of flesh.

'Scarface. Been following a while.'

Colin glared at his friend. 'I thought you...'

'What?'

'Doesn't matter now.'

The sun was higher in the sky and Scarface swam at a leisurely pace about ten feet from the stern, no companions, no fear. With one eye on the shark, Ken poured three ounces of water and gave it to Colin. Both had noticed yesterday how few tins there were, but neither had voiced his concerns. Only three. How long would they last? Fortunately neither had the energy to work it out. Colin realised this might have led to their foolish seawater consumption. Trying to avoid using those final three water tins.

When Colin had supped his portion, Ken drained his. Scarface was the best deterrent against further seawater. Though black and skeletal now, hands wouldn't be safe cupping drinks from the ocean with him there.

'If he attacks,' said Ken, 'I don't reckon I've the strength to spear him, lad.'

'He knows,' said Colin.

'Knows what?' Ken split a bit of chocolate in two, handed one to Colin.

'That it's just us two now.'

'So why not attack?' croaked Ken.

'He doesn't need to. He'll wait us out.' Colin paused, sucking his chocolate square. Though tiny, the twice-daily chunk perked them up for at least half an hour. 'We'll not make it like this, you know.'

'What do you mean?'

'With what we're eating. If a ship comes in a week we'll not live to meet it. They'll find this boat and our corpses and a few tins and bits of chocolate and Bovril. We can up the rations again now there's just us.'

'But isn't that risky? We already did ... was it last week?'

'Look what a difference the food makes when we have some,' insisted Colin. 'We can almost function. An hour later we're washed out. No strength to talk, to watch. Set rations to tinier portions but five times a day.'

'He's gone,' said Ken, nodding towards the stern.

Colin did not hate Scarface. The shark did not mean

them harm, he only followed his instinct, lived his ocean life. He had become as much a part of their existence as log writing and rations and morning and night and prayers. Colin imagined that should he make it home, he might miss the great creature, might wonder whether he still swam these waters, looking for prey, for them.

'So? The rations?' insisted Colin.

'We up them,' agreed Ken.

Colin tried to change position, but none lessened the ache that tortured his whole body. 'Did you hear it?' he asked.

'Hear what?'

'That sound. At dawn. Curious. Sure I heard it.'

'No. Nothing ... but ... the sea...'

They slept again. Like babies, they now napped as much as they were awake. Half an hour of existing needed half an hour of recovery, and sleep, when dreamless, was escape. When dreams did come they were mostly an endless sequence of nightmares, tortured visions of the passed away crew, of great pools of crystal water, of home, of parents, of childhood places visited.

Colin searched in the dark for the girl, yearned to hear again her softly saying *Grandad*. But it was as though the more he looked the farther away she went.

He heard instead his companions' many dying words; Scown begging him to hear the message he'd given Ken, and Young Arnold saying, *Ken, may I pray*, one last time, and always Fowler. Fowler glaring at him, Fowler holding his arm after the punch, Fowler dead against the mast – again and again and again. Was this where the cliché that your life flashes before you as you die came from?

When Colin woke the sun had reached her peak and bore down from cloudless skies. Ken was already awake, trying to hold the pencil stub between his blackened fingers so he could write on the torn canvas sail. Colin leaned closer and read over his pal's shoulder.

Not seen a ship. Where is our navy patrol? Looking for a ship or plane any day now. We must be near land. Many sharks around. Still two of us left, but we are getting very weak, can't stand up. We will stick it to the end.

'If this outlives us,' said Colin, 'it'll make quite a read for someone one day.'

'Don't say that!' Ken threw the pencil down. 'We're getting home! Stop that talk!'

'Would it be so bad if we didn't?'

'What?'

'Get home.'

Colin's mood was not depressed. Rather he felt calm, accepting of what might come. How good might it be to sleep forever? A vivid recollection came to him now. He recalled plunging through the dark, straight like an arrow, to the sea, as the *Lulworth Hill* sank too. Strange words had come to him then, but made no sense.

I'm just going to go and lie in bed from now on and that's it. Stay there and wait for my long-forever sleep.

Colin had thought they were born of fear and adrenalin. Now he recognised the voice; it belonged to the girl who said Grandad, the girl with sunlit straw hair. Had she been inviting him to sleep forever?

'What about your ship?' demanded Ken. Colin saw in his eyes that he too tasted the beauty of escape, of no more thirst, of no more feeling pain at every breath and every movement, of sleep.

'It's so beautiful.' Colin looked out over the ocean's soothing ripples. 'And it would be quick and merciful relief. A quick dip, just like you did that night so long ago. Shall we?'

'I don't...' Ken faltered, but his eyes looked longingly at the water.

'We can probably only last another two or three days on what rations we have, lad. I could do it. Go into the water. We'd not have to wait long. Think how cooling the sea will be on our skin. I could do it.'

'But Scarface...'

'Don't worry about him.' Colin smiled, felt his body go limp at the thought of finally surrendering. 'He won't get a decent meal off the pair of us. Only make it quicker. Shall we? There'll be no ship, Chippy. I've looked and looked. I've counted fish and sharks and waves.'

Ken listened, tempted, resisting, tempted, resisting.

'Our chums are waiting for us.' Colin's eyelids grew heavy with weariness. 'I might see our Stan again. We might ... lash ourselves ... together ... we could not struggle ... that way ... be over even quicker...' Half-heartedly he reached for the line as though to bind his body to Ken's and go there and then.

'Tell them I died a true Christian,' said Ken. 'Some of you are going to be saved.'

'What's ... that ... you say...'

'Not me, lad – John Arnold.' Ken sat up, the jolt causing him to wince in pain. 'He said it to me once. It just came to me now!' He shook Colin roughly. 'Don't you realise what it means?'

'Let me be.' Colin was barely conscious. 'I'll swim ... later ... rest first ... then swim ... escape...'

'No, don't you see? He said *some* of you are going to be saved – more than one. That means us. So we must hang on!' Ken watched Colin sleeping, the line still in his hand. 'You rest, lad. Do you good. Need it.' Then he repeated softly to himself, 'Some of you are going to be saved', and slept too.

When Colin woke again the sun was approaching the horizon and though he couldn't remember his dream it must have been a good one for he felt considerably more hopeful than he had earlier. Breaking their general synchronistic behaviour, Ken was snoozing still, spear at his side as though to make sure Death didn't attack while he slept.

Something drew Colin's attention to the rope trailing astern. How long had it been dangling there? Why did it matter? What made him care so now? Still, something made him crawl to the foredeck and grasp the line to reel it in. Made fast to the bows, it had dragged right under the boat and was out of reach.

'I'll lie across your legs,' said Ken, behind him. 'Not got the strength to hold them. What do you hope to find?'

'Let's just get it in,' said Colin.

'Be quick,' said Ken, and Colin knew he feared letting him go. What price they were prepared to pay for Colin's random instinct.

'Got it!' cried Colin. 'Help me!'

For a moment he thought he might slip under, but Ken grabbed his shoulder. 'This had better be worth it,' he said.

It was. Shellfish had attached to the length of submerged rope, dozens and dozens of them. Delighted, the two men opened their shells and slowly munched their fleshy contents so as not to lose any of the flavour.

Tackling the long, juicy stems, Colin winked at Ken and said, 'Water, lad, they're full of fresh water,' and they devoured every one.

As was always the case with any amount of water, they felt immediately stronger, able to think more clearly, look for a ship again.

'What made you think of it?' asked Ken, as they enjoyed the coolness of twilight and their meagre late meal.

'Not sure, lad.'

Ken studied him. 'Are you alright now?'

Colin nodded. He knew how close he had come to jumping earlier. It had never come over him quite like that until then, and he feared it happening again. At the time all he'd been able to think was that not being there anymore would be purest bliss. Now it served to comfort as an escape plan; if the water ran out before a ship or land was seen, then he meant to take control and see out his own end.

Caw-caw-caw disturbed his thoughts. *Caw-caw-caw.* That sound again, the one that had woken him so brutally earlier. *Caw-caw-caw.* He frowned, looked around, and realised Ken was searching too.

'You hear it?' said Colin.

'I do, lad.' Ken pointed. 'Look, there. Seagulls. I think three of 'em. How lovely they are.'

The birds circled the boat like white kites. Colin pitied them – what morsel did they hope to find here? Nothing here but tins and wood and two wasted seamen. Still it was nice to have a different creature to look at; how soft their feathers were, how bright against the sky. So long since he'd seen a bird. His father could name most types, just from a flash of wing or beak. He had often taken Colin and his brothers bird spotting in the nearby woods.

'If only *we* had wings and the land instinct they have,' said Ken.

Colin slapped the deck next to him.

'Now what are you grinning at?' Ken was not in the mood to be mocked. 'Have you gone stark raving mad? Am I to throw you overboard myself?'

'Birds!' said Colin. 'What chumps we've been. Their sound woke me this morning. Neither of us realised they were here. And now we have we're just sitting and saying how lovely they are. What a pair of bloody fools! Don't you realise – those are the first birds since we've been at sea.'

'Of course!' Ken grinned too. 'The seagull is never far from land.'

'We must be closer, Chippy.' Colin held onto his mate's arm. 'We did right to up the rations last week else we'd not be here now to see the gulls.'

'Thank God.'

The water from the barnacles, their small evening meal, and the sight of birds gave the two men immense hope. They watched the gulls swoop and dive, looking for fish, as the sun sank beyond. Scarface surfaced about fifteen feet away but didn't stay for long. The sea calmed, the boat stilled, and night fell.

'Maybe we don't need a ship,' said Colin. 'Maybe land will come first. Maybe tomorrow land? I just hope we can last it out.'

'We must,' said Ken. 'We simply must.' He sighed, his breath barely enough to move a leaf. 'The excitement ... has left me ... tired...'

'How curious it would be if happiness was what killed us,' said Colin, still mad with joy at seeing the birds. 'After all this time we die in joy.' He paused. 'It's what's left when the excitement passes that concerns me. It's too bleak to bear. That's why you're tired. Hope's just as cruel as despair when it lifts and then drops you again. But without it, we're done for. No, you rest, lad.' He looked over at Ken, a thin shape half-lit by stars. 'Those birds mean summat. They do. More than just land. They've come to ... well, to give us hope.'

Colin lay back and counted stars. He recalled that first night on the lifeboat, when he'd thought he might be the only one and it had seemed the stars laughed at his efforts to survive. They had not changed – but he had. Now he only managed to count twelve of them and knew no more.

25

A NEW SNOWFLAKE

Great hopes today. Hope it will soon end.

K.C.

And so, with another Christmas done, Rose returned to school.

She got dressed in her customary manner, leaving a trail of items in her wake. She cleaned her teeth and chose the bobbles she wanted for her ponytail and then let me brush her hair, as if the last few weeks hadn't happened.

I looked out at the small patches of grass where the snow had melted. New snowfall if it came would look identical. But its invisible-to-the-human-eye design would mean it was unique. Rose did all the things she'd always done, but I knew she was different.

She now did the majority of her injections, mostly so I'd not have to go in to school at lunch.

'It's just embarrassing,' she'd said last night. 'Everyone will say to me, oh, why does your mum come in, are you a baby, are you like stupid?'

'I doubt anyone would say such things,' I'd said, sad.

Now she pulled away as I finished her hair and then packed her Hello Kitty bag. I'd bought her a gaudy spotted make-up purse to keep all the lancets and insulin pens safe during lessons. If only the pretty colours could lessen the severity of the accoutrements inside. She put them in her bag and zipped it up. I'd just hoped to make the diabetes less obvious to others, but Rose told me she didn't care about that anymore.

'It's just me now isn't it?' she said. 'Diabetes. It's me, full stop.'

'I suppose,' I agreed.

She put on her coat. 'If Dad comes home when I'm at school,' she said, 'will you get me straight away?'

'No, because he'll be here when you get in.'

I'd still not told her that I wasn't sure when he'd be home. Jake hadn't called since our Christmas morning conversation and I had no clue when he next would. It could be February; it could be Easter for all I knew. The sadness that our ocean story would end with no Jake grew fatter and heavier. I carried it around, unable to share it with Rose, not knowing if he'd even get back at all.

'He's going to be dead proud of you doing all your injections,' I said. 'He won't expect it at all.'

Almost at the door, Rose dropped her bag and let her coat fall to the floor. Had I upset her?

She went back to the book nook where crumbs from breakfast were still scattered across the cushions, tiny clues that we'd been there. Kneeling, she took Colin's diary from the shelf and held it to her chest. I realised it was a goodbye. Though we were not yet quite at the end of his story we had agreed last night that I should today give the diary to my father. We had read all of Colin's words; we had opened every page; we had heard every syllable.

'We can still borrow it anytime,' I said as Rose continued to hold the book. 'It's not like a goodbye forever.'

'I don't want to read it again,' she said. 'That's why I just want to remember it – what it looks and smells like.'

That morning, with breakfast, we had shared day forty-two. So little happened aside from Ken and Colin sleeping that we talked mostly of previous days. Rose told me she had dreamt she told Grandad Colin to look for barnacles on the trailing rope the night before we did day forty. She'd been reading a story at school where sailors had done this and had hoped she'd dream of Colin so she could tell him – and it happened.

Now Rose put Colin's diary back on the shelf and headed for the door. 'If only I still dreamt about him like I used to,' she said, halfway down the path. Three snowflakes landed in her hair, sticking to it and looking like frosted hair slides. 'I'd be able to close my eyes every single night and see him. I'd tell him off for saying he'd jump over with Ken that time. I'd say – you can't talk anymore about jumping in the sea! Do you hear me? You're not allowed!'

I went towards her, my feet bare on the icy path but she shook her head, said, 'I'm fine, I'm just saying,' and went off to school, her bobbly scarf flying behind her like a barnacle-covered rope.

I closed the door, got dressed and took Colin's diary from the shelf. I wondered about keeping it to show Jake when – *if* – he finally came home, but Rose had said last night that even though she loved her dad, he wasn't the dad who needed this book. She said it belonged to my dad now.

So I went to him.

e~

My father lived alone in the house where he'd been born sixty-four years earlier, a life come full circle. It had changed less than he had and seen much. The cool larder was still home to a variety of cordials, the kind I'd nagged for as a child; the high-backed chairs were those my grandma had favoured, sitting with knitting on her lap; pictures of my dad's brother Peter and sister Jane lined clean surfaces and flock walls; and the kitchen floor tiles had witnessed many years of muddy shoes, wet Wellington boots, and worn slippers.

That day, when he came in from the garden, flushed from chopping wood, I saw more of Colin in my father. It must have always been there, but now I'd relived almost all of his story, I could see details I'd overlooked. My father is fairer haired and skinned than Colin was but something in the eyebrow, in the jaw, made them alike today. He washed his hands and put the kettle on.

'I have something for you,' I said. 'It might be a bit of a shock.'

He doesn't like fuss or melodrama so I simply handed him the soft, brown diary and said no more. For a moment I paused, not wanting to give it up, and the lifeboat and Scarface and the ocean flashed before me, a cliché turned on its head because it was not my life I saw but Colin's.

'Well, well,' said my dad, studying it, then turning it over and looking at the inky C.A. initials. 'I know what this is.' He didn't open it though.

'You do?' It was I who instead experienced shock.

'Of course. It's my father's notebook.'

'You ... but...' I could not seem to get any coherent words out.

'I recall that it was tied in two thick ribbons,' he said, frowning.

'Yes,' I admitted. 'It was.' I paused. 'You've seen it before? I thought no one ever had because the ribbons were so knotted up. I thought perhaps it had got mixed up in the box of things Grandma left me, forgotten until we...' I wondered how to describe Rose finding it and said simply, 'Until we came upon it.'

'Your grandma knew about the notebook too,' my dad explained. 'She knew Colin had written in it during the months following his lifeboat rescue. But he never wanted to talk very much about it and always kept it hidden away in a desk – so she felt she might have been intruding if she'd opened it.'

I wondered if maybe she'd been afraid to, knowing more than anyone what he must have gone through. I also began to worry that I had done the wrong thing in undoing those difficult knots to get to it.

It occurred to me for the first time that Colin had been in this house. So long ago now, he had slept here, been a father here, written in his diary and remembered the lifeboat here. How had I not sensed him more? Do we go when we die to the place we were born, a place we love best, the place where we lived longest, or some other faraway place?

'When did you decide to look for the book?' my dad asked. 'It's been...' He thought about it. 'It's been seven years since your grandma passed.'

'I never looked at anything in that box,' I said, watching him make tea in the flowery china teapot that was probably older than I was. 'I felt too sad. So I just put it away and never went back to it. Until Rose ... a couple of months ago.'

'Have you read it?' he asked me.

'Yes.'

'What made you read it now?'

My father was a pragmatic, no-nonsense man of rigid opinions. Would he think me now a little silly – slightly crazy – if I told him of Colin talking to me at the hospital and to Rose in the night, and also appearing in dreams?

But I did not want to lie.

'After Rose was diagnosed,' I said. 'I began ... *thinking* of Colin. No, more than thinking. At times it was as though he was here, somehow. When Rose was fighting her injections she came across his book in the shed. More than came across really. Rose had dreamt about Colin and he told her to go there. So I've been telling her his story to get her ... well, really, *us* through the injections. It's been ... quite incredible. She's loved it.'

While I talked my father sipped tea and took in the information, and his eyes never showed surprise or disbelief or judgement. I could not tell anything from his even gaze but that was the way of my paternal family. Colin had viewed me similarly at the hospital. I wondered, did I look at Rose like that? Was I as difficult to read?

'We're almost done,' I said. 'We're at day forty-three and I

know the rest. I know how it will go. I've finished the diary.'
I paused. 'So you should have it now.'

'Thank you.' It was all he said.

Then he went into the back room and I followed, watched him stoke the fire and put a stray book in its proper place. We drank our tea and looked out at the frosty garden, at the tangled, leafless bushes behind it and the factory beyond that. He told me about the ridiculous grammatical errors in a local newspaper article last night, and I said I'd decided to go back to work now that Rose was gaining independence. I'd called my boss Sarah and she'd agreed that I could return in two weeks. My time off had not been even half as long as maternity leave but I worried that I'd forgotten what I did there.

'Won't it be difficult without Jake at home?' asked my dad. 'What about evening work? Weekends?'

'Vonny helps,' I said.

'I will too. When will Jake be back?'

'I don't know,' I admitted.

He put Colin's diary in a drawer, separating it from the numerous other hardbacks on his shelf. 'I've always thought solitude is good for a person. If you're not contented alone then you'll never feel secure in partnership.'

I agreed. I had always found peace in being alone. But also we need companionship. Would a person survive for many days on a lifeboat if they were there alone?

'I'd best get back,' I said. 'Rose will be home from school in half an hour.'

'Story time?' asked my dad.

'Yes,' I said, a half-smile shyly emerging.

He walked me to the door and saw me to my car. The front garden was neatly kept. In only a few months I knew daffodils and crocuses would burst through the soil; suddenly I longed for spring. This winter had been far too long.

'I think I have a few books that belonged to Colin,' said my dad as I started the car up. 'Dickens and such, from when he was a boy. Rose might like them.'

'She would,' I said.

'Good. I'll find them for her.'

I pulled away; he waved as I did. That he had made no comment was his way of saying he accepted that some curious, unexplainable link had been formed between my family and Colin, crossing more than sixty years, a bridge built of imagination and memories and DNA. I wanted to stop and ask him if he would now read the diary too but decided he might not even know yet. And if he did, maybe that journey was one he would take privately.

Weren't all books supposed to be like that?

Back home, I prepared chilli con carne for tea and when Rose came in from school we took a portion to the book nook.

'Will I have to eat at the table again when we're done?' she asked.

'Yes,' I said. 'You know how your dad is about meals at the table, so don't tell him how bad we've been.' I paused. 'How was school? What was it like doing your blood and injection without me?'

'Fine,' she said. 'Don't ask me every bloody day, will you?'

'*Language*, seriously, Rose. No need at all.'

'No,' she said, 'but you've got to stop asking and watching

and fussing like all the time. It's just all *normal*. Diabetes is just my life.'

Rose was right. Only I held her back now.

She prepared the finger pricker as ably as I'd learnt to do so. Her hands moved like they'd always been meant to do this. Mine, however, faltered. For a moment I felt lost without Colin's dairy. I reached to touch the soft leather and found nothing but smooth, colourful paperbacks. Even when we hadn't actually opened it I'd always known it was there, like an actor with his script in case of forgotten lines. I panicked, feared I wouldn't know the story.

'You don't need the diary,' said Rose.

I had kept the one string of lights up at her request and she shone gold and red and purple in the glow.

'I'm scared,' I admitted.

'But don't you know?' she said. 'It was never the diary or the newspaper bits or what anyone else told you. It was always you. Just *you*. You're the storyteller and I love you.'

26

GET UP AND KEEP LOOKING

Good news at about 10.30 this morning.

K.C.

Once away from it, the ocean's many colours fade. No paintbrush or pen can ever quite recreate their intensity. And yet, while on the lifeboat and surrounded by them, Colin dreamt of otherworldly tones and tints, of unnatural shades manufactured by companies wanting to lure children into their pages.

During those final nights at sea he saw a shelf full of books. The place he'd been so often now. Some were neatly placed in alphabetical order; others were piled high more carelessly. They were as real as though Colin could have taken one and read it. But when he tried to it melted like snow.

Then he wasn't alone; he never had been.

Sitting on two cushions were a woman and the beautiful girl with her sunlit hair, her eager, imploring eyes, holding a box full of tiny needles and other strange things. Seemingly unaware of him, they shared a story. It must have been one they loved for they barely stopped talking, taking turns and then interrupting in excitement.

Colin didn't want to disturb the moment. Yet he also wanted to reach out and let them know he was there too. On and on they went with their story, their sentences flowing, building, bouncing. He couldn't hear what they said but, as with the other curious dreams, the words were somehow familiar.

It began to fade and he panicked.

Don't leave me, he tried to yell.

But darkness stole the books, their faces.

Then he heard it: *You have to get up and keep looking, Grandad!*

The girl. His great granddaughter. Where was she?

He could hear the sea's current. Her watery hands rocked and tipped the boat. No, he didn't want to wake. He knew what awaited him there.

Do you know the story of Noah, said the girl. *Remember what the bird meant. Get up and keep looking, Grandad!*

Colin woke to find Ken staring at him. His eyes were lifeless, hopeless, apathetic, shrunken into their sockets. After the dream, Ken's face shocked Colin. Having watched forty-three days of deterioration he rarely noticed Ken's gaunt appearance, but that morning, after the fresh faces in his dream, Ken looked like him. He looked like Death. Colin realised then how ill they were and knew that without land or a ship they wouldn't last longer than another two or three days.

Ken bravely tried to smile at his chum and Colin attempted to return the effort. The sun was already halfway across the sky – how had they slept so long? Never before had Colin missed dawn; and when had he last said to Ken, *Maybe today a ship?* He tried to say it now but his tongue filled his mouth, trapping the verbs and muffling the nouns. The effort he anticipated would be needed to reach the final water tin kept him from moving.

In the last twenty-four hours Colin had felt the will to live leaving his body as acutely as if he were physically bleeding. He no longer cared that he didn't care. He did not count fish or sharks or clouds. He did not miss food or water or home. He did not see his brothers, all different sizes and heights and colours, united by the subtle family trait of firm chin and heavy brow.

It was easier to give in and sleep. To wake only to sip the tiny bit of water Ken made him take and nibble on scraps of chocolate given. Each man would, upon finding the other alive, nod weakly. Colin was not sure he would care now if he woke alone, left drifting on the lifeboat until someone came for him.

Who would that be?

Not his mum; he had called her many times, but she never came. Maybe the sunlit-straw-haired girl would take him. She came often. Maybe she was Death prettied up in his head to make his end gentler? Maybe Colin had hallucinated her. Maybe he had hallucinated the whole journey, every one of the six weeks, and he was still on the *Lulworth Hill*, whistling and writing letters home?

But no. There was Ken, skeletal, desperate Ken. His friend.

Ken crawled now to the final water tin and came back with it, no moisture left in his body even to sweat after the action. He opened the lid as carefully as they had each one, lest a single drop got wasted. The temptation to drink it all in violent gulps never died; that they hadn't was probably the only reason they still existed. They looked into the clear liquid now, their grim faces reflected back more kindly in its mirror.

'Two ounces,' croaked Ken. 'Two ounces four times a day might get us to another five days.'

'No ... point...'

'No?'

'We'll be dead by...' Colin couldn't finish.

Ken appeared to think about this. 'You're right, lad. You were right that other time and saw us through.' It took him a few minutes just to say these words, saying only two at a time and pausing for breath between. The heat shimmering on the midday deck drained every last bit of energy they had. 'We'll have four ounces now then. Assess what we can get by with each time we serve it up. You go first, chum.'

'No, you,' croaked Colin, and so they argued back and forth until Ken took his share.

It barely wet their throats.

'Rest,' said Ken. 'Then ... watch.'

'But ... the dream,' Colin said. The memory of it sparked sudden hope.

'The dream?'

'She said ... get up ... and keep looking.'

'Who did?'

'That girl. The one ... who said ... Grandad.'

'Chum.' Ken closed his eyes. 'If I believed all the dreams I'd had on here, we'd have been picked up weeks ago and I'd be in Kath's arms now.' A dry sob broke from Ken's chest.

'Kath,' he said. 'Kath, why don't you help us? Please help us. You're with the RAF. Send someone. Send a ship. Help us.' And then he passed clean out.

Colin tried hard to stay awake. He took the brown button from his pocket and sucked on it. Not so much to lessen the endless thirst – which, really, it had probably never done – but to do something physical that would prevent sleep but not overly exhaust him. He turned the button over in his mouth – click, clack, click – and watched the water until his eyelids began to droop.

Remember the bird and what it meant. Get up and keep looking, Grandad.

Click, clack, click.

'I'm trying,' he muttered. 'I'm trying hard.'

But in the end he fell asleep.

A persistent buzzing noise woke him. It throbbed in his head like a fly had got stuck there. He decided he had gone mad; that the occasional drinking of seawater and lack of food and too much sun had finally fried his brain. But then the lifeboat was moving in a way it never had and a rhythmic thudding that kept time with the sound in his head made Colin open his eyes.

Ken was pointing, his face one of joy that even parched skin could not dull. 'Can you hear it?' he cried. 'Can you hear it? A plane, a plane!'

Together they searched the clear skies, methodically, from port to starboard, up a few degrees and then starboard to port, seaman on watch again, on proper duty, eyes tired but eager.

'There she is!' Colin and Ken broke into insane laughter

at the realisation that they had spoken at exactly the same time.

The plane was astern of them, flying very high. Ken clapped his hands and slapped Colin on the back, who in turn shoved him almost over the side. Wasting no time, Colin grabbed one of the three smoke-floats. He pulled the firing-tape and dropped it into the water. Like two children watching a bonfire, they smiled as the dense red smoke drifted in the breeze.

Scarface surfaced to investigate the smoke-pall but disappeared as quickly as he'd arrived when no food materialised.

'No plane can miss that,' cried Ken.

'No matter how high,' said Colin.

'I reckon that smoke could even be seen from below the horizon!'

They clasped hands together, jubilant. The plane continued her journey. Was she going to slow down? Circle overhead? Signal an acknowledgement somehow? She must, *she must*.

'Where are you going?' whispered Colin.

'Don't leave us,' begged Ken, and Colin felt sadder for his chum in that moment than for himself.

Not wanting to believe their eyes, they watched the aircraft grow smaller and smaller until it was a dot in the sky and faded from ear and then eventually sight.

'They left us,' said Ken.

Colin could not look at him; could not stand to see in his friend's face the desolation that crushed his own chest. He turned instead to port where the dying smoke-float slowly drifted, increasing distance from the lifeboat, until with a few sputtering gasps of smoke it died.

With it went all hope.

Ken flopped to the deck, head in hands. Colin had no words. He sat too, the exertion of joy leaving him broken. Neither man spoke all afternoon. Scarface trailed the boat as though also waiting for the plane to come back. The sun began her descent. Water was consumed, chocolate eaten.

Colin picked up the length of line and ran it through his fingers in grim silence. Ken watched him, knew his thoughts. How quick it would be to lash themselves together and go over. Colin twisted the line, over and over, wrapping it about his arm and then letting it slide through his fingers again.

He looked at Ken.

'It's the quickest way home,' Ken said.

'Are you ready to go there?'

Ken didn't answer.

'I don't think I'm ready yet,' said Colin. 'We can't let our friends down, can we?' He looked about the boat; he saw Weekes joking about eggs for breakfast, Fowler on watch, Platten issuing rations, Arnold praying fervently, and Officer Scown in his final moments. He saw them all chatting after rations, egging Ken on with his spear, sleeping, praying, surviving, living, dying.

'Who else will tell everyone how brave they were, Ken? We owe it to them. How will anyone ever know what went on here. What we all endured. What we saw. Who we were.' He paused. 'I don't think I'm ready yet.'

Colin put down the line and closed his eyes. How long he was out can't be known but buzzing disturbed his slumber again. Not daring to open his eyes, he thought he must be dreaming about the plane.

But the sound continued.

Then Ken shook him. 'Two more!' he cried. 'There, two more planes!'

Colin leapt to his feet. Energy returned so fast when immediate survival required it. He set off the last two smoke-floats, hoping this would make certain that they were seen. In his haste, one ignited while he still held onto it. Yelping in pain, he went to plunge his hand into the sea, but Ken grabbed him and pulled him back.

'Scarface,' he said.

Once again, as Colin nursed agonising burns, the two planes continued overhead and eventually disappeared, oblivious to the smoky red signals that died like the other had. Colin's hand swelled up and blistered fast. They had nothing to ease it. No creams, no bandages, and only saltwater to pour on it, which caused greater hurt. But the pain lifted Colin as though any feeling, even bad, was something.

'We may see more planes,' he insisted. 'Look Ken, we've been forty-three days on this lifeboat without seeing another sign of human life. Then in one day we spot three planes. Maybe we're in a patrol area. It's a good sign.' He paused. 'You do think so too, don't you Ken?'

Ken nodded with effort. 'Of course, you're right. We'll be picked up tomorrow, you'll see. Tomorrow.'

When they retired at sundown, Ken wrote on the torn canvas.

30ᵗʰ April – 3pm – Two more aircraft passed over but gave no sign of seeing us. But we have greater hopes now. If there are any tomorrow, we shall know it for the RAF Coast Patrol, and then we can expect to be sighted any day. We are both very ill.

e

Morning brought 1ˢᵗ May. Colin wasn't sure what prompted his thinking of the date for he'd hardly noted the others. Time had become meaningless. He watched their limp sail hanging from the mast, a forlorn and colourless Maypole. He thought about those back home, celebrating under England's gentle skies. Oh, for kind weather, for less heat.

He must have spoken the words because Ken croaked, 'Without the heat we'd have been dead long ago.'

Colin knew it to be true. If their journey had been through the Arctic it would have been much shorter. Immersion in those seas resulted in quick death. Still, he longed for cold, for cool air, for icy drinks.

The men drifted through day forty-four, eyes closed to the sun's cruel glare, ears open for another plane. When they felt strong enough to talk it was mainly of planes; when they might return, if they'd been spotted, and what might result.

During midday rations Ken watched a young dolphin swim playfully alongside the boat. He nudged Colin and the two men enjoyed the gorgeous creature's dance. How silvery his skin shimmered beneath the waves, how his tail flashed through surf. Joy was tempered by concern that Scarface would appear.

'Go swim away,' whispered Colin. 'Sharks here.' He leaned over the boat edge to watch the dolphin dive there and saw a cluster of four large goose barnacles attached to the wood.

'Ken,' he cried. 'More barnacles! Look!'

Ken leaned over. 'They're a good foot away,' he groaned. They looked so juicy and succulent that Colin's jaws automatically moved, imagining the delicious meat in his mouth.

'Grab my legs,' he said. 'I'll see if I can get them.'

'What about Scarface?'

'It's worth the risk. What beauties they are.' Colin paused and gave a bitter grunt. 'What does it matter all that much if he *does* get me?'

Weak as they were, it was an operation of magnitude. Merely thinking about how to do it was exhausting. They first passed rope over Colin's shoulders and fastened it to the mast. This alone needed a ten-minute rest. Then, doused with seawater to energise them, Colin edged himself over the gunnel while Ken used every scrap of energy to hold his legs. Getting the barnacles was no issue but bringing Colin back onto the boat proved hardest of all. When they did, it was worth it – he'd managed to retrieve five.

They ate them as slowly as possible, savouring every bit of liquid and meat. Satiated, they then slept a while. The faint beat of a plane again woke them. Colin sat up so fast he screamed in agony but Ken ignored him, cried, 'Look, there, he's coming directly towards us.'

So he was, not high, not low, speed neither fast nor slow, his wings black against the blue.

'If *only* we had another smoke-float!' cried Colin. 'Why the hell did I let two off at once? He'll pass so near he couldn't possibly miss one if we had it!'

'So we wave,' said Ken.

Wave they did, barely able to stand, voices so dry their cries of help were likely not heard further away than ten yards. The plane passed directly over, so close they saw the underside of his wings. He continued his course, leaving only the dying sound of engines like distant thunder.

Ken dropped to his knees, muttering a prayer or curse at the heavens. Colin tried to remain standing another moment, watching the plane's departure. As he began to turn away, to give in, something stopped him.

The plane was turning.

'Ken,' he cried. 'He's spotted us. Look, he's coming back!'

The plane banked around in a slow, easy turn to port and continued circling until he'd made three complete rings around the lifeboat. Then, satisfied something warranted more investigation, he dropped to a lower altitude and passed right over. He dropped something that stained the nearby sea with red dye and Colin realised he was marking their position. Just to have been seen was enough.

'They're dropping something else,' cried Ken.

A package landed close by.

'Can we get it?' said Colin, terrified it would sink or drift away.

'The spear!' cried Ken.

This time he leaned over the boat edge while Colin sat on his legs. He was able to fish it out of the water with his spike hooked into the wrapping. The package contained a kite, a wireless set, a balloon to support an aerial, and a rubber dinghy. Exaltation at being spotted gave way to despair at the drop not including water. They watched the plane depart and felt more alone than they had in a long time. Contact with another human – even inside an aircraft – brought such joy that when it ended, emptiness deepened.

The balloon was useless without gas to support it, so they could not work the wireless and get out a message. And what good was a rubber dinghy? Water was all they wanted. Exhaustion set in, and with it came anger, despair.

'Perhaps we can fix the aerial to the mast,' said Colin.

'How the hell are we to do that?' snapped Ken. 'Stand on one another's shoulders? We can barely support our own weight, lad.'

Neither could concentrate enough to think of another solution. They settled into the well of the boat.

'We've been seen, Chippy,' said Colin.

'Aye, lad.'

'That's all that matters...' Colin's words trailed off as sleep stole speech.

'Aye, lad.'

'Now we ... wait...'

It was all they had done.

'Maybe tomorrow ... a ... ship...'

'Maybe.'

Get up and keep looking, Grandad.'

27

THE LAST SUPPER

Have been expecting to be rescued today but no luck.
K.C.

There were two of us that night.

I wore old leggings and Rose had on her new lilac one-sie covered in purple hearts. There was no ambulance, there were no paramedics asking questions, and no hospital trip.

Like Colin and Ken, we could not wait. At the beginning of the story I had paced the chapters, attached them to meals and injections, exchanged them for Rose's blood. I had wanted us to slowly discover Colin, to meet Ken and the other twelve men who shared their journey. I'd let the days gently unfold. I'd tried to do it right. Tried to set the scene and build tension and describe characters.

Now we couldn't wait for the end.

That morning I'd crossed 10th January off the calendar, just as Ken had marked the passing of their time on the canvas log. Each time I'd done it since Jake's Christmas phone call I'd wondered when the next call might be, what news it would bring. Rose knew now that his homecoming might be delayed.

Two days ago she'd asked, 'Why isn't Dad here yet?' and I'd had to tell her the truth. That I had no clue. She'd surprised me with her acceptance and said he was probably waiting for us to finish Colin's story first.

And now we were almost done.

Rose came down with her diabetes box and looked at the book nook. She didn't sit on a cushion though. I knew why. We were at the end. This was the last time we'd sit together and visit the ocean. The last time we'd be lit up by the string of colourful bulbs and the magic of what had happened. The last time we would see the lifeboat. I knew Rose would likely go back to reading secretly, under her covers, and our book nook would end up forsaken, dusty, haunted by words passed.

I saw then as clearly as a vision that we would pack her babyish hardbacks in a box for the loft and put the bookshelf and cinnamon cushions in her bedroom. We would clean the area, paint it and think of a new purpose for it. I might stand in the sunny corner and hear the sea if I tried. I might drink tea and look out onto the garden and feel the whip of breeze from the lifeboat's sails. But I'd be looking back, and now it was time to look ahead.

This was our last supper.

Rose went into the book nook first and I followed with her piece of crusty bread covered in peanut butter. She broke it in half and said I should have some, that she was way too excited to eat it all. Then she patiently prepared the finger pricker and drew blood, rich and thick, which I gathered onto the strip. Five-point-two – it was the perfect reading, the number of someone without diabetes. She had, for now, conquered this complex and difficult and random condition.

I knew there would be difficult days ahead. I knew there would be times when she'd hate the injections, cry at her sore finger ends. Times when hypos would surprise us and debilitate her. When someone might point to her bruises and ask who had done it. When her eyesight might be affected. Her heart. Her kidneys.

But for now we had won.

'I think I know why I got it,' said Rose suddenly.

'Got what?' I asked.

'Diabetes.'

'What do you mean?' I asked.

'I was thinking and thinking in bed last night and I think maybe I'm supposed to not never forget how thirsty Grandad Colin got at sea. Or how much we need to eat to survive. I think I needed to know that you always need one other person cos I'm so bad at having help. And I think it's so I got to understand Colin and not never forget him.'

'No,' I argued. 'It can't be that at all. It's just bad luck. Just a faulty pancreas. Not something you deserved or needed. Just one of those things.'

'Don't be an idiot,' she said.

'*Language*, Ro...'

'No, I mean there's no such thing as just one of those things.'

'Maybe I didn't eat the right things when I was pregnant with you,' I said. It was something I'd thought about a great deal. That maybe I had done something that caused it.

'No, it's all for a good reason,' insisted Rose. 'I know it's to do with Grandad Colin and you can't say nowt that will stop me thinking so.'

'Anything,' I corrected.

'Nowt,' she repeated softly.

She measured the right dose of insulin; the creamy bubbles within the pen frothed like the sea. Then she held an area of tummy fat with one hand and pierced it with the needle in her other and pressed the lever in, as though she'd been doing it since the beginning of time, as though she'd known how all along and I was merely there to learn from her.

With lunch and tea we had shared days forty-eight and forty-nine on the lifeboat. Breakfast on day forty-eight had consisted of nothing – no water, no food. All rations had gone. Empty tins taunted them, clanking together in the boat's motion. There was nothing to do but wait for death. At midday another plane had flown towards them but with no smoke-float, no energy and no belief that anything would result, Colin and Ken had merely watched it approach in delirium.

But this one had dropped supplies. Parcels fell, gifts from the heavens. Some dropped close enough so Ken could use his spear to retrieve them; others were too far to even try and get. They remembered the dinghy they'd harshly disregarded days earlier and realised it had was supposed to be used for picking up these provisions. But neither man had the energy to inflate it, navigate it, and get out of it again.

Amongst the supplies were cigarettes and matches. When Ken and Colin smoked they felt like civilised humans again. They coughed violently, but didn't care. There were also boiled sweets and chocolate, and most deliciously of all, water. They rashly consumed a whole tin of water. Fearing the effects of overindulgence after starvation, they were slower with the food.

'They might have tried to land,' said Ken, angrily.

'Shut up,' snapped Colin. 'Don't be silly. What if they'd crashed? Not been able to get airborne again. Then where would be? Anyway, there's a note. Here, read this, chum.'

Ken quietly read the words.

Sorry we can't get down to pick you up – sea is too rough. Have sent signals from overhead for shore base to get a fix on you. If any shipping seen on the way back to base will direct them to you.

The note sustained them through the rest of that day, and the next. Hopes of rescue were real now and they had another two days of food to nourish them. Sleep proved difficult though, with such expectation. Neither wanted to risk missing another drop of supplies or seeing a ship finally arrive, so they drifted in and out of dreams, in and out of conversation, each starting sentences that the other knew exactly how to finish, and so not having to say the words.

Now we were at day fifty.

Rose ate her portion of bread and I picked up the crumbs after her. I ate my slice, savouring the nut spread like it might be my last. Through a full mouth I began to say, 'And so on da...' when out of nowhere the coloured lights fizzled with a sharp snap and died. The kitchen light went too. Darkness swallowed us. I waited, expecting them to come back on.

After a moment Rose said, 'What's happened?'

'It must be a power cut,' I said. 'Good job you've done your injection already.'

'Ooh, exciting,' she said.

'Not really. The heating will go off. It'll get cold quickly. Let me get you a blanket and see about some candles.'

I made my way upstairs, holding the bannister for guidance, and got Rose a blanket from the airing cupboard. Then, halfway across the kitchen tiles, a soft knock on the door stopped me. In the blackout it was hard to tell who stood on the doorstep, until April said, 'Oh, yours are off too, lovey.' I could just make out her curly hair against the sky.

'Looks like it's the whole street,' she said. 'It must be an electricity shortage. Do you need anything? Is Rose okay? Is she scared, lovey?'

'I think she's quite enjoying it actually,' I said. 'I'm just going to find some candles. Do you need any?'

'No, I've got plenty. I'm going to go and sit with Winnie. I was right in the middle of "Coronation Street" too. I hope the power comes back on in time for the plus-one viewing.'

I laughed.

'If it hasn't come on in another hour I'll bring you some lemon cake. That'll cheer you both up.'

'There's really no need,' I insisted.

I watched her black shadow depart.

'April,' I called, and she turned. 'Thank you for everything.'

This was why I'd always favoured the dark. I loved its anonymity, its safety. Like the men on the boat, we're all the same in the dark. None of us is less or more. We can all say thank-you here and ask for help.

'You're welcome, lovey,' April said. 'Look after that little girl of yours.'

I closed the door and went to find a candle. The only one in the drawer was from the pumpkin we'd made the night Rose went to the hospital. The one I'd worried would set the house alight. The one we were sure Colin had blown out. How perfect that I'd kept it. I felt about for a pack of matches and took them both back to the book nook.

'I'm not scared at all,' said Rose. 'Even on my own.'

'Of course,' I said, smiling at her forced words.

I wrapped the blanket around her like I had when she was first born. In the dark I breathed in the scent of her hair, knowing she'd not see and shove me away. She smelt of her room, of wax crayon and bed and new material. I lit the candle and put it on a book between us. It blessed us both with its soft, mystical glow; everything flickered like sunlight does on waves.

'Day fifty,' said Rose.

'I know,' I said.

We were there. We were there and we could let go. Shelley had been wrong about the story being a crutch. Yes, we had needed it. It had given us hope, helped us get through the last weeks. But I knew we could live on it forever without having to go back.

'I'm a bit scared,' Rose admitted. 'Well, not *scared* ... never scared ... more, you know, all twisty inside.'

I knew exactly what she meant. 'It's such a big day,' I said.

Rose knew rescue was coming because I'd accidentally described the story as Colin's fifty-day ordeal at the weekend. She had slammed her off-pink door and told me I'd ruined it. When we shared diary extracts, the pages had never randomly opened on Colin's description of day fifty. I knew how the end happened; Rose didn't.

Later she forgave me, admitting she'd known really and hadn't wanted to tell me. Said Colin had whispered *fifty days* in a dream and now she knew what he meant.

'I really hope Ken's with him until the end,' said Rose. 'That's all I'm wishing for now. That he can last as well because you always need two of you. Can you tell me if he gets there? Now, before we start? Please?'

'No,' I said. 'Let's go and find out.'

'I'm ready then,' she said.

I closed my eyes. Tried to go to that place I always did. To where I was Colin and knew all the words he'd never had the courage to record in his diary. Rose squeezed my hand, clammy and encouraging.

I opened my eyes again. Her face was gold in the candlelight. In the darkness behind her was someone else. I wasn't afraid. He put a hand on her shoulder and she smiled. I couldn't see his face, but I didn't need to. I could hear the sea. Smell the salt. Feel the breeze. He whistled and I knew the song. He whistled and Rose tried to do the same but couldn't and instead softly sang her own song, one made up from a top-ten hit and a hymn they once sang in Christmas assembly.

And we were on the lifeboat.

28

TODAY A SHIP

The greatest day of all my life and the day I shall never forget.
K.C.

There were no dreams that morning. There were no heavenly signs. No calm. No extra glorious sunrise. The light came up as it had every day. The stars died. The boat rose and fell, rose and fell, rose and fell. No relent, no clouds.

Colin woke in great pain and doused his eyes with seawater just so they would open. His burnt hand throbbed ceaselessly but acceptance dulled the pain in his head. It wasn't surrender. He did not give in. Rather, in the deepest black of night he had realised that there might be far worse ways for a man to go. He could live a hundred years and not witness what the lifeboat had shown him in seven weeks. He could make a thousand friends and not know mates like the thirteen men he'd known here. He could travel to every land on earth and not see such beauty and brutality as on the ocean.

If a ship didn't show today Colin had not lost. How could a man who had looked so hard for one die with regret? If no one came he was not alone. He never had been. One truly great friend was worth a dozen more.

With an agonised groan he rolled over, looked around the lifeboat. A place that eyes have beheld so many times becomes forever imprinted there. He knew that wherever he went he would be able to see it as clearly as if he were still here. The wood caked in salt, the rows of empty tins, the life jackets of mates gone, the greying sails hanging limp from their masts, the foredeck where hope of a ship drove each man on lookout; and Ken.

His friend slept in the well, curled tightly, feet bare and black as the fireback at home. Colin knew that calling out would not rouse him; there was not enough strength in his voice now. So, bracing himself for more pain, he crawled across the wood. At Ken's side he rested a moment and then poked him. Nothing. Again, he jabbed his friend in the back.

Nothing.

'Wake up, Ken,' he croaked.

Nothing.

Colin put his head on his mate's shoulder. There was nothing to rest against but bone. They must have each lost a quarter of their body weight, their fat and muscle wasting away like butter in the sun.

Colin remembered how back home he had occasionally criticised his mother's stew, moaning about some bit of gristle or hard carrot. How he longed now to taste that meaty meal. To thank her profusely for making it.

Perhaps it was better he never got home. What pitiful sight would he make? How much would he scare his mother with his burnt skin and gaunt frame? Though he so wanted to get there, to see her again, might it be kinder to go as Stan had – forever young.

The boat moved suddenly and Colin fell off Ken, cracking his head on a bench. He sat up and looked for Scarface but the sea was shark free, gently rolling and dotted with amber diamonds.

'If you're gonna wake a man, wake him with a ciggy.' It was Ken. Ken had moved, not the boat.

'Christ,' said Colin. 'I thought you were a goner, mate.'

'Any cigs then?'

Colin reached for the tins. 'Two left,' he said. He opened one of the water tins they had retrieved from the plane drop, poured a cupful and passed it to Ken.

'You first,' said Ken, but Colin made him drink.

Then he had a full cup, savouring the plentiful portion. He found some chocolate in the new rations and they shared a piece, the sugary chunk giving Colin and Ken the energy to scan the horizon, east to west, then west to east, seeing only the unmerciful expanse of the rolling Atlantic. The sharks were increasing in number, led by Scarface. Rows of sleek fins cut through the surf. Colin once read somewhere that a shark's fins are used for balance, that their movement is much like an aircraft's flight and if they stop moving they sink.

'So what about them cigs,' said Ken.

'Should we save them?' said Colin.

'For what? How many tomorrows do you think there are now, lad?'

'What say we share one and save one?'

'Suppose, lad.' Ken lit one and inhaled, coughing hard but shaking his hand at Colin when he tried to take the cigarette off him. 'No, I don't care,' he said. 'So what if it kills me.'

Colin took his turn. Their smoke spiralled into the blue like an Indian signal for help. Around the boat the sharks continued their surveillance. It occurred to Colin that they sensed something. Perhaps Scarface knew the two of them could not last much longer and had invited his friends to the feast. What a disappointing meal he and Ken would make.

When their eyes grew tired of scanning the sea, they crawled to the foredeck – at least if they slept they were eternally in position for lookout.

Half-heartedly, Colin played his game. He counted waves hitting the boat edge – one, two, three, four, five, six, and lost count and started again. If he could just get to ten he'd see a ship. One, two, three, four ... Come on, lad, get to ten, and a ship. Try again. He'd keep trying until he died or a ship turned up, whichever came first. One, two, three...

'Today a ship,' he said, sleepily.

'You said it wrong.'

'What?'

'You missed out ... the ... maybe,' said Ken.

'Did I?'

'Yes ... chum.'

'Couldn't ... think of ... it...'

And so they fell asleep again. When they woke, in unison, the sun still watched over them, a cruel but constant guardian. Sharks continued circling on all sides. One of Ken's most painful saltwater boils had come to a head and burst. Wearily, he cleaned it with a bit of rag and threw the dressing over the side.

What resulted was a frenzy and it very nearly killed both

men. The water around the material reddened as blood merged with salt. A small shark swam to investigate. In a watery flash Scarface was upon the creature, rows of vicious teeth smashing together. Water churned and the small shark raced off, blood streaming from an injury hidden below the surface. He got no farther than a few feet before sharks, large and small, devoured him.

Around them the water frothed and bubbled. Colin recalled each of their mates' sea burials and how the water had whipped that way then. He covered his ears, realised Ken had done the same.

'They'll turn the bloody boat over,' mouthed Ken.

Perhaps it was best. Perhaps it had all come to this. Perhaps Scarface, their constant companion, would be their end. Perhaps he was Death and not the sunlit-straw-haired girl.

Where *was* she? Why hadn't he seen her since yesterday? Had it been yesterday or the day before that? Maybe she had given up. No longer believed he'd get home. No longer cared.

And then he saw Scarface, away from the others and heading straight for the boat's stern. He hit before Ken had seen and the two men fell into the boat's well. They grabbed the gunnel and pulled themselves to their knees, in time to see him returning at speed. At the last minute he dived beneath the boat.

'Where'd he go?' cried Ken, eyes full of horror.

'Christ! He means to sink us!'

Fight returned to Colin. He got Ken's spear to fend the brute off if he resurfaced, but realised the fight was only in his head. His body was still as weak as ever, and he dropped the weapon.

Scarface lashed out with his tail, spinning the lifeboat on its axis for two complete circles. Pausing as though to tease them, he then dove beneath before emerging to strike mammoth blows to the side. Finally he dropped back to his usual position, swimming astern, watching. Then he disappeared.

'He's leaving,' croaked Ken.

'Thank God,' said Colin.

'He'll have us by the end of this day, I tell you.'

'He knows it's his last chance,' said Colin.

'How could he know that?' snapped Ken. 'You're talking daft, lad. It's just another day to him.'

'I just *know* it,' said Colin.

'I'm all in.' Ken slumped in the well. 'How can we keep on with this? How can we do it anymore? They're not coming for us. Don't you realise it? So what if another plane comes. They can't land, can't pick us up. What they gonna do – keep dropping bits of water and food. They'll be dropping it for corpses soon.' He paused. 'I'm all in, chum. All in. Tell my Kath I was...'

'No.' Colin grasped Ken's arms, hard.

He couldn't bear the thought of another night with no ship. The feeling was so acute he thought he might pass right out. Where could he find the strength to hope when all muscle had gone? How could he find enough for two if Ken didn't believe?

'No,' he said. 'I won't hear any more messages. Do you understand, I won't hear it. You'll tell her yourself and I'm going to be with you, do you hear me?'

But Ken had fallen asleep.

'Do you hear me?' Colin said softly. 'You and I are going to get home, lad, either when a ship comes or because we reach land.'

He crawled to the foredeck and fell asleep there, posed for watch. And this time he dreamed, not of home or a kitchen or a strange book-filled place, but of the lifeboat. All the men were present and they were as healthy and well as when they'd been on the SS *Lulworth Hill*.

Weekes wore his hat the wrong way for comic effect and joked about their quarters not having flush toilets. On a bench the young gunners, Bott, Bamford and Leak, shared a ciggie and teased one another. Nearby King listened to them with a smile. The Second sat astern, quietly mending his trousers. Stewart played a game of cards with Platten, arguing back and forth about whose hand was better. Davies, his ribs not broken, lounged against a mast, contentedly reading a book. John Arnold stood, reading a passage from his bible, and Officer Scown sat on the boat edge and cleaned his boots to a shine and smiled at the men before him. Only Ken slept, curled up in the well, perhaps dreaming this very vision himself, perhaps watching Colin sleep on the foredeck.

In the middle of the boat was Young Fowler.

He watched Colin. His hair was brushed flat as though for church and his cheeks pink with health. Joy filled Colin's chest.

He said over and over, 'Am I ever glad I got to see you again! By, lad, you do look good! I really wanted to say ... well, I really ... I never meant to...'

'No need to say anything,' smiled Fowler. 'I know it. We went through a shocking time, mate, but we're over the worst now. You've got a bit to get through yet though. You have to wake up.'

Colin didn't want to wake. This felt like home now. It would be easy to surrender and stay here, among friends. He looked down at his hands and they were smooth, not blackened or burnt or calloused. He touched his stomach and it was muscled, firm and well fed. His clothes were the day-to-day uniform he'd worn on the ship. And he was not hungry or thirsty.

You have to wake up, Grandad.

Colin turned around.

On the foredeck sat the girl. She wore a strange kind of one-piece suit made of fur-like material, with a zip up the front. It was the colour of his mother's garden lilacs and had purple hearts all over it. She squinted in the sun and pointed out across a sea so calm he leaned over and looked at his face in its mirror. No beard, no sunburn, no shrunken skull. He was a young man again.

'You have to wake up, Grandad,' she said again.

'Am I really your great grandfather?' Colin smiled at her and there was no pain in the action.

'Yes, you will be, but only if you wake up and see the ship.'

'I don't want to wake up.' Colin's voice was strong. 'It's good here.'

'It *is* good here.' She smiled, her hazel eyes flecked with gold. 'But you're not supposed to stay. You've still got stuff to do.'

She jumped up then and came to him. 'I wanted to stay asleep one time,' she said. 'But then there was this amazing story that I just had to get up for and it's about to end now and if you don't wake up it won't end right.'

Colin wanted to pat her head but felt shy. He'd never had much to do with children, especially girls. Boys he knew. Brothers he'd plenty of.

'Let's get to ten,' she said, tugging on his sleeve.

'Ten?'

'The waves,' she said. 'You said if you could just get to ten...'

She led him to the foredeck, her small hand around his larger one. Colin sat next to her and she began counting waves. Behind them the crew began singing a sailor's hymn that Colin knew well. Young Fowler whistled and Officer Scown ruffled his flat hair.

'One...' said the girl. 'Two ... three...'

'What's your name?' he asked.

'Rose,' she said. 'Four ... five...'

'Like my mother,' he said.

'Is it?' She seemed surprised.

'Yes. Six ... seven ... eight ...' He paused.

'No, you finish,' she said.

'Nine...'

Colin woke. Pain again. Raw skin. Dry eyes. Tight bones. Empty belly. Burnt hand. No girl. No Fowler. Just the sun beating down and the waves moving the boat. Waves. He opened his eyes. Watched one break at the bow.

'Ten,' he croaked.

Then he looked to the horizon, at the shimmering heat. Nothing. That's what he had woken for. Nothing. He sat up with difficulty. Saw Ken sitting opposite him, staring morosely out to sea. Had he died sitting there, eyes forever open? Was he going to have to put his friend to sea? He could not do it.

Behind Ken, far away: something.

Something.

Colin got to his knees, shaded his eyes and lo oked harder. Grey against blue.

'A ship.'

Colin realised his voice had failed altogether.

'A ship.'

Excitement had killed his words.

'A ship,' he managed to croak.

Ken turned. He was not gone. He looked at Colin and then towards the horizon. His face broke into a gash of a smile. With the aid of the mast, Colin got halfway to his feet. It surely was a ship. It could not be a vision like all the others he'd seen on the lifeboat, not when Ken had seen it too. It could not be a cruel mind trick. If it was then the dream and the girl – Rose, her name was Rose – had lied, and that was more than he could bear.

No, it was a ship, on the horizon. Today a ship. Today a magnificent white ship cutting through the water, heading their way.

Colin had won the game.

'A ship,' he cried. 'A ship, Ken, a ship!'

'She's heading this way.' Ken crawled to the mast. 'She must have seen us. She knows we're here.'

'Isn't she the most beautiful sight?' Colin grinned. 'Can you really believe it? Is it really and truly a ship?'

'See the white ensign,' cried Ken. 'She's British Navy!'

'God bless the British Navy!'

'A bloody ship, lad!'

'We're saved,' said Colin.

Nearer and nearer she steamed, until they could plainly see the numbers on her bow – H32 – and recognised her for a destroyer. She blasted several whoops of greeting and Ken and Colin whooped back. Across the water came the wonderful sound of her engine telegraph, and screaming as her forefoot lessened so she could slow down.

'Let's stand,' said Colin, gripping the mast harder.

'I don't know if I can, chum,' admitted Ken.

'You can.'

'I really can't.'

'You will. We'll do it together.' Colin put an arm about Ken's waist and, much as he had fifty days earlier when pulling him from the water, helped him stand. 'We'll be standing when she meets us, by God we will.'

And so they were standing when HMS Rapid pulled up alongside their small lifeboat. They heard orders being shouted aboard, saw cheery, smart, well-fed sailors rushing around, following commands. Nets were dropped and heaving line thrown.

A gentle, well-spoken voice came from above. 'Are you alright there, chaps? Can you make it up here by yourselves?'

Ken waved cheerily and began to climb but fell back into the boat's well. Colin tried and failed too. But there was nothing more to worry about. No more fight needed. Agile sailors climbed down the netting and carried them both onto the ship, to the robust cheers of its crew.

'Come on up,' grinned one of them. 'Nice little craft you have there. Shouldn't fancy crossing the Atlantic in it myself mind.'

'Never did see owt like it,' said another.

'Blimey, me old China,' said another. 'I've heard they starve you blokes in the merchant navy but I never knew they did it as proper as that.'

Colin wanted to say thank you to the blond-haired baby-faced sailor who carried him, but could find nothing. He looked back at the ocean as he was lifted over the railing; their lifeboat seemed so tiny.

How had they lived so long on it? Was this ship a dream and he'd wake up, asleep next to Ken? Ken. Where was Ken? He tried to see where he'd been taken but he was so tired he could barely stop his eyes closing, afraid if did he'd wake back on the lifeboat, alone.

One last look back at it and there was Rose, waving, her hair bouncing in the gentle breeze. He tried to whistle but nothing emerged. Yet even from so far he heard her singing, some song he didn't know. But it didn't matter because the ocean did and her words merged with its endless sonata.

❧

In his log that day, Ken wrote – *The greatest day of all my life and the day I shall never forget. We were rescued this day by* HMS Rapid. *To our Lord we can only say Thank You.*

29

HOME

It was with great pleasure that we were able to wire you today that it has been reported that your son was landed aboard yesterday from one of HM ships, which has rescued two members of the crew, and no doubt your boy had had a very trying time.

In the book nook, bathed in the candle's playful light, Rose and I danced around the cushions as though a gleaming white vessel had picked us up too.

Rose cried, 'A ship, a ship, a ship, today a ship!' Then she clapped her hands, sang it again and danced anti-clockwise, her shadow flickering ghostlike.

I flopped onto a cushion and laughed at her joy; eventually she tired and sat opposite me. Excitement submitted to sadness. We were done; it was over.

But I didn't want the blackout to end, the lights to come on and reality to hit.

'I'm so glad Ken was there too,' Rose said, still breathless.

'Me too,' I said, 'Neither of them would have survived without the other.'

'Even though I *knew* Grandad Colin would live, I felt

dead nervous,' she admitted. 'But that's what happens in ace stories. Like when I read the last Harry Potter book and everyone had told me what would happen. It didn't matter, because you can never *really* be sure until you get to the end.'

She was right; even with a true story, there are different versions and there are parts that get exaggerated or left out. In the end all you can do is believe the parts that sound right to you.

'Did you name me after Colin's mum?' asked Rose.

'No,' I said. 'That truly is some strange coincidence.'

'No such thing.'

'Maybe. But we named you after the lovely colour of your face.'

She pulled a scornful expression. 'Why do parents have to be so stupid over names?'

'Rose!'

'At least it means I'm like Scarface,' she said. 'We both got names because of our face. The best reason. So what happened to him?'

I sat closer to her, wrapped the blanket around us both.

'It was actually said – by Ken afterwards – that *HMS Rapid* gunned Scarface down when he attacked the lifeboat one last time. But I just couldn't bring myself to kill him like that. Even if it happened – and we can never truly know – I prefer to think of him still swimming out there in the Atlantic Sea. Don't you? Isn't that how it *should* be?'

Rose nodded. 'Will he still be there? How old do sharks get to?'

'Not sure. Maybe twenty? So, no, he won't be.'

'At least he maybe got to be an old man.' She paused. 'Did Colin?'

'No more story right now,' I said, getting up. 'I'll have to find more candles and ring and find out what's going on with the electricity.'

'Because the story's not over,' Rose said, more urgently. 'There's always the end and then what happened *after* the end.'

'We can maybe do that tomorrow.'

'In bed,' she insisted. '*Soon.*'

'We'll see.'

'We'll see!' she mocked.

'Rose, you said you'd be able to let it go,' I said.

'This isn't me not letting it go,' she said. 'I just want to know about the medals and stuff.'

'I know,' I said softly.

I understood her needing those final threads to be tied up neatly. I could feel Colin fading already, leaving us, returning not to the lifeboat but perhaps home. Even though I hated them, I also felt there should be one last goodbye.

'I know,' I said. 'We can do that, but the house is cold and dark and I need to warm and light it.'

'When I'm in bed, *please?*'

'Maybe,' I sighed. 'We cou...'

A knock on the door finished my sentence. I remembered April earlier on, promising lemon cake if the lights didn't come back up. Such treats only reminded me that Rose would need extra insulin to enjoy it or she'd have to wait until her blood sugars were low. Perhaps I'd just hide the cake away so she didn't nag for the smallest piece, as she so often did, breaking my heart.

How fast the reality of injections and blood readings and power cuts replaced our visit to the lifeboat. I was almost afraid of the lights coming on again. When they did, like those in the theatre after a play is done, I felt like the magic would die altogether. It would be like none of it had happened.

A knock on the door again. An impatient April, with cake.

'Don't go too near that candle,' I warned Rose, 'and when I come back I'll guide you upstairs so you can clean your teeth and get ready for bed.'

'Not bedtime,' she moaned. 'Can't I ...'

'No,' I snapped, and went to the door.

In the shadow I could barely make April out. What was it Colin had written in his diary? That at sea it wasn't the darkest before dawn but when the sun had just gone. Yet it seemed blacker now than when April had called earlier, even though my eyes had had time to grow accustomed to it.

'April,' I said.

Then the lights flickered, came on, went off, and came on again.

'I'm not April,' he said.

No, it wasn't. It was a ghost.

It was Jake.

Jake with his two oversized bags. His thick red hair was cut short for the tour, his freckled skin was sunburnt and his hazel eyes so like Rose's, full somehow of both mischief and sadness. He dropped the two bags. I put a hand out and drew it back, afraid that my touch would make him disappear again. He held my face and I closed my eyes, smiled.

He was real. He was home. He kissed me.

'But ... how?' I managed to ask, still afraid to believe.

'Aren't you going to invite me in?' he said.

'Oh, yes.' I shivered in the wintry draught. 'Of course, yes.'

'What did you do with all the light?' Jake picked up his bags. 'The house was dark as I approached. Did you forget to pay the bills in my absence?'

'Oh, no. It was a power cut. But you ... when did ...how...' I could hardly talk; I was Colin when he saw the ship.

'I only found out yesterday,' Jake said, still bright in the new light, so sudden, so real. He stamped his feet on the mat. 'There wasn't time. Anyway I thought it would be like that night in the snow. Remember? Me showing up when you didn't expect.'

'Of course I remember.'

I had thought of it so many times while he was away. Now Jake had given me another moment to save for dark times alone – the night he arrived with the light.

I began to close the door, but paused. On the street, in a growing mist that curled like waves, another ghostly shape. Colin? I tried to focus, make him out in the silvery haze, a familiar shape, a smile. But it disappeared. Perhaps my imagination.

'What is it?' asked Jake.

'No, nothing,' I said softly, and closed the door.

Then, shy at first, I put my head on Jake's chest. Like Rose, he smelt of things familiar, of him, and of faraway places I'd never know. I could hear his heart through the thick jacket, as rhythmic as the sea – or maybe I imagined I could.

'I can't believe you're here,' was all I could say.

'I am.' He squeezed me, hard.

'I don't want you to go away again,' I said softly.

'We can talk about that,' he said.

'We can?' I looked up at him.

He nodded. 'It might be time.'

I remembered Rose, waiting by the candle. As though reading my mind, Jake said, 'So where's my girl?'

'She's going to be so happy.' I pulled free, wanting to share this wonderful surprise. 'Rose,' I called. 'Can you blow that candle out and come here?'

Come and see what happens after the end, I thought.

30

BACK TO THE SEA

Two of us left. We will stick it to the end.

K.C.

'I don't want to go to bed yet,' Rose called from the back room.

Then she appeared in the hallway, hair all messed up from being wrapped in a blanket, and her mouth fell open and her eyes blinked three times. 'Dad? Oh, Dad, it's you!' And she ran and jumped on him.

Jake picked her up and swung her the way he had since she could walk. 'Gosh, you've grown,' he said, pretending she was too heavy for him to lift.

Rose play punched him. 'I'm light as a feather!' She looked at me. 'Did you know, Mum? You should have told me!'

'She didn't know,' said Jake, kissing her forehead and putting her down. 'I thought I'd surprise you both. I'd never have missed the looks on your faces now. So what have you been up to then? What's new and what's happening?'

'Don't say happening, Dad,' said Rose. 'It makes you sound ancient. We just had a power cut – it was aces. We had to light a candle to finish our story.'

Jake came into the kitchen, Rose dancing around him, and I closed the door. The radiators clanked and warmth filled the house again. We had light, we had heat, and we had Jake. I still wanted to pinch his arm, touch his face, and make sure he was real.

I switched on the kettle and fussed about how hungry he must be, but he said he was fine and he'd eat supper with Rose.

'I've had it already.' She was still dancing about. 'Done my injection and blood and everything.'

Jake looked sad at the word injection. I remembered that I'd had two months to get accustomed to it, to her diabetes, to blood tests. This would all be new for him. It would likely be a shock to see his little girl drawing blood for the first time, to watch her pierce flesh with needle. He'd have to get used to the dark.

He sat at the table, motioned for Rose to sit on his knee.

'I'm nearly bloody ten,' she said.

'*Language*,' I warned.

'You're never too old to sit with me,' he said.

So she did.

'Tell me all about this here diabetes then,' he said, his voice light but his eyes pained. I left them together, Rose talking animatedly about what she had to do and what it all meant and showing him her blood machine, and Jake listening intently. I washed the tea and supper pots and put the laundry away, and when I returned they were talking about Colin.

'Today the ship came,' she explained. 'I swear, Dad, I

thought my heart was going to jump right out of my mouth!'

'Speaking of stories,' he said, going into his holdall. 'How about these?' He took out a handful of new paperbacks. 'I got them for you at the airport. If you've already got some of them, don't worry.'

Rose viewed them quietly. 'Thanks, Dad,' she said.

Jake frowned and looked at me. The old Rose had always clapped her hands in joy at new books. This one – the one Jake had to get to know – hadn't read a book in weeks. I shook my head to let Jake know I'd explain later.

'I know your dad's here, but it's late,' I said.

'Do I have to go to bed?'

'Yes,' said Jake. 'Come on, your mum's right. I'll be still here in the morning.'

'But it's school then!'

'How about I take you and meet you after?'

Rose danced around the kitchen again, scattering her new books.

'Shall I put these in your book nook?' asked Jake.

'No,' she said, looking at me, nervous. 'I don't want to keep my books there anymore. Do you mind? I want them in my room now.'

'Of course,' I said. I had expected this.

'I loved being in the book nook,' she said. 'But I don't think any other stories would be quite right there now, would they?'

I smiled, and she smiled back.

Then we all went upstairs. On the landing Jake frowned at Rose's new off-pink door. I waited for the question I'd dreaded since that horrible day, the answer I had to give ready in my throat. But Rose said, 'Oh Dad, do you like my new door? I had a really bad hypo one time and kicked the old one shut and broke it up. Don't be mad – I can't help how I am in a hypo.' I tried to interrupt her with the truth. It wasn't fair that she take the blame. But Rose talked more loudly over me. 'So Mum got me this new door. What do you think?'

Jake shook his head and laughed. He looked around the room and his eyes moistened. I knew how he felt. Even her bedroom had changed. Chaos had calmed. The once choppy sea of papers and DVDs and pens and books and clothes was now a smooth expanse of folded jeans and orderly items.

While Rose was cleaning her teeth he said, 'She seems so grown up, Nat. How can she have grown so much in only three months? I feel so bad that I missed all of this. What you two had to cope with.'

'Don't.' I shushed him with my finger to his lips. 'You did what you're supposed to do – your job. And I did mine. I know I made things difficult for you at first. I was a pain in the arse. But now I wouldn't change any of it.'

'I'm so proud of both of you,' he said.

'I am of you.' I hugged him. 'I'm glad I had to do this on my own. I needed to.'

Rose came back into the room, toothpaste smeared above her top lip. She climbed into bed, said, 'Can Dad stay with me for ten minutes?'

'Okay.' I tucked her in. 'Just ten minutes though.'

The Lion, The Witch and The Wardrobe fell from under her pillow, its bookmark still at the title page.

'Will you read this now instead?' I asked her.

'Maybe soon.' She paused. 'It just won't be as good though, will it?'

'As Colin's story?'

'No.'

'I don't suppose anything ever will be,' I said.

'I was wrong,' she said softly.

'What do you mean?'

'I said animals in stories are more interesting than people. And I still think they're great – like Scarface was. But people are the only ones who make you feel *everything*. Especially your own people.' She paused. 'In the morning will you tell me about when Colin got home?'

'Yes,' I said. 'We'll do that tomorrow.'

'But tell me ... did he get better? Please tell me that.'

'Yes, he did,' I said.

'Did he find a sweetheart?'

'Oh, yes,' I said. 'Your great grandma. And they had three lovely children.'

She smiled.

So I left her and Jake; their heads bowed close like two sails on a ship blown together. I watched them for a moment, sharing jokes. It occurred to me that a person doesn't have to be physically present to be with you. You can be separated by time or miles and still affect one another.

I closed the off-pink door.

Then I went to the book nook and took all the paperbacks from the shelf and put them in a box. I put both of the cinnamon cushions on top and put the box near the stairs. I polished the wooden bookcase until it looked like new. I closed my eyes and pictured Rose in her room, reading again. Words devoured secretly once more, beneath her duvet, with a torch. She might read slowly at first, grumbling each evening that the sentences were too clunky and the build-up too slow. She might say that the story didn't make her heart dance. But I knew then she would remember how to enjoy made up books and everything would fall into place.

When a hand gently touched my shoulder, I smiled. Jake. I looked up.

It wasn't Jake. It was the other ghost.

I looked into dark eyes, and the ocean and a tattered boat sail and my own face, but no colour, as though I viewed the images through a black-and-white filter. I readjusted my focus, took in his face, and all the sea colours flickered – jade and turquoise and amber.

Colin.

Grandad.

He was young and unlined and cleanly shaven. He had on a suit with thick lapels, kept together by four buttons forming a square, over a hand-knitted jumper and finished with a striped tie. Two medals were pinned to his chest and he wore his hair the way men had in the forties, swept to one side with gluey gel and cut short around the ear.

I heard the gentle roll of waves. A breeze caressed my ankles and moved the curtains at the patio doors. Salt tickled my nose, filled the air. Colin smiled and it softened the penetrating study in his eyes. It was like the sun after a long, cold night. He was so close I could have leant forward and kissed his cheek.

He bowed then, courteous, a little shy, and looked towards the back door.

'I don't want to say it,' I cried, because I knew. I'd learned to say thank you, but I'd never get used to people leaving.

'You mustn't be scared of goodbye,' he said, his voice just like that night in the hospital, his accent beautifully rich Yorkshire, familiar in its flow, like mine only from a time gone by. He smelt of musky aftershave. 'I'm just going back to the sea. To meet my brothers. My mum and dad. My Kathleen. My friends from the lifeboat.'

He didn't belong to us anymore. I knew this. He had to go where he was supposed to, and I had to let him. Hadn't I insisted Rose let go?

'Don't be scared,' he whispered.

Back at the hospital that night I'd lied and told him I wasn't afraid. Now I realised we don't get less scared, we just find it easier to admit it when we've been as brave as we can.

'I'll try not to be,' I said.

'Good lass.'

'Young Rose is really the bravest of us all.'

'Thanks to you,' I said.

'No, it is thanks to her,' he said, gruffly. 'Tell her I got the drawing she did on the sail cloth and I read her words – *You have to know how to be happy to know how to be sad and if you know both of those things you'll know how to be brave.* They're good words. Very good.' He smiled.

I heard the waves building, the breeze about my ankles more urgent.

'Have you always been with us?' I asked.

'Always,' he said. 'Watched you folk come and go, seen you get born and some pass on. But I miss the sea. Once you've been on it, you can never quite let it go. It gets *in* you, in your blood. Even when it sinks your ship, takes your friends, your hope.' He straightened and patted his tie. 'Christopher

Columbus once said, "You can never cross the ocean until you have the courage to lose sight of the shore." I thought of it often, you know.' He paused. 'I couldn't go back there after the lifeboat. I couldn't even think of it without great pain. I hated it for taking my friends, our ship, my youth, most of all my little brother. But I know now the sea wasn't to blame. The sea just ... *is*. We can either live on it and try and survive, or away from it and never know her lessons.' He paused. 'And I'm ready to go back there now.'

The night at the hospital I had wanted to put a hand over his but feared it might seem forward – now I did. He patted it and he kissed my forehead. He smelt of faint tobacco and wool.

'I won't look back,' he said, 'but it doesn't mean I'm not watching, Natalie.'

The breeze picked up again and my skirt fluttered about my knees. He turned and headed for the back door, but I didn't want to look. His presence faded the way it had when I was small and someone opened the bedroom door.

It was like the last paragraph in a favourite book. I didn't want to look at the words because I didn't want to say goodbye. But it surely wasn't goodbye because I could think of the story whenever I wanted. Creating it for Rose was over. I'd never create it like that again. Never trade blood for words. Never go to the lifeboat. But I would know we had done.

'Goodbye,' he said, at the back door. He opened it.

I wouldn't say it. I couldn't.

Outside, the winter dark whispered to me. It's time, it said. The candle is out, smell the promise of new days, of snowdrops coming, of changes, of spring, of beginnings.

Colin stepped outside. The ocean waited, its swirls a sweet roar that I knew he didn't fear. I ran to the door. Spray dampened my face. Salt hung in the air. He walked up the garden, through the mist. For a moment I thought I saw the lifeboat, on a shimmering horizon in the wispy haze, and men there lifting their hands in a salute. In the rush of water I heard the final roll-call of every man. Their fourteen names floated over the endless ocean and soared into the sky.

I had to say it. He belonged to the ocean now.

I called, 'Goodbye, Grandad.' I knew that he heard me over the waves, even though he never turned around.

And then I closed the door and went home too, back to my sea.

AUTHOR'S AFTERWORD

Young Rose is right. In a story there is always the end and then a *what happened after that*, because really there's never an end at all. Stories don't stop dead and no one lives happily ever after. Even when we die the things we did live on after us, like the spray from a homeward-bound ship.

After their rescue Colin and Ken recuperated aboard *HMS Rapid* for some days, until she reached Freetown, in West Africa. There they stayed for two weeks at the Disabled British Seaman's Rest Hospital. Only then, at the end of May 1943, did they board a troop ship bound for England.

Once home, Ken and Colin parted ways to return to their loved ones. They united again to deliver the many messages for their lifeboat brothers' families. Together they visited Officer Scown's wife and handed over his broken ring, with the words, 'He was courageous, and a gentleman to the last.'

Mrs Scown had the ring repaired and today their daughter Wendy cherishes it; along with her father's medals and many letters he gave before setting sail from Hull. One paragraph written in curled script might have been written with poetic foresight: *Don't forget your Daddy whilst he's on the sea, for he'll always think of you, his darling one – Wendy.*

For a while after their return Colin and Ken gave help to

the Ministry of Information in promotional work, recounting their tale in numerous factories across the UK. But Colin found it increasingly difficult to talk repeatedly about his ordeal. Reliving it impacted his health, and he eventually stopped.

Colin didn't return to the sea; he trained as a joiner and married his sweetheart, Kathleen. They briefly broke their honeymoon to go to Buckingham Palace, where Colin received the George Medal. His bravery also earned him the Lloyd's Medal, which gave the Armitage family a unique record. Brother Alf, a Captain in command of the tanker Scalaria, was also given this award for his gallantry. When the ship was bombed, he carried the third officer to safety, and ordered the anchor to be lowered so the crew could cling to it for five hours while a fire blazed above.

Colin fathered three children, two sons and a daughter, who then went on to have his six grandchildren. Sadly he only lived long enough to see his children reach four, three and one. They grew up with barely fleeting memories of him, his absence felt as acutely as their mother's presence.

Six years after he was rescued from the sea Colin died, aged only twenty-seven, of heart failure and asthma. He left behind his medals, a worn wallet, an identity card, a legacy of bravery, and an incredibly proud family.

ACKNOWLEDGEMENTS

Thank you to the incredible early readers who helped shape and improve the book: my beloved sisters Grace Wilkinson (the first reader!) and Claire Lugar, my (crazy) mother who wishes I would describe a blade of grass in six pages, Scott Derry, Daniel Ash, Ruth Dugdall, and Jacqueline Grima.

Thank you to my father for the sharp and helpful edits. He and my aunt, Jane Leng provided a rich wealth of family information and some wonderful stories. Thank you to the late Peter Armitage for all the beautiful family photographs, footage, newspaper cuttings, and letters. Thank you also to Wendy Scown for sharing with me her father, Officer Scown's, letters, medals and stories. How wonderful that this story brought us together. Thank you also Vivien Foster for your support and help, and for allowing us to march on Colin's behalf at the 2014 Remembrance Sunday parade in London.

I owe thanks also to Kenneth Cooke. His incredible memoir, *What Cares The Sea*, gave me much information, background, and facts, from which I was able to build my story and imagine what he and Colin went through.

Thanks for the support my daughter and I have had from Hull and East Yorkshire's HEY Parent & Child Diabetes

Support Group. This book is a tribute to all the brave kids with Type 1 Diabetes. Thanks also to the Juvenile Diabetes Research Foundation – support them at www.jdrf.org.uk .

I want to remember every brave merchant seaman on the lifeboat in 1943: Basil Scown – First Officer, Unnamed Second Engineer, Platten – Chief Steward, John Arnold – Apprentice, King – Apprentice, Kenneth Cooke – Carpenter, Colin Armitage – Able Seaman, Davies – Able Seaman, Weekes – Engineer's mate, Fowler – Cabin Boy, Stewart – Cabin Boy, Bamford – Army Gunner, Bott – Army Gunner, Leak – Army Gunner.

Thank you to those who helped on this writing journey, either by encouraging, inspiring or more actively guiding: Carol Macarthur, Roy Woodcock, the Luke Bitmead Bursary team, especially Elaine Hanson, the Hull Truck Women's Writers and the crazy and creative Ushers, Gill Sennett, Ann Marie Jibson, Fiona Mills, Lesley Oliver, Claire Nolan, the Five Fecks gang, Nick Quantrill, Chris Miller, Jennie at number 1, Carl Wheatley, Lizzie Buckingham, the WF Gang, Carrie Martin, Tom Steer, Rachel Harris, Russ Litten, Cassandra Parkin, Morgan Sproxton, Fawn Neun, Burnsey, Louise Brown, Dave Windass, Sam Hartley, Bryan Marshall, Will Ramsey, Vivien Foster, Brenda Baker, Beate Sigriddaughter, Sarah Louise Davies, Eddie Roberts, and the beloved much missed Kathleen Roberts.

I can't forget two important men in my life; my husband Joe who put up with me in the throes of all that writing involves, and my brother Colin who broke text tradition and sent happy emoticons when I told him I'd be published.

Thank you to the wonderful Karen Sullivan of Orenda

Books. I'll never forget the day (right down to the time) when she told me she would publish *How to be Brave* and made my lifelong dream come true. Thank you also to her incredible reader, Liz Barnsley of LizLovesBooks who championed me right from the start. Also to West Camel who worked with Karen to provide some great edits and suggestions. Without all of you, the book would not be what it is.

And last, but absolutely not least, I want to thank my children, Conor and Katy, both of who inspired the book. Katy has to live forever with Type 1 Diabetes, but Conor grew up in a family where a lot more attention had to be given to her because of this, and he never complained, only loved her. I love you both more than you'll ever know.

e